BEAUTIFUL

Crazy

KASEY LANE

sourcebooks
casablanca

Published by Sourcebooks Casablanca, an imprint of Sourcebooks, Inc.
P.O. Box 4410, Naperville, Illinois 60567-4410
(630) 961-3900
Fax: (630) 961-2168
www.sourcebooks.com

Printed and bound in Canada.
MBP 10 9 8 7 6 5 4 3 2 1

For Jeffrey, my big, bad handsome man.
Thank you for pushing me to chase my dreams and
cosigning all my crazy.

I love you.

Chapter 1

KEVAN LANDRY COULDN'T CATCH A BREAK. No matter how hard she tried to alter her fate, everything just got worse. Same shit, different fucking day. Case in point: her self-destructive brother Bowen. At the moment, the bruised and bloodied idiot was sleeping off an epic and near-fatal high in a local rehab center, New Beginnings. She and two of his buddies had dragged him half-conscious into the bright, sterile admitting room the night before during a typical Portland fall downpour.

She'd lied to the counselor about being able to pay the whopping bill for treatment. Truth was she did have some savings that would help, but the bulk would have to come from somewhere else—what she made at her part-time job at the tattoo shop and her full-time gig as an event marketer wasn't going to be enough. Unfortunately, the one promising opportunity had gone down in a fiery ball of flames when she'd had to choose between saving Bowen and making a meeting with an up-and-coming band. She'd just have to find another better-paying promotions job.

Which is exactly how Kevan found herself hurrying into the Tiki Torch Bar and Lounge with a new plan to keep Bowen in treatment and save Jolt Marketing, her fledgling company. Somehow she had to convince the headlining band, Manix Curse, they couldn't live without her marketing genius. Fortunately, she knew most of the band members. Unfortunately, according to Jax, Manix's drummer, all business decisions were made by the band's manager, Joe McKellan, whom she didn't know well. Now she just had to locate him and pitch her services.

Searching for Joe, she felt the eyes of another man watching her. Hair rose on the back of her neck, but she wasn't cold. It was practically a sauna in the packed club. She smoothed her clammy hands down the front of her dress and glanced over her shoulder. *There*. A handsome stranger's gaze followed her movements through the room. Their eyes locked and she held her breath. She turned and forced her eyes back to the crowd, trying to locate the man she needed to find.

Her pulse quickened, and her heart slammed against her ribs, either from the man's perusal or anxiety from approaching Joe. Maybe both. At first, she'd thought her excitement was from being in a club again. She loved the way music cast its spell, allowing her baggage to drop away as it swept her up in the magic of the moment. The pounding drums and gyrating bodies filled her with freedom as she swayed to the fantasy created by the instruments.

Damn, she loved live shows.

The opening band, Toast, worked the capacity crowd into a frenzy of sweat and thrashing bodies. Careful to steer clear of the widening mosh pit, Kevan leaned against the end of the battered wooden bar. Turning her head, she attempted to catch a surreptitious glimpse of the striking man who'd tracked her from the shadowy edge of the club.

Yep. He was watching. Not leering. Just observing

her with a slightly amused curve to his lips. He leaned against the wall, with his long legs crossed at the ankles. Arms folded against his broad chest in a way that might make another man appear surly. He didn't look surly.

Oh no. Mr. Hot Conservative Suit Guy looks interested.

Two words: goose bumps. Her nipples hardened, tightening just from some suit eyeballing her across a crowded, dingy club. The lights dimmed, and the bodies moving between them made it difficult to get another good look, but he seemed familiar. Unlikely, though. She'd remember a looker like him, especially if he'd been walking around in an Armani suit. Suits did things to a girl. Good things.

Kevan tried to gather the butterflies twisting in her belly and summon her saucy minx persona—as Bowen called it—the one she used to use to cover her nerves and get guys to buy her drinks. Before she slipped her mask into place, her former coworker and token jokester, Tyler, staggered up and bent his long, lean body over her.

"Haven't seen your tight ass around here since you quit and started your little business." He reeked of cheap whiskey, and his sour breath assaulted her nose.

"You're a real charmer," she said. "You always work drunk, or is that something new?"

"I'm not bouncing tonight."

"Good. You're so wasted you couldn't bounce your way out of a paper bag." She shifted to peer around him. Tyler followed her gaze until his eyes landed on her target across the bar. When she pulled away, he wrapped his fingers around her upper arm.

"Stick with your own kind, Kev." Tyler moved to block her view and raised his slurred voice over the crashing guitar solo. "That one is way over your pay grade, sweetheart."

"I have no idea what you're talking about." She turned her attention to the band onstage. The band her brother had started with his childhood friend, Nathan, and had eventually been kicked out of after too many missed practices and shows. Bandmates tend to frown on guitarists who don't show up for paying gigs.

"A suit like him will only use you and break your heart. He'll kick you to the curb with your cute little tail between your long, hot legs. Play it safe and come home with me, gorgeous."

Kevan ground her teeth. She'd been good-natured about dodging Tyler's lines for years because he was related to her assistant, Tina. But this shit was getting old. Her cheeks burned as she clenched her fists and stuck her chin out.

"Knock it off. I like you. As a friend."

Tyler flinched and took an uneven step back, stopping short against the bar. "A fucking friend? I don't want to be your friend."

"You think you're any different from any other guy who's tried to get up my skirt? You're not. You're all the same. Him. You. You're all arrogant jerks who think you're so damn hot. Get over yourself, Tyler."

Covering her mouth with her hand, Kevan took a deep breath as regret, tinged with maybe a little righteous courage, filled her chest. Once again she'd gone too far and said too much. His withering glare shifted over her shoulder.

"Sorry, Tyler. But you're acting like a dick," she said, hating the shake in her voice.

"Well, so are you, Kevan Landry," he said. And then he was gone. Absorbed by the writhing mass of bodies screaming and jumping to the band.

It wasn't his fault she was on edge. Tyler wasn't a bad guy, just a bit needy. And grossly inappropriate. Like a new puppy wanting to sit in your lap and lick your face all night, then take a dump on your carpet. More than once he'd come to her defense by fending off drunk and overly aggressive frat boys. Now, she had another mess to fix, because she couldn't hold her tongue. Add it to the list.

Before making her way to the ladies' room she ordered and drank a glass of water to help loosen the tightness her chest. Time to shake off the awkward exchange with Tyler and get her head back in the game.

After waiting in line for almost twenty minutes and carefully avoiding at least two of her brother's jilted lovers and one of her own, Kevan finally made it into the grimy bathroom with the chalkboard walls scribbled with profanities and silly doodles. In the mirror, she checked her face for makeup smudges and steeled her nerves, which felt raw and exposed, arcing like downed electrical wires after a storm. Attempting to appear playful, yet professional, she practiced a smile. It wasn't great, but it had to be good enough. She ran her tongue along her teeth and patted the front of her violet fifties-style pinup dress.

In the past, a night like tonight had been all about letting loose, letting her hair down, getting tipsy, maybe even hooking up with someone and getting lost in the shallow promise of a potential romance. Superficial goals she'd fully embraced once upon a time. But that wasn't her anymore. Sometimes she longed for the past, when she and Bowen could hit the clubs and party with the metalheads or the rockabilly crowd, where she didn't have to worry about responsibility. But the fun was over for good if she couldn't sign Manix Curse tonight.

Taking a deep breath, the warm air filling her lungs, Kevan smiled weakly at her reflection, ditching thoughts of loan payments, past-due rent, and rehab costs. Tonight was about finding a solution to her problems and calming the chaos swirling around in her life. Signing her first on-the-rise band would give her a chance, and she would fight like hell to save her fledgling business and keep her brother in rehab.

Kevan exited the restroom, intent on finding Joe. As she scanned the room for the older, gray-haired man, she stepped forward and looked down as her foot caught on a tear in the thinning carpet. She lurched forward, arms flailing and grasping for purchase.

Frickin' shoes. They were too damn high. But so cute, and they made her legs and ass look amazing...or so she'd been told.

Her cheek collided with something solid. She lifted her chin and met the whiskey-colored eyes of Mr. Hot Businessman. Her heart raced, and her breath quickened. When he swept his tongue across his full bottom lip, it glistened the way his eyes did, and she nearly stopped breathing altogether. His large hand fanned across her lower back, a single finger resting above her waistband.

What a cliché. Only she would nearly fall into a *mysterious stranger's* lap.

Kevan clutched the fine material of the man's pressed shirt. His tailored suit looked like it easily cost more than the monthly rent on her tiny apartment. Her fingers rested on the hard muscle of his chest, reminding her more of a solid wall than a man's body. Time suddenly felt frozen as his hot breath feathered against her cheek, and she noticed the thick, dark lashes and soft crinkle of laugh lines around his eyes. The man was hot, definitely. But there was kindness mixed with the darkness in his calmly amused expression.

"Don't worry, darlin'. I won't let you fall." His voice was a low drawl, dripping honey and sex.

For a heartbeat, she wished his reassuring words meant more than they did. They were like sandpaper and silk smoothing her jagged nerves and carried over the thumping of the club's music. All bass…matching her increasing heart rate from the reassuring grip of the breathtaking man's hold on her. A woman could lose herself in those mesmerizing dark eyes. A woman could forget he wasn't her type. For a minute, a woman could, but shouldn't, imagine a white picket fence with a man like him.

Shifting her feet, Kevan cleared her mind of the fall-induced tunnel vision clouding her head. "Thanks for saving me from total embarrassment," she said, her face heating to the point of fever. She hoped her words got lost in the loud club. But, of course, that wasn't her luck, was it? Righting herself, she tugged her crinoline skirt straight and looked around.

They weren't alone. They were in a crowded club surrounded by dancing bodies, pickup lines, and bleak desperation wrapped up in combat boots, skimpy

clothes, and copious amounts of sweat. And the ridiculously handsome man with the angular chin and firm
grip on her waist was not Kevan's date, nor was he some
kind of modern-day Prince Charming. He was a polite
man who happened to catch her—a career klutz—before
she fell on her face.

"My pleasure, Ms…?" His deep voice dragged out
the words as if expecting her to offer her name. And
still, he didn't remove his hand from her waist. Instead,
he brought her hand to his lips, almost delicately, and
brushed a kiss across her knuckles.

Oh. My. God. Who the hell does that anymore?

His soft lips caressed her hand in a simple, old-
fashioned action, but jolts of desire shot from where his
mouth lingered, down her arm, through taut nipples, and
straight to her sad and lonely sex.

This man was not safe.

*The man's middle name has to be Sexgod. Holy
mother.*

"Kevan Landry," she mumbled before her brain
kicked in and had a chance to reconsider.

Making an effort to keep her wits and avoid embar-
rassing herself further, Kevan closed her mouth to prevent drool from running down her chin. She was used to
a little male attention, but never had her body betrayed
her so quickly. Reacting with such strength to an almost
innocent and chaste action was not a good sign, especially since she was there for one reason: to find the
band's manager for a brief meeting and get the heck
out before she got into trouble. And even more so since
she'd sworn off men for the foreseeable future.

She didn't belong in his arms. The more comfortable

she became with his hands on her body, the faster she should run away. But his strong arms around her and the sweet kiss on her hand had somehow rendered her stupid…and more than a little horny.

"Nice to meet you, beautiful Kevan Landry. Mason Dillon." A slight smile touched his full mouth, sending more tingles of warmth down her arms at the mere thought of those lips on her body. Mr. Classy Businessman definitely had her teeny tiny panties in a twist.

Toast finished up their first set, and the club echoed with the excited chatter of fans mingled with random yells for songs and chanting for Manix.

"You don't look like a cowboy at all." The heat in her face spread down her neck.

Cowboy? Really, Kevan? That's my clever intro to the hottest guy in the history of forever?

A vague recognition of his name and maybe his face drifted in the back of her mind, but it quickly evaporated the moment she stared into his enticing eyes. Maybe she knew him from somewhere.

"I *am* from Texas." He grinned. A heartbreaking, light-the-room-up, panty-melting smile. For a moment, he didn't seem so serious or dangerous at all. He seemed kind, approachable, and full of life.

At the front of the room, the band started their second set, tearing into a spirited cover of Korn's "Coming Undone." The woman standing next to them squealed, loud even over the noise of the band. As she jumped up and dragged her friend into the roiling mosh pit—a quilt of undulating flannel, black T-shirts, and denim— Kevan was pushed against Mason. Again.

As soon as the heat from Mason's intoxicating touch began to warm her frigid soul and dormant libido, all hell broke loose. Tyler rushed up and grabbed her arm. As he dragged her toward the front of the crowd, he leaned in close. "I'm sorry, too." Then he flashed a sloppy bad-boy grin.

"You know you're a letch, right?" She laughed as he pulled her farther into the audience. Tyler had always been good to her and Bowen. And it was probably best to leave her new *friend* before she decided to drop her latest resolution like a bad habit. One minute to dance with Tyler wouldn't kill her, then she would go back to finding the band's manager.

Kevan flashed a stilted grin at Mason. Thankfully, he met her silent apology with that damn smile and waved before pointing to his watch. What did that mean? Did he want to meet with her again? Or did it mean it was time for him to leave?

She didn't have time to process the sexy man's cryptic gesture. Tyler turned her toward the band. Nathan, Bowen's best friend, raced his fingers like lightning across the guitar neck. Before Bowen's life disintegrated, her brother would have been up there jamming next to Nathan, performing the same complex dance they'd executed flawlessly for years onstage. Closing her eyes, she let the music take her. The notes collided and churned as the tune took over, and her busy brain stopped thinking and focused only on the melody. Her hips, her legs, her body swayed.

With half-open lids, she watched Nathan. His long black hair fell over his face as he concentrated on his mistress, his love, the guitar and the melody it created.

He flipped his sweat-drenched hair back and gave the audience his patented wolfish smile. The smile said he could make a woman scream with pleasure and then make her beg for more. If they ever decided they wanted to be more than an opening act, his grin had rock star written all over it.

Kevan was pretty sure every straight chick in the room got a little wet thinking about Nathan Carter. The dude was hot. Not that it mattered to her. Kevan looked at Nathan like a brother. Just like she did all the guys at the tattoo shop.

Once again, she found herself scanning the room from one corner to the other, involuntarily searching the dark club for Mason. She dropped her shoulders, and her stomach clenched. He was nowhere to be found. Not that she'd intended to do anything about the attraction, but he was nice to look at.

He's gone. Damn. Now focus on your future.

It was for the best, really. Kevan needed to quit looking around for Mr. Wrong and get back on her A game. Tonight was her Hail Mary pass to sign the coolest local metal band as her first major entertainment marketing client. Time to go big or go home.

Chapter 2

TONIGHT WAS KEVAN'S ONE CHANCE TO SIGN MANIX Curse before they were out of her league forever. Over the last four years, they'd played the local music circuit so often that fans joked they were Portland's official house band. In the last six months, though, the band had honed their sound and built a substantial fan base in Portland and the surrounding areas. They'd scored a dream gig—opening act later that year for metal superstars Pagan Saints.

The tour would catapult Manix Curse into the heavy metal music stratosphere with bands like Five Finger Death Punch and Volbeat. They were that good. Maybe even great, and someday might reach both the commercial and artistic heights of Avenged Sevenfold.

Toast finished their set with a big flourish, and Kevan spotted Joe as he strode toward the back of the club. Moving quickly, Kevan snaked between the bar and the edge of the pit. Avoiding flying elbows and spilled beer, she made her way to the Tiki's small green room.

"You fucking rock! We're Toast!" Nathan yelled, his voice gravelly and thick. Glancing up at the stage as she passed, she saw him fling his damp hair back, strands sticking to his heated face like a time-traveling '80s rock god in his Slayer T-shirt and ripped jeans. The crowd roared. "Thanks for coming out tonight. You guys stoked to check out Manix Curse before they hit the road next week?" The crowd went even more berserk. "You should be. Now, go get a fucking drink and buy our new CD."

Pushing past fans in various stages of drunkenness, Kevan followed Joe through the back of the club. After opening the door to the wrong room, an office where the night manager was entertaining two "regulars," she located the band members and their manager crowded around a small Formica table. Kevan patted her blue-streaked, victory-rolled hair before pulling a folded brochure and contract from her clutch. Trying to ignore her sweaty palms and the thunderous pounding of her heart, she stepped into the room, ready to do battle.

"Well, if it isn't the lovely Kevan Landry. Everyone's favorite metal billy pinup." Joe winked, his open grin bolstering her confidence.

The band—and more important, Joe—had to believe she could promote them and take them to the next level. She tried not to focus on the dollar amount float-ing in her head—the one from the bottom of the page she'd signed at the treatment center. Pulling in another deep breath, Kevan cleared the sand from her throat and smiled.

Joe's eyes narrowed. "We thought maybe you were too good for us, girlie. We haven't seen you around the clubs. Seen that troublemaking brother of yours, but not your pretty face."

Hiding a cringe at Joe's reference to Bowen's epic crash and burn at the club the night before, Kevan threw back her shoulders and moved deeper into the room to hug the guys she saw practically every day at the shop. This was different. This was their element. And really the guys were Bowen's friends. Not hers.

"Work's kept me busy. I've been doing all the pro-motions for Tatuaggio—"

"Hell yeah," Marco shouted.

Kevan winked. "And I was working with Toast before Bowen left. Put together a few shows for them." Her lips felt tight, sore, as she tried to form them into the smile she'd practiced in the mirror.

"Glad to see your brother's getting some help," Joe said. "He's a good guy and an amazing artist when he's not wasted."

She swallowed again and wished she had a drink. "Thanks. It means a lot. But I want to talk to you about Manix."

His playful demeanor evaporated instantly. Joe was all business as he leaned forward and waited for her to continue.

"I've always been a fan but really followed Manix Curse closely for the last year. You guys, and Mandi"— the young, petite, pink-haired guitar player smiled as Kevan gestured toward her—"have really tightened your music and taken your stage show to a more pro-fessional level. You've gained such a huge local, and even extended, following. I hoped you might be ready to discuss a marketing and public relations campaign." Sitting down in the one open seat next to Mandi, Kevan crossed her legs and willed her restless hands to be still by folding them in her lap.

"Kevan." Joe held up his hand as she prepared to launch into her pitch. Her heart sank. *That doesn't sound good. At all.* "We were kind of thinking the same thing. And we know you. You know us. We like you."

Awesome. "If you're on board, I'd love to discuss

some ideas I have," she said as she set her brochure on the table in front of him. Damn. And why hadn't she thought to bring along her tablet to give them a short presentation?

"Honestly, we've been approached by a bigger, more established firm," Joe said. Her gut dropped, and her heart melted into puddles around her four-inch purple heels.

"Oh." The room began to shift suddenly, and the smell of stale beer filled her nose, making her stomach pitch.

Think. Think. Think. Don't panic.

She could do this. She pulled deep for her most authentic smile and pointed it right at the man holding her future in his hands.

"That illustrates my point. Manix Curse is ready for the next step. And you need someone in your court who's not only a fan, but who knows this industry, this genre, and promotions. And that someone needs to understand the importance of not spending your band's money before they make it. I can do it, Joe. You know I can."

She hoped the deep breath she took was disguised as a normal one—not the sucking-for-life type it felt like.

Kevan looked around the table, gauging each band member's expression. Nothing. Both the singer, Marco, and the bass player, Conner, watched Joe for his response. Jax made eye contact but showed no indication of how he felt. Only Mandi opened her mouth to say something but snapped it shut. Waiting. Confirming Kevan's suspicion that all business decisions were clearly Joe's domain. Maybe it was better. She didn't have to convince five different people—people she was kind of friends with—how badly they needed her, only one very savvy businessman.

"I don't disagree. However, I need to do what's best for this band. These kids trust me," Joe said, and his nephew, Conner, rolled his eyes but stayed silent.

Kevan felt like she was drowning, could almost feel the water filling her lungs. "Joe, give me a chance—"

"I didn't say no, hon. I'm saying we have another option to consider. We'd be fools not to at least see what this other company has to offer. Come by my office tomorrow, say, around three? We'll sit down and discuss it."

The breath she didn't know she'd been holding escaped on a silent sigh. She was still in the game. She had tomorrow morning to fine-tune her pitch, make it perfect.

"Thanks, guys. Joe, I think you'll love what I put together for you." Kevan tried to hide the anxiety and excitement running rampant through her veins in an epic battle for supremacy. She shook Joe's hand and hoped he couldn't feel the dampness of her palm.

Jax, the band's tall, roguish drummer and Mandi's older brother, unfolded his long frame and pushed up with a grunt. "Now that the business shit is done, let's go rock the fuck out of this place."

The double hoops piercing one brow above his deep brown eyes glinted in the low light, and he flashed a wide grin worthy of a pillaging pirate. His bandmates jumped up, their chairs scraping against the ancient linoleum floor, and a cacophony of "fuck yeah" and "rock 'n' roll, bitches" filled the small room. They danced and hollered around her, their excitement and energy vibrating through to her core. This right here was why she loved what she did.

Music was everything to Kevan. Before her mother died and her dad turned into a bitter asshole, her mom would turn on the radio, and she and Kevan would dance through the house, sometimes waltzing, sometimes singing, always laughing. Kevan heard poetry in the words of her favorite songs. The lyrics sang of her frustration, her pain, and her joys. After her mother's death, instead of losing herself to the streets or to the almost-crippling anger, she found refuge in the local music scene. Not only did it keep her connected to her mother, it kept her close to her brother. Through the magic of music, she never felt weird or alone. Music was her escape and her sanctuary.

As she followed the band single file down the narrow hall, she wished them a great show. Jax leered down at her, his meaty paw finding its way down her lower back and landing firmly on her butt.

She looked into his mischievous face. "Jax Paige, please remove your freakishly large hand from my bottom. If my brother were here, he'd kick your ass. I'm not one of your groupies, honey."

"No, you're not anyone's groupie. But you can't blame a guy for trying." He winked. This was their way. Unlike Tyler, Jax's flirting was strictly for show. He'd had his heart broken by some mysterious woman in college and was a one-night-only kind of guy. And their growing friendship was too valuable to both of them to mess it up. She wrapped her fingers around his wrist and guided his hand away.

"Even as hot and sexy as you are, you know I don't date musicians anymore."

He laughed before leaning down and whispering in her ear. "I'm not really a musician. I'm a tattoo artist." He held his finger to his lips. "Does that make a difference?"

She laughed. "Bummer. I don't date ink slingers, either."

He looked down, almost sheepishly—if it was possible for a fully tattooed, impossibly tall ruffian to look sheepish. "Maybe one day you'll change your mind, or I'll be lucky enough to find a woman like you."

The expression on his face evened out; his smile faded as he lowered his voice. "Have you heard from Bowen today?"

She shook her head. "Our first visit is tomorrow."

"Lemme know how it goes and if you need anything, okay?" With a friendly swat to her behind, Jax ran over to the stage, pulled his drumsticks from his back pocket, and began to drill a beat against the wall as he bounced from one foot to the other. She wished she knew Jax a little better so she could ask his take on the meeting. Find out who the other company was. Did Kevan even have a chance? But although she worked with him and he hung with her brother, she didn't feel comfortable pushing for info.

Kevan needed to shake off her unsettling mood from the short meeting. She pushed her way back toward the outskirts of the crowd where she could observe the band and the audience. The whole time, she scanned the club for her mystery man, hoping he might reappear. Not that she had plans to do anything about him.

No. Not tonight.

Not ever.

Focus and stay away from supersexy men in fancy suits.

When the club's hipster owner hopped onto the stage and announced Manix Curse, the screaming and cheering was deafening. Despite the fact that Kevan would hear ringing in her ears the next day, she smiled. The wall of noise rose to a roar. Definitely ringing for the next few days.

The stage lights, silhouetted the band in a foggy glow. Noise in the dark club fell to a dull murmur, waiting, anticipating the first chord. Suddenly, the long wail of Mandi's guitar rang out and built into the primal riff of their intro song, "Punch Drunk." The audience went wild, jumping and pumping their fists frantically in the air. Hundreds of tiny light beams merged into one focused spotlight, revealing Marco at his retro-styled microphone with his head bowed, his long dark hair falling forward over his angular face.

"Show me your horns!" he screamed before jerking the mic from the stand.

Marco tossed his head back and started singing their fast and furious signature power song. A surge of rock-and-roll devotees thrust their hands up with their fingers held in the worldwide recognizable sign of heavy metal. Kevan let herself become caught up in the sound and power built by the band and their adoring audience.

Manix played song after song, working the crowd into a lather, only to bring them down again with a heart-rending ballad full of angst and longing. They didn't lull the crowd for long, building the swell of notes into a tidal wave of sound, cresting and breaking over the spectators. They teased and cajoled their fans, pummeling them with their music and taunting them to beg for more. And they did.

Kevan took stock of the hodgepodge of people—punkers and metalheads mixed with rockabilly rockers and coffeehouse hipsters. They validated her belief that this band had universal appeal. Now, how to get them to recognize that she was the one to bring them to the next level?

As she surveyed the crowd, her gaze snapped back to a familiar stranger leaning against the wall. He hadn't left. Everyone watched the band, but he was watching her. So intense. She was his prey, and he was ready to pounce. Instead of feeling exasperated as she had earlier with Tyler, or amused like with Jax, Mason's overt perusal made her feel desired and sexy.

Unfortunately, he wasn't her type. No, after the debacle with Ethan and the string of losers before him, Kevan had learned her lesson. No more "normal" guys or guys not interested in a real relationship. Men from outside her little world of tattoo artists and music could never see past her curves and pinup-girl style. They had no problem chasing her; they just weren't interested in keeping her. Most of the tattoo artists were friends with her brother, so they wouldn't date her seriously. Musicians appreciated her "quirkiness" but couldn't stay faithful. So she'd stopped believing in the happily ever after and focused on work. Until Mr. Right came along, she was done wasting time on Mr. Right Now.

A shiver ran up her spine as she felt Mason behind her before she heard the loud whisper in her ear: "I've been so patient. I can't wait any longer, darlin'. Come have a drink with me."

A command. Not a request.

"I'm watching the band," she answered without turning.

"They're almost done with their first set. We can watch from a balcony table."

Kevan turned to protest his bossiness and the sheer audacity of his tone. He was standing so close she had to crane her neck to see his face. They didn't touch, but heat rolled from his broad body in waves, blanketing her in its warmth.

What was it she was going to say?

Instead of volleying a snappy retort, she brought her hand up and brushed against his tightly trimmed beard, barely more than manicured stubble, the texture rough under her fingertips. As she snatched her hand away in surprise, he grabbed it and turned it over, his eyes never leaving hers. His lips touched the center of her palm, then he turned and pulled her after him, up the steps into the lounge area of the club.

"Please," he added over his shoulder, a polite afterthought as he tossed her a sincere smile. They stepped into the quieter lounge—a spot obviously reserved for more prurient pursuits.

Okay, well, as long as he said "please."

Mason glanced right and left, apparently spotting an open booth hidden in a dark corner. He tugged her toward the table and slid elegantly into the booth. When she went to scoot into the torn Naugahyde seat across from him, he pulled her to his side and held her hand on his leg, gently caressing her knuckles, sending hot tingles of electricity shooting through her body. Again, who knew such a thing could be so erotic? The tingling between her legs was a foreign friend that sprang to life under his soft touch.

"So tell me something about yourself, Kevan." She liked the way her name rolled off his tongue like a poetic title and not just a boy's name. He leaned forward to look into her eyes. "Tell me what brings such a beautiful woman out to a club like this."

His longish wavy hair, the only outward sign he might not be a typical "suit," fell forward over his forehead. She nearly reached for him again to brush it aside but twisted her fingers into her skirt instead.

"Does that line usually work? I figured a fancy man like you might have something slicker, more original." She lifted her brows and cocked her head to the side. "I gotta say I'm a little disappointed."

He laughed, his eyes gleaming. "It did sound like a line, didn't it? No, I'm serious. What brings you to the Tiki Torch tonight?" He looked directly into her eyes and waited.

What the hell? Where's the harm in a little flirting?

"I love music, especially live shows. I work with some of the guys in both bands." She studied his face, gauging his attention. "My brother was in Toast, the first band. And I'm a huge fan of Manix Curse. They're insanely talented, don't you think?" Mason reached up to push a stray curl behind her ear, his long finger lingering on her cheek, the heat threatening to burn her skin as he dragged it over the curve of her earlobe. "I'm totally babbling, aren't I? I tend to do that."

He leaned in closer. His eyes swept her face, landing on her mouth. Oh God, he was going to kiss her.

His lips parted, and his tongue brushed his full bottom lip.

God, those lips. That mouth.

"Hey, Kevan, haven't seen you around in a while," a female voice interrupted. "You guys want a drink?"

A familiar, petite waitress had decided the perfect time to take their order would be right when the Big Bad Handsome Man was making his move.

Kevan couldn't decide if the interruption was good or bad. Good because she should be concentrating on her meeting with Joe tomorrow and not on the fascinating man next to her. Bad because, uh well, she kind of wanted him to kiss her. A little.

She looked up at Dana, meeting the waitress's forced grin with an equally manufactured toothy smile. Before Kevan could answer, Mason ordered a cranberry juice and a water. He smiled politely at Dana and then turned to Kevan; apparently, Dana's famously magical cleavage had no effect on him. Score two more points for Mr. Mason Dillon.

"I hope you don't mind that I ordered you juice. Saw you drinking it earlier and wanted to get rid of the waitress so I could have you all to myself."

She nodded, surprised he'd paid attention to what she was drinking. "No drink for you?"

"Water's fine. One scotch was enough."

She smiled, staring down at the table for a moment before looking into his expectant face. "So what were we talking about?"

His mouth twisted into a teasing smile, and little crinkles appeared around his eyes, making him even more gorgeous. Mason reached up and brushed her hair back again, tangling his fingers in her locks. Instinctively, she rolled her head back into his grasp and stared into his eyes. She could swim in his sultry gaze for days, like a parched nomad during an extended drought. In the desert. And no oasis in sight.

"We were talking about the bands," he said.

"Right. What did you think of the bands?"

Dropping his hand to her neck, he began to rub in small, gentle circles with rough, calloused fingers. His warm fingers on her cool skin melted her tense muscles, and she tried unsuccessfully to suppress a moan. When Dana delivered their drinks, Mason paid the bill and included a generous tip.

"Both were quite good," he said. "Toast needs some time to mature as a band, but Manix Curse is phenomenal. Great sound and stage presence."

Her chin dropped, and she looked down her nose as he reached for his water. "You're a fan of metal, Mr. Armani Fancy Pants? You seem as conventional as a vanilla shake."

He coughed, water splattering the table. "Wow. That's what I look like to you?"

Pulling a handkerchief from his pocket, he patted his damp face. *Classy. Of course he has a frigging hanky.*

"I happen to like vanilla shakes. And, yes, you're a very good-looking, tall suit. How tall are you? Six and a half feet?"

Tucking the damp cloth back into his pocket, he nodded. "About. I assure you I'm far more interesting than plain vanilla. Come home with me."

His hands gently caressed down the sides of her face and pulled her in for a kiss. The heat from his hands told her one thing: together they would be an inferno. He looked into her eyes, silently requesting her compliance by agreeing to spend the night with him. She nodded, or at least she thought she did. He pressed his full mouth over hers, caressing her lips with his before parting them. Her galloping pulse shot to a sprint and was bolting for the finish line. His tongue explored her mouth with tenderness and determination. It was the slowest, deepest kiss she'd had. Ever. The man could kiss. That was for fucking sure.

The tiny remnant of Kevan's capacity for reason that still remained told her she should push him away. This was moving way too quickly. But it was hard to deny the magnetic pull of her body to his that she'd felt even before almost landing in his lap.

As the kiss deepened, all rational thought seeped away, leaving only her need. Kevan pushed her palms up under Mason's coat, and his solid muscles flexed beneath his shirt. She was definitely considering throwing her self-imposed celibacy to the wind and jumping this man. Her eyelids floated shut when one of his hands brushed her neck and swept down her back, his mouth catching her moan. She could feel the dampness starting to build between her legs and the flutter in her lower belly. Was she really allowing a stranger to practically feel her up in public?

Yes, yes she was. For now, it was such a relief to let the world—her brother, her financial problems—fall away.

Mason pulled her closer, his hard body against her soft one. For the first time, Kevan felt small and delicate next to his overwhelming size. She couldn't shake the sense of safety and protection that engulfed her as he cradled her in his strong arms. Which, of course, was ridiculous, since he was a complete stranger.

She knitted her fingers through his thick curls, and her

other hand skated over his shoulder, slowly outlining his rigid and defined body beneath her fingers. Compelled to see his face, she opened her eyes and was surprised to see him looking at her with hooded lids, watching her every wanton reaction. She felt him smile against her lips, and he moved his mouth delicately across her jawline and to her neck.

"Please come home with me." His deep voice implored her to give in. He leaned in and kissed the tip of her nose gently, almost chastely. "I promise I'll be worth it." One hand held her tightly above the waist and traveled up her rib cage, where his thumb brushed the underside of her aching breast, making her clit throb and her knees tremble with want. His other hand on the back of her neck tilted her head so he could have unrestricted access to her throat. His mouth touched her skin and his nibbles increased, turning more aggressive when he suddenly bit her earlobe.

She gasped the word no.

He leaned back to look at her face. His sexy smile fell. She took perverse satisfaction in realizing this man was not used to being told no. She chose to ignore the voice in her head telling her, *No shallow hookups, no normal guys. Focus on business and business only.*

"But I might bring you home with me," she said. Screw her plan. Why couldn't she have one night in the arms of a really hot guy? She could totally do a one-night stand. Right?

The corner of his lush mouth jumped, and those eyes twinkled with mischief. "Oh, you will."

His hand found her knee and began to stroke her inner thigh. His palm felt heavy and hot, as if he meant to brand his touch into her oversensitive skin. She glanced around the dark room. Could anyone see them?

"No one can see us. I wouldn't let anyone catch me with my hand up your pretty little dress."

His assurances were sweet. Protective. But the idea of someone catching them making out like teenagers in the darkened booth added a little spice, danger, to their illicit encounter. She smiled. "Not into public displays of affection?" she teased.

"Not into sharing." His smile was both sexy and predatory. And she liked it. A lot. Maybe Mason was the answer to gaining back some of the sexual confidence she'd lost with Ethan.

"Why?" she asked, nearly panting.

"Why what?" Mason's fingers began to knead her soft flesh, so close, but so far from where the ache grew at her core.

"Why me?" she asked, shaking off the spell he was weaving around her. "I'm obviously not your type. You could go home with anyone—here or the theater across town."

Her insecure-tinged words spilled out before she could stop them. A shadow slipped behind his eyes, but his hand under her dress never stilled. *Is that doubt?* Had she hit too close to home?

"Darlin', you have no idea what my type is. Didn't think I had one until I met you. Gorgeous. Voluptuous. Vivacious. That seems to be my type now. I want to bury myself in you until you forget whatever keeps you up at night." He drew his fingers down her neck and traced her collarbone. The butterflies in her belly took flight as his other hand continued to casually stroke her leg until the tips of his fingers barely brushed the silky seam of her panties. Shivers shot up from her toes and ran all the way to her hardening nipples. She could give herself this. One night of passion and abandon before the real world came crashing back down again.

Kevan said nothing. Not a word. She couldn't. She could hardly breathe. Grabbing his hand from her thigh, she dragged him from the booth and back down the steps. Ten minutes later, she found herself speeding down the highway in Mason's sleek black car, his hand holding hers against his leg, thumb rubbing her knuckles.

They shared few words on the drive across Portland. Kevan spoke only to give him directions to her rundown apartment building. She tried to ignore the rising heat between her legs and the burn of his hand on hers. Just like she ignored her conscience reminding her about no one-night stands.

Instead, she struggled to remember what condition she'd left her apartment in. In her haste to put together the perfect sexy but professional outfit, she might have left a number of bras and panties thrown about. On the bright side, she'd worn her sexiest retro undergarments. Sexy enough to distract any man from the cyclone that had hit her bedroom. She'd saved for months to buy them, and wore them only occasionally to give her confidence, make her feel pretty. With the way she felt, he could tear the damn things off now. Well, not really, but maybe.

Chapter 3

MASON STEPPED INTO THE SMALL, DARKENED ENTRY behind Kevan, watching as her ass swayed back and forth, her dress emphasizing every soft curve and angle of her shapely figure. Usually, his alert gaze would wander over a new environment. Tonight, he couldn't be bothered. He was mesmerized by the unsteady but stunning woman in front of him. Without turning, he reached behind and quickly locked the door. Kevan jumped when the sharp click echoed through the room.

She spun to face him, an eyebrow raised. Her glossy lips quivered and parted, full with the promise of paradise, but she couldn't disguise her rising anxiety with a coy facade. Her eyes widened, and her hands shook as she fumbled with her handbag.

Funny, she'd been so overtly sensual and vivacious at the club. All innuendo and smart mouth. Where had the confidence gone? And where had this shy, vulnerable young woman come from? Didn't matter. Both versions of this woman were hot and fuckable.

He couldn't remember the last time he'd had such a compulsion to be with a woman. Maybe never. Where her earlier bravado had been the gauntlet thrown down to challenge him, this new, more cautious woman was one he wanted to protect. Nurture. Pleasure. Either way, he wanted her out of her clingy fucking dress before he tore it off.

First, Mason needed to assuage her fear and wipe away her uncertainty. He was a man of action. That's how he'd been so successful in business. Well, up until yesterday, when he'd been notified of his apparent incompetence at the job that had become his life. Before the buzzkill of his employment situation could take hold and overshadow his lust, or before Kevan's anxiety became more tangible and derailed his intentions, he made a decision.

He caught her hand in his and pulled her close before turning her. Moving his hands to her curvaceous waist, he gently, but firmly, pressed her against the door.

More than anything, he wanted her to say yes, but he'd give her another chance to back out. Mason looked directly into her eyes for a confirmation or rejection. He would walk away if she really wanted him to, but it might kill him. Brutally. Could a man actually die from blue balls? He really didn't want to find out.

Kevan nodded, but her hooded eyes and parted lips gave the real approval. Her face lit with an eager, almost greedy smile. Mason went in for the kill, meeting her mouth with his, instantly attacking her with his tongue. He hoped that later he'd have the chance to show her how painfully slow and gentle he could be. But not now. Now he needed this woman. Needed to show her how much he wanted her. Needed to be in her. Fuck her until she screamed his name and clawed her cherry-red nails down his back. Marked him. She made him lose all control, this strange, radiant woman he'd just met. He prided himself as a thoughtful—although dominant—lover. It was all about the control. The control that was seeping through his fingers like melted ice from her searing heat as he gripped the soft material at Kevan's waist.

Mason didn't just kiss her. No slow work up once she parted her soft lips and opened to him. Her invitation was clear. Take me. So he took. Plundering her mouth, he nipped at her full lips. The soft intake of air spurred him on as he demonstrated with his tongue what he was going to do with the rest of her body. Take. Give. She showed no hesitancy. No slight withdrawal or push. Her hands grasped his shoulders as she pulled him to her. Her full breasts and luscious body pressed into his hard, firm one. Like she aspired to merge with him. When her hands wandered down his chest and started pulling at his belt, he realized if her sneaky fingers made it inside his pants, the night would be over before it even started. So much for his legendary control.

Reaching down, he grabbed her narrow wrist and placed it by her head against the door. Pulling back briefly, he looked into her dilated eyes. Her breath hitched when she realized she was pinned. Her chest heaved as her panting increased. Apparently, his new saucy friend liked his little show of dominance. He filed that juicy tidbit away for future use. No, not the future. Tonight. There was never a future with him.

Her eyes sparkled as she licked her swollen lips. Her jaw tensed and eyes widened when his fingers gripped her wrist tightly. Eyes locked, she took her free hand slowly, deliberately from his shoulder and placed it on his hardened cock. The corners of her mouth twitched, and one brow rose. His face warmed. Mason attempted his most wolfish smile and grabbed her other wrist and placed both in his much-larger hand just above her head.

Her eyes widened again, and he swore she quit breathing for a second.

"Oh my God, Mason." Her chest continued to heave, and her eyes were glassy. "Please. Let me touch you." Not ten minutes in the door, and she lowered her lashes and melted into him. Her nervousness evaporated and morphed into desire as she gave herself to him. *Holy shit, this girl is amazing.* Gorgeous. Energetic. And hot as fuck.

Her need ratcheted up his desire at the same time it gave him back a little of the control he craved. She pushed her hips toward him, and his erection collided with her belly. Well, so much for his control.

Her want, her touch, fueled him. Mason had to stop acting like some college freshman with his first hot chick. Been there. Done that. He wanted nothing more than to show this amazing, writhing woman with the preoccupied eyes how fucking beautiful she was. To prove his conservative exterior was a front for a power-ful and sexual man. Then he'd worry about all the other shit floating around in his head. Like the idea that kept bugging him about tomorrow. And more.

"You are the sexiest woman I have ever seen," he said. "We need to slow down."

She frowned, and he instantly regretted his tone. But the pink glow on her cheeks was adorable.

What the fuck? Adorable? When did he ever think anything was adorable?

His gut churned with anxiety. The kind that makes a person introspective and a little uncomfortable. What was it about Kevan Landry that twisted him up like a Twizzler? He cleared his throat, needing to stall a minute and regain some semblance of dignity. *Get your shit together, Dillon.*

Probably best to go with honesty here. "I want to fuck you, Kevan, probably more than I've wanted anything in a long time. But if we don't slow down, I'm gonna lose it like a teenage boy. Understand?" He tucked his finger under her chin and gently tilted her face up. She nodded, and her cheeks turned an even darker shade of red. Yeah. Fucking adorable. He smiled. She grinned back, and he crushed his mouth to hers once again.

"Now take me to your bedroom," he said.

She pulled her hands free and ducked under his arm. Flashing a shy smile over her shoulder, she pushed past, knocking him off balance as her warm, lush body left an absence he didn't care to analyze. Then she winked and ran, legs and arms swinging, her playful squeal ringing out across the room just as the little jacket from her dress getup flew past him and landed on a lamp. Damn. Such a wicked girl.

Mason was all for a game of hide-and-seek. What red-blooded man didn't enjoy a little sexy chase? But truth be told, they'd had enough foreplay at the club. He was more than ready to get her underneath him. And then maybe on top of him, where he could grasp her hips and watch her tits bounce as he thrust into her. Maybe mark her as his. *Ohhh. Enough of this torture.* It was time to find his girl and make sure she never forgot him. Instantly, he dismissed the slip "his girl." Sort of.

He let his eyes adjust to the dark and looked around the room before following her down the hall to the right. Thankfully, the apartment was small, and it wouldn't take long to track down his prey. The streetlights outside shone brightly, casting elongated shadows against the walls. The thud of his heavy steps echoed down the narrow walkway.

"*Kevan?* Where are you, naughty girl? Know what bad men like me do to pretty girls who misbehave?" He hoped he didn't push her too far...before he had a chance to really get...to what? Fuck her? Get to know her?

From somewhere down the hall came a gasp and a giggle. He smiled to himself. She was on board. Somehow, he knew she would be.

"Do you want to know what I'm going to do to you, Kevan?" No answer. He stomped through the bathroom doorway and yanked the shower curtain back. Loudly. "If you're not naked by the time I get to you, I'm going to rip that sexy little fifties number off your delicious body." He opened and shut the cupboard doors, noting how chaotic and out of order Kevan's toiletries were. All types of colorful and glittery tubes and bottles, in addition to piles of clothes, were strewn across the darkened counter.

Mason stalked down the hall, careful not to walk on her discarded dress in a pile on the floor, and stepped slowly to the closed door of what had to be her bedroom. He was out of rooms to explore in her tiny apartment. His ear against the door revealed quiet rustling and heavy breathing. He knocked twice, smiling and chuckling at Kevan's muffled screech and then a slight thud. Another quiet giggle.

"If you're not going to answer me, I'm going to tell you, my little Bettie Page." The knob, cool to the touch, turned easily. He pushed the door open, and a cloud of flowery scents flooded his nose. A woman lived in this room. This was definitely her bedroom. No doubt.

"Since you've already driven me past the breaking point, I'm only gonna make you come once before I take you." He felt the aging carpet give underfoot as he stepped into the room. No sound except for her labored breathing.

"First, I'll spread you out on the bed and run my hands over your body. Then I plan to squeeze those beautiful tits and pinch your nipples to see how hard or how soft you like it." He ran his fingers along the textured wall and moved toward the soft moaning sound emanating from the corner of the room.

"When you're squirming under my hands, I'm going to pull your tight little peach ass to the edge of the bed and push your legs apart. I cannot wait to lick my way down and finally find out how you taste."

Kevan popped up in the corner and leaned over to turn a lamp on, flooding the room with a soft light that made her pale skin glow. She was fucking beautiful. *Beautiful*. Like a wicked pinup angel or a colorful rainbow breaking through the clouds after a nasty storm. A nervous smile flitted across her face. She breathed deeply, and her chest rose and fell.

"I'm not naked. Are you going to punish me?" She angled her chin down and batted her eyes. Her darkening cheeks gave hint to her battling nerves.

A brave girl. No smile, just a mischievous gleam in her eyes. He stood still for a moment, admiring the way her dark hair fell over her shoulder and contrasted against her pale skin. No, she wasn't naked, but she was standing there in the sexiest lingerie he'd ever seen. She wore lavender silk and gray lace with the garters he'd felt under her dress at the club. Good God, did women even wear those anymore?

And the shoes. She had left those impossibly high, shiny purple shoes on. Mason was a pretty self-aware guy who recognized his virtual plethora of kinks. But not until he'd seen those shoes on her did it even occur to him to add shoes to the list. *Or maybe it's the woman in the shoes, Mason*. Again, he pushed his errant thoughts to the side. Instead, he took one long stride toward Kevan.

Her faltering smile was his cue. No more games. He spread his arms wide. "Fucking perfect. Come here." And it was the truth. He'd assumed she was different— unique—when he'd watched her work her way through the club, but he suspected he'd never met a woman like her before.

She tipped her head down but couldn't hide the relief in the upward curve of her full mouth. He wanted to devour her. Wanted to worship her. Wanted every single bit of her. And she was going to give it to him.

She took two shaky but resolute steps toward him. Arms still down, she slowly raised her gaze to his. Then he cupped her face in his hand. So gently, though he wanted to yank her to him hard. She deserved better. She deserved more. Without words, he implored her with his gaze, asked if she was ready. Ready for him. She nodded almost imperceptibly.

Thank the fucking universe.

Mason caressed the smooth skin of her cheek with his thumb, then slowly and deliberately dragged his index finger down her face, feeling the downy texture under the soft curve of her jawline and down the slender slope of her neck. Her skin was satin under his weathered fingertip. She shivered. Her chill lit a fire in him that he'd kept in check until the moment he felt her shake beneath him.

He gently stroked her collarbone and traced the colored hearts tattooed there with his blunt fingers, as he'd done in the bar, and then dragged his fingers to her chest and over her breasts. The fullness of the bottom of her tits fit effortlessly in the palm of his hand. So heavy and full.

She gasped, a soft exhale of a sigh from her open mouth as his thumb abraded her swollen nipple through her silk bra. "Do you like that? Gentle or rough?"

Her head fell back, but still she kept his gaze. No answer.

Mason tugged slightly harder with his thumb and forefinger. Giving enough of a pinch of erotic pleasure and pain to bring her back into the moment. Back to him. She smiled around a quick intake of air. God, she was sexy.

"Answer me, beautiful girl. Gentle or rough?" His voice sounded alien to him. Low and gruffer than his normal tone. If he wasn't careful, soon he'd give up all pretense of seduction and rut her like a wild animal.

"Rough." Her voice was barely a whisper. Her dark lashes brushed her cheek as she arched into his hand. "Please."

The growl rose deeply from his belly, surprising him when it burst from his mouth. It wasn't that she wanted his hands on her roughly. Oh no, it was the soft but resolute "please" following her answer. This beautiful dark angel with the blue streaks and pinup body liked it how he did. Rough. Passionate. Hopefully dirty.

Using more force than he intended, Mason reached around to unsnap her lacy bra and tossed it to the floor. Before he went into complete caveman mode and threw her on the bed, he pulled back to take in her naked breasts pressed together by her arms and presented to him in the glowing light of the dull lamp.

"Jesus Christ, Kevan, you're a goddess," he said.

Her cheeks already pink and warm from desire turned almost red. Her contradictions were refreshing. One minute, the sexy, voluptuous woman was a siren, and the next she was shy and innocent. A woman as stunning as Kevan must have had plenty of lovers. What man wouldn't worship her body? For some reason, thinking of her with another man burned like acid in his gut. He didn't usually care about a woman's history. But for a moment he imagined what it would be like to claim the effervescent woman in front of him as his own.

Mason pinched her rosy nipple. Hard. He leaned forward to soothe the sting with his tongue, quieting her sharp cry. The woman tasted like vanilla and sugar. So fucking sweet.

"God, yes," she keened. "Feels so good." Her hand spread on his chest as she looped the other around his neck. He didn't want to leave her gorgeous breasts, but he needed to get her into bed. Now. He swept her chest and neck with kisses to find her mouth waiting. Ready for his.

Mason attacked her mouth with his tongue and reached under her knees to lift her into his arms. She squealed. Protesting. "No. Don't. I'm too heavy."

At her withering, guilty expression, he asked, "What idiot told you that? You're perfect. Fucking. Perfect." He gently laid her on the bed covered in piles of pillows and a soft floral comforter.

Lifting her leg with one hand wrapped around her delicate ankle, he ran his hands up and down the silky stocking, savoring the softness of her body beneath the thin barrier, before guiding her shoe off and tossing it to the side of the bed. "I'd love to take you in these heels, but I want you to be comfortable, so let's take them off." He caught himself before he said "this time" as he gently removed the other shoe, adding it to the one on the floor.

In his world, there was rarely a second time. Women were lovely, and he enjoyed their company, but when you added sex to the equation, it became too complicated. Too messy. But it would be nice to have more than one time with Kevan. This woman pushed almost every hot button he had. He wanted more, but he'd have to be satisfied with their time together tonight. He didn't have time or room in his life for a commitment. He had work, and that would have to be enough for him.

"And we wouldn't want my sharp heels to poke you in that fine ass when I wrap my legs around your hips, now would we?" She'd found her voice. Albeit, it was lower and suppler than earlier. The sassy pinup was back in play.

Good girl.

"But you have the advantage, Mr. Dillon. I'm almost naked, and you still have your suit on. So unless you plan on tying me up with your overpriced tie from Needless Markup, I suggest you take it off and commence with the ravishing."

Hmm. Another rough-and-tumble sex reference?

Her playfulness threw him off balance a little, but it made him laugh. His encounters with women were usually much more serious, with him in control and his partner not. But not this one. She liked to give as much as she took. Too bad he hadn't taken the chance to get to know her better before taking her to bed. Within a few brief moments, he could already tell she was funny and sweet, and saucy and sexy.

"Ah, there she is." He smiled, catching the slight sparkle in her eyes. "I have to admit, there's something very sexy and very dirty having you laid out naked and me dressed. I find it awfully appealing." He undid the knot of his tie slowly, taking time to pull it from his collar, then laid it at the head of the bed.

"And I have to admit to having a bit of a suit-porn addiction."

She laughed and drew her toe down the front of his shirt before settling her foot back on the bed.

Carefully, he removed his coat and hung it across the old-fashioned velvet chaise adjacent to her bed. When he reached down to pull his dress shirt out of his pants and unbutton the top button, she hopped onto her knees and crawled to the foot of the bed in front of him.

She knelt before him and her cherry-tipped fingers brushed his hands away. She unhurriedly undid his top button. And then languidly worked the next. By the time she reached the third button, he'd lost all patience with her slow tease.

"Fuck it," he growled and ripped the shirt open, a button clicking against the side table.

Her shriek, accompanied by a grin, was filled with

half surprise and half joy. He kicked out of his shoes and pulled his socks off. Then he yanked down his slacks and boxer briefs, his eager cock bouncing against his lower belly, painfully ready for action. Kevan's eyes scrutinized him.

He bent forward to join her on the bed, but she held up her hand. Was she having a change of heart? Now?

"You are an insanely good-looking man." She covered her smile with her other hand. "It hardly seems fair to the women of the world that you hide such a gorgeous body under those overpriced, boring suits."

Her genuine reaction warmed him. Working out and running were his outlets, almost like meditation. He often found his most creative solutions during a run. Other women, even other men, had complimented his physique, but he couldn't care less. It had never really made a difference to him. Kevan's open appreciation and honest compliment gave him a feeling he couldn't quite identify. Pride? Gratitude?

File it away. For later.

He shoved the new emotion aside but smiled as he pushed her compliant body gently against the bed. Mason pulled himself up and over her, his elbows on either side of her head, and gazed directly into her blue-gray eyes. Brushing a kiss on each eyelid, he continued planting small kisses down her throat, into the soft hollow behind her ear, and on the curve of her neck. She shivered. Her already-hard nipples puckered into perfect tight buds.

"Looks like I discovered one of your hot spots, sweet girl." He continued kissing down her breasts. He caressed and licked each swollen nipple and then moved down across her belly.

She pushed her hands down to cover herself.

"There's no reason to hide from me."

Sighing dramatically, she moved her hands into his hair. When she tugged sharply and he nipped her belly, her moan of pleasure rolled up in him and added itself to the earlier, unidentified feeling. What was this little vixen doing to him? She had his brain all twisted up in knots. Not to mention what she was doing to his cock.

When he pulled on her panties, she lifted her hips and he caught the scent of her arousal—spicy woman with hints of vanilla and sugar. His already-racing pulse quickened, the blood throbbing in his ears. Enough fucking around. He needed to have this woman. Now.

His prize was within his grasp. "Do you know how badly I've wanted to lick your sweet cunt?" When she smirked at his dirty words, he continued, "How badly I've wanted to see if you're curly or if you're smooth?" No answer other than a sharp intake of breath as he placed his hands against her upper thighs and pushed to spread her legs open, reveling in the feel of her delicate, silky stockings under his calloused fingers.

"Jesus Christ, woman. You have the prettiest bare pussy I have ever seen." He cupped her, the warmth from her body soaking into his hand as she pushed into him with a slight thrust of her hips.

She chuckled, a low, sultry sound—not at all like the twitters of other women he'd been with—that grabbed him deep down in his chest. "I'm not sure that's a compliment in most circles, Mason."

"Trust me. It's a fucking compliment."

She arched up as he drew his index finger down her smooth crevice and through her honey and spread it back up again. She gasped when he pushed in the first time and continued to pant as he pumped it in and slowly drew it out several times. He added another finger when she pushed into his hand harder, and her eyelids fluttered closed. He plunged in and out, deliberately keeping the pace unhurried and loving the sounds of her wetness and pleasure.

She was beautiful and unapologetic in her sexuality. The way she gave herself over to him completely made him feel powerful and protective. When he moved his hand out and slid his thumb over her slippery, hard clit, she cried out and dug her heels into the bed, lifting her ass off the mattress.

"There it is. I'm going to taste you now, because I don't think I can wait any longer." Dragging his tongue up and around her plump, pink folds, then down the center of her core as he rubbed his thumb over her hard nub, he was rewarded with the sweet and tangy, uniquely Kevan taste. *Damn*.

When her hips began to thrust into his mouth and her breaths became shallow pants, he placed a hand on her hip bone to steady her and plunged his fingers from his other hand deep inside her channel and sucked her clit. "Give it to me, darlin'. Come for me." Her legs shook and her hands grasped his hair. Sharp tingles of pain ran from his head straight to his dick.

"Yes." Her breath escaped on a hurried rasp. "Oh God, yes."

Kevan came with a rush of heat and a keening cry as her honey flooded his tongue. Her eyes slammed shut, and her mouth formed an *O*. The gravelly cry that tore from her throat was his invitation to grab the condom he'd pulled from his wallet and suit up. He quickly rolled the protection over his painfully hard cock and moved up and over her again.

Her chest still heaved from her orgasm as she panted soft puffs of air through her parted lips. She smiled, and he rubbed her cheek gently.

"That was seriously…yeah. I just don't know. Amazing. Thank you," she said.

"We're not done. Spread wider for me." He brushed his fingertips over her soaked pussy to make sure she was ready for him.

She looked down between their bodies, the peaks and valleys perfect complements to the other. "I'm a little afraid."

He tugged her chin back up to make eye contact. "Of what? I'm not going to hurt you. Just the opposite."

"Don't get a big head… You know what I mean." She giggled nervously. "But you're kind of big."

He pecked her nose with his lips, relief flooding his body. "We'll take it slow."

Pushing the head of his cock into her slick opening, he parted her swollen folds, and her pussy clenched around him. She was so tight, so warm, so fucking wet. Mason's biceps began to tremble as the delicious torture of her heat surrounded him. It took all his control not to shove himself into her willing body. Kevan's neck arched, and he bent down to bite the tendon there. She wrapped her long legs around his hips and dragged him into her.

"I need you in me now. I need to feel you." As she pulled him in fully, he throbbed with the compulsion to move, to thrust deeper into her soft body. Instead, he cupped her face in his hands and let her adjust to his size, allowing her to set the pace. In truth, he needed a second to catch his breath. Her tight sheath clutched his length like they were made for each other. At that moment, he felt like maybe they were. She moaned. "Please, Mason. Please fuck me now."

So he did. He dragged his dick out from its new home and plunged it into her perfect, wet cunt over and over with jarring strength, racing for the finish, but desperately trying to hold on to the feelings surging through his body. He covered her as she clung to his shoulders and his waist, their eyes never losing focus of the other. He reached under and clenched her round ass in his hands, pulling her up and into his body. Over and over. In the back of his mind, he knew he should be gentler; she deserved to be made love to and not ravaged, but his control had thinned, an unraveling rope barely holding him together. Only this moment with her mattered and his driving need to brand himself on her. In her.

He mumbled dirty and sweet words, mingled together in a song of sex and sounds and all-consuming fire. Their connection complete, she cried out again as she arched her back and her body stiffened under his. Nails clawed into his shoulders, sending sharp whips of good pain straight to where they were joined. Her body pulsed around his, launching him into a torrential wave of pleasure so strong it bordered on agony. He shouted her name on an orgasm so ferocious it stole the air from his lungs—from the room—and white lights danced across the insides of his eyelids.

Instead of looking for his clothes and planning his exit like he usually did, he kissed her nose and rolled off the bed to dispose of the condom. He smiled to himself at her quiet whimper. She felt it too. This thing that had just happened between them. When he returned, he lay down next to her on his back, tucking her against his side, the pounding of her heart thumping against his ribs.

Kevan peered up at him through her long dark lashes, her eyes alight with something akin to joy…satisfaction. For a long time they stared at each other. Then she sighed, exasperation permeating the sound. She grinned, her swollen lips without lipstick but shiny from his kisses and bites. Damn sexiest woman he had ever seen. That was the fucking truth.

"What the hell was that?" she groaned. And they both laughed. Happy. Exhausted. Nervous.

Mason's eyelids felt heavy and his body relaxed. More relaxed than after his most brutal workout. This woman had some kind of special narcotic sex mojo. He might even be able to sleep for a few minutes before he snuck off into the night. The thought of leaving this soft, sweet woman tonight made him feel dark and a little alone. Whoa. Again, with the weird thoughts.

Push that shit right on down, Mason.

Yeah. Later. Maybe he'd close his eyes for a minute. Relish the time with Kevan before he went home to fight his insomnia and put together his career-saving plan. He closed his eyes, listening to the slow, steady breathing and heartbeat of the delicious woman wrapped in his arms.

Chapter 4

LONG AFTER SHE HEARD THE QUIET RUMBLING OF
snores emanating from the big man lying next to her,
or more appropriately, wrapped around her, Kevan lay
awake. An unexpected cloying darkness filled her heart
as she realized the fences of her life prevented her from
spending more time with Mason beyond this one night.
She definitely didn't regret the best night of sex with
the hottest guy she'd ever met. But she marveled that it
had taken under two hours for Mason to turn her from
mission-oriented businesswoman to wanton sex toy.
That had to be some kind of record.

No matter how delicious he was, Kevan wasn't looking for casual, and her last attempt at serious had been a
failure of epic proportions. Besides, there was no place
in her life for a super bossy, boring business guy who
would eventually lose interest in the novelty of banging the tattooed pinup chick. But Mason wasn't really
boring, was he? Bossy, yes, but in a good way. Boring?
Not so much.

Once she'd dreamed of a time when she wouldn't
feel so lonely. For a little while, Bowen had held it
together and been there for her. Not the same as sharing her life with someone, but still, it was good. And
then his demons had taken over, and he couldn't take
care of himself, let alone her. When she had met Ethan,
the sexy-in-a-nerdy-kind-of-way art history professor,

she couldn't get enough of his wisdom and experience. Kevan had thought he might actually love her...until she met his fiancée. In the arena of love, she was definitely not a winner. From friends with benefits who didn't hold her interest to serious relationship contenders who cheated, no one lasted in her life.

It would probably be wise to label this what it was—the best one-night stand in the history of one-night stands—and then call it a night. Kevan stroked the surprisingly soft down of Mason's chest as it slowly rose and fell, and stared at his beautiful face. He was so peaceful and relaxed in sleep, unlike the intense expression he seemed to normally wear when awake. Soft, dark waves of hair fell across his strong forehead, brushing his straight, aristocratic nose and resting softly on his darkly stubbled cheek. It wasn't right for a man to be so effing hot.

Kevan stretched under the weighty leg thrown over her thigh and smiled at the gigantic hand palming her breast. The big, bad, handsome man was still in her bed. Better yet, his warm body was draped over hers. God, he felt good. Heavy? Yes. Geez, the man was huge, but delicious, like tomato-soup-on-a-cold-rainy-day good.

Careful not to wake the sleeping, godlike giant, Kevan shimmied out from under Mason to use the bathroom. On the way back to bed, she paused in the doorway as the low rumble of Mason's breath raising his broad chest caught her eye. With the sheet tangled around his waist, she had a chance to really appreciate the man in the low light shining through the parted curtain. From his wide, tan shoulders to his muscled chest, with the light dusting of hair, and his steel-like stomach to his trim waist and those erotic little dips at his hips—this man was almost perfection.

He seemed like the kind of guy who was all business. Up at dawn for a quick ten-mile run, then off to work, and in bed after midnight. Just another reason why this needed to be a one-night deal. He'd likely be gone by the morning anyway.

Should she wake him, kiss him gently, and send him on his way? She could put on her sexy sashay and detached demeanor to save her dignity and push him out the door before he realized how intimidated by him she really was. Or even worse, before she grabbed on to his beefy arms and begged him to stay. No. She crawled into bed, back into his embrace. She should wake him up, but a few more minutes in his strong arms couldn't hurt, right?

✫ ✫ ✫

The early morning light peeking around the drawn bedroom curtains and the faint twittering of birds drew Kevan from her deep sleep. It was barely dawn, but a large, warm hand stroked her breast, and someone's morning wood rubbed against her butt. She reached her arms over her head in a languid, satisfying stretch and peered over her shoulder. Mason grinned wickedly.

"Morning, darlin'," he said, his drawl thicker than before. God, he was sexy even in the morning. The man didn't even have morning breath.

He reached his free arm over her waist and petted her smooth mound. Parting her legs, she pulled one knee back over his thigh. To make access easier for him. It was only polite, right? His grunt of approval was all the confirmation she needed. He nipped her earlobe with his teeth, the sharp sting igniting the growing heat in her core.

"Good morning, pretty boy," she said, cringing at the squeak in her voice. She'd been going for sultry and ended up with mousy.

"Boy? Really? After everything I've done to you, with you? I'm a boy?" He reached behind to grab something off the side table. She heard the rip of foil and assumed it was a condom. Somehow he managed to get it on one-handed, because the other dragged through the pooling liquid between her legs. How could he be both dominating and considerate at the same time? How could he finger her and pull a rubber on simultaneously? Again, the man was gifted.

"Goddamn, woman," his deep voice growled. "Ready for me, aren't you?"

She arched into his hand, desperate to get even closer, for him to be inside her, soothing the bottomless ache in her belly. How could she not be ready for him? With one arm cradling her head and the other heavy on her hip, he plunged into her from behind. All she felt was him, pushing into her, overwhelming her with his whispered naughty words and hard, commanding body. The sensuous undulation of his hips colliding with her backside drove away her worries and created a place where only they existed. The pleasure-pain of his fingers digging into her hip bone and his teeth on her neck shoved Kevan over into the abyss, with Mason following immediately after with the shout of her name bursting from his mouth.

It was going to be a really great morning. At least

until it was time to say good-bye, because this feeling of contentment never lasted beyond the bedroom.

Hours later, her eyes burned. Blinking into the golden light saturating the room, Kevan knew immediately that she was alone in her bed.

He was gone.

Her stomach knotted with unexpected regret. She'd known it would be a one-time deal with Mason. But deep down, she'd hoped he might stick around. She pressed her fingers against her temples and massaged away a brewing headache. Then she pushed off the bed still clouded in a heady mix of their sex and her perfume.

Kevan grabbed her favorite vintage silk robe she'd picked up for a couple dollars at an estate sale last summer and stepped over her discarded clothes to the bathroom. She took care of business, first brushing her teeth. The reflection in the mirror surprised her. Instead of the bride of Frankenstein she'd expected, the woman peering back looked dewy and fresh faced.

Dear God, that was not good. She scrubbed her face of any remnants of makeup from the night before and padded out of the small bathroom. A cold cloud expanded in her chest, reminding her of the bleak reality of her life and the presentation she needed to put together for her meeting with the band. Kevan's fantasy night of frivolity had come to an abrupt end, and real life was once again rearing its ugly head. Losing business, brother in rehab, rent due. *Bleck*.

Later that morning, after taking a shower and putting on her best retro power suit, Kevan sat down in front of her laptop to work on the graphics for her pitch. When she glanced at the clock on her computer, it confirmed that she was running out of time. Dammit. Her assistant, Tina, was late bringing the rest of her presentation from her office computer. She stood and paced her living room. Poor Tina had no idea that her meeting with Joe would mean the difference between employment and unemployment for her one full-time paid employee.

But Kevan's mind kept flashing bits and pieces from the night before. In the harsh reality of day, she understood how the darkness of night protected people from seeing the things they'd rather not see. At the club, she'd been too caught up in the heady mix of music, fear, and adrenaline to realize bringing Mason home might be a bad idea. A really bad idea. Besides, why was a guy like him hanging out at a dive club in suburban Portland?

She glanced at the digital clock on the microwave and drummed her fingers against the kitchen counter.

Where the fuck is Tina?

Her assistant was a bit flaky on a good day, but she was getting worse, more and more undependable. Time to have a heart-to-heart with her about her behavior. Of course, if she didn't sign Manix Curse today or the meeting didn't go well, the talk they'd likely have would be about unemployment.

Insistent knocking at the front door forced Kevan from her trance. *Oh shit, what if he came back? What will I say?* She froze, staring at the closed door before realizing her assistant was finally making an appearance.

"Open up." Tina's shrill voice cut through the wooden barrier and grated on Kevan's frayed nerves.

Both disappointed and relieved, she pulled the door open, and Tina swept into the room, holding two paper coffee cups. Sunlight glinted off her sequined top, and her ever-present stilettos clicked on the tiled entry. As usual, she was dressed like a tiny drag queen.

"Seriously, it's butt-ass cold out there. What took you so long to answer? I know it's not because you have a man in here." Tina sneered, then laughed.

"Where have you been?" Kevan shut the door and walked into the kitchen. "Did you bring the presentation?"

"Yes, princess, I downloaded the presentation from your computer and brought the thumb drive." Tina's scrutiny shifted to the piece of clothing on the lampshade and then swung to her dress still in the hallway. "What happened?"

"Is that coffee for me? I need this so badly." Kevan held out her hand, ignoring the pang in her chest. When had her pseudofriend gotten so antagonistic toward her?

Tina handed her the coffee with an exaggerated sigh, then plopped down on the couch like she owned the place. "Start from the top, and don't leave anything out."

"There's nothing to explain. Except where the hell have you been?" Kevan's patience with Tina's snark had about run its course. Since Kevan had hired her, their tenuous relationship had begun to fray immediately under the burden of the boss-employee dynamic. Obviously, she'd been too wrapped up in her new business and her brother's spiral to see the growing resentment right in front of her.

"I'm not your lapdog," Tina mumbled, took a sip of her coffee, and locked eyes with Kevan. One pencil-thin eyebrow lifted. "Is that your underwear posing as a lampshade?"

Kevan snatched the sweater and threw it down the hallway. "No. It's the shrug from my purple dress. I meant to toss it on the couch when I got home last night. Guess I missed."

"Wow, your lying is as bad as your aim." She snorted. "And your aim's as bad as Bobby's."

Looking down at her hands, Kevan felt the burn in her cheeks. "Really? You're bringing up that asshat now?"

Tina just loved bringing up Bobby Calvin, like a bull-horn in Kevan's face, reminding her of that mess from high school. Tina had been the one person who hadn't turned her back on Kevan when Bobby, the school's quarterback, had used her and dumped her. They had forged a long-lasting, but awkward friendship as two mis-fits in a town of cookie-cutter cheerleaders and preppies.

"Hey, I'm trying to lighten the mood. That douche can't hurt you now." She smiled a toothy grin. "I'm your friend. You can tell me what has your knickers in a twist—or on the lamp."

Trusting Tina had never come easy, and it was becom-ing more difficult, but Kevan didn't have anyone else.

"What do you know about any of the bigger Portland entertainment marketing companies?" she asked.

Tina looked down her nose at Kevan. "Just what you do. There's GEM, of course, and those two dorks from Los Angeles—Argyle Artist Associates, or something. That's about it." She leaned back, closing her eyes. "Dude, have you ever seen the guy who runs GEM?

He is so freaking hot. Like burn-your-eyeballs-just-looking-at-him hot. Like hump-his-leg-like-a-horny-little-puppy hot."

Warmth crept over Kevan's cheeks, and she faced the window. As usual, Tina was missing the bigger picture. The one where companies like Global Entertainment Marketing and Argyle were the evil overlords of the entertainment marketing world, aimed at crushing her entrepreneurial dreams. "No, I've never seen him. You realize he's the competition, right? His company's ginormous and could flatten us for fun."

Tina snorted and rolled her eyes. "Why would they give a shit about our dinky little agency?"

Kevan took a long sip of her coffee, letting the heat warm her from the inside. "Someone big is supposedly pitching to Manix. Do GEM or the L.A. guys even sign indie bands or heavy metal acts?"

Shrugging her slim shoulders, Tina seemed far more interested in chewing the tattered end of a nail.

Kevan blew out a long breath, lifting her bangs off her forehead. "I think GEM might be interested in Manix."

Tina stopped chewing on her nail and gaped up at her. "That doesn't make any sense. They only go after established stars."

Exactly what Kevan had been thinking.

"I know. But somebody is courting Manix. Has to be GEM. And we're fucked if they get serious about it."

Kevan watched her assistant's face instantly transform. Her eyes changed from unfocused to razor sharp, and her slack jaw tightened. This cunning version of Tina scared Kevan and forced her to keep her boundaries firmly in place.

Hell, she'd only agreed to hire her on Tina's promises of vast connections in the music industry through a cousin Kevan had never met. Turned out her cousin was a professional groupie, and screwing a bunch of local musicians and roadies wasn't exactly considered business networking. By the time Kevan figured it out, Tina had proven to be a cheap and semicompetent office manager. She also had the occasional deviously brilliant idea, which Kevan was counting on right about now.

"How do you know this?" Tina asked.

Kevan rolled her eyes. "You're missing the point."

"Then indulge me. What *is* the point?"

"The point is that a huge megacorporation, or some slick, experienced yahoos, have our band in their sights. They may just end my company before it even gets started." Kevan stood and paced the room. Catching sight of her wadded dress in the hall, she pushed all thoughts of one big, sexy man out of her head. She had to focus.

"Again, how do you know this?"

"Joe told me last night at the club that another company had approached them."

"Doesn't mean anything." Tina waved her hand, dismissing Kevan's wariness. "Could be anybody. And he could be trying to get us to up our game."

"Maybe." It had occurred to Kevan that Joe was bluffing.

"I wouldn't worry about it." Tina's shrewd eyes narrowed, and her pink-slashed lips twisted into a smirk as she looked around the room. "You're never this paranoid about landing a client, especially when you've mind-fucked half the band."

"That's not true, Tina," Kevan said. "And way out of line."

"Something has you twerking and twitching." Tina stood and clacked her way from the living room, down the hall and back. A know-it-all, shitty grin plastered on her face, she said, "You got lucky last night, didn't you?"

"No," Kevan said, dragging out the *O* sound. Nothing even slightly tainted with the possibility of gossip ever got past Tina.

"You're so full of it. Who was it? Do I know him?" She smiled. "How *did* your clothes end up all over your apartment?"

Oh sure. As if she'd share anything personal with Tina the Tiny Talker. "It's none of your business. Focus. Someone big is going after Manix, and we need to figure out who."

Tina's expression of excitement evaporated and was quickly replaced with a tight grin. "Why would they care about some midmarket metal band?"

"How the hell do I know?" she snapped, regretting asking Tina anything about the competition.

"Both GEM and Argyle do big names, acts that sell out arenas. We do local and small-time. Companies like GEM are the lobster to our peanut butter sandwich. Even Argyle is champagne, and we're day-old canned beer. We're ghetto, and they're—"

"Okay, okay. I get it. They're awesome, and we suck."

The room spun a little. Was it true? Maybe she really didn't have a chance at signing the band. Maybe Manix Curse would jump at the opportunity to work with someone sporting more impressive credentials.

Pushing down her doubt, she looked Tina in the eye.

"I don't have a choice. If I don't do something, we lose our lease, the company, and my brother will never get clean."

"That's not what I meant. They're both big-time. Maybe we could partner with them instead of fighting over the same sorry-ass bone."

"Are you on fucking crack? Both those companies would chew us up and spit us out. They don't want to be our buddies. GEM never collaborates with small agencies; they obliterate them. And the Argyle guys are such pompous asses, I'd never want to work within fifty feet of them. We need to do this on our own."

Tina looked away. "You mean *you* need to do this on your own. Your business. Your band. Your brother."

"Not true." Kevan could hear the frustration edging into her voice and tried to cut it back. The stress of Mason bailing and now Tina's obstinacy was wearing on her last nerve. "It's for all of us." It was true. If she couldn't sign the band, she couldn't keep her bitchy assistant on. She let out a huff. Maybe that wouldn't be the end of the world.

Tina stood and walked to the small kitchen, tossing the thumb drive on the counter. "Whatever you say, boss. But we both know you'll always have a job at Tony's shop." She turned and looked Kevan up and down, hand on her hip. "At least you look ready to do battle."

Although Tina's compliment seemed to lack sincerity, Kevan said, "Thanks. Hopefully, I'll get this straightened out, sign the band, and we can get to work on a kick-ass promotional plan."

"Sure. So what *is* the plan?"

Tina had dropped the subject of Kevan's possible

hook-up. Relieved, Kevan recounted the brief discussion with Joe the previous night and shared her pitch for later that afternoon.

Kevan walked to the door, then swung it wide. "I'm going to put it all out there and give it my best shot." She leaned in to embrace Tina, who stood there placidly. Her frosty demeanor sent icy spikes of uneasiness through Kevan's chest. Damn, her friend ran hot and cold. With a quick squeeze and pat on Tina's back, Kevan pulled away.

Well, that was awkward.

Once she figured out this mess with her brother, she'd do some serious housecleaning—and not just the mess strewn about her apartment, but the people in her life. And maybe that would happen sooner than later.

After Tina left, Kevan plugged the memory drive into her laptop and scanned the presentations she'd spent the last week putting together for Demon Hill and Manix Curse. She clicked through the slides, faster and faster, and realized several of her graphs and bulleted data were missing. *What the hell's happened to the slides I worked my ass off to perfect?* Obviously, Tina had copied the wrong file.

Kevan checked the computer clock one last time. She had ten minutes before she had to leave to meet Joe at his downtown office. Maybe she could still catch Tina, have her get the right file, and bring it. She dialed her number, but the call went straight to Tina's voice mail.

What the hell? She left five minutes ago.

Leaving a short message, she jabbed the "end call" button and packed up her laptop. She was out of time. She'd have to improvise.

Chapter 5

MASON REVIEWED HIS PRESENTATION ONE LAST TIME before saving it and shutting down his laptop. He pulled off his reading glasses and rubbed his weary eyes. When had his living room become so cold and sterile? So different from Kevan's tiny but colorful apartment, which had been full of warmth and character. How had he never noticed the precise placement of his furniture and overpriced art by a popular artist he couldn't even name? Who was the interior decorator he'd used? He didn't care to even remember. But what he did recall was instructing her to make it understated and functional. Somehow he'd ended up with stark and arrogant. On second thought, maybe the designer had nailed it.

The phone on his desk rang, startling him out of his thoughts. Other than his sister, only his board members and his parents called his home line. Since the phone was a refurbed antique from the forties, it didn't have caller ID, and answering meant he risked dealing with his robotic parents or one of GEM's board members. But it could also be Jami.

"Dillon," he barked into the receiver, a little harsher than he'd intended.

"No kidding, Mason, since it's your house I just called, and you're the only one who lives there," his sister's clipped voice answered, and he could picture the smirk on her face.

"Hey, Jami. What's up? I'm on my way to a meeting."

"What's up? That's the question, isn't it? What happened at work?"

The last thing he wanted to do was recount his humiliating meeting with the board of directors and their subsequent ultimatum. But when his tenacious pit bull of a sister wanted information, she wouldn't rest until she got it. It's what made her a good attorney and also a pain in the ass.

"Fine." He pinched the bridge of his nose. "I met with my board, and basically they said I need to increase revenue or I'm out."

The expected gasp on the other end of the line never came. Of course not. He was talking to his no-nonsense, all-business sister. "So what's your plan? You *do* have a plan."

"I do. I've been trying to get the company to diversify our talent for a long time. And now suddenly they realize we're behind the curve and need to step it up," he explained.

"And…"

"I signed a band called Demon Hill that might have some potential. And I've found a local heavy metal band that's on the cusp of hitting the big time. I'm going after them—without the board, because they'll just fuck the deal up. They're already trying to micromanage the developmental deal with Demon Hill."

"And?"

"And what?" Mason blew out a breath. "I gotta go, Jami. I'll talk to you later."

"I know you're not telling me something."

God, how she irritated him with that sisterly sixth

sense bullshit. Except she was right, but he wasn't willing to talk about Kevan. Or what he'd learned about Kevan and her connection to his band.

Finally, she said, "We'll talk about it later, okay?"

"Sure. Love you. I'll call you later."

"You better. Love you too," she said before hanging up.

Yeah, he was still processing his night with Kevan Landry. In truth, he'd considered taking her to breakfast. Maybe even asking her on a real date, hoping for a repeat of their sexual acrobatics.

He laughed into the empty room. The hollow sound bounced off the slate-colored walls. A date. What a joke.

When he'd gotten up after dawn in search of water, he'd seen a printout on Kevan's kitchen counter of her pitch to Manix Curse's management. The same band he'd gone to the Tiki Torch the night before to sign. Never one to panic, he was surprised at the myriad of scenarios that had flooded his sex-fogged mind. Had she targeted him after reading that damn "Most Eligible Pacific Northwest Bachelors" article in the paper last month? That was ridiculous. He'd been the one to pursue her, zeroing in on her the moment she'd walked into the club.

In the end, it hadn't mattered what had brought them together. The pitch on the counter had served as a reminder to keep his head in the game and only proved his need to refocus on the work, like always. Without work, without his success as a star maker and top earner for GEM, what else was there?

The momentary distraction of Kevan could have easily cost him the band and maybe even his job. The stakes were too high to worry about her hot body. Hell, had she known he was pitching to Manix today? Maybe her game had been to make him lose concentration. As he stuffed his laptop into his briefcase, he shook his head, attempting to dislodge thoughts of her and turn his attention back to the pitch. He wasn't easily bewitched. Success was the only option, and sex with a quirky rockabilly vixen did not factor into that equation.

As Kevan maneuvered her ancient Volvo into the nearly empty parking lot of the Nob Hill area, a much nicer section of Portland than her sad, little dilapidated Belmont apartment, she reviewed the plan in her head. This was a shoot-it-all, go-for-broke, play-to-win gamble. And she had to win.

Hopefully, she still had an icicle's chance in Hades to get this deal done. For all she knew, one of her competitors had already swooped in and stolen her band. Maybe this was a "thanks, but no thanks" kind of meeting. Anxiety flowed through her belly like a bubbling lava river.

Shaking off her nerves and any thoughts of the morning's disappointments, she pulled the door open and stepped into the clean but aging office building where Joe ran his business as an accountant. Kevan's eyes watered as she stifled a yawn. Looking and acting sleepy was not a good way to start this meeting. Another reason why last night had been such a bad idea and why it was probably good that Mason, the love-'em-and-leave-'em asshole, had left.

She pushed the door closed and turned toward the desk in the small reception area. *Dammit.* She should have known better than to take a man home. Thank God she hadn't made him breakfast. She made it a practice to cook only for Bowen and close friends. Never for someone she dated. Well, not that what she'd done with Mason actually qualified as a date.

Laura, Joe's assistant and an acquaintance from high school, met her with a wide-open grin as she struggled to stand and waddle forward. Kevan stood transfixed, gawking at Laura's gigantic round belly before the woman wrapped her in a hug. Warmth grew in the dark cavern of Kevan's heart and battled for space next to the ugly jealousy already mounting. She buried her uncomfortable feelings and smiled.

"Damn, girl, when are you going to have that baby?"

Laura blushed and wobbled back to her desk and plopped back into her chair. "I know, right? She still needs to bake another three weeks. Paul and I are so excited. How have you been?" Her lowered tone made Kevan wonder if Laura had heard the gossip about Ethan. Didn't matter. He was the past. And Laura's glow was contagious. Kevan's stomach settled, and her muscles relaxed. The pure adoration in Laura's eyes when she'd mentioned her husband gave Kevan hope. Even if she never found love, she was glad for some it was real and tangible.

"I'm so happy for you guys."

And she was. They deserved to be happy. Laura and Paul were a couple years ahead of Kevan in school, so they'd never been close, but she'd watched them battle so much to be together, with her wealthy parents doing everything to get rid of her "white trash" boyfriend. Kevan was pleased that someone from her part of town had made it out and found love. And a family. There were years they had struggled with multiple jobs so he could get through school, but finally their dreams were coming true.

Kevan's heart tightened. Their happily ever after, though, highlighted how lonely her own life had become. *No matter*. It was time to nail this gig and save her company. Definitely not the time to start feeling sorry for herself. Again.

"So, they're already in the conference room. You can go on back." Laura smiled and winked. "And then you can tell me who the new hottie is when you're done."

New hottie?

Who was she talking about? Kevan smoothed down her soft black pencil skirt and arranged her fitted silk blouse and trim jacket. With a deep breath, she shook off the dark clouds of doom she'd been dragging around all morning.

Move forward, cupcake. That's what her mom had always told her and Bowen.

She knew this band, and they knew her. This could be the perfect partnership for both of them. In addition, signing the band would give her access to a much higher-level clientele as Manix Curse grew in popularity and, thus, build her client list. She just needed to convince them that her plan was better than GEM's or Argyle's plans. Because it was.

No pressure. I got this.

Straightening her spine and leveling her shoulders, she marched through the conference room doorway. Bolstered by her inner badass pep talk, Kevan added a confident swing to her hips. At exactly the same moment, her shiny new shoe caught on the short pile carpet, snapping her head back and throwing her body forward. Instead of a graceful entrance, she flew through the air toward the floor. Closing her eyes, she braced for the inevitable impact and connected with something solid. She smelled fresh soap and mint.

"Are you okay?" That voice.

Her heart sank into her gut, and the hair prickled on the back of her neck as she opened her eyes and rolled her head up to look up at her rescuer. She glimpsed the concerned expression of a serious, but gorgeous—like so fucking beautiful—man with glowing hazel eyes. And just stared. What the hell was he doing there?

Mason.

"Are you all right?" he asked again. One corner of his mouth turned up as if slightly bemused by her puppet flail.

Against her will, she felt the warming between her legs from the rumble of his voice. Pulling her upright, he slid her body up against his. Not only was she staring at Mason, but her traitorous body leaned into him. With her breasts pushing against his lower chest and his erection growing to attention at her belly, her thoughts drifted back to their morning and night together. Why was she such a klutz around this man? And why the hell was he here in Joe's conference room? Did he work with Joe?

But then he smiled his light-up-the-room smile. "I've got you, darlin'. Don't worry. I won't let you fall."

And his magic spell solidified into glass and shattered into a million little pieces. Dark realization slipped through her mind with blinding clarity. He was the competition.

"Actually, no, Mason, you don't." She pushed away from him and smoothed her hair. "I'm fine."

And go away.

Inside Joe's conference room, the band sat around the battered conference table, staring with open interest at the exchange. Jax cleared his throat. "Well, you always do make an entrance, don't you, Kev?"

The heavy tension in the room thinned as she laughed and greeted the band members and Joe, who motioned for her to take a seat directly across from the man who had recently vacated her bed.

"Kevan, thanks for coming. We've also invited GEM's CEO, Mason Dillon, to join us."

Oh, hell fucking no. Mason Fucking Dillon. CEO of Global Entertainment Marketing. I was a fool not to have realized who he was.

Her blood boiled and her pulse raced as she ground her teeth and tried not to glare at the tall, smug man across from her. His expensive and professional manner exuded the powerful aura of someone used to winning.

Dammit. Had he known who she was when he'd watched her in the club last night? Had he known who she was when she'd taken him home?

She needed to keep her cool and not act like the hormonal mess she actually was. She tilted her head in acknowledgment and fake-smiled in Mason's direction—where he looked oddly uncomfortable, almost like his perfectly tailored suit was too tight—then back at Joe.

Whatever. You won't ruin my presentation, fucker.

Her heart beat so hard she was sure they could hear it pounding against her ribs. All the reasons she'd decided to stay away from guys—especially guys like Mason—came flooding back to her in her father's voice.

You're lucky you're pretty…

Boys will be boys…

Don't think he can't find a million more like you, only smarter…

She looked to Joe as he smiled, ignoring the palpable strain in the room and blocking out her father's taunts. "I'll cut to the chase," Joe said. "We'd like to hear both of your plans. If we like what we hear, we can talk about moving forward."

"Both of us?" Kevan and Mason asked simultaneously, his deep voice overpowering hers. She felt her eye twitch slightly and heat rise up the back of her neck. The air thickened again, weighed down by the growing tension between her and Mason as she launched her most vicious glare his way. This was not going the way she'd wanted it to.

Time to pull up my big girl panties and fix this clusterfuck.

Pretending she hadn't spent the night with the deceitful man sitting across the table and that Joe hadn't just blown her world apart, she smiled at each of the band members. "Look, Joe. Guys. I understand why you might be interested in a more conventional firm like Global Entertainment Marketing. They're big business and have industry connections. I get it. But I know the players in this industry well, and I know GEM has never signed a heavy metal band."

She took a deep breath and glanced toward Mason. He didn't look happy. He might actually be trying to bore holes in her with his laser-like eyes. Not her problem.

"In fact, they've never come close to signing a hard rock band. Their clients are strictly pop or easy listening—"

"I have one of the largest client bases in the industry, Joe. And, contrary to Ms. Landry's claim, we recently signed a metal act to a developmental deal." Mason looked pointedly in Kevan's direction and smirked. "I'm sure you've heard of Demon Hill." Everyone nodded, like a table full of bobbleheads.

Well, fuck.

While not quite the caliber band that Manix Curse was, Demon Hill was a popular draw in the Portland area. Kevan had been so close to signing them until Bowen's fiasco. The band had made it clear they wouldn't be rescheduling their meeting with her.

Now she knew why. And Mason Dillon suddenly became even more of a threat.

As he flipped open his neat little leather dossier, she felt the muscles in her neck and shoulders tighten.

"Demon Hill is a good rock band, more mainstream and definitely less hardcore than Manix. GEM is designed to cater to mainstream artists. Which is cool. For them." Her words were coated with just the right amount of disdain. The metal community was tight-knit and loyal. Painting Mason as the outsider might help her make her case. "But you guys aren't mainstream or even hard rock. You'll never be easy listening, and you're sure as hell not pop. Your music may be melodic and hit a broader audience, but it's hardcore. Mason wouldn't know the first thing about positioning you for long-term success."

Had he known before he'd taken her home that they were competing for the same contract? The thought was momentarily soul crushing. How could she have been so gullible? Again.

Joe pointed to a cable next to Kevan. "Why don't you plug your laptop in and show us what you have first? Then Mason will present." She pulled out her laptop and set it at the end of the table, plugging the projector cable in and focusing the image on the screen at the opposite end of the room. Launching the slideshow she'd prepared, feeling proud of the cell phone images she'd asked for from the attendees and instantly received over social media from last night's show. She glanced up at Joe. He looked impressed.

"Not only do I know Manix Curse, but I love your music. I'm a fan. I recognize how to market a cutting-edge group like Manix, and it's not going to be through prostituting yourself to frat kids, or by fronting boy bands or playing footsies with radio execs. It'll be through social media, authentic follower interactions and events, and playing your badass music to fans who love badass music and want to buy your awesome merchandise." Her throat felt dry, her voice raspy in her ears. She glanced around the table, and Jax rolled a water bottle her way. And winked. *Sassy man-boy*.

Mason tapped one finger on the table. "That's all very quaint, but sending a tweet about concerts won't get you a recording deal—"

"No, of course not." She smirked, pleased she was getting to him. Glad she could make him feel just a little of the discomfort she felt. Damn. Had he seen her meeting notes on her kitchen table before he'd left?

"But building a solid support base and packing every show you play will. As you can see on the graphs, here"—she pointed to the screen—"marketing metrics show a direct correlation between a bands' fan base growth curve and their engagement in social media.

"The great thing about using social media is the costs are measured in time, not dollars. Bands have a lot of down time, which is a prime opportunity to engage current and potential fans." She looked directly at Conner, who was looking down into his lap, maybe at his phone. The full tattoo sleeves on his muscled arms tucked under the table and his hair pulled back into a man bun. To win this battle, she had to appeal to all the band's members, including the distracted bass player. And ignore the jerk threatening to steal her one chance to fix her mess of a life.

"Three years ago, Chris Kael, the bass player of Five Finger Death Punch, was a bartender at a Hard Rock Café, now he has a drink named after him there and more than fifty thousand followers on Twitter. He's sold hundreds of thousands of albums in the last year. In addition, his personal merch product line and distilled whiskey business are growing franchises."

At the mention of one of his rock heroes, Conner sat up and tucked his phone away, his handsome face still drawn, but paying attention. "So what does tweeting have to do with Kael's success in business or as a bass player?"

Score. Finally.

"He grows his band's brand by interacting directly with his fans. Jolt Marketing specializes in social media and can help fine-tune a program designed for this kind of success." She continued through the slides, showing the different statistics and graphs supporting her ideas.

Kevan assessed the interest of the group. Everyone, including Joe, studied the charts on her screen. Mason's foot tapped against the carpet and jiggled the table, but his face remained expressionless. He was obviously a master at hiding his emotions. Or maybe he didn't have any.

"Another great way to effectively build interest in Manix without spending outrageous amounts of money is through fan-centered events, such as meet and greets. Video, too. I'd love to make a couple of low-budget videos—personal behind-the-scenes kind of stuff— and get them to go viral on the web. Growing local interest outside of your core fan base could be done through community events like social activism, charity performances, and volunteering. Sabbath, Slipknot, and Godsmack are all bands well known for giving back." She cycled through the bulleted slides featuring overly happy pierced and tattooed people.

"Finally, I can revamp your merchandising. I have an in-house graphic designer with an eye—"

"GEM has an entire design department. I personally handpick the designers assigned to each brand." Mason leaned his elbows on the table, his eyes locking with hers.

"Yes, but do any of your designers have a father who once played studio guitar for Anthrax? Someone who understands the metal scene because she grew up in it?" Kevan glared and Mason pressed his lips into a tight line, his eyes stormy and filled with something like anger. That shut Pretty Boy up.

"As I was saying, the day of rock star advances is long gone, and touring, videos, and merchandising are how bands make their money nowadays. So, I propose we take a look at your current branding." Apparently, they didn't like that idea as her words were met with groans. "Hey, I don't want to change Manix. I want you to stand out above all the other noise out there."

At least Joe nodded. He got it. Her heart slowed a little from the near-constant pounding against her chest. *Breathe*.

"What does that mean? You don't like our logo—the skull with bleeding eye sockets doesn't get you hot?" Marco asked with his trademark playful smirk.

"Shut up, dickhead. She's trying to help us." Mandi threw her empty water bottle at the longhaired singer.

"No, it's a good question." Kevan was ready for their resistance to updating the band's look. "I don't want to change everything, but help refine it. I love the logo. It's totally brutal. We need to clean it up a bit. We can talk about updating your other stuff—shirts, CDs, posters—in the coming weeks."

Mason's foot still fidgeted, but his expression had changed. He looked different. Impressed? Nervous? Could the CEO of GEM actually be threatened by little ol' Jolt Marketing?

Time to wrap this up and seal the deal. No way could she let the big asshole and his pitch steal her thunder. "In conclusion, I think you need to focus on a few key issues—how to get the most bang for your buck and how to grow your fan base organically." She paused and looked around the table. They were listening. Waiting for her to finish. Interested.

"Jolt is not only the hands-on kind of agency you need, but I love your music, and I'm part of your target market. You can't buy that kind of authenticity."

Turning to look directly at Mason's reddening face, she drew a deep breath. "I know why a big firm is interested in you guys. You're going to be huge without Jolt or GEM. But signing with a monolithic corporation means getting lost among all the other major label acts they cater to. With Jolt, you'd be the main act, and our time and resources would be devoted to promoting you. Besides, Mason Dillon wouldn't know cool if he woke up next to it."

Chapter 6

MASON WAS TORN LIKE A DAY-OLD CONCERT TICKET. On the one hand, he was pissed at Kevan's low blows and repeated hits to GEM and his leadership. On the other, she was right in oh so many ways. Even more, she wasn't just a pretty face anymore. Nor was she only a hot, pinup body with curves he could get lost in. She'd proven she had the brains to back up the bod. In a word, she was a challenge.

And he liked a challenge.

The idea that she knew who he was shouldn't bother him, but it did. Was the connection they had even real? Had she felt what he had felt last night, or had it all been bullshit? It had been a long time since someone had pulled one over on Mason "The Ice Man" Dillon.

Nail this, Dillon. Doesn't matter if she knew. You got this.

Standing, he took the cable from Kevan and plugged his laptop into the projector. His pulse was a steady thrum in his ears. Whoosh, whoosh, whoosh. The screen displayed the vibrant colors of the paused video demo his creative group had put together for prospective clients.

He cleared his throat and rolled the tension out of his shoulders. Time to go to work.

"Thank you, Ms. Landry, for highlighting GEM's assets and illustrating the vast resources and connections we utilize to make our artists money. A lot of money."

Mason smiled at Kevan as she sat rigidly in her seat. Her flinty stare never left his face.

"The ability to send a tweet and gather a thousand Facebook friends doesn't make you a marketing expert, but Ms. Landry does have a point. GEM has a long, successful history in the entertainment industry, and in the past, has targeted more established, conventional artists."

Mason clicked the projector, and the slide changed just as Kevan turned her chair to face the screen and crossed and recrossed her legs.

Fuck. Those legs.

Ignore her. Do your magic.

"The music business has transformed over the last decade, and we've rolled with it. We'd really like to make Manix Curse the cornerstone of an edgier brand of our client portfolio, one that targets a younger demographic, but still utilizes our established industry expertise to help grow the band's fan base and earning potential."

To emphasize his point, he gave his patented "trust me" grin and pointed it at the band, desperately trying to blot out the aggravating woman sitting at the end of the conference table. Her jabs and unyielding attack had set everyone on edge.

"And how do you plan to do that, Mason?" The tall, wiry drummer asked, a glint of defiance in his eyes.

Had the drummer realized the tête-à-tête between him and Kevan had gone beyond the boardroom? He'd seen Jax with Kevan before the band had hit the stage last night. Yes, he'd noticed her earlier but had assumed she was just a fan.

"Great question, Jax. After studying your band and your fans, we've concluded we should focus on three key areas—sponsorship opportunities, greater exposure through higher profile events and tours, and a record deal with an established recording company."

"Who is 'we'?" Marco threw in, tossing back his long, braided hair.

"My market research team was responsible for the data in this video. As you watch, keep in mind we can produce professional-grade videos for the band, too."

"Putting something on the Internet doesn't mean anything. Contrary to popular belief, videos don't go viral by themselves," Kevan interjected, her voice rising. "It takes strategy and planned effort."

"I can also distribute them through the traditional media channels, like MTV. Regardless, I'd like to take a more boutique approach and work with you directly."

Joe nodded his head. Apparently, he liked the idea.

"One of the benefits of going with GEM is our relationship with potential sponsors and industry media outlets. We could explore opportunities with equipment manufacturers, drum and guitar makers, energy drink distributors. The list is endless." He had their attention now.

Kevan appeared to examine her nails, except for the occasional burst of air from her mouth, which sounded suspiciously like disbelief.

"Our mainstream media connections can be useful, as many of those groups also own metal and hard rock media properties, both print and online."

"Dude, like *Metal Maniac* magazine? How fucking cool would it be to be their featured bassist?" Conner grinned widely at his band members, who stared at him in disbelief. Did he not smile often, or were they all already on Kevan's side?

"You're such an egomaniac," Mandi said. Obviously, it was her job to keep her metal men in line, because Conner looked duly contrite as he bowed his head, but Mason caught him throwing a secret thumbs-up to Marco.

Mason's usual confidence grew as the band radiated enthusiasm for his plan. "*Metal Maniac* is owned by a media conglomerate we do a lot of work with."

These guys wanted to be rock stars, and he was their answer to the big time. Now to clinch the deal. "The biggest piece to your success puzzle entails ascertaining a substantive recording contract. I'd like to shop you around and try to negotiate a plan that would include an advance, travel cost, and support, as well as the best royalty options. Maybe some higher-end equipment."

Check and mate.

"Which of your partner labels would be interested in Manix? I mean, do you think Lady Gaga's label is going to take a second look at a heavy metal band?" Kevan scoffed. Mandi and Jax laughed. Kevan was starting to play dirtier, and he was fighting the call to lower to her level.

His face flamed, and he nearly lost his tightly held control. Instead, he replied, "Actually, Ms. Landry, I have a lot of success signing artists with almost every major label, several of which cater to the markets Manix Curse entertains, including both Metallica's and Korn's labels." *Take that, little Ms. Music Diva.*

"And now here's a short video we put together, highlighting some of our successes over the last several years." He flipped off the lights and pressed the play icon on his laptop before sitting across from his former lover and current business enemy. The sweet vanilla smell he'd whiffed when she'd fallen stayed in his nose, wreaking havoc with his concentration.

As everyone focused on the film, Mason glanced around the table at the rapt faces of Joe and his band. He smiled to himself, pleased he'd begun to win them over. His eyes latched on to Kevan, the colors from the demo reflecting on her unblemished porcelain skin. Her body language showed strength and control, but her shadowed eyes gave hint to a gloomy sadness within. *Not your problem, Dillon.* This was business. He was a take-no-prisoners kind of guy.

After the fifteen-minute presentation finished, Mason stood and flipped the lights back on. He turned to Joe and the band. "Any questions?"

They all shook their heads. "I'd really like to thank you for meeting with us today," Joe said. "You both have great plans for leveraging the momentum of this band. It would be extremely difficult to decide between the two paths suggested." Joe paused and took a deep breath.

"Which is why I'd like to take both of you on tour with us. We have a small marketing and PR budget and want to see what each of you brings to the table—not just in theory, but in practice. The tour is eight shows over a week and a half, but you'll get a chance to show us firsthand what you're capable of doing for the band." He looked from Kevan to Mason. "What do you say?"

The room was heavy with silence. Kevan's eyes were wide, and her mouth formed a grim line. She was definitely not happy. In fact, she looked like she might hate him. Was she as off balance as he felt? Strange. Off balance wasn't usually a feeling he had to deal with.

People usually sought out his expertise. He wasn't used to being pitted against newcomers and minor agencies. For years, he'd had a reputation as the marketing golden boy because of his ability to pluck seemingly unknown acts from obscurity and catapult them into superstar status overnight. Pop bands and coffeehouse musicians definitely wanted him on their side. Promoters and marketers wanted to work for him.

Kevan took a long pull from her bottle of water as her eyes darted back and forth between the people at the table. Was that panic starting to flood her expression? Mason knew she'd never go for the tour, since she could hardly stand to spend five more minutes in his presence, let alone two weeks. For some reason, the fact that she looked like she might dart from the room—and he might never see her again—rubbed him the wrong way.

Even though, technically, he was the one who'd left that morning. And he didn't do repeat nights with the same woman. And Kevan was now the competition.

"Honestly, Joe, I appreciate the opportunity, but I need a little time to think this over," Kevan said quickly before Mason had a chance to respond.

"Well, why don't you both take a day and give me a call? We hit the road at daybreak on Tuesday and head for Eugene first, then down the West Coast. Laura can email you the schedule."

After some hurried handshakes, it was over. Before he could stop her, Kevan said her quick farewells and charged out of the room, reminding him of those cartoon characters with bright red faces and steam shooting from their ears. He remained professional, but cut his good-byes short and rushed out after her. What was it about this woman that got under his skin? Even after she had tried to gut him in the meeting, he still couldn't stand to see her walk away.

I walked away first.

He'd been irritated and even a little angered by her confrontational attitude, but throughout the meeting, she'd held her own, sharing innovative ideas and a clear concept of her plan for the band. A completely different, more grassroots plan than his, but still good—very good. Her contrasting and conflicting facets fascinated him. Light and dark juxtaposed with hot and cold. Despite his initial impression of her good-time-girl personality, she was all business in the conference room—professional and polished—so unlike the spirited woman who'd come apart beneath him hours before. Her genuine shock at his presence in Joe's conference room led him to believe that maybe he'd misjudged her. Perhaps she hadn't known who he was.

Since joining GEM right out of college, his passion and business acumen were well respected throughout the entertainment industry. Or had been until he'd learned his job was in jeopardy. For the first time, the heavy pall of doubt had clouded his usually razor-sharp decision-making skills. Then the stunning Kevan Landry had wiggled her curvy, inked ass and blue-streaked hair into his head and had stayed firmly embedded there for the last several hours.

Mason had been waiting for her when she'd swayed into the room. When she'd walked in, she'd been even more mesmerizing in her business attire—sexy fifties secretary—than she'd been the night before. Warmth had flooded his chest at the pinkish bite mark peeking out from under the edge of her blouse. The image of her naked on his lap, his cock buried deep inside her, and the thought of sinking his teeth into the sensitive spot on her shoulder had triggered one hell of a hard-on.

And then she was falling. Again.

A few quick strides, and he'd caught her before she'd fallen too far. Again. Secretly hoping it would become a trend. Her falling. Him catching.

The meeting had passed too quickly, in Mason's professional opinion. Joe's request to accompany the band on tour should have offended him. However, he understood their hesitancy with his inexperience in their genre of music and with their demographic. He also understood they might have some loyalty to Kevan's company. But eventually, he'd obtain the contract, even if it took more time and work than he'd anticipated.

Mason pushed out the door of Joe's office, brushing off the colliding thoughts he had about Kevan. When he finally caught up to her, she stood next to her car, fumbling with her oversized purse.

"Kevan," he called, hurried but not out of breath.

Jogging up, he saw her glance up and her eyes narrow, just before she yanked her keys from her purse, sending them flying from her hand onto the pavement. "Dammit," she said. Hiking up her skirt, she leaned over to pick them up and flashed her lickable rack.

Quickly, he stooped next to her, grabbed the keys, and stuck them in his pocket.

Her pouty lips curved down as she straightened herself. She looked pretty pissed, with a pinched scowl marring her delicate features.

"Give me my keys." She thrust her hand out palm up, and her other hand fisted on her hip.

"Not until we talk."

"About how you're a fucking liar? About how you're poaching my band like you stole Demon Hill? Did you know I was there to sign Manix? Did you creep around my house, looking for my presentation?"

"No. I had no idea who you were. Did you know who I was?" His voice was getting louder.

Breathe. Don't let her get under your skin. Just another day at the office.

"Are you for real? You snuck out of my house like you were ashamed to spend the night with me."

Wow. Toxic anger dripped from her tongue. This might be harder than he'd thought. And who the fuck would be ashamed of banging a smart, smoking-hot woman like Kevan?

"Oh, or do you want to talk about how we aren't spending two weeks together on a smelly, dirty tour bus? About how I hate you and never want to see your smug face again? See, nothing to talk about."

Kevan spun on her heels and stalked down the street. She probably wouldn't get half a block before her feet started bleeding in those mile-high fuck-me heels. God, even in all her glorious anger, she was sexy as all hell.

Then something occurred to him. Sometimes his brilliance surprised even him. Maybe he could have some fun with Kevan, since he'd missed her warm body the minute he'd closed the door on her tiny apartment. What was wrong with mixing a little business with pleasure? They were obviously compatible in bed. And they both wanted to sign the same band. Close quarters with his fiery little wet dream might be exactly what he needed to end what was becoming a tiresome trudge of women and gratuitous dates. Especially now that he was pretty sure she hadn't had any idea who he was when she'd taken him home last night.

"Kevan. Stop running away from me." Damn woman. She had him yelling again. "I didn't know you were interested in Manix Curse until I saw the papers on your table this morning. And I definitely didn't know about Demon Hill."

Without turning, she raised her arm and extended her middle finger. She continued stomping away from him toward the strip mall bordering the parking lot.

"So, that's it? You're afraid of a little competition, so you run? Never pegged you as a coward."

Immediately, she stopped and swiveled.

"I'm not afraid of you," she yelled and took a few steps back toward him. "You're the past, Mason, and I'm the goddamn future. You don't know a thing about repping a band like Manix." Her high heels stomped that asphalt as she marched up to him and stabbed her red, manicured finger in his chest. "Your pressed Armani suits will get you laughed off the tour bus like a bad fucking joke. How long has it been since you've been on the street with one of your clients? You can't just take Manix Curse for overpriced gin and tonics at the club," she said, her voice full of venomous condescension.

What the hell does she know?

"I may have been growing one of the biggest West Coast music marketing companies, but that doesn't mean I've forgotten how to get shit done, sweetheart." It was none of her business that his company had needed new talent for some time, and unless he delivered fresh blood, he was going to be their sacrificial lamb.

Hot anger boiled in his veins and battled with the memory of that same finger dragging down his chest early that morning.

"You don't get to call me *sweetheart*. You don't get to call me anything. You are *exactly* who I said you were." Her voice dropped low.

Mason grabbed her hand and tugged her close. Her sugary scent washed over him. "You didn't seem to mind when I called you sweetheart last night and early this morning." He cringed at the drawl that crept back into his voice, along with his increased arousal. She was messing with his head. Or heads.

She yanked her fingers from his hand. "Go fuck yourself. Because one night with me is all you're ever gonna get."

A surge of anger crackled in his veins. Before he could stop himself, he said, "One night is all I usually offer, darlin'."

Without warning, the sharp sting of her palm met with his face. Surprised, he took a step back. Kevan gasped. Her eyes widened in horror. Then sharpened again. "I know I should be sorry, but I'm not. You are a smug asshat."

"Maybe. But you don't see me acting like a pissed-off teenager." A prickle of guilt for leaving this morning without an explanation crept into his head.

She clenched both fists, but a quick shadow of desperation, or maybe regret, shone from the depths of her eyes. He wanted to take the desperation from her and chase it away. But he was too pissed, and he knew soothing her would only force her to push him away again. A lyric from the White Stripes song "Prickly Thorn, But Sweetly Worn" popped into his head.

Goddamn infuriating woman. Sweet one minute and freaking out the next. He knew he could convince the band to sign with him, especially if they saw him in action. But wouldn't it be sweeter if he could work out his lust for Kevan *and* get the band? But at this rate, she wasn't going anywhere with him.

"You're a liar, and you used me to get ahead of the competition. Just like the sneaky corporate suit you are," she said.

"Don't remember any talk of business or competition. The only thing I remember is your hot little body writhing under mine, crying out my name." Leaning forward, he bent down to eye level and heard her quick intake of breath as he looked directly into her eyes. "I didn't know your connection to the band."

Her eyes shot icicles at him, but their gazes remained locked. To convince her to go on tour, he needed to do it in a way that she felt she was the making the decision. Not him. And he couldn't pin her hands behind her and kiss her into agreeing. Nor could he bend her over his knee and spank her beautiful ass until his hand stung. He'd never earn back this fiery woman's body unless it was completely on her terms. Or, at least, she thought it was. This was a whole new animal for him. He'd never pursued a woman. Kevan Landry presented him with yet another challenge. A new plan bubbled up and took shape.

"You need this contract, don't you?" he asked, and she bobbed her chin tersely. "Then why would you say no?"

She shifted her dainty shoulders, the bite mark flashing him as her blouse shifted. Yeah, he needed to get this band signed and get into Kevan Landry another time or two. She stared at her nails, turning them from front to back, examining them. She muttered inaudibly.

Time to ratchet this up a notch. "I can't hear you. One minute you're screaming and slapping at me like a madwoman, and the next you're practically whispering and shuffling like a nervous child." Trying for his most imperious and intimidating look, he stood tall, arms across his chest, one eyebrow drawn up.

"It's none of your business. I'm none of your business."

"I asked a simple question. Why won't you go on the tour? What's the harm?"

She peered up at him through her dark lashes. "Look, I know I was an easy hookup. But you're a dick for leaving after looking at my presentation and then showing up here. I'm not going anywhere with you."

"Why?"

"I…I can't."

"Afraid you might have to actually work for this contract, Bettie?" he scoffed, grabbing her hand and placing her keys in her palm. "Then run away, little mouse. Now who's the liar? Your whole cheeky-chick thing is all a front, isn't it?"

Once again, she squinted, and the scalding heat was back in her eyes. Inwardly, he smiled. *Now we're getting somewhere.*

Her face darkened, and the knuckles on one hand turned white as her fingers grasped her handbag. "No, you jackass. I'm not wasting my time going on a tour, battling for a band that'll end up signing with you anyway."

"Giving up that easily? Thought you had more fight in you." He pivoted on his foot as if to walk away, hoping the lump in his chest would dissolve.

"I can't compete against you and a company like yours. You have a staff; I have one full-time assistant and a part-time intern. You have money and resources I don't have. I can't waste my time on a job I don't have a shot at." She huffed back to her battered Volvo and tried to shove the key into the lock.

Mason moved up behind her, resisting the urge to wrap his arms around her shoulders, and instead stilled her frantic movements with his hand on hers. The soft skin of her cold fingers sent a punch of tight awareness straight to that knot his chest. He longed to enfold her cold body in his warm one.

"What if I make you a deal?" What his board didn't know, right? They had barely agreed to the superficial development contract he'd offered Demon Hill. So why not make it fair?

Skeptical, she glared at him over her shoulder. God, she was so beautiful it made his heart ache a little. *No, not my heart, dumb fuck, my dick*.

"What kind of deal?"

He removed his hands and stepped back, giving her some space. She turned and leaned back against the car. "We compete for the contract fair and square. Mano a mano. Your wits against mine. I promise a fair fight."

It was a stupid idea, but for some reason he really wanted her to say yes. He held his breath. Waiting. He hoped her long exhale indicated her resignation.

"No." Her eyes, the color of blue steel, held his gaze

unflinchingly. Why was her first response always no? "I…I can't risk it."

But her hesitancy convinced him of an opening, so he went in for the kill. "So you have some other low-hanging-fruit opportunity waiting for you?"

She pushed off from the car and stood with her shoulders thrown back, her chin tilted up. Her face began to redden from his taunts, but she said nothing.

"Or maybe it's because you're afraid you can't keep your hands off me?"

"So this *is* about getting into my pants…"

Good question. What *was* he doing? "No, it's about—"

"What is it about then, Mason?" she asked, suspicion dripping from her simple question. "You're the one who left without even a polite good-bye. I wasn't expecting flowers and poems. Let's just call it what it was: a misguided one-nighter. But now this. What am I supposed to say?"

Misguided? He leaned forward. The side of his mouth brushed her ear, sending jolts of sensation straight to his cock. "I shouldn't have left this morning. But this tour is a great opportunity. For both of us. And even if you lose the band, which I'm not saying you will, there might be other potential acts and venues you can book."

Her breath hitched, but she didn't move. "Why should I trust you?"

"Because you don't really have a better option, do you?" he said softly.

"Maybe," she said finally and put both her hands on his chest to push him away.

"Really?" He couldn't help the smile threatening to

take over his face. So much for his reputation as the cool, collected negotiator. Willem Maxfield, GEM's founder and chairman, had nicknamed him The Ice Man years ago, but this woman got under his skin like a blowtorch and melted his calm, cool shell to a big, messy puddle.

"Under one condition. Okay, two conditions," she said.

He tried not to roll his eyes, but as she'd reduced him to a teenage boy, it was more difficult than he would have thought.

Instead, he narrowed his eyes. "What conditions?"

"If you lie to me one more time, the deal is off. You walk away, and I sign Manix Curse without a fight from you or GEM."

"Didn't lie, darlin'. I honestly didn't know you were there last night to see Manix until this morning." He paused. "What's the second condition?"

She stood up straight and tilted her head to peer directly into his eyes, and that sugary vanilla smell filled his nose. "We forget last night ever happened, and we don't repeat it."

Uneasiness trickled down his spine, pooling and souring in his belly. How could he ever forget the best sex of his life? How could she? Impossible. Ridiculous, even. Hell, he'd agree to just about anything to be near her for a little while. At this point, he'd take what he could get and work on her resolve later. Work her up until she was ready to scratch her nails down his back and scream his name as he pulled her hips from behind and pounded into her.

"Fine. I'll agree to it. For now." He stood there, feeling awkward. If he couldn't kiss her or dry hump her against the car, what now?

She provided the answer by offering her slim hand.
Really?

"After I had my fingers and cock in your perfect little pussy and you were quaking with lust in my arms, you want to shake hands?" He quirked an eyebrow.

Her hand shook slightly, but she kept it in place.

"Don't be an ass. This is a business deal. Shake."

So he did.

"You're agreeing to go on tour?" he asked, trying to keep his tone even.

"I'm agreeing to think about it."

He stood, numb, while she unlocked her car and pulled open the door, cringing at the sound of metal grinding against metal. She threw herself into the car and revved the engine. Then nothing. After a second try, the engine turned over and chugged to life. He stood watching her through the window as she busied herself on her phone, presumably waiting for her old heap to warm up. Finally, she put the car into gear, and without another look in his direction, drove out of the parking lot.

Mason didn't want to question why he wanted her to go on tour and why he'd made such a ridiculous deal. He'd worry about that later. First, he'd save his job and have some fun with Kevan. Then he'd move on with his happy little life. Feeling half-heartedly positive about his path, he watched as her car drove out of sight. Finally turning away, he climbed into his BMW M5.

He punched the band manager's number in his phone and spoke. "Hey, Joe, it's Mason. I think we're both good to go on the road with you. I'm definitely on board and you'll probably get a call from Kevan soon. What time should we be there?"

He wasn't letting this opportunity pass, and he sure as hell wasn't letting Kevan move on. Not yet.

Chapter 7

LEAVING MASON STANDING IN THE PARKING LOT WAS hands down, one of the most uncomfortable things Kevan had ever done. The physical ache in her heart was a surprise, like the almost overwhelming desire to run her fingers through his hair while screaming in his face. She wanted to wrap her hands around his throat at the same time she wanted to kiss his beautiful, lying mouth.

Go figure.

Kevan parked in the lot next to the small cottage she'd rented to house her fledgling business. This part of town was just off the main drag of the trendy Hawthorne area, with retro houses turned into boutiques and small firms. The shabby but cute and funky bungalow wasn't a traditional office. Sort of like Kevan, which was why it felt so special to her. Her space. Her office. Her dream. If Mason Dillon and his robo corp didn't put her out of business.

Her little office had been home to a number of businesses long gone, but she loved the lighting and its turn-of-the-century style. Because it had housed a salon, a toy store and—before that—a record store, the small rooms hadn't required much work to make them serviceable.

She enjoyed working at Tatuaggio part-time and loved that it was less than a block away. The camaraderie and energy of the tattoo shop was so positive, but this place was her future and true passion, where she wanted to build her own thing, make her own stamp on the entertainment and business fronts.

She pushed on the front knob, and the door swung in without any resistance. The door was unlocked. *That's odd*. "Tina? Sindra?"

Her voice echoed through the small building. It was the middle of the day, and no one was in the office. Why had Tina left the door unlocked? So unprofessional. How were they ever going to be taken seriously if they couldn't even lock their own doors?

Hopefully, her assistant had her schedule somewhere on her computer. Walking to Tina's desk in the small lobby, she punched the password on the keyboard and received an error. After three more attempts, Kevan gave up and huffed down the short hall toward her office. She'd talk to Tina tomorrow about locking her out of her computer, especially since she was probably going to have to let her go anyway.

Kevan would have to wait until she got Tina's password to print out her schedule for the next couple of weeks. She was fairly certain there wasn't anything on the calendar that would prevent her from going on tour with Manix. Other than driving out to see Bowen at the treatment center that afternoon, her schedule looked pretty bleak.

She glanced in the other small office, a creative arts space for her graphic artist intern, Sindra, and continued past the kitchen-turned-conference room that still served as the place to eat. A lot of scrubbing, some rearranging of shelves and storage space, and several buckets of paint had turned the inside of the dated bungalow into an elegant and quirky office. Kevan was a firm believer in using color as a design element, especially when money was an issue. And money was *always* an issue.

At her desk, she threw herself into her chair and sighed loudly. Usually, she felt immediately centered and filled with purpose in her office. It was a space where her creative juices flowed and her best ideas materialized. A girl with her stellar history of failure — failed family, failed relationships, failed schooling — had built this beautiful space with her brains and tenacity. She'd taken the shit life had given her and turned it into something for herself. Even if she did still have to work at the tattoo shop to make ends meet.

Today she felt none of that self-confidence. Icicles of doubt and the acidic bite of fear had settled into her chest and taken root after Mason had snuck out that morning. It was camping out for a while, eating away at the foundation she'd forged, revealing and reigniting the heartache of never being good enough — always the curvy girl with the pretty face. *All beauty and no brains*, her father's voice echoed in her head.

Now that Mason had provided her with a fighting chance by offering a battle of wits and skill, she had more to worry about. Even if he didn't have some sneaky hidden agenda, he could change his mind about their flimsy deal anytime he wanted to. It would be much easier for him to bring a team in to romance Manix Curse. He was the kind of guy who never lost. He probably didn't even know how. Unlike Kevan, who was practically an expert.

While she couldn't afford losing the money from not working at the tattoo shop, she couldn't afford to lose the opportunity either. Another issue was whether or not she could stick to her condition of hands-off. The man was hot. But Mason had probably lost all interest once he'd seen her pitch sitting on her kitchen counter. Besides, he was a jerk. Yeah, that ship had sailed and sunk.

Boy, she had a shitty track record with men, starting with the football captain in high school, then various tattoo artists and musicians. The latest, a little over a year ago, had been Ethan. She could almost hear her dad's voice chiding her on her pathetic first attempt at a serious relationship, laughing at her public humiliation as the ever-present cloud of cigarette smoke engulfed him and he sloppily chugged on a beer. She'd ignored the warning signs, including her lukewarm reactions to Ethan's sexual prowess, and had kept plodding along, trying to make it work.

The mind-numbing pain Kevan had felt when she'd met Ethan's lovely little fiancée had seemed debilitating at the time. Sweet Jessica was everything you'd expect a professor's fiancée to be—smart, pretty, quiet, polite. Nothing like Kevan. The shock on his face when Kevan had run into them at the movies had been priceless. Almost enough to dilute the agony of betrayal. He was the reason she'd sworn off men, especially Suits.

Instead, she'd taken her anger and worked her ass off to finally finish her bachelor's degree, while working as a pinup model for a local retro clothing designer and running the tattoo parlor Tatuaggio. She had taken her shiny new certificate, applied for and received a small business loan from her local credit union, and hung out her shingle for business while still holding down another job. But her loan was coming due, and she had major cash-flow issues. Then there was Bowen.

Looking around the office she loved so much, her eyes fell on a picture of her, Tony, and Bowen at a pool party last year. Their tattooed arms were wrapped around her shoulders as she smiled up at her big brother with affection. Bowen had his head thrown back in laughter. Bowen on a good day. Tony Martelli, the owner of Tatuaggio, and all the employees had thrown her a surprise party in celebration of her new business. They were the closest thing to a real family she and Bowen had had since their mom died.

The memory filled her with warmth and sadness, and tears began to well in the corners of her eyes. Minutes after the picture was taken, Bowen and Nathan had tossed her in the pool. She'd been furious about her ruined hair and makeup and her soaking dress for all of two minutes. Then she'd looked at their happy, laughing faces, and her heart had filled with overwhelming love for the family she and Bowen had built themselves from the ashes of their ruined childhood.

Kevan jumped when the front door slammed.

"Hello?" Tina's voice pierced the otherwise quiet building. "Kevan?"

"Back here," she yelled, her gut swirling with acid. She was sick of Tina's bullshit but still didn't relish the idea of letting her go. Maybe she should wait until after the tour.

A few seconds later, Tina peeked her flushed face into the room. "*So*, how'd the meeting go?"

"The presentation went well." She frowned. "Even though half the slides were missing."

"Oh no. I must have copied the wrong one. Maybe *you* should be responsible for your own files." Tina had the grace to appear mildly apologetic, but as usual, made it Kevan's fault. "But the meeting went okay?"

"Sure." *If you consider a total nightmare okay.* "Where were you?"

Tina looked down at the mail in her hand and shuffled through the envelopes. "I went to see my grandma. She's sick." She looked up at Kevan and narrowed her eyes. "So if everything went great, why do you look like your dog died?"

"Mason Dillon, GEM's CEO, was there."

"And…" Tina tapped the stack of mail she was holding against her leg.

Kevan wasn't in the mood to rehash the meeting or her confrontation with Mason, so she cut to the chase. "They want me to go on tour with them."

"Cool. Why don't you sound excited?" She leaned her short, narrow body against the doorframe, her mile-high stilettos crossed at her ankles.

"They invited him, too. They want a marketing cage fight between the two of us. Old school versus new school. Very heavy metal." Kevan snorted.

Tina rolled her eyes. "And that's a problem? If you can't compete in the brains department, you could always screw him."

Kevan's pulse pounded in her ears, and her jaw nearly dropped. Before she could respond, Tina continued like she hadn't just verbally slapped Kevan. "Oh chillax, I was just kidding. Have you considered this might be a gift? At least it's not the Argyle douchebags. You know, you might learn something from him. Even steal some tricks from his fancy marketing bag."

Kevan crossed her arms on the desk as she counted

to five before speaking. "I am not interested in stealing anything from his bag of tricks." Except maybe another kiss. Whoa, where had that come from? She couldn't let those kinds of thoughts sneak up, especially with Tina nosing around in her personal business. "And teaming up with them is not going to happen. Besides, I can't afford to leave Jolt for two weeks to go on the road with a metal band and some arrogant business guy. I need to be here, running this business."

Tina's grin returned. "You slept with him, didn't you?"

"Who?" Kevan asked, looking away and hoping Tina couldn't see the truth on her face.

"Dillon. GEM's CEO. You screwed him didn't you?"

Kevan sighed and looked back at Tina. "We are not talking about my sex life. I'm talking about Jolt."

"I freakin' knew it. But whatever. So if it isn't because you screwed him, it's because of the business?" Tina taunted, wrinkling her nose and curling her lips. "News flash, sweetie. We don't have any business. We have bills, not clients. A couple of bands, a freak-show entertainer, and a tattoo shop are not enough to keep us going. We'll be closed in a month if you don't do something now." She took the stack of bills she held in her hand and tossed it on Kevan's desk.

Kevan held her breath for a moment. Tina's blunt words had hit their mark. It hurt, but it was true.

Before she could respond, Tina said, "I don't mean to be harsh, but what happens to me? And Sindra? And your brother—"

"Stop," Kevan ordered, keeping her voice even. She stood and stepped around her desk to stand in front of Tina. "Look, seeing as I don't know whether or not I'm going to be able to sign Manix, maybe it's best if you start looking for something else."

Tina's mouth dropped open, and she pulled back. "Wait. You're fucking firing me?" She stared in disbelief. "After everything I've done for you?"

"No. I'm letting you go. You're right. I'm out of money. This tour is a last-ditch thing, and who knows what's going to happen." Kevan felt like her heart had been ripped from her chest when she admitted her possible failure aloud.

"Whatever," Tina practically spat. "Good luck, princess. I hope you know what you're doing." Tina turned to walk away. "I'm beat and going home."

"I'm sorry. I'm so sorry," Kevan said. As Tina stomped down the hall, Kevan remembered the locked computer. "Hey, you changed the password on your computer. Make sure you email it to me."

The building shook as the front door slammed shut. Tina had every right to be pissed, resentful—whatever she was—but Kevan was almost to the point of not giving a shit either way. The constant battle with Tina had long begun to overshadow any value she'd once had as an employee, let alone as a quote, unquote friend.

Her thoughts drifted to Bowen. Regardless of what happened with Jolt, Kevan couldn't let her brother down. Until the last year, when his addictions had gotten out of control, he'd always been there for her. Like when their mother had died from breast cancer. Or when their dad had gone off the deep end and buried his grief in a bottle. A teenage Bowen had done his best to keep their abusive father from dragging them down into his abyss.

Her phone alarm sounded through the quiet office, snapping her attention back to the present. Time to stop wallowing in her own self-indulgent misery and drive out to see Bowen at New Beginnings. A noxious blend of emotions had been boiling in her gut all week. She was terrified that the man who used to be her brother would be different, and even more terrified that he hadn't changed at all.

As she locked the front door and turned to her car, she marveled at how easily she rolled from one clusterfuck to another. Like a champ.

Walking into the treatment center almost an hour later, Kevan took the time to let the surroundings sink in. Short walls painted in soft pastel colors and a lobby crowded with tattered furniture reminded her of a high school teacher's lounge. More industrial than medical. Behind the glassed-in reception desk, the room opened up into a hall of sorts with a dozen or so people scattered throughout the room—reading, dozing, or playing games. There was little, if any, discussion going on. And Bowen was nowhere to be seen.

"Can I help you?" A voice inquired.

"Huh?" Kevan turned to face the older woman seated behind the desk. She didn't recognize her from that horrid night earlier that week.

The woman smiled warmly. Patiently.

"Are you here to see someone?" The woman looked down at something in front of her, maybe a list of visitors.

"My brother. Bowen Landry."

The woman typed something on her computer

before a frown settled on her face. "New patients aren't usually up for visitors during the first week." The woman studied Kevan, her eyes still kind but her frown deepening. "Didn't the admitting counselor tell you that?"

"Yes, but I thought he might want to see me."

Was there something wrong with him? Fear pounced on her heart, piercing it with sharp claws. *Oh God, please let him be okay.*

Her panic must have shown on her face, because the woman reached through the open window and patted Kevan's arm with her soft hand. "I'll call him, okay?" She squeezed Kevan's hand and smiled again. "We'll see if he's up for a visit."

Kevan swallowed, her throat lined with dusty sandpaper, and nodded.

"Sign in, and I'll buzz you through."

Several minutes later she was seated at a wobbly card table in the corner of the room, picking at the torn vinyl covering. Anything to keep from letting her mind wander, or worse, bursting into tears. What if he wanted to go home already? Her aching shoulders bunched tighter, the tension pulling across her back and neck like a vise. Who knew if he had another shot at recovery?

Sadly, this wasn't his first rodeo. He'd attempted sobriety a couple of other times. Granted, this time his bottom was far lower than all the others. Before it had always been just alcohol, but this time he'd added speed to the mix, and it had been game on. That scary drug-dealing gangbanger, Santino, and his buddies had almost broken Bowen's jaw when they'd beaten him so severely he'd lost consciousness. Thankfully, the guys from Tatuaggio had shown up as the goons were about to crush her brother's hands. Without his hands, he couldn't hold a tattoo machine or play the guitar. Without his hands, who knew what would happen to him?

Two battered, black skater shoes appeared where she focused on the carpet. She took a deep breath, not looking up, and stopped picking at the table.

"Kev?" Bowen's voice was a pale imitation of his once-strong bass. Slowly, she raised her eyes to meet his and exhaled. She barely recognized the stooped, battered man before her. *No. No. No.* Tears threatened to fall. Taking another deep breath to quell the storm welling in her chest, she stood and smiled.

"Bobo, you look like shit." Her words held bite, but her tone was soft, and her voice quivered as she reached up to embrace her brother. The man who hugged her back was a shell of her once-vibrant and larger-than-life Bowen. Pulling back, she stared into his handsome face and reached up to rub her thumb across his cheekbone. The swelling had gone down, and the bruise had begun to fade to a watercolor mix of green and yellow. His usually bright eyes were dull and had dark shadows underneath. His clothes hung from his gaunt torso. Where had her brawny big brother gone?

Bowen gestured to her chair and plopped down into the one across from her. She reached over and gripped his clammy hand. Though sitting, Bowen's body moved constantly, not like before with a bounding kinetic energy infecting everyone around him. No, now his feet shuffled, his fingers picked and smoothed the jagged edge of the fraying table. He twitched and stretched as if so uncomfortable in his own skin even his shadow didn't belong to him.

"Kev," he said drawing out the single syllable, "I can't stay here. I will fucking die here."

Kevan knew right at that moment that Bowen had to stay in rehab. No matter what. He would fail if he left. His battle had suddenly become life and death.

Kevan sighed. "No. You'll die out there. You're staying."

His haunted eyes widened, and he yanked his hand away. Big brother was not used to her refusing him anything. Ever.

"The fuck? I can stay sober. And I'm totally done with the drugs. I'll go to meetings. I promise." His gaze swept from left to right, and back to Kevan. The table and his chair rattled from his knees bouncing up and down. "I don't fucking fit here, okay? Bunch of whiny pussies crying about how their wives won't let them have a girlfriend and how they lost their vacation home. How's that supposed to help me not drink or use?"

"I don't know how it's supposed to work. It just does. Please don't do this." They'd been through this before. And if they could make it past this point, maybe they'd actually have a shot at being a family again. She leaned forward and peered directly into blue-gray eyes identical to hers. "And I won't let you die."

He was on that path if the night before last was any indication. If the guys hadn't interrupted Santino beating the shit out of Bowen, who knows if her brother would have survived. Bile burned the back of Kevan's throat. The thought of living a life without him sent chills down her arms. Even a sick Bowen was better than no Bowen.

"What about my job? What about the band?" His face was flushed, and he looked wild. "What about you?"

"The band will still be there, and Tony already told you your station will be there when you get out. We all want you to get better." She sighed. When had she gotten so damn tired? "None of it matters if you're dead."

Crossing his arms, he turned his head to stare at the wall to the right of her.

She leaned forward and grabbed his chin, pulling it toward her. Looking directly at him, begging him with her eyes to hear her—really *hear* her—she said, "I love you, and I won't watch you kill yourself. And I won't help you do it."

He opened his dry, papery lips, but she raised her hand. He closed his mouth.

"I need you to get better. For real this time. I can't lose you, Bo." She paused and watched as the words sank in. "I cannot survive without you. I'm barely holding on as it is."

"Not sure I'm strong enough, Kev. Maybe..." He looked away.

"Maybe what?" she demanded.

"Maybe I really am like Dad." The whispered words hung in the air, ready to drop on her at any moment.

"You're nothing like him. Bowen, look at me." She placed her palm on his sunken cheek, tilting his face toward hers again. "That's a cop-out. Life's getting hard, and you're tired of fighting it. Well, suck it up, buttercup."

He rolled his eyes. "Easy for you to say."

"You think it's easy for me?" Her raised voice attracted stares from the other patients. "I'm losing my business, and the one band I thought would save me is making me fight for their business."

"Wait. What? Manix didn't sign with you? I'll kick Jax's ass."

"It's not just up to him." She shook her head. "And I don't want to talk about them. Or me. This is about you."

Bowen stood up, knocking the chair over. "I have to get the fuck out of here. You need me. I need to be there. I'll tell Jax and the others—"

"Sit. Down." She practically growled the words. "Now."

His sudden burst of energy drained away as he picked up his chair and crumpled into it, defeated. But she couldn't let him quit. They had only each other.

"I need you sober. I need you back. If you can't do it for yourself, then do it for me, Bowen." The tears she'd kept damned up so tightly for so long were fighting to get free.

"Please," she begged. "Please fight for me."

Bowen stood up and crouched in front of her; reaching up, he cradled her face in his battered hands. "It kills me that I'm the reason you're so afraid. Fucking soul-crushing knowing I can't help you, protect you from in here." His voice hitched.

"You haven't been there for me for a while." She watched his eyes widen and lines form on his forehead as the whispered words sank in.

He knew the truth. "I'm sorry."

"So you'll stay?" She held her breath again.

Moments passed as he peered into her eyes while stroking his thumbs slowly across her cheeks, like he had when she was young. "If I stay, how will we pay for it?"

A wave of relief flooded her body as she took a deep breath. "I'll sign Manix. End of story," she said, infusing her words with a confidence she didn't feel.

"But you said—"

"Jesus. Shut up. I'll handle it. Promise me you'll try. Really listen to the counselors and make it stick this time."

He nodded stiffly. She circled her hands around his wiry biceps and pulled Bowen to his feet as she stood. Wrapping her arms around her brother, her best friend, she hugged him tightly for several minutes, wishing she could let the tears fall.

Kevan's heart felt as battered as her brother's body looked. She wished she could stay longer, hold on to any connection still holding them together, no matter how tiny and frayed. Anything would be better than leaving the treatment center and being on her own again. Completely alone. But she had work to do.

After saying her good-byes and making a promise to visit again in two weeks, she sat in the parking lot, sorting through her thoughts as her car sputtered to life and warmed up.

She was out of options. She'd have to go on tour if she wanted to keep her brother in rehab and save her business. If she didn't go, she was screwed.

Could she really compete with someone like Mason— shrewd, experienced, and educated? Maybe she should stop trying to prove them all wrong and give in. Or, perhaps it was time to pull up her big-girl panties—her pretty lace-and-silk panties—and bite the fucking bullet, so to speak.

She laid her head on her steering wheel, the dark surrounding her with its choking emptiness. She felt so alone. She was totally on her own and staring directly into the abyss of losing everything.

Kevan rubbed her slick cheek. The warm river of tears running down her face surprised her. It had been a long time since she'd allowed herself the luxury of a good cry. So many nights in tears, worrying about her brother and whether he was safe. So many tears she just didn't cry anymore, and yet there she was, sitting in her car, crying. Alone. So alone.

She had only one choice. In her gut, she knew Manix Curse was the key to her success. She didn't want anyone to steal her opportunity. She'd have to do her best to keep her walls up and keep that damn man out of her pants and away from her band.

The only thing to do was fight like hell for Manix Curse and for her company.

She stabbed her phone with her Rebel Red finger-nails, looking for Joe's number to confirm that she would be joining the band on the road. *Thank you very much*.

Then it was time to get home and back to work, fine-tuning the plan for the band with solid details. She needed to be at her best in order to compete with the intelligence and experience of big, bad Mason Dillon and beat GEM at their own game.

Chapter 8

THE FOLLOWING AFTERNOON, MASON WAS NOT AT Tatuaggio looking for Kevan. No way, he told himself for the tenth time. He was there on business. Pulling open the glass door, he marveled at the surprisingly quaint building ideally located on the main strip of the trendy Hawthorne district. A retro-styled neon sign hung in a window framed with ivy trailing from the covered arched wooden entryway. Moss lined the bricks of the walkway and lent the warm, inviting curb appeal of a café instead of the more intimidating ambiance of most tattoo parlors. The shop's welcoming feel balanced equally with its high coolness factor.

Though he lived less than five minutes away, Mason spent more time commuting back and forth to downtown Portland than he did in his own part of town. He was shocked he wasn't more familiar with the businesses in the area. He made note of a couple of bistros on the block and vowed to spend less time in the city center and more in his own backyard. That, of course, might be all too easy if he didn't sign the band and secure his position as GEM's top gun.

The boisterous vibe of the shop quickly greeted him. A bell over the door announced his arrival, and heavy metal music pulsed from the speakers, mixed with the buzz of tattoo machines and the banter of loud voices. The waiting area at the front of the shop contained two

well-worn black leather couches, arranged perpendicu-
lar to each other and set around a chrome coffee table
covered with black-and-silver photo albums and a stack
of tattoo magazines. The rest of the shop sat behind a
long wood-and-chrome counter that ran across the width
of the large room.

Although fluorescent lights hung from old-style
rounded shades throughout the building, hanging in the
center of the high ceiling was the most badass glass-and-
chrome chandelier Mason had ever seen. Conner, Jax,
and an older man with a long gray beard and short dark
hair worked on clients in three of five chrome-and-gray
reclining chairs set along the walls, much like stations in
a beauty salon. All three men looked up. Jax waved with
his free hand as Mason greeted the singer and drummer.

"If it isn't big shot Mason Dillon. Here for some
ink?" Jax asked, sarcasm painting his words.

"Not this time. I'm looking for you, actually. Well,
you and the rest of Manix." Enthralled, he watched the
bearded man spread goo on what looked like an old-
school-style mermaid before focusing on Jax. "Joe said
I could stop by the shop. I hope that's okay."

The older man placed a sheet of plastic wrap on the
young woman's shoulder and then secured it with some
tape. He stood and pulled his heavily tattooed arms over
his head and stretched with a loud groan.

"Getting too old for the long hauls, old man?" Conner
said without looking up from a man's leg he was working on.

"Watch it, punk, or I'll put you on clean-up duty."

Conner cringed and continued working on his client.
The older man peeled off his latex gloves and tossed

them in the garbage. Then he gave aftercare instructions to the pretty young woman he'd been working on and told her to wait up front. Turning to Mason, he held his hand out over the shiny counter. "Tony Martelli. And you're welcome to talk band business here with the boys as long as it doesn't interfere with tattoo or piercing business," Tony said. His warm, friendly grin contrasted with his weathered leather vest, worn motorcycle boots, and multitude of colorful tattoos.

They shook hands. "Great shop you have here," Mason said. "How long have you been here?"

"Over twenty years. Before that, I managed a shop in the Bay Area."

"Seems like you got a good crew."

Tony smirked. "These assholes? Bunch of slacker metalheads." He laughed when Jax tossed a towel at his head. Turning toward the back of the shop to a hall Mason hadn't noticed before, Tony shouted, "Hey, doll-face, we have a customer here ready to check out." Then he said to Mason, "Both Jax and Conner should be done shortly if you want to hang out and wait." He gestured toward the waiting area.

"Hold your pants on, old man," a woman's familiar voice called back, coming closer as she moved into the room. "I'm working on your next ad, you old geez…" She froze, and the glossy smile on her lips dropped as her eyes narrowed when they connected with Mason's face. She looked from Mason to Tony and back to Mason again. "What the hell is he doing here?"

"Well, hello to you, too, Kevan. A pleasure as always." God, she looked gorgeous in a pair of loose jeans rolled up at the ankles and a red plaid cowgirl top that highlighted her never-ending curves. Her long dark hair was tied back into a high ponytail, those streaks of blue glowing bright under the fluorescent lights. Instead of the mile-high heels, she had on a pair of beat-up, red Chuck Taylors. And still the woman was hotter than a freaking volcano on the sun in the middle of summer.

Again, why had he left her apartment? At the moment, he was drawing a blank.

"Um, Tony said I should pay you and schedule my final appointment to finish the color." The young woman who'd been waiting for Kevan squeezed past Mason and sashayed to the register.

"You really should get some ink," the girl said. He swore she glanced over her shoulder and winked, but Mason was paying attention to only one woman in the shop. Tony snorted and sauntered out the front door, yelling something about grabbing dinner.

As if remembering she was actually working and not in a perpetual sparring match with Mason, Kevan shook her head and walked to the counter. She handed the woman her invoice and rang her up on the modern register. When they'd said their good-byes and the bell tinkled over the door, Kevan turned back to him with ice so cold in her eyes he could feel the chill between them. She was like a broken thermostat capable of only two settings: hotter than hell and colder than fuck.

Pushing through the gate attached to the counter, she stepped forward and reached for him. When she grabbed his hand, he was momentarily stunned by the zing of electricity that sparked instantly between them. Apparently, the other night had not been a fluke.

She pasted an obviously forced smile on her glossy lips. "Can I talk to you for a minute?"

When he stood there dumbly, saying nothing, she added, "About the tour."

As she dragged him across the room and down the back hall, he didn't resist or pull his hand free.

"Where are we going?" He wanted to know. She didn't answer but continued tugging him down the hall and past an open storage closet. "You're glad to see me then?" he teased. "Trying to get me alone so you can have a repeat of the other night?"

"Shut up," she hissed between her teeth. "It's unprofessional to yell at each other in the front of the shop."

"True. You were very unprofessional."

She stopped and turned, forcing herself into his personal space—not that he minded—so close he could smell her vanilla-sweet scent. "Seriously. Why are you doing this? You are such an arrogant ass."

"Me? I call 'em like I see 'em, *dollface*."

The sneer curling her pretty mouth was almost comical. He was beginning to enjoy how easy it was to read her expressions. When she leaned forward, he felt his breath hitch, and the air nearly crackled. Kevan pressed her palm to his chest, but instead of moving closer like he wanted her to, she reached around and opened the door at his back and shoved him inside. A little roughly. His body instantly reacted.

Dick hard? Check.

Stumbling backward, he grabbed her wrist with one hand and her hip with the other. He twirled her and pushed her up against the door, closing it with a click. He pinned her hand above her head and looked down at her heaving chest. "Well, this feels familiar, doesn't it, Bettie?"

For a moment—barely a couple of bats of her long lashes—her guard was down, and he saw the woman from the other night, the wanton seductress with the hooded eyes. But just as quickly, it was gone. He could almost hear the click as her mask fell firmly back into place.

She pulled against the hand he had above her head. "Let me go, Mason. I'm at work. And we're not happening ever again."

"Never say never."

"I didn't. I said ever… Never mind, just let me go." Kevan shoved her hip bones forward, pushing against his upper thighs and rubbing her body dangerously close to his dick. God, he wanted to fuck this woman again. Preferably sooner than later. But almost instantly, she realized her mistake. Her lips parted, and her breath hitched before she groaned in despair and leaned her head back against the door. "I can't do this. We can't do this."

"Why?" Mason asked, his tone like that of a petulant child sounded unfamiliar to his own ears. Goddamn, her soft curves molded against his taller, harder body so perfectly. Something about this woman sucked him in, made him want more. Trying to salvage control of the situation, he tried a different tactic. "We're both consenting adults. We obviously have chemistry. Why not have some fun?"

As he leaned down closer, their lips were a hair's width away from touching. All the pleasure receptors in his brain fired as the memory of the other night flooded in. Images of their bodies tangled for hours in pleasure.

From the moment he'd heard she was going on tour, he'd decided he needed more time with her…to work her out of his system. Pressing his mouth against hers, he whispered, "Live a little, Bettie, and have some fun with me."

For a moment, she pressed back, her lips and her breasts pushed against his body. The contact sent familiar sparks of desire through him. Dragging in a deep breath, she closed her eyes and turned her head, pulling her face away from his. When she opened her eyes, he was no longer looking into pools of desire, he was—once again—looking into the eyes of a very pissed-off woman.

"Fun, Mason? This is my work. I'm not here to have fun. And signing Manix Curse is not something I'm doing for shits and giggles. I take my business seriously. I'm sorry if you don't." She shoved at him again, but this time he stepped away and silently mourned the loss of her body heat against his.

Irritation at her rebuke began to bubble up and turned a little darker, a little redder, and felt a little more like anger.

"Don't kid yourself. I take everything seriously." He waved his hand back and forth between them. "You. Me. The band. Don't make the rookie mistake of under-estimating me." He put a hand on either shoulder and gently but firmly moved her away from the door. Before releasing her, he kissed her cheek, savoring the sweet smell and soft give of her skin. "This isn't over."

Fixing her steely gray stare at him, she took a deep breath and asked, "Why are you here?"

"Just checking in with the band before we start the

tour." He nudged her to the side and pulled the door open. "Nothing nefarious or underhanded. Not the villain here, Kevan."

He turned and walked out to the open work area, hopefully leaving Kevan staring at his back.

Luckily, both Jax and Conner were done with their clients and were standing at the glass display counter, talking with Mandi. Time to get down to business.

Kevan stood in the combination office and privacy room the guys used for piercing and more intimate tattoo work, feeling like she'd been hit by a freight train. A six-and-a-half-foot-tall, all-bossy man-train named Mason Dillon, to be specific. How the hell was she supposed to stay on track and keep her resolve when that kind of man candy was doing everything he could to sabotage her success? And why the hell was he here of all places? Was he here to see her? More likely, he was there trying to get closer to the band members, despite his claim of innocence.

The thought of him getting to Manix behind her back flung her into the present and into action. She couldn't trust that man as far as she could throw him. After a moment to catch her breath and compose herself, Kevan marched into the front room and found Mason standing at the counter with Mandi, Jax, Marco, and Conner grouped around something in front of them. His deep voice rumbled loudly, but not loud enough for her to make out the words over the Butcher Babies song blaring over the sound system. There went her plan to eavesdrop without being too obvious.

Her circumstances dictated that Kevan had a choice to make. Either she was out of the loop and left to wonder what sketchy card Mason had tucked up his tailored sleeve. Or she was going to have to interject herself into the conversation without seeming nosy or awkward. Great. Now she was back to being the dorky kid that never quite fit in, having to perform the adult equivalent of "hey, guys, whatcha doing?" without actually seeming like that was exactly what she was doing.

Fanfuckingtastic.

"Hey, Kevan, come look at what Mason brought." Yeah. Saved by the pink-haired pixie. Mandi, a full-time college student at PSU, didn't work at Tatuaggio, but lived over the shop in an apartment she shared with her brother, Jax. They'd formed a bit of a bond over the last year, not quite friends, but definitely on the way there.

Kevan pasted on her biggest, brightest smile and sauntered up to the group, with her hips swinging and her head held high. She couldn't avoid the smirk pointed her way when Mason pushed the black, glossy, embossed folder across the counter.

"It's the proposed tour itinerary. Each folder contains details of the city, venue, as well as scheduled and potential promo opportunities." His eyes gleamed in triumph. Really? That's all he had—a pretty folder with maps and locations? Maybe he'd be easier to beat than she'd thought.

Mandi's grin split her face, and her eyes nearly sparkled with glee. "Check it out, Kevan," she said, flipping to a page titled "Sponsorship Opportunities."

Kevan scanned the page. Holy shit. Mason already had the band scheduled to meet with several product sponsors. "Very impressive," she mumbled. And then her eyes settled on one line:

Eugene, Oregon—National tour opportunities, Dan Carver 6 p.m.

Holy hell. Mason had a meeting set for possible tour sponsors. She was totally screwed. Brushing her clammy palms down her jeans, she willed her jagged heartbeat to slow.

"I have a copy for you." The smirk had been replaced with "all-business" Mason as he handed her a similar folder with her name decorating the cover.

"Thanks. I assume you have an electronic copy. In fact, if you can email it to me, I'll append it to the one I sent to the band this morning. Sorry, I forgot your copy."

Mason's cool demeanor slipped. For barely a fraction of a second. But it was there. A tiny chip in his ice-cold armor. Maybe Mr. Perfect wasn't so perfect after all.

Before she had a chance to celebrate her brief victory, Mason handed her a thumb drive. "Of course."

He said good-bye to Conner, Jax, and Mandi, promising to see them the following morning, before he winked at Kevan, turned on his heel, and left. Leaving her standing there staring after him.

Chapter 9

TUESDAY MORNING, MASON WAS EAGER TO GET ON the road, especially with one spicy, rockabilly hot tamale. Once he'd decided to move forward, he'd put his plans in motion, made the arrangements, and was impatient to test his marketing know-how. He had a company to save and a woman to seduce. And less than two weeks to get both done.

Bigger feats have been accomplished by lesser men. Right?

But would she show up? Although Joe had mentioned she was on board, Kevan hadn't confirmed or denied whether she was going when he'd seen her at the tattoo shop. Merely having the thought irked him. Either way, he'd end up with the band. And while there was no denying Kevan's magnetic allure, she was turning out to be quite the challenge — an emotional, clever, passionate challenge.

He pulled up behind the tour bus and trailer as the band and their crew milled about the lot, bundled up against the crisp Northwest fall morning. Workers loaded equipment into the truck, and bags were packed into the cargo area of the bus. Despite the early hour and frigid temperature, the crew exchanged good-natured taunts as they worked, buzzing with a familiar energy. Something he hadn't felt since he'd signed his first act over ten years ago as an agent's intern.

Before today, he hadn't realized he'd missed this—
the thrill of identifying a rising star, then formulating
a plan for an artist who'd put their faith in him, put
their career in his hands. Sure, Mason had a job to
salvage, but he looked forward to recapturing some of
his old enthusiasm.

Manix Curse was more than his ticket to keeping his
job. They might also help him rediscover why the hell
he'd wanted to get into this business in the first place.
The music. The excitement of watching a young band
find itself and hit their stride. Maybe Kevan might be
part of that too. Maybe her passion for this band would
rub off on him—reignite his zeal for the industry. Now,
if he could just get her to forgive him for leaving—oh,
and "stealing" Manix Curse.

Mason hopped out of his car and walked over to
his rented RV to meet with the hired driver. Scanning
through the chaos of people shuffling around, he spotted Kevan.

She was bent forward, reading over something with
Jax and a heavily made-up petite woman in a very short
skirt and the highest heels he'd ever seen. Kevan looked
up and laughed at something Jax said. The garish woman
scowled, but like Mason, Jax was riveted by Kevan's
gregarious laugh. Jax lifted his hand, tattoos peeking
out from his shirtsleeve, and pushed a dark blue lock of
hair back behind Kevan's ear. Mason again felt a pull,
an almost instantaneous draw to run over and rip Jax's
hand from her face.

Okay, that was ridiculous. Where was this posses-
siveness coming from? Why was he suddenly upset
when another man barely touched Kevan? For whatever

reason, the action twisted his gut into knots and had him seeing through a fog of red.

Damn. He needed to get his shit under control.

So instead of acting on his stupid impulse to pummel Jax—whom he actually kind of liked—into the cement, he forcibly spun and went to locate Joe and confirm the travel schedule.

By the time he returned, Kevan was standing in front of the band's bus, surrounded by her bags, gripping what looked like a fifties version of a laptop bag. *Geez, even the woman's gadgets are retro.*

He snuck up behind her and leaned over her shoulder. "You look perturbed, Ms. Landry. Something wrong?"

Fumbling her bag and almost dropping it, she spun to face him. "You mean other than you trying to hijack my band?"

"*Your* band? If they were your band, I wouldn't be here, would I?"

She shook her head, long dark waves of shiny hair brushing the tops of her breasts, making his breath catch in his chest. "Wow, for a second I almost forgot you're a total dick. Thanks for the reminder."

"Ouch. You wound me, Bettie." He leaned down and whispered, "How about I show you what I can do with my dick?"

Planting her palms against his chest, she pushed him away. "Been there, done that. And then you ran off, remember? Speaking of running, why don't you run along to your pimped-out motor home thing over there, Mr. Fancy Pants."

"Well, actually, since you asked…"

"I didn't."

"I rented the RV and hired a driver, because according to Joe, the tour bus is short on space."

She placed a hand on her hip and cocked her head. "So?"

"So there's room for you too." He smiled. Hopefully not in a creepy, lascivious way. Well, not too lasciviously, anyway, since he was shooting for sexy.

"On your RV? You've got to be kidding me," she hissed and turned away. "No, thank you. I told you, no funny business."

"Did you really just say 'funny business' in reference to our fucking?" Mason's chuckle quickly transformed into an all-out belly laugh. *God, she is adorable.* "Geez, woman, what are you, eighty?"

She rushed up to confront him, the ruddy flush of her checks making her skin glow. "Stop talking about the other night. And don't make fun."

"You mentioned it. Or am I the only one not allowed to talk about the night we bumped uglies?" He said it before he had a chance to filter himself, not quite sure why he was trying to rile her up.

"Are you for real? You may dress in a fancy grown-up suit, but you're a pig boy like the rest of them," she said, her voice rising.

"Look, sweetheart, there's no room on their bus, and I have plenty on mine. And a driver. You'll have your own space to sleep and your own place to work," he said.

She looked skeptical but didn't walk away.

He continued, "I won't touch you. I won't do anything to you." He paused and lowered his voice. "Until you beg me to."

"As if. I will never beg you for anything." She

snorted, but her eyes dilated, and her breath caught. She wasn't completely unaffected by his overtures.

"We'll see about that." God, she was so cute and feisty.

The small blond woman from earlier strutted up to them and hip-checked Kevan, but her eyes brushed over him without bothering to hide her interest. "Aren't you going to introduce me to Mr. Dillon?"

"Mason, this is Tina Blalock," Kevan said and flashed him a withering look.

"Kevan's former assistant." Tina thrust out her hand, her long, glittery nails like talons, her eyes darting to Kevan before looking back at him. "Charmed, Mason. I've heard so much about you."

"You have?" Mason's eyebrows arched as he shook her hand. So maybe Kevan had been kissing and telling with her assistant friend. "Like what?"

"Nothing from me," Kevan said and then addressed Tina. "Thanks for dropping by the media list for the Redding event. You didn't have do that…and I really appreciate it."

"Yeah, sure. No problem," she said, still eyeing Mason.

With a terse "Thanks" and a quick shake of her head, Kevan grabbed two of her suitcases and struggled up the steps of the band's tour bus.

Mason had assumed she would be excited to have an option other than the worn and torn, possibly radioactive, tour bus. Unless she wanted to be on the bus to be closer to Jax. Or maybe she wanted to get as far away from him as possible. Mason planned to untangle that little puzzle right away. So far, all of his assumptions about her had been wrong.

Tina brushed up against his side and shivered, reminding him of a wet Chihuahua. He'd forgotten she was still there. "Brrr. It's cold out here." She looked up and actually batted her eyelashes.

Man, this chick was ballsy. Mason didn't care for anyone invading his personal space without an invitation. "I need to make sure we're all set to get on the road. It was a pleasure meeting you."

She grabbed his arm and leaned up to whisper loudly, "You know, Kevan let me go. I'm an awesome assistant and have a lot of insight into the band and their market."

Was she offering to work for him? Right here with her former boss less than a hundred feet away?

He extricated himself from her grasp. "I'm sure you're very skilled; however, Kevan and I have a deal."

"What deal?" she asked, reaching for his hand.

Tugging out of her surprisingly strong grip, he looked around the lot for his driver. "Ask her. Now if you don't mind—"

"Oh, I don't mind. And I already have several good opportunities, so you might miss your chance," she said, not bothering to look offended.

"I can live with that. Now we need to get on the road."

"Whatever. If you change your mind, you can always ask Kevan for my number." Then Tina twirled and strode off to her car, leaving Mason agitated.

Finally locating his driver across the active lot, he started toward him, but before he could take more than a few strides, Kevan called his name. He turned, brow raised, to see her standing in the doorway of the band's bus at the top of the retractable steps, a determined look on her face.

Dragging one bag behind her and shoving another down the steps, she made quite a picture, her hair wild and her nose scrunched up. She was the antithesis of Tina, who was all angles and innuendo. And, apparently, the conditions on the tour bus didn't meet Kevan's delicate standards. *Aw, too bad*.

"The bus is full."

"Is it now?"

"Apparently, Joe's decided to go with the band on the bus instead of in his own vehicle."

"Oh really." He didn't bother mentioning it was at his suggestion that Joe keep a closer eye on his band and start working on their media training during travel times.

"I guess he wants to keep a tighter rein on them."

Mason crossed his arms over his chest and nodded.

"And it stinks." She wrinkled her nose.

He smiled. He couldn't help himself. "Offer still stands, unless you're planning on driving your car all the way down the coast?" Mason tried not to hold his breath as he watched the different emotions roll over her expressive face. *Come on, you know you wanna say yes*.

She gave him a long, calculating look, her deep sigh accentuated by the frosty burst of air accompanying it. "Yes."

He ignored the look of disappointment on her face and maintained his cool indifference. He wasn't going to make this too easy for her.

"Yes, *what*, darlin'?"

"Yes, I will share your RV for the tour. Happy?" she asked. He nodded, trying not to look too smug. "We may be shacking up together, but the terms of our deal still stand."

His pulsed spiked. He focused in on her lips and the mere thought of "shacking up" with her. Then her words began to sink in, evaporating his smugness.

"Deal?" he asked weakly.

She looked at him like he had two heads. "No. Sex. Remember?"

Now he remembered. He straightened and grinned. "Whatever turns you on, sweetheart."

"Don't just stand there looking pretty. Help me with my bags." She gestured to the pile of suitcases on the sidewalk.

"Say 'please.'" Instead of taking the bait, she rolled her eyes and flipped him off.

He smiled, walking over to the RV. "Your wish is my command." Before she could respond, he stuck his head into the rented motor home and called out to the driver, "Ben, can you please take Ms. Landry's belongings into the room at the back?"

Ben, a stocky man in a too-tight black suit, with thinning gray hair, exited the vehicle and bobbed his chin at Kevan. She grinned and stuck out her hand to shake his, but her words were for Mason. "I don't want any special treatment. Mr. Dillon will keep the stateroom, and I'll take the guest bunk."

Mason shrugged, and Ben picked up the bags.

Ben's face was a tight grimace as he tugged on her heavy bags. "Whatever you say, boss."

Mason stepped up on the first step and offered his hand to her, palm up. Kevan's lip curved slightly, but she smacked his hand away. "After you, *boss*."

As Ben gave Kevan a brief tour of the bus, Mason sat at the small built-in table. The driver indicated where the food was stored, where the office supplies were located, and the dresser and closet areas she could use to house her many bags.

Really, how many suitcases does one person need for a nine-day road trip?

He counted at least four. Four full-size suitcases. The woman had high maintenance written all over her.

According to the itinerary, they were to make the short drive to Eugene, where the band was headlining a small show to be opened with the college-town favorite, Chaotic Reign. They'd play until eleven, pack up, and get back on the road for tomorrow night's stop in Medford and then on to California.

It was another hour before they hit the highway through the Pacific Northwest. After a quick call to Joe, Kevan flopped down across from Mason and set up her laptop, using her phone as a WiFi hotspot to do God knows what—Tweet? Facebook? Mason didn't know how to use Twitter. He let his admin, or Steve, GEM's VP of client relations, do all that. Or he had. He'd kept Steve out of the loop on this. No one knew he was on the tour with Manix.

Needing to keep his mind from wandering, Mason booted up his laptop, got onto the Internet, and made a half-assed attempt to check and respond to email. He occasionally glanced at the beauty across from him, absorbed in her own world as she tapped away at the keys. They worked in companionable silence as the RV rolled along the winding highway. Well, it was mostly silent, except for the occasional lyric Kevan would sing off-key, forgetting the accompanying band was in her headphones. He should have found the distraction and interruptions annoying. Instead, it was comforting to have someone working next to him. Not alone.

Yep. Push that one down, too, buddy. Add it to the little pile of stuff not to think about now. Label it "Later." Or "Kevan."

Except, he enjoyed looking at her, watching her twirl blue-streaked lengths of hair around her finger while obviously deep in thought—probably pondering some element of her strategy.

Catching him staring, she yelled at full blast, "What?"

He smiled. Should he tell her he was thinking of dragging her back to the bedroom for a repeat of their all-nighter? Probably not.

"You look hungry," she yelled.

So fucking hungry...for you.

"I'll cook," she said even louder.

He winced, and she gave him a quizzical look. He pointed to his ears. She laughed, hopefully forgetting for a moment she didn't like him. She ripped the large pink headphones off and smiled.

"I'll cook for you. For us, I mean. And Ben," she said at a more tolerable volume. When he scrunched his brow, she added, "You know, for the ride and every-thing. I don't want to feel like I owe you for the RV."

"You don't owe me, dar..." He caught himself. "Kevan."

"So you say. Let me cook, and I'll feel like things are more even." Kevan's eyes brightened as she pursed her lips in a beseeching manner.

"How can I possibly refuse? I'm a horrid cook, and it's not one of Ben's responsibilities."

The sweet, satisfied smile that lit up her face was

stunning. Damn woman, twisting up his brain again. making him want more than a couple of more tumbles in the sheets with her.

"Thank you."

"Under one condition." Mason grinned.

"Now what?"

"You promise not to throw any food or utensils at me."

Kevan stared at him, her face an emotionless mask. And then she burst out laughing again. She picked up her pencil and threw it at him. "Where's the fun in that?"

Mason chuckled at her and tossed it back.

This trip is looking up already.

Chapter 10

THE COLLEGE TOWN OF EUGENE WAS A VERITABLE launchpad for up-and-coming bands in all genres. Acts like Tool and Korn had started out in small clubs similar to the one Manix Curse planned to tear up later that night. With only a day to lay the groundwork before the tour, Kevan feared she wouldn't have enough time to properly set up the promotional opportunities.

The best way to spread the word in a college town would be through the media and word of mouth. Kevan emailed both the rock and college stations to set up on-air interviews. Then she emailed Streetlight Vinyl and CD, a popular music store and hangout, to gauge their interest in promoting the show. As the bus chugged down the highway, she called Joe to confirm their earlier conversation about taking over the band's social media. As soon as he agreed, Kevan had her phone in her hand, shooting off tweets and Facebook posts about the show.

Eugene was a music-friendly town. It was the hometown of bluesman Robert Cray, after all. Kevan didn't receive any resistance. The enthusiastic reception filled her with energy she could feel zinging through her veins. Already, the buzz was building online. Fans had reposted and shared her updates, and her first Tweet alone had over one hundred retweets.

I can totally do this.

Over the top of her computer, Kevan snuck a glance at the maddening man sitting across from her. She studied his strong, muscled forearms through the fringe of her bangs. What was it about a man's forearms? So hot. He'd donned a pair of chunky, black-rimmed glasses that might look hipster or just plain dorky on a different man. On Mason, they looked distinguished. He was typing intently at his very posh laptop. Well, he was more like stabbing at his keyboard than typing. Seems Mr. Perfect was a hunt-and-peck typist. Deep in thought, he pursed his beautiful mouth and ran his hand through his messy dark hair.

Oh, please do that again.

Oh no, please, don't *do that again.*

The obnoxious ringtone Bowen had set on her phone blared through the RV. Mason looked up in time to catch her ogling him before she grabbed the offending gadget and turned toward the window. The passing scenery was a blurred smear of greens and browns as the RV raced down the highway.

"Hello?"

"Ms. Landry? This is Mike Dean, the programming manager at KMTL."

"Thanks for calling me back. As I mentioned in my voice mail, I'm on the road with Manix Curse, and we're in town for a show tonight. I'd love to bring the band down for an interview this afternoon. I can offer some free tickets to listeners as incentive." Kevan held her breath. She hoped she had sounded confident and businesslike, even if this was her first attempt at getting free on-air promotion for a client. Or not-yet client.

"That would be awesome. Could you bring them

in around four p.m.? That's when Corby hosts *The Underground Steel Hour*."

Her heart beat faster, and her pulse raced. A win. Finally. "Excellent. We'll be there."

After sending a group text to the band and Joe, she set down the phone and stared out the window, realizing they were already off the freeway and headed into town.

As she turned back to her laptop, Mason stared at her as he rocked back against the leather seat, arms crossed and glasses balanced at the end of his nose.

"What?" she asked. "I'm supposed to tell you, the friggin' enemy, what I have planned? I don't think so." He must really think she was naive. Or stupid.

"It doesn't take a rocket scientist, which I happen to be, to ascertain your plans, sweetheart," he said, a smug grin plastered on his face.

"Shut the front door. Now you're totally full of shit. You're not only the entertainment marketing kingpin of the West Coast, but also a flippin' rocket scientist?" Barely able to keep her eyes from rolling back, she gaped at him. "What, are you the Tony Stark of everything?"

"Forget it," he muttered, looking back down at his computer. But one eyebrow lifted. "You think I'm Iron Man?"

"Oh, please," she teased. "Are you pouting?"

He continued typing, and without looking up, said, "I don't pout, Bettie."

"Really? 'Cause it sure as hell looks like you are. In fact, if your bottom lip stuck out any farther, I could use it as a table. Hmmm. Maybe I'll have dinner on it."

He lifted his fingers off his keyboard and dramatically dropped his hands into his lap with a sigh. "I got my BS in aeronautics from MIT before I realized I hated science and transferred to Harvard for my MBA."

Kevan's mouth dropped open, and she was pretty sure her heart stopped beating for a second. She had known he was smart, but not rocket-scientist smart. Damn, maybe the Stark comment was a lot more accurate than she'd intended. "For real? So you have degrees from MIT and Harvard?"

"Well, no." He glanced back at his laptop and shifted his hands nervously in his lap. "I dropped out of the MBA program before completing my master's and went to work as an intern for BEA."

"I hate you even more, now," she mumbled. This man was smart-smart. And totally out of her league.

He flashed an aggravating smile and looked back at his computer screen.

Against her better judgment to keep her distance and not dig, she asked, "Who does that? Switches career paths so drastically? Seems kind of indecisive."

He shrugged but didn't respond.

Leaning over the small table, she poked his arm. "Seriously, what made you change like that?"

He grimaced. "What, drop out? I realized I was done with school, and I was there only because it was expected of me."

"By who?"

"By whom."

Kevan flipped him off. There was no need to show off.

He ran his long fingers through his hair, leaving the tips standing up, making him look like a mad scientist. "My parents." He sighed. "My mom is an astrophysicist with NASA. I was expected to follow in her footsteps and become an aeronautical engineer, but I found the whole industry soul-sucking and overly political. And I kept coming back to my first love. Music. I wanted to do something in the music industry. So I did."

"But—"

"Drop it," he interrupted. "It's not complex. There wasn't any big existential crisis. Let's talk about your interview this afternoon. What time do we need to be there?"

Pushing, Kevan continued, "No drama? You weren't running away, because you seem kinda good at that. So why won't you tell me more? It doesn't make sense. Weren't Daddy and Mommy Stark pissed when their golden boy went off the rails?"

"Yes. They were upset. Cut me off, for fuck's sake. It's not like I was going to community college. I transferred from MIT to fucking Harvard."

Ouch. The derision in his words was a sharp dagger in her chest, but she swallowed the hurt down before he could see it. She was proud of her education and wouldn't let anyone take that away from her. "Yeah, I got it. You're smart. Mommy and Daddy disowned you, though, because you were throwing your life away on sex, drugs, and rock 'n' roll?"

His laugh sounded hollow and didn't reach his eyes. "Basically. And they're still not thrilled. But it's not my problem."

Nailed it. Mason had parent issues. "Is that why you went so far away from home to intern? I mean, BEA's in LA. Might as well be a different planet, cowboy. Or maybe it was for some chick."

"Give the tattooed girl a prize. You're right about getting away from my parents." He swept his hand across their work area and stared at her for a moment. "Kevan, I left Sunday morning because I thought you might have known who I was all along. A mistake. I blew it."

Wow. Another near-apology from the guy who was always right.

Don't let him fool me.

"Can we get back to work now, Dr. Freud? What time do we need to be at the radio stations and record store?" he asked, an impatient tone edging his voice.

"So no fair-haired coed enticed you to leave Texas?" She winked, trying to lighten the dark mood hanging over them.

"I told you I don't do long-term. Never works out." He ran his long fingers through his already-mussed hair again. Guess Mason had a tell. "And now this conversation is really done. What time do we need to be at the station?"

She'd let it go. For now.

"We?" Did he seriously think he was invited?

"Yes, we. I'm assuming you'll be along for my events. We are both here to help the band, aren't *we*?" He smiled that deliciously evil grin again, a hint of a dimple in the shadow of his now-scruffy beard. "Maybe you'll learn something. You know, since I'm a rocket scientist slash entertainment-marketing Iron Man and all."

For about two seconds, she had actually started to like him again. And then not so much. "Or maybe you can learn something from me, hotshot."

"Maybe. Now quit trying to distract me with your cleavage and requests for kinky sex and tell me the details of this afternoon."

Who knew Mr. Grumpy had a sense of humor? "Have I mentioned within the last ten minutes how much I hate you?"

He pulled off his glasses and wiped the lenses with the hem of his T-shirt, giving Kevan a brief glimpse of chiseled muscle. She had to resist the sudden urge to lean over and lick his solid abs.

Shaking her head and focusing on Mason's face, she said, "Fine. We need to be at the campus radio station at three for an interview and then go to the rock station at four. I thought we'd offer some meet-and-greet tickets and maybe a grand prize of joining them onstage to jam for a song."

"Now, was that so hard?" He winked and put his glasses back on.

Turning back to his laptop, he grinned wide as he pecked away at the keyboard.

"Now, why are you so happy?" she asked.

"Looks like we're going to have a special guest at tomorrow's show."

An icy finger of apprehension slid down her spine. "Who?" she asked.

"You'll see tomorrow night."

"How the hell is that fair?"

"I'll tell you tomorrow. It's your turn tonight." His eyes softened at the apparent strain on her face. "Don't worry about it, Bettie. Really."

"Whatever," she mumbled as the bus pulled into the club lot and parked. When the RV stopped, she jumped from her seat and darted out the door. She drew in long pulls of the fresh air. Hopefully, some deep breathing and stretching would quell the churning in her belly. She had to focus on the interviews today and the meet and greet tonight, not whatever card Mason had tucked up his sleeve.

The band's tour bus pulled up behind Mason's RV and came to a stop. A couple of minutes later, Mandi sauntered down the steps in hot-pink yoga pants and an oversized T-shirt. Peeling a banana, she waved at Kevan and walked over.

"Hey, chica, how's it going over there on the love bus?" she asked, brushing back a few wisps of her pink pixie 'do, managing to goad and appear the picture of innocence at the same time.

"You're kidding, right? We're competing for your business, remember?" Kevan replied, hoping the heat in her cheeks didn't show.

"And if you keep telling yourself that, we'll all believe it." Mandi nudged her with her shoulder. "Oh, relax, the guys are clueless. No one else can tell but me, and I'll never say anything." She drew her finger and thumb across her mouth like a zipper closing. Kevan gave her a weak smile. She didn't really have any close girlfriends and liked the idea of being friends with Mandi, even if Kevan was a few years older.

"Everyone awake?" Kevan asked, and Mandi nodded. "I set up a couple of interviews this afternoon. I'd really love to hand out an opportunity for a musician fan to join you guys onstage for a song. Think the band's up for it?"

"Definitely. How cool is that? Girl, you know I like your way of thinking." Mandi laughed. Her energy was contagious. "We're all eager to see your marketing stuff on this tour. Because *most* of us are serious about getting out of the garage and into the arena."

"Most of you?" Kevan asked.

"My brother's been acting kind of weird."

"Weird?"

"I don't know. Noncommittal." Mandi drew her brows together and rubbed the back of her neck. "He won't really talk about anything beyond this tour, and he's not chasing the girls like he used to."

"He likes to stay in the moment. It'll work out." Kevan stepped toward Mandi and put her hand on her shoulder, giving her a reassuring squeeze. They made arrangements for everyone to meet an hour before the interview to discuss details and expectations and then said their good-byes.

After a quick walk to clear her head, Kevan returned to the kitchen area of the RV. Mason still sat working on his laptop. There really was no way around it. The man was hot. And the casual version of Mason was sex-on-a-stick in old faded jeans hanging low on slim hips, beat-up Doc Marten boots, and a Portland Timbers henley shirt. Give the man a sexy tattoo, and she'd be done for.

Done.

For.

Too bad she'd declared him off-limits. Maybe she should have thought that decision through. Was there really anything wrong with sharing some sexy times with this man, especially since he seemed remorseful for leaving? She could keep her heart fenced off. *Right?* Well, no, probably not, but she could try. Besides, he was kind of a jerk. A sexy jerk.

Kevan rubbed her thumb across the faded love bite he'd left on her shoulder. His mark. *Hell's bells*. Just thinking about his teeth on her, his lips sliding against hers, his tongue in her, his hard dick...*oh my God. Stop*.

She was in big trouble if simply standing there observing him work was making her nipples pucker and her pussy wet. Thinking about the strength in those hands and the power of one look from him had her practically moaning in desire. No. Think about what a band-stealing, smug, player fuckwit he was.

Mason looked up from his laptop, and their gazes locked in mutual surprise. *Dammit*. She must have sighed or mumbled.

Holy hell, this is going to be a very long trip.

He smiled, almost tentatively, his hesitancy endearing for such an overbearing man. Without thinking—as usual—she let her mouth curve up in response, but then broke eye contact and sat back down in front of her computer. The look was too intimate after everything they'd shared. He could see too deeply into her with those demon eyes.

Remember, he's the enemy.

She forced her thoughts back to obtaining Manix Curse and their business. There wasn't any room in her life for a fling, no matter how aflame the flinger made her feel. Better to focus on preventing her life from going down the toilet. She looked over at the tall man across from her as he chewed on the end of his pen. Was it weird to feel slightly jealous of the mangled plastic between the man's perfect teeth?

It was time to get lost in her drug of choice—music. Pulling her headphones back on, she turned up the volume on her iPod and scrolled through her playlists for something all consuming. *Rockabilly? No. Hmmmm*.

Maybe some metal will help tune out the noise of my thoughts? In This Moment? Butcher Babies? No, something more melodic…yes, In Flames.

As the dulcet opening riffs of "Come Clarity" built and then roared through the earpieces, her head cleared, and a familiar warm, almost meditative calm fell over her. Yes, music was her happy place. At that moment, it enabled her to turn her mind away from the distracting man and back to building interest for the Eugene show and the rest of the tour.

Later that afternoon, the entire crew, including Mason and Joe, met at the college station. The band was ushered into a tiny recording studio to discuss the show that night and give away tickets to callers. The next interview at the local rock station exceeded all Kevan's expectations. For the first time in forever, everything was aligning properly.

The band members were perfect rock stars, silly and full of mischief, but interesting and passionate about their music. At the radio station, lead singer Marco had taken his usual interest in the nearest hot chick and set his sights on the redheaded deejay by turning up the charm to ten and breaking into an impromptu performance of their most popular slow song. The rest of the band had joined in for an a cappella metal ballad. It had been sublime. Kevan had cringed, hoping Marco's on-again, off-again girlfriend, Sabre, hadn't been listening in.

Other than a professional, dignified smile, Mason showed no emotion as they walked single file out into the station lobby. He surprised her with a catlike wink when their eyes met. What was it about this straitlaced businessman that made her belly twist and nether regions damp?

It's a wink, Kevan. Just a wink.

Joking and laughing as they stumbled out into the darkening evening, they were met by a group of young metalheads. Disjointed chants of "Manix, Manix, Manix" rolled through the crowd, and the energy surge for the "hometown" heroes was palpable. As usual, pink-haired Mandi was immediately surrounded by her adoring fans, both male and female.

Content with the flush of success, Kevan didn't resist when Mason grabbed her hand and led her back to the RV. For a moment, she wanted to forget he was out of her league and the enemy.

At the bus, he whirled her around with her back cold against the textured steel vehicle, and placed his hands on her hips. She held her breath as he stared directly into her eyes—damn cobra-charming man—and leaned into her. *Oh God, he's going to kiss me. Please let him kiss me.*

Her eyes fluttered shut, and she leaned her face up to his. Waiting. Her belly churning, she felt him shift, and the soft, scratchy hair of his beard brushed her cold face. When his lips finally made contact with her neck, her skin tingled, and the electricity arced between them. He dragged his mouth down the slope of her neck, burning her frozen skin and making her want so much from him. Her hands made their way from his strong shoulders to tangle in his hair. Then he pulled away and kissed her gently.

On the cheek.

Disappointed, she opened her eyes, silently asking the question. *Why?*

A wave of regret rolled over his face but quickly dissipated into the stoic, unreadable look he usually wore. "You're so lovely when you're happy. All your walls drop, and I can see the real you for a moment."

She longed to lean her tired head against his solid chest. She yearned for his strong arms to pull her into his embrace and his always-warm body to thaw her constant lonely chill. She ached for the soft kisses he'd placed at the top of her head the other night and his sharp nibbles at the tender spot on her shoulder. She wanted the committee in her head to quiet for a while as she lost herself in the bliss of Mason's body, his touch.

But, no. They weren't meant to be. There was the band, of course. But, also, they didn't live in the same world. He was Ivy League, and she was community college. He wasn't relationship material, and she was done with flings. There was not one damn thing between the two of them that aligned.

Kevan stiffened in his arms. "Just because I smile and let you drag me away from all Manix's fanboys doesn't mean you know me, Mason. Don't think for one minute because you know where I like to be touched that you see the real me."

From down deep, she pulled the strength to duck under his arm and march back onto the bus to get ready for the show.

In the RV, Kevan took over the bathroom and the vanity in the bedroom to prepare for the concert. Her show-night ritual consisted of hot rollers, curling irons, vats of hair spray, and her "war paint," as Bowen called her going-out makeup. Next came choosing which ensemble to wear—fancy floral pinup-girl dress with a bright red crinoline and red patent leather peep-toe stacked heels.

When she stepped from the vanity into the living area an hour later, Mason was leaning against the small kitchen counter, tapping his booted toe against the linoleum floor and flipping pages on his phone. As he looked up at her, his gaze grew heated and his foot abruptly stopped. His usually unreadable face gave a brief hint of fire before he shut it down. He drew his gaze from Kevan's hair, over her breasts and curves to where they landed on her feet. And stayed there. Her lips twitched with amusement.

Note to self: Mason Dillon likes high, shiny leather shoes. Not that I care.

"Shall we?" he asked without a trace of leftover tension from earlier. He offered his elbow, and she wrapped her fingers around his arm. The man cleaned up—or was it down?—well. Decked out in an untucked dark flannel shirt over a Black Sabbath T-shirt stretched tight across his wide chest, Mason looked edible.

"Are you planning on going to the after-party?" she asked as they walked across the long lot to the venue.

"Wouldn't miss it. And I want to keep an eye on you and the winners." His innocuous smile hinted at the dimple hidden in his trimmed beard.

"Huh?" Her face burned, and she stopped walking.

"The contest winners. I want to evaluate the success of your program."

She clenched her teeth and forced herself to answer in an even tone. "You're going to evaluate me? Geez, who the fuck do you think you are?"

"No. No…" he stammered. "I like your idea, and

I want to see the results. The guy who won the song with the band could be really cool or an epic failure. Let's hope for your sake it's the former, not the latter," he teased. She smiled. Good, let him be arrogant. It would be all the more satisfying when it worked out in her favor.

"Sure, Mr. Marketing Iron Man," she said. Untangling herself, she smacked his tight denim butt and sashayed off into the club, calling over her shoulder, "Watch and learn."

As usual, Kevan was a flurry of activity—checking merchandise sales, posting Instagram fan pictures and short videos, charming the local media. She gleaned the occasional brief glance of Mason throughout the night. She knew he still watched her like the first night at the Tiki Torch. She could feel the slight tingle at the back of her neck, the telltale sign that he had his eyes on her.

She wanted to be annoyed by his attention. Normally, she would be offended. She could take care of herself, right? It was obvious he wanted to get her into bed again. And, yet, she took comfort in knowing he was thinking about her, looking out for her. Even if it was to get his hands on her boobies again or steal her band out from under her.

As a conversation with the opening band's manager ended with a promise of a meeting after the tour to discuss a promotional plan, Kevan realized she hadn't seen or felt Mason for at least an hour. She glanced around the spacious room and caught sight of him in the back corner with Joe and a younger man, talking animatedly. The well-dressed younger man smiled broadly and shook Joe's hand, then shook Mason's hand. The other

man stood grinning like the cat that had eaten the proverbial canary. But Mason didn't look happy. In fact, he
wore a deep scowl and glowered, with his arms folded
tightly across his chest.

Before she had a chance to run over and eavesdrop
or process what might be going on, the lights went low,
and the opening act took the stage. The packed club
was primed by Chaotic Reign's set and went wild on
the first note.

When Manix finally went on after ten, the crowd
went ballistic. The sultry swell of Mandi's guitar filled
the venue, and the lights at her feet washed her in a shadowy glow. Slung low across her front was a shiny new
purple Gretsch Kevan had never seen before. Conner
added in his long, slow bass line which drew in the hard
drums of Jax, followed by Marco's whiskey-smooth
growl. The pit opened, and the crowd turned into a mass
tornado of sweat and music.

The fourth song into their set, Marco introduced the
contest winner and invited him up onstage. The guy
obviously knew their music but wasn't nearly as skilled
on the guitar as Mandi. But after an awkward start and
some patience on the part of the band members, he
seemed to settle in. They let him play along for a few
songs and then sent him offstage with the crowd cheering for him. It was awesome.

Kevan could hardly believe ninety minutes had
passed when the lights came up and the sweaty crowd
shuffled toward the door, like a congregation exhausted
and excised at the altar of heavy metal. She gathered the
winning callers and the grand prize recipient from the
radio show and took them back to meet the band.

Joining the after-party group at the bar, she introduced the winners and the band members. As she stood back and watched, she realized that regardless of what happened, they would all look back at the tour as the "good times." Her heart sank into her belly when her sense of urgency and all that loomed over her threatened to steal the warm, fuzzy feeling she should have had from the experience.

Her thoughts brought her back to the present. She needed an edge, something to tip the odds in her favor. She had hoped her friendship with the band members would help. Maybe she could appeal to their metal-scene lifestyle as well as their hardworking ethic.

Like her, they lived and breathed the music, but they all had real jobs, except college student Mandi. They all loved the music, got off on the energy and the vibe. But no one had been more surprised than the actual band members when their hobby had become a little something more.

She focused on Mandi, sitting on a battered barstool, holding a beat-up acoustic guitar, the pretty new one probably packed up on the bus. She'd lovingly signed the aged instrument and was plucking at it while talking with two of the meet-and-greet winners. Kevan didn't hear the entire conversation but assumed the guitar belonged to one of the fans.

Kevan smiled. Yep, no matter what happened with the contract—who won or lost—she would always remember this time with them. If they gained in popularity as quickly as she thought they would, Manix Curse would be huge. She would be proud to have known them, to have been part of their grand adventure and thrilled they had let her come along for the ride, even if her personal circumstances had sullied it a bit.

She felt Mason's warmth before he even spoke. "Looks like your meet and greet is a big hit, Bettie." The cadence of his deep voice sent shivers down her spine, threatening to chip away at her weakening walls.

"Thanks. Not too shabby for being thrown together at the last minute," she said without facing him. She didn't want him to see the way his compliment warmed her cheeks. Gathering the courage and the right words to ask about the man at the show, she tried for casual. "So, uh… who was that guy you and Joe were talking to earlier?"

His warm chuckle wafted gently over her scalp. "Were you looking for me earlier? I'm flattered."

"Don't be, only keeping my eye on the competition." She cringed at her harsh tone. "And you're kind of hard to miss, being such a ginormously huge man and all."

"Yes, we've covered how big I am, haven't we?"

Ignoring his innuendo, she asked, "Seriously, who was that guy?"

"That guy is no one you need to worry your pretty head about."

Acid pooled in her gut. "Why was he talking to you and Joe?"

"Fuck if I know."

Why is he lying?

"You're not breaking our deal, are you?" she blurted before she could craft her words more carefully.

"No, darlin', I'm not." He paused and leaned down to her ear, pulling back a lock of her hair. "Are you?" He took her lobe between his teeth and nipped; a sharp spike of desire shot through her like a bullet.

She shivered and felt her heartbeat triple. Did he mean their marketing deal or the hands-off deal? Did it really matter? How was it possible he could be burying her with his success and, at the same time, getting her as hot as melted chocolate? Her life was spiraling out of control, and all she could think about was how close his warm lips were to her ear. How his teeth felt on her body. How close his mouth was to that spot, the one spot on her shoulder he'd discovered.

The feel of his erection pressed tight against her lower back made her pussy pulse. When she pushed her hips back into his body, Mason's low growl in her ear spread through her like a forest fire. His fingers found her neck and painted flames across her collarbone. It was getting harder and harder to deny her visceral reaction to him.

She laid her head back against his solid chest and was reaching her hand up and around to touch his hair, when Ben, their driver, walked up, prim and proper as usual. Abruptly, she jumped away from Mason. The cool air between their bodies was a shock to the warmth that had just inhabited them.

"Sir, ma'am, we're ready to get on the road. The band should be about fifteen minutes behind us. Are you ready to depart?" The older man was as professional as an English butler, in spite of the metalheads yelling and laughing throughout the room. Apparently, nothing fazed Ben. Nothing yet, anyway.

After they said their good-byes and were preparing to walk out into the cool night, Jax snuck up, grabbed her arm, and dragged her off to the side.

"I hope you know what you're doing," Jax said in a loud whisper.

She pulled her arm back, clutching it against her chest.

"I don't know what you're talking about." She looked toward the door where Ben and Mason had walked out. "I'm not *doing* anything."

"Bullshit, Kevan." His pointed glare dug into her like a sharp stick. "Look, I really do care about you." When she rolled her eyes, he held up his hand in protest. "That's not what I meant. Yes, you're hot, but I love you—like a sister."

She nodded, and the sincerity in his face lit his eyes.

"I see the way he watches you. I see the way you look at him. He's a nice guy. I get it. But…"

"But what?" But he's arrogant? But he's a love 'em and leave 'em kind of guy? But he's too smart for me?

"He's a suit. Dabbles in the metal world, but he's not ready to move here, if you know what I mean."

"Yeah, then why are you making me compete against him for the band's business?"

"You know if it were up to me we'd sign with you. No question." Jax released a frustrated sigh. "But it's not up to me. We signed financial and business decisions over to Joe, when we couldn't even agree on a stupid logo."

"I know. Had to ask." She squeezed his hand. "But why all the crap about him being a suit, blah, blah, blah? Aren't you being a little hypocritical? Seems I remember you in law school for a couple of years," she blurted, sounding more like she was defending Mason, even admitting she was interested. Which she wasn't. "I couldn't care less what he is or where he lives or whatever. There's nothing going on between us."

Jax bent over and brushed a light kiss on her cheek. "It's not the same. And I was there when the asshole professor tore your heart out and played baseball with it. Remember?" She felt her cheeks heat with the humiliation Ethan's public betrayal still elicited. "Birds of a feather and all that. We gotta stick together. We can play in their world, take their money, but we need to remember who our real friends are."

She shoved his rock-hard arm. "Why are you suddenly all mushy and worried about my feelings? Weren't you acting like you wanted in my panties a couple of days ago?"

His face transformed back into the rock star, and his dimples winked as he smiled. "Well, you're as hot as a winter campfire, and I want s'mores."

Kevan made a gagging noise and laughed. "Does that ever work?"

"Every time." He looked directly at her with his chocolate-colored eyes. His rock-star persona dropped again as his face filled with genuine sincerity. "Promise you'll be careful."

"I promise." She winked and smiled, attempting her sassiest grin. "I promise you don't need to worry about me getting my heart broken again. Especially by some bossy, know-it-all suit. Now let's get on the road to the exciting metropolis of…where are we going next?"

He threw his arm around her and pulled her toward the door. "Medford, baby, we're going to Medford."

Chapter 11

BACK IN THE RV, MASON'S BLOOD STILL BOILED. THE surprise visit from his vice president had led to a nasty confrontation. He'd promised Kevan a fair fight. How was that possible if Steve Revell was checking up on him? Fucking board of nosy fucking directors.

And where the fuck is Kevan anyway? Probably still with Jax.

Mason made a half-assed attempt to read his emails, but his mind kept drifting back to Revell and the show tonight, then back to Kevan. He should go find her and convince her to jump back into bed with him. The need to drive out his anger and aggression was all consuming. Sitting back, he ran a hand over the top of his head. No, he should do the honorable thing and stick to their hands-off agreement. And not drag her into his dark anger.

Honor blows. Was his frustration over Steve's surprise visit or something else? Someone else?

In his fractious state, he wondered if she had ever spent a night or two in Jax's arms. Not that it was his business, but the thought of her with him, or with any other man, made his stomach turn and his brain hurt.

This must be what jealousy feels like. And, yeah, jealousy sucks too.

He needed to fuck Kevan Landry again. There was no other way he could justify his behavior. He was pissed about work and the board interfering with his deal. But more than that, he craved Kevan with an insatiable hunger. Despite everything going on with Manix and GEM, all he could think about was his primary goal that night: Kevan.

His whole life had been a series of identifying and achieving goals. He discovered something he wanted, determined the value, and then devised a plan to get it. And he had always succeeded. Until now. Now everything was different. When the hell had he ever waited for anything? Work. Women. Never.

Frankly, he was already tired of waiting for the band and even more exhausted by his own impatience and constant desire for that damn woman. Watching the way she affected other men only made the sting sharper. Silly as it sounded, it was like she walked around with a spotlight shining over her head. He either needed to move the fuck on or get her back into his bed. And soon.

While musing on his lust for the brunette with the blue streaks, a message with an earlier time stamp caught his attention:

Mason,

The chairman requested I notify you that he has tasked Steve Revell to act as President of Talent Development. He is overseeing your current responsibilities at the corporate office and abroad while you pursue your current project. In that capacity, he has taken an interest in your activities. He has made arrangements to attend your event this evening and suggests you schedule time to meet with him and formulate your plan for acquiring the contract for Manix Curse.

Best regards,
Simone Talley
Executive Assistant to Steve Revell

So his former VP had been promoted to president of the artist division and was somehow Mason's boss now? What the fuck was going on? Mason wished he'd read the email before that blowhard had shown up at the club and tried to snow Joe with his smarmy bullshit. He hoped he'd chased him off for good, but when he'd threatened to fire him for interfering with his deal, Revell had laughed. Dared him to give the chairman a call. Frankly, the last thing he needed was Revell's interference. Not with Dan, the Hellfire event rep, coming to see Manix play the next night in Medford. So Mason had sent him on his way with a threat of censure.

The squeak of the motor home door got his attention, and the real source of his discombobulation walked onto the RV and into the kitchenette.

"Ready to go?" she asked with an upbeat lilt to her voice. Was that courtesy of Jax? One more asshole's teeth to kick in.

"Go?"

"Leave for Medford. Ben says any time."

"Could you go up front and let him know we're ready?"

When she returned, Kevan filled a glass with water before sitting across from him.

"I'm sorry," they both started at the same time. Then

she laughed, her voice as shaky as the hand gripping her glass.

He smiled. "Ladies first."

"Look, I got a little carried away." She ran her purple-tipped finger around the top of the glass, watching like it was the most fascinating thing in the world. "The music gets me amped up, and I forget how to behave some-times. It won't happen again."

He should be relieved, really. Getting involved with her while they were on the road made everything much more complicated. He didn't like complicated. *Remember?* He liked simple, honest, professional. Or, *boring*, as Kevan would call it.

"Promise?" he teased.

"Of course," she snapped. "I'm sure I can manage to keep my hands off you."

"Whatever you say," he said, looking back at his computer screen, closing out GEM's email server. He didn't need Kevan learning his bosses had sent his pro-tégé to undermine his progress. No telling how she'd take the news.

"What the hell does that mean?" Her glare made him want to smooth the lines on her forehead.

With his mouth.

"It means we made a deal, and I'll keep to it. Unless…"

"Unless what?" She scrunched up her nose and tilted her head.

"Unless, maybe you'd like to break that part of the deal." He held her gaze, his tone even, not wanting to give away his plan.

"What part? I'm not giving up on my band." Her face flushed with the telltale sign of a woman ready to do battle. Yeah. He wasn't going there, today. The RV was too small, and maybe her aim had gotten better.

"I just meant…oh, never mind."

"What? Say it." Her voice was husky.

"I thought maybe…" He started praying the warmth he felt creeping up his neck didn't show as a blush. Because he didn't blush. Not ever.

"What?" She got up and rinsed her glass in the sink. As she leaned her fine ass against the counter, the bus stopped short, sending her into Mason's arms with a grunt.

"I got you, darlin'."

She looked up into his eyes, her face so serious, and said, "This time you do, don't you?"

He nodded and cleared his throat. "I'm starting to get used to you landing on me."

Kevan's lush body perched on his lap like it was custom-made to fit him. On impulse, he almost asked her to dinner on their first day off. Maybe it was best not to.

"I bet you are," she said. God, the feel of her in his arms felt so fucking right as images of their bodies entwined flashed through his mind. He almost moaned when she looked away and struggled back to her feet, her ass wriggling right over his suddenly attentive cock. Fucking hell.

When she sighed and yawned, Mason reluctantly allowed her out of his hold.

"I need to get to ready for bed."

Minutes later, she emerged from the small bathroom wearing a faded, holey Reverend Horton Heat T-shirt and sweats cut off at the knees. She'd wrapped her hair up in a knotted handkerchief and removed all her makeup. With the protective layer of paint gone, her skin glowed. Her freckled face looked young and sweet.

He couldn't win. She had stunned him in her tight pinup dresses, but standing there without makeup, she devastated him in her sweats and grubby T-shirt. At that moment, he wanted nothing more than to strip her of her cute pajamas and fill her with his cock, brand her with his come, show her what she was doing to him.

Instead, Kevan moved toward the side bunk and said quietly, "Good night, Mason." Then she pulled aside the bunk's curtain and ducked inside.

He shut down his laptop, walked over to her bed, and bent over her bunk to brush a chaste kiss across her cheek. "Good night, darlin'."

He lay awake for hours, staring at the ceiling, tortured by images of Kevan asleep a few feet away. It drove him crazy listening to her toss and turn mere feet away from him. He'd have to wait until she fell asleep so he could take matters into his own hand, so to speak, and relieve some of the pressure she'd created. Sometime later, his mind finally shut down, and he drifted off to sleep.

Close to dawn, the tour caravan pulled into Medford. All three vehicles lined the rusted fence surrounding a small armory—tonight's venue—next to a row of military vehicles resembling props from a war movie. After a fitful night of punching his pillow into submission, Mason dragged himself to the kitchen and made coffee. An early riser, he tiptoed around, trying to let Ben—in the front bunk—and Kevan sleep as long as possible.

Being on the road could wreak havoc with a person's

sleep cycle and, sometimes, health. For Mason, exercise was a form of meditation. When presented with a problem he couldn't solve, he often found it would untangle itself easily through a run or some weight training.

A good, long morning run was the therapy he needed to get his head around his job, this thing with Kevan, and the deal with the band. After leaving her a note, he stretched outside the bus. He was about to take off for a trek around the area, which wasn't much more than a cozy community in a lush valley, when Jax loped off the band's bus and started stretching.

"You run?" Mason asked the tattooed drummer.

"Don't sound so surprised." Jax laughed. He bent down and touched his toes.

"Actually, I am. A little anyway. Doesn't seem very rock star. Aren't you supposed to be in bed with two groupies until late afternoon?"

"Not enough room in my bunk for two fangirls. And I'm on tour with my sister, dude. Besides, don't tell anyone, but I'm a bit of a health nut. Have been since college."

"Now, I am surprised," Mason said. "I wasn't aware that tattoo artists went to college."

Jax gestured to the road, and the two jogged down the street through the shadowy fog. "Most probably don't. I was pre-law at Oregon State. Go Beavs! Graduated with a degree in poly sci, but art was always my thing."

"I can relate. More than you know." Mason nodded. "Didn't go to law school though?"

"Almost the full three years. I fucking hated it," he said with a shallow laugh.

Mason laughed, surprised he was starting to like the

tattooed drummer. "My sister's an attorney. It's definitely a personality type."

Jax made a show of fake shivering and laughed. This time more genuinely.

Mason slowed, remembering the news he had for the band. "Before I forget, I wanted to let you know the events VP from Hellfire is coming to the show tonight."

"The possible tour opportunity from the itinerary?" Jax lifted both eyebrows.

"The one and only. Want to know why?"

"For real, dude? Hell yeah."

"They're interested in the band for their big festival tour next year."

Jax grinned. Then his smile fell, replaced by a frown. "The band will be stoked."

"So why don't *you* looked stoked?" What was going on with this guy?

"No, it's totally cool. I'm busy as hell at work and have some commissioned paintings I need to work on. No worries. It's all good." Jax smiled again and increased his pace.

Mason raced to keep up with Jax as the burn of cold air filled his lungs. His chest expanded and expelled the warmed air in cloudy puffs. They ran for two miles before Jax glanced repeatedly at Mason as if he wanted to say something but didn't quite know how to start. Mason assumed he knew the topic.

"Spit it out already." He breathed heavily.

Jax doubled the pace. "Look, Kevan acts like a badass, and sometimes she is, but the truth is she's had it rough." Jax started breathing heavier but didn't sound winded.

"Her mom died when she was young, and her dad has

always been a loser dickhead. She's an amazing girl, and she doesn't need another douchebag slumming it with the edgy chick."

Did Jax just call him a douchebag to his face? "Don't hold back. Tell me how you really feel."

"You have a sister, right?" Jax asked. Taking the pace to another level, Mason welcomed the burn and stretch of his muscles as they heated and tired.

"What does that have to do with anything?"

"Answer the fucking question." Jax's face darkened— either from exertion or from anger. "Do you or not?"

"You know I do."

"Do you feel protective of her? Want assholes to steer clear? Keep her out of trouble?"

"What's your point?"

"Kevan is super sweet, smart, and sexy. She's also impulsive." Jax glanced sideways at Mason and took several deep breaths. "It's a recipe for disaster. And the one person who's supposed to look out for her, Bowen, fucked up his life. While he's trying to straighten his shit out, she has no one to turn to. No one she can trust."

How was he supposed to respond? She didn't need him messing around with her life. Jax was right; he should walk away from her.

"What about you?" he asked. "You two seem pretty close."

"We've all been friends for years—through the shop and music scene—but really it's Bowen and I that are tight."

Mason wanted to pump his fist in the air and yell his relief.

"What's the deal with her brother?" he asked as they looped around toward the bus and RV.

. "Bowen's the guy everyone likes. Life of the party. But he's an addict and alcoholic like his old man. The pressure of trying to be all things to all people got to him. He hid his insecurities in a bottle of booze and then got hooked on speed." He slowed and looked lost in thought. "Then he got his ass kicked by a local dealer. It was bad. Thank God Kevan got him into rehab."

They ran two blocks in silence before Jax said, "Damn waste of talent if he doesn't get clean. He's one of the best artists I've ever met."

"Do you have any of his work?" Mason asked.

"Why? You thinking of getting some ink?" Jax laughed.

"Maybe."

Jax peered at Mason's face, maybe trying to gauge his sincerity. "Yeah. He and Nathan did most of my tattoos. Bowen is obsessed with traditional Asian art. He did all my Chinese and Japanese stuff. I'll show you sometime. He's gifted."

Mason smiled absentmindedly, thinking of Kevan's body art. "I've seen Kevan's koi and cherry blossoms. They're insane."

"So you did bang her." Jax slowed and glared at him, veins bulging in his neck.

Mason threw his hands up in front of him. "None of your business, bro."

"It *is* my business, *bro*. Her koi wraps around her back and over her rib cage. No way you can see it with her clothes on. Motherfucker, I should kick your ass."

"She's a grown woman, Jax. And I'm pretty sure I've got at least twenty pounds on you, so relax."

"Like I couldn't kick your white-bread, beamer-driving ass." Jax sneered and then laughed humorlessly. "I'll back off, for now. But if you hurt her, I will make you suffer." Then he turned and looked him in the eye as they approached their line of vehicles. "The last guy who messed with Kevan will never forget his fuckup. My upbringing affords some moral ambiguity. If you get my drift."

A wave of dark anger surged through Mason at the thought of another man hurting her, causing her pain. So unexpected. These odd, possessive feelings toward Kevan were frustrating and uncomfortable. He needed to get her out from under his skin.

"Point taken. She's not going to give me the chance, to be honest. I don't know what the fuck is up or down with that woman. But I have no intention of hurting her. I promise you."

"Make sure it stays that way."

As they cooled down and stretched, Mason's thoughts kept drifting back to Kevan.

While she might be inexperienced and a little naive, she was definitely creative and inspired. She was more about action and less about the hype and bullshit that tended to get attention in their industry. She would make an excellent employee. That is, if he got to keep his job. Too bad he wanted to screw her again so badly. Unfortunately, he had a strict no fraternization policy. Since he didn't date seriously, he couldn't have a string of one-night stands working for him, now could he? Too messy.

Mason didn't like messy. He liked neat and tidy. Kevan was as complex as they came. And the more he

discovered, the messier she got. Jax's information was
proof. It was probably best for him to keep his interest in
her strictly horizontal. No, vertical. He'd like to take her
up against the wall with her long legs wrapped around
his hips. Oh, the dirty things he'd like to do to her. No.
Maybe he should think about backing off a little. Yes,
she was sexy, and yes, he would love to get her back into
bed. But Jax had had a point. And despite how obsessed
he was with her body, he'd meant what he'd said to Jax.
He didn't want to hurt her.

It was all becoming so much more complicated.
And messy.

Outside the RV, he was in the middle of his final
stretch when he heard a loud crash from inside the bus,
followed by some muffled yelling. He skipped the
steps and burst into the RV, colliding with a sleepy-
eyed Kevan.

"I seem to always be falling on you or crashing into
you." She lifted her hands from his damp chest.

"You okay? I heard a noise." His heart raced from his
run and the sudden close contact with Kevan.

She laughed. "I'm fine. I was trying to make breakfast
and dropped a plate." Her eyes suddenly turned glassy
as she took in his sweaty T-shirt and the board shorts.

He peeled off the wet shirt and wiped his brow.

"I'm food," she mumbled.

Ha! She was frazzled. He couldn't resist taking
advantage of her discomfort just a little. "You're food,
Kevan? Like a tasty ripe strawberry?" he teased. She
was flustered and distracted. Affected by him. He liked
that. Oh yeah, he liked it a lot.

Shaking her head, she stepped back to the stove to

stir something. "I'm making food. For you. For us. Remember, I said I would." Her words tumbled out of her mouth in a rush.

"Dammit. This is your fault." She pointed her now-blue fingernail at him.

How many times a day does she paint her nails?

He looked down at her bare, very sexy feet. And toes? The purple polish on her toenails matched the outline of flowers tattooed on one of her feet.

Mason pursed his lips. "What's my fault?"

"You. That body. It's distracting. And turning me into a dork." She looked back toward the scrambled eggs on the small stove. "Go take those clothes off and take a shower. Oh, shit, that's not what I meant." He caught a glimpse of her flushed crimson neck when she moved to stir the eggs.

"Wouldn't you rather get creative with kitchen utensils?" He winked before she turned around to wash the dirty spatula.

"You're such a perv," she mumbled as he stepped up behind her, not touching, but desperately wanting to.

He bent over her and whispered, "What do you mean, darlin'?"

She spun and pinched her nose. "I mean, you stink. Go get cleaned up so I can feed you."

When he rubbed his slick chest up and down her arm, she feigned indifference and pushed him toward the bathroom, but her hand shook, and her breath hitched. "Gross. Just go, you dumb, sweaty man. Get cleaned up."

"Yes, ma'am. Sure you don't want to join me?" He lowered his voice to the level that always got her eyes a little hooded and her breath raspy.

"Don't try your magic Texan voodoo on me. Go."

He winked and followed her command, wondering how he could possibly last another week in such close quarters with her. Didn't his wicked little pinup know she was the one casting spells on him?

Chapter 12

MASON COULDN'T CONCENTRATE. ACTUALLY, THAT was only partially true. For the first time in his professional life, he couldn't focus on work. Instead, he was hyperaware of Kevan as she sat across from him at the RV table. After breakfast, they spent their day typing on their laptops and occasionally stepping outside to use the phone. There was something about having her so close he found both reassuring and unsettling. Her presence seemed to fill those empty spaces he'd never noticed were there. The ones he'd filled with nonstop work and the occasional sexual tryst.

That afternoon, when Kevan's phone starting playing Metallica's "One," she stared at it buzzing on the table and covered her mouth with her hand. She punched the answer button and sucked in a deep breath. "Bo?"

Mason glanced up from his laptop when she sniffled. Watery tears filled her eyes, and she nodded her head in response to whatever her brother was saying.

She looked at Mason with a raised brow and pointed to the back room. Her smile was weak, hopeful, but hesitant. He smiled and mouthed "of course." When she ran back to the bedroom and shut the door, sealing herself away from him, a shard of sorrow unexpectedly ripped through him. If only he could be there for her.

He tried hard to give her the privacy she deserved, but caught bits and pieces of the conversation through the thin door. The RV was a pretty small living space, after all.

After his conversation with Jax earlier that morning, and hearing a few things slung around backstage about Kevan's brother, Mason doubted Bowen's chances of getting and staying clean and sober. Over the years in this business, he'd seen a lot of talented people throw it all away when their addictions consumed them. He hoped for Kevan's sake that Bowen took his recovery seriously. She needed dependable people on her side, people she could count on. Bummer it couldn't be him.

He forced the feeling away before it took seed in his conscience. No; he was here to do a job. He wasn't making promises he couldn't keep or falling for a woman who was wrong for him on every level. Nope. Not gonna happen. Sure, he'd like to get her back into bed, maybe even a few times, to get her out of his system. But long-term wasn't his thing, and Kevan deserved something real. She may play up the provocative vamp act, but Kevan had white picket fences and happily ever after written all over her.

Sign the band. Bang the girl. Get out of Dodge. No harm, no foul.

Kevan was still on the phone, listening intently, when she walked back into the room, and Mason was struck by his intense reaction to her. He suddenly realized cutting his losses and moving on was easier said than done. No makeup, and the girl was a stunner, all glorious curves and creamy pale skin with a smattering of freckles across the bridge of her nose. Had he ever spent this much time with a woman and still felt like it wasn't enough? No. Never.

Mason loved women, but he was a man focused on his career. With work overshadowing everything, he lost interest in relationships quickly. And after bearing witness to the twenty-year civilized existence of his parents' cold, clinical marriage, he could never see himself settling for that type of business arrangement. So he was always up front and honest.

The more time he spent with Kevan, the more he felt compelled to peel back the layers of her quirky personality. Fuck, peel back the layers of her crazy clothing. He wanted more. More of her. If someone had told him he'd feel this way after a onetime hookup, he would have laughed hysterically. Yes, she was a stunner, but he didn't have room in his life for a complicated woman like her.

Kevan walked back into the room as she ended her call. She stood in front of the window next to the built-in couch and stared out the window, lost in thought. He would have never chosen this near obsession with her. He must have snorted or laughed aloud, because her gaze snapped to his, and she looked at him strangely, with her eyes soft, her head cocked to the side. He would always associate that stance with Kevan. Even when this tour was over and they'd both moved on.

She tried to smile, but it looked more like a sad grimace.

"How's your brother?" he asked.

The smile spread on her beautiful face but didn't reach her eyes. "Oh, just peachy."

"Not very convincing. Tell me. I know he's a big part of your life, but what happened with him? Really? I hear he's a phenomenal artist and a great guitar player.

Although, I guess he has a bit of a wild side. That's what they say anyway."

"*Them*. That amorphous blob of gossipers." She took two short steps, stationed herself against the kitchen counter, and toyed with her hair.

"No, it wasn't gossipy. People really like him. It sounds like he's going through a rough spot."

She snorted. "Yeah. A rough spot."

Kevan breathed in deeply. Maybe she was debating how much or what she could tell him. She could trust him. Didn't she know that? No, dipshit, she didn't, considering they were going after the same goal. So, no, she couldn't trust him. But for some reason, he really wanted her trust.

"Tell me. I want to know you better," he said before he realized what he was saying.

"Oh, really," she said, dragging out her words in disbelief. "The only thing you need to know about me is I'm going to kick your ass and send you home wiping tears from your face with your Hugo Boss tie."

Regret burned in his gut. Fucking hell, would she ever lower her guard? "Tell me."

"No. God, you're the bossiest man I have ever met." She frowned. "I don't work for you."

Pushing his laptop aside, he stood and grabbed her hand. It was small and soft in his much larger, rougher palm. When she pulled back slightly, he held firm. "Tell me."

She sighed so deep and long he could almost see the fight leave her, an unwelcome ghost that she nevertheless clung to out of habit.

"Bowen is awesome. After my mom died and my dad

was anywhere but at home, my brother practically raised me. He sounded so much stronger, healthier on the phone, but addicts are natural liars. Fish swim. Addicts lie." She tried to hide the tears welling in her eyes again by pivoting toward the window, but it was too late. "I'm so afraid I've lost him this time. He's terrified he's like our dad. And I think he might be right." She turned back and glared like she expected him to agree or condemn her for her honesty.

He moved to the built-in couch and patted the seat next to him. When she sat, he covered her bare knee with his hand, the action meant to comfort, but instead it felt more intimate. She didn't respond, but she didn't pull away this time. He squeezed gently, the familiar zing traveling between their touching skin. *Come back to me, Kevan.* She faced him with a small, shy smile.

"Go on, darlin'."

"My dad turned into another person after my mom died. He was never superdad or anything, but after mom passed away, he was always drunk or on pills. And he could get mean. Bowen tried to shield me from my dad's toxic bitterness, but…" Her haunted gaze drifted back toward the window.

What she didn't say filled the RV with more truths than the few short words she had said aloud. Mason ground his teeth and felt like punching the wall. Knowing his rising anger would send her skittering away, he schooled his features and waited for her to continue.

As if in a trance, she said softly, "The anger wasn't as bad as the unpredictability. We never knew when he'd go off, or if he'd forget to leave money for food, or if he'd show up at school totally wasted. More than once he stole the money Bowen made cleaning up nights at the Tatuaggio."

Lost in the past, she didn't speak for a minute. He covered her hand with his and rubbed his thumb over her delicate bones, tracing each bump and fighting the urge to take her into his arms and wrap her in his warmth. If only he could go back in time and ease her suffering.

"His abuse was mostly verbal." She looked up and smiled weakly.

Mason tried not to hold his breath and asked, "Mostly?"

She nodded. "One time. About ten years ago. He was probably coming down, tearing up the house looking for booze money or a hidden stash. He started choking me, when Bowen came in and beat the shit out of him. Told him to never come back or he'd kill him. Haven't seen him since."

Motherfucker.

"And now you're afraid your brother is turning into your dad?"

She shook her head and then nodded slightly. "He's so lost right now. When my dad left, Bowen promised me we'd always have each other. That he'd never leave me. He worked hard to take care of us. He sacrificed a lot, and now it's kind of taken its toll. He's had a drinking problem for a while, but the speed is new." She shrugged.

"Booze and speed? That's why he's in rehab? To straighten out and be there for you?"

"I guess. But it's hella expensive. And he's having a hard time."

Cold fingers of dread wound around his heart, making it difficult to breathe. "Are you paying for Bowen's rehab?" he asked quietly.

"Yes. And the first full payment is due soon."

Mason sighed. It was getting worse and worse. He wondered if the reason Tina was her former assistant had anything to do with her money problems. On top of that, Kevan was struggling to help the one person she loved get well—and Mason knew he stood in her way.

Kevan smacked Mason's knee and jumped up before he could stop her withdrawal. She grabbed his hand to tug him after her. "Let's get the show on the road, Gloomy Gus. I've got to start getting ready. Need to look my best while I'm kicking your ass and signing Manix Curse." She winked and started off toward the tiny closet pretending to be a bathroom.

"Hey, Bettie?" he called after her.

She turned, hip pushed out and her eyebrow cocked.

"Go to dinner with me." So much for keeping his distance.

"Are you asking me out on a date?"

Damn, the warmth was creeping up his neck, again.

"Yes, I suppose I am." Her agreement meant everything.

"Like a date date?" She raised her eyebrows in confusion.

"Yep. Well, no. Just as colleagues." When her face dropped, he added, "Whatever you want it to be. No expectations, I promise." He placed his glasses on the table and scrubbed his hand down his face. Maybe it hadn't been such a great idea after all.

She looked at the ceiling of the bus and tapped her plump bottom lip. "I'm not saying no, but how would that work? I mean, we don't have an off night for a couple of days."

A warm glow filled his chest, feeling something like hope. "We have a night in San Francisco. We can go to dinner or go dancing or walk along Pier 39 and eat shrimp. Well?"

"Yeah. Maybe."

"Yeah? I'll take that maybe." And he smiled, even though he knew he was breaking every one of his damn rules. And for once, he didn't really care, as he stood and stepped toward her with one long stride. Her eyes widened—either in fear or arousal—it didn't matter. Instead of giving in to his maddening desire to pick her up and drag her into the back room, he wrapped his hands around the sides of her face, cradling her head in his palms and caressing her jawline with his thumbs. Her clear blue eyes softened as he leaned forward and brushed his mouth across hers, sending shivers of arousal straight to his cock.

Kevan's dilated pupils and breathy sigh betrayed her rigid stance. She was all in, just like he was. But he didn't want to scare her off—because he finally realized that's exactly what she was. Scared. He wanted only to give her a taste of what they'd been missing since that first night. So he kissed her lips fully and pulled free before pressing his mouth to the heated skin of her forehead.

"You are so beautiful," he said. Then with the strength of a circus strongman, he turned and walked into the back room, shut the door, and dropped his head forward with a thud against the hollow wood of the wall.

An hour later, Mason read emails while Kevan put the finishing touches on the night's look, when his phone rang. Without looking up from his computer screen, he hit the speakerphone button. "Dillon."

"This is Cora Taylor from Hellfire Energy Distribution, Mr. Dillon. I'm calling to confirm your meeting with Mr. Carver. He'd like to meet you at the armory back door at six." Mason glanced at his watch. He had ten minutes.

Mason settled back in his seat, letting the satisfaction and excitement blanket him. This was going to be an awesome night.

The smell of vanilla and honey hit his brain, and his head lifted instinctively toward Kevan, where she stood in a checkered top tied snug below her round breasts and jeans rolled to her ankles, her very sexy, tattooed ankles. Her dark hair spilled in waves over her shoulder and was pinned on one side with a huge velvet rose. Mason's mouth went dry, and his heart beat faster than a hummingbird on speed.

A very awesome night.

"Mr. Dillon? Are you there?" A voice crackled over the speakerphone, snapping him out of his trance.

"Yes. Tell Dan I'll be there in a few minutes."

"I'll do that," the secretary said.

He ended the call and fixed Kevan with a stare. "You look fantastic."

She frowned. Not the reaction he expected.

"Who was that?" she asked, setting her jaw and squaring her shoulders in her classic fighting stance.

"My surprise. Dan Carver's secretary. Dan is the event director for High Energy Bottling."

"The guy you said might be interested in sponsoring the band?" Her face looked even paler than usual.

"He's an old buddy of mine and interested in adding Manix to the Hellfire tour next year," he said, trying to make his words sound casual.

"Wow, cowboy, that's serious firepower. Some of the biggest bands are featured at Hellfire. Marco and Conner go every year. Honestly, I'm shocked you even know Hellfire exists."

Ignoring her dig, he grinned. "My company pursues fiscally viable commercial talent as a business model, but I personally enjoy a lot of different music genres. I've gone to the Hellfire festival several times and personally sponsored one of the VIP tents."

Her face sank a little more. "Gotta hand it to you—you're good. Really freaking good."

"I know." Mason instantly regretted sounding smug. Her uneven smile and dropped shoulders made him suddenly want to wrap his arms around her and tell it would be okay.

Unsure why he felt like comforting his competition, Mason ran a hand through his hair. This rivalry was starting to fuck with his head. The wrong head.

Instead of responding with her usual sarcastic remark, she gave him a determined nod. "Okay. Shall we go?" He could hear the defeat in her voice as she grabbed her clutch, and he followed her down the steps of the RV with his hand on the small of her back. The need to touch her was too powerful to ignore. They walked out to the parking lot in silence, touching, but miles away from each other. When they reached the side entrance, Mason dropped his hand. The always impeccable Dan stood waiting for Mason.

"Thanks for coming out." Mason grinned and shook hands with his old friend.

When Mason introduced Kevan, Dan smiled and made an obvious effort not to stare at her. Even a guy still in love with his college sweetheart couldn't ignore Kevan's dark beauty and curves.

Kevan excused herself on the pretext of checking in with the armory's management. She rushed off in the opposite direction, her tall heels clicking on the cement.

"Holy shit, that woman's hot." Dan grinned. "I wanna live vicariously through you. Please tell an old married man like me she's yours."

Mason smiled. *Do I wish she's mine?*

"You know me. I don't do serious." His words sounded hollow, even to his ears, as he leaned against the old cement-brick building.

The shorter man reached over and socked him on the arm. "Good ole Mason never changes, right? Still stupid and single?"

"I guess." For the second time that night, Mason tried to tamp down the warmth creeping up his neck. He suddenly felt somber and not so confident in his answer. "How's Julie? And the kids? How old are they now?"

Dan laughed. "They're great. I'm the luckiest man in the world. But we're talking about you. I can tell that woman is under your skin."

"She's not." Was she?

"Then why are you blushing?" Dan smirked.

"The fuck I am," Mason spit out, shifting uncomfortably to avoid Dan's direct stare.

"You're so full of shit your eyes are turning brown. I saw the way you followed her when she walked away. And I saw how she looked at you before she left."

Mason pushed off the wall to face his friend. "How?"

"That got your attention." He snorted. "Drop the crap. Who is she?"

Explaining the competition to Dan might tip the scales in his favor. Mason couldn't risk telling him too much. Instead, he shared the basics—they were both interested in signing Manix Curse, and his company was taking a more hands-on approach to expand their talent pool. It was the truth. Kind of.

"So you're not screwing her?" Dan asked. Never one to beat around the bush.

He looked around as the parking lot began to fill with cars and fans lined up outside the venue. "I didn't say that."

"So you are?"

"No." Mason looked down and kicked a stone with his boot. "But I did. It was supposed to be a one-night stand. I left without saying anything when I figured out we're both competing for the same band's PR business. Shit went downhill from there."

"Total dick move, dude. But you like her?" Before the automatic "no" could roll from his tongue, Dan held up his hand.

"What? Are we in high school?"

"Don't bother trying to distract me. Do you like her, Mason?"

Did he? Yes, probably. Maybe more than he had any right to. He nodded. "I do."

Dan grinned and smacked Mason on the shoulder. "She doesn't look like she'll go down without a fight. You're totally screwed."

"What the hell? You said she was eyeballing me."

Dan quirked his eyebrows. "She was, but she seems a little fierce."

Mason smiled. True that. His girl *was* a badass. "She is."

Dan gave him a sympathetic look. "Welcome to the club, brother."

"What club?" Mason asked, not really wanting to hear the answer.

"The one where you can't think about anything but the woman. All your hard work and drive becomes laser-focused on her. And you won't stop until you convince her she belongs to you." Dan turned and put his hand on the door handle.

"Whoa. I don't think it's that serious—"

"Of course you don't, but you will." Dan pulled the door open, and a sea of sound crashed over them. "Now, let's go see your band."

Numbly, Mason led him into the club and tried to forget Dan's words. Tonight he needed to sell Manix, not get flustered by Kevan.

Hours later, long after the Medford show, when Kevan was tucked into her bunk and the RV hummed down the freeway, Mason sat at the table and checked his email one last time before he headed off to bed. He clicked on a new message from Dan.

Hey Mason,

It was great meeting up with you tonight. It's been too long. Thank you for inviting me to see Manix Curse. After watching their show and meeting with their manager, I feel pretty comfortable telling you they'd be a perfect fit for the Hellfire Heavy Metal Masters Tour. I'll need to coordinate with our booking committee, as well as my boss, to confirm their inclusion on the schedule, but I would like to informally offer your band a spot on next year's fall tour.

Once I have the proper approvals in place, I'll have the contracts sent to you to present to the band's management.

I'm looking forward to working with you again. I'm also very excited about working with Manix Curse. They're an awesome band with a wicked blast beat.

On a personal note, I wanted to remind you to get a life. And by life, I mean quit being an idiot and go after Kevan. Before she wises up and finds someone else.

Give your girl a kiss for me and give me a call.

Dan

Some good fucking news to end a good fucking night. Mason wasn't sure what to make of the dig about Kevan, but his meetings with Dan and then with Joe had gone off without a hitch. The whole night vibrated with the energetic pulse of making the deal. Mason felt young and full of fire again. He'd remembered instantly where his passion—the same zeal Kevan breathed into everything—for entertainment marketing had come from. He loved this business.

Luckily, Dan had been able to secure flights in and out of town. And even more luck, the band had killed it. They were perfect, and with all Kevan's work online to pack the venue, Manix was staged exactly how he'd wanted them. Dan had been obviously impressed enough to quickly put together a deal for the band to join the Hellfire tour.

The tour package was the surefire way to seal Manix's business. A high-caliber booking like Hellfire could launch the career of any band with the right sound and marketing support. Manix Curse would go from local band to opening act to headliner in under a year. More important, this kind of publicity and exposure could secure them a solid recording contract with a big label.

Before he proposed the idea to the band, he'd have to put together a plan that secured their contract for GEM and ensure he didn't hurt Kevan's business. He wanted to walk away with the contract in his pocket and Kevan Landry in his bed. At least for a little while.

Thinking of Kevan was like dumping a cold pail of water over his head. Yes, this was excellent news for him and phenomenal news for Manix Curse. But definitely not good news for her and Jolt Marketing. Not at all.

Chapter 13

MASON WAS KNEE-DEEP IN EMAILS AND HIS STRATEGIC plan when a cry sounded over the dull hum of the RV's engine, startling him. Was that Kevan crying? He pulled his tired body from the table and stood outside her bunk, listening. The dark burgundy curtain swayed gently with the rocking of the RV, but no more sounds came from her bed. Just as he was about to give up and chalk the noise up to the late hour and his ping-ponging thoughts, he heard a low sniffle and groan. A sad sound from a normally upbeat and energetic woman.

"Kevan?" he called quietly, not wanting to wake her up if she was sleeping. "Are you okay?"

"I'm fine. Go away. Just a bad dream."

Bullshit. He pulled the curtain back. "Hey!" she squealed, scrambling to cover her exposed legs. "Get out of here."

"I heard you crying. What's wrong?" He could barely make out her reddened eyes in the shadows of the darkened bunk.

Instead of looking away, she squinted her eyes and squared her chin. "I wasn't crying. I was sleeping. I had a bad dream. And, no, I don't want to talk about it."

"Why are you so fucking stubborn?" he growled. Why wouldn't she let him help her?

"Why are you so damn bossy?"

They stared at each other in the darkened RV for what seemed like hours but was only moments.

Enough of this crap.

He reached one arm beneath her knees and the other under her arms and scooped her up. The startled look on her face was almost worth the payment he knew she'd render from his hide later.

"Put…what…stop…" she sputtered as he clutched her against his chest and marched to the bedroom. His heart thumped in his chest, beating double time, perfectly in synch with hers.

Settling her on the bed, he gathered her wrists in one hand and looked her in the eye. "Stop," he said simply.

She quit squirming but didn't break eye contact. Her scowl dug deep lines bisecting her brows.

"I still don't trust you."

"I know," he said as he caressed her wrist with his thumb. Her quickening pulse told him a different tale.

Leaning down, he kept eye contact and brushed his lips across hers, skin just touching, but the ever-present spark arcing between them. Her quick intake of breath and the arch of her back signaled her interest.

"Let me comfort you. Let's pretend—just for tonight—that none of the other stuff matters and there's only us."

"It's not that simple, Mason." The sadness in her sweet smile wrapped around his chest and squeezed just a little too hard on the bindings he kept tightly around his emotions.

"Tonight, it can be," he whispered, his voice scratchy and rough with need. He leaned down again to kiss her in that special spot but rubbed the bridge of his nose along the long, elegant line of her neck instead. "God, you smell so good."

"We don't get to make the rules. They're already set, and we have to play by them."

He smiled and slid his tongue along the delicate shell of her ear. "What does that even mean?"

Her body shuddered. "I. Don't. Know." Each word was delivered on a gasp as he continued exploring her with his mouth.

She shivered, and her skin pebbled under his hand as he began to stroke up her arm. She closed her eyes and tilted her head back. Her body was magnificent, made just for him. A gift to be unwrapped and discovered over time. Too bad she wouldn't let him take the time. The thought momentarily jarred him from the erotic task at hand. Did he want more time with her? No, impossible.

Ridiculous even. Take what she's offering now and move on.

When he finally reached her mouth, Kevan's hands were weaving though his hair and tugging at his T-shirt, frantic to get his clothes off. Her heavy breathing and glassy eyes lit him from the inside and spurred him to match her pace. Had it been only days since he'd touched her, felt her satiny skin beneath his fingers? Having her so close and so untouchable had messed with his head. He had to slow down now that he had her beneath him again. He wanted to savor her body, but she seemed to have other plans.

He took her mouth, demanding control back before he came in his pants and completely ruined the moment. Tugging her against his body with one arm under her, he cradled her head with his other. He swallowed her moan and pushed back on his knees.

The look in Kevan's eyes dimmed with confusion until he dug the condom out of his wallet and tossed it onto the bed. As he pulled his shirt off with one hand, she grabbed at his belt and began to undo his pants. The wicked grin from their first night together spread across her beautiful face as she pulled his belt free and tossed it aside. Mason moved over her and yanked on her nightshirt.

"Off," he demanded. "Now."

She pulled her nightshirt off and lay on the bed in her Wonder Woman panties and her full breasts on display, hard nipples begging for his mouth. A wanton goddess just waiting for him to ravage her. He smiled down at her as he stepped out of his jeans and underwear.

"Holy shit. I forgot about that body," she said. Giggling, she reached a hand toward him.

"Holy shit. I couldn't forget about yours."

Her shy smile was a reminder of the constantly changing and contradictory beauty that was Kevan Landry. And her gasp as he pinched one nipple and sucked the other into his mouth was his cue to keep things moving.

"This doesn't change anything." Her words were rushed and delivered on heavy breaths.

"I know, Bettie. Just enjoy it," he said. Reaching down, he parted her wet lips to stroke her pulsing clit. "Oh, I think you already are."

He pulled her other rosy nipple into his mouth and bit a little less gently as he pinched her hard clit. Her body stiffened, and she sang his name as she came apart in his hands. He dragged out her orgasm by plunging two fingers into her quivering canal, absorbing her cries as if they were feeding him straight adrenaline. Oh, the power he felt when he brought her some relief, some joy, like he could conquer the world.

If Mason wasn't careful, he could become addicted to this woman.

Kevan was a lot of things; stupid wasn't one of them. She knew she shouldn't be here with him, but she couldn't muster the energy to feel any regret for falling into bed with Mason again. He'd shown up right when she'd needed him. The nightmare that had frightened her from a sound sleep had continued to linger until Mason had bullied his way into her bunk and carried her off. Her pathetic attempts to pull away were just her going through the practiced motions she used to keep everyone away. She'd wanted him. Desperately.

There would be time for personal recriminations and self-flagellation later. At that moment, she was riveted by the image of the glorious man kneeling between her parted legs. Watching as he stroked his long erection with huge—but somehow still elegant—hands and seamlessly rolled on the condom. He really was a massive, gorgeous man with broad shoulders, sinewy taunt muscles, and a tapered waist.

"If you're not inside me in the next five seconds, I swear I'm taking matters into my own hands and leaving you out of the equation," she blurted.

He laughed, never taking his eyes off her or his hand from his cock. "Now who's the bossy one?"

Mason's hand wrapped around her knee as he

stretched her legs wide before laying her ankle on his shoulder. His grin took on a scandalous, almost feral tilt, before he leaned forward, caging her in, and lifted her bottom. He stared directly into her eyes with an intense heat that made her want to look away. But she didn't. She needed this connection with him, even if it was transitory and superficial. Needed to feel part of something and not alone. Just for a while.

Kevan grabbed Mason's shoulders as he plunged deep inside her, deeper than she thought possible. When he began to move slowly, the tingling sensation building in her core surprised her. Apparently, the man had a magic penis. She felt her muscles relax, unfurl, with his increasingly demanding motions. Kevan's body no longer belonged to her, she realized, as she arched into his and her fingers scored his back.

His thrusts became more erratic. He groaned, "I can't last much longer."

The urgency in his voice and the fact that a powerful man like Mason could lose control with her pushed her over the edge. Her world sparked a million colors, going from shades of gray to a rainbow in seconds. He called her name as he spilled into her, stroking two more times before he stilled inside her, on top of her.

It took all of about three minutes before the panic set in and she pushed him off her, which he let her do. Avoiding his stare, she gathered her nightshirt and sifted through his tangled sheets for her panties.

His warm hand pressed on her back, calming her enough to stop and look at him. Warmth flooded her cheeks—embarrassment from the sex or from her panic?

"It's okay, Kevan," he said quietly, as if talking to

a frightened animal. As if knowing her better than he should and sensing her fear before even she could identify it. "We don't have to talk about it. We don't have to try and figure anything out. Just lie here with me."

His hand rubbed circles on her lower back. God, he really did have some strange hold on her. Better to own up to the mistake now and get the fuck out before she lost her heart to him.

She cleared the cobwebs from her throat and stood next to the bed with her shoulders level. "Thank you for the distraction. But I think it's time for me to go to my own bed."

His eyes widened, and his face flushed. "You're thanking me? *Thanking me* for fucking you? Jesus. Why can't you just let go for one night? Just let me fucking hold you."

The anger in his eyes was all the justification she needed to rationalize her escape.

"You know why, Mason. We…" She pointed to him and back at herself. "We aren't a thing. We can never be a thing. You don't do relationships, remember? And I don't do this! Don't even get me started on the whole 'you're taking away my livelihood' thing." Hating the shake in her voice and knowing there wasn't anything left to say, she smiled weakly and stomped out of his room.

She yanked her gown over her head and threw herself into her cold bunk. Alone. Always alone.

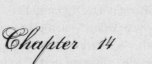

Chapter 14

WELCOME TO LIFE ON THE ROAD, KEVAN THOUGHT WRYLY as she pushed the off button on her phone's alarm. She drew open the curtain and dragged her achy body out of her narrow bunk. They'd only been on tour two days—three now—but Kevan was exhausted with an unnatural weariness that left her bones heavy and her muscles fatigued. And now the ache between her legs matched that of her heart.

Grabbing her iPad off the bunk shelf, she reviewed the schedule for Redding that day, which included an all-day charity home build. Then she shot off a text message to her intern, Sindra, reminding her to follow up with the media, and set her tablet back on the bunk. The clank and clunk from the kitchen alerted her to Mason's presence. She smiled, knowing how hard he tried to be quiet in the morning, but his big body in the small RV was the proverbial bull in the china shop. Then she remembered how she'd thrown a tantrum and stomped off in the middle of the night. Yet another impulsive act meant to salvage her bruised ego and shield her wounded heart gone wrong.

She trudged into the kitchen, stretching her arms over her head. Mason handed her a steaming cup of coffee, which she accepted gratefully. They exchanged niceties, ignoring the awkward morning-after tension that swirled around them. She sipped her coffee as she prepared for the low income Home for Good project build she'd set up through Bowen's ex, Lynn Bale.

They moved around each other as if they already knew the other's carefully choreographed routine. She smiled to herself, allowing herself to imagine them as a real couple. He was beautiful and graceful, where she was all clunk and sparkle. Her manufactured glamour and klutziness. His natural sophisticated style and class. What would it be like to wake up with a man like him every morning? A real man. A grown-up. Would she get up early to make him his morning coffee every day? Or would he let her sleep in and deliver her favorite blend to her in bed?

Kevan shook her head and moved into the bathroom to finish getting dressed. As she pulled the bathroom's pocket door open and called out to Mason, "Hey, you ready or wh..." Mr. Punctual was already standing in the kitchen with her enormous boho bag hanging from his index finger, smirking.

"Of course you are," she said wryly.

They stepped out the door into the foggy early morning and piled into the rented van. The band, a few roadies, some woman she hadn't met before, and Joe were already there waiting. While some warmed their hands with paper cups of coffee, others shoved their hands in their pockets, hoping to find warmth in the cold fall morning. Kevan pulled her phone from her pocket and fired off a few more texts to the local media attending the build.

"Let's get this party started!" Jax yelled, laughing when the rest of the sleep-deprived group winced, groaned, and slid down in their seats. Maybe September was the wrong time to plan an event like this.

Once they reached the build site, Kevan climbed out of the van first, and checking the time on her phone, she realized they were running slightly behind. She pointed Mason, Joe, and the band toward the coffee and donuts while she located Lynn, Bowen's old high school girlfriend and the community relations director for Home for Good. The thin, tall blond squealed and threw her arms around Kevan, rocking her back and forth and squeezing her tight. The earnest reception warmed her heart and melted some of the tension knotting her shoulders. Kevan had always liked Lynn and, at one time, hoped she might be the special woman to quell Bowen's restlessness and stop his downward spiral. Despite it not working out with her brother, Lynn had stayed in touch, and they'd remained friends.

"I can't believe how great you look." Lynn was always complimentary and sweet, despite always being the hottest chick in any room. With her long, straight hair and big green eyes, she was the quintessential beach babe. The California girl with model looks and a heart of gold, who dedicated herself to improving the lives of others.

"Right," Kevan said, rolling her eyes. She laughed and looked down at her vintage Social Distortion shirt and torn, baggy jeans. Yeah, she looked lovely today. "How have you been? Heard you're getting married. Who's the lucky guy?"

"He's a cop here in Redding I met at a fundraiser a year ago. It was love at first sight. Plan on having a bunch of his babies and living happily ever after." Lynn's smile grew even wider, if that were possible. "So who's the sexy, broody giant you came with?"

"No one," Kevan said shortly. No reason to open that can of worms. "Just another marketing guy."

As her eye instinctively sought him out in the growing crowd, Mason raised his head and glanced at her. He stood next to a young woman wearing a sheer yoga outfit that was completely out of place on a cold housing build. The woman talked animatedly, waving her hands and her hammer in the air. Maybe she was one of the volunteers from the local gym. Maybe she was more Mason's type. He didn't smile at Kevan but nodded and turned back to the overly chatty woman. Kevan clenched her jaw. Maybe the hammer would slip out of blondie's hand and land on her foot. Or his.

Catching Kevan watching him like a love-starved teen, Lynn raised her eyebrow. "Really?"

"Really." But maybe she should pair Mason with someone more helpful. Like another guy. "We might have gotten together once."

"And?"

"And then he found out I was trying to sign Manix and left without a word."

"And?" Damn Lynn and her tenacity. The woman was like a pit bull.

"And now he keeps cornering me and kissing me. And maybe he dragged me out of my bunk on the bus last night and then I ran off like a scared bunny. It's all a mistake. He's the CEO of a really big company, and now we're sharing an RV and competing for Manix's business." She explained the meeting with Joe, the deal they'd made, and how she'd ended up sharing his motor home.

"Girl, you have a knack for jumping in the shit

feetfirst, don't you?" Lynn laughed. "I give you two days at the most."

"Two days? For what?"

"Before you're back in his bed again." She winked.

"Shut up," Kevan mumbled and shoved her friend's shoulder. Nope, she could totally stay away from him.

"Don't look, but he's been staring at you the whole time we've been talking."

It took all of Kevan's self-control to keep from looking for him again, to not dwell on the constant heat in his eyes and the sexy glower she knew was on his face. "He's watching me? How?"

"Like he wants to eat you up." The two women dissolved into girlish giggles. Then Lynn's smile faded, and her brow furrowed as she leaned in close to Kevan. "How's Bowen?"

Though they hadn't stayed together after Lynn had left Portland for college, Lynn and Bowen had stayed friends. Her brother was so charismatic it was difficult for anyone to dislike him for too long, even a jilted ex. Until he'd bottomed out, of course. Then it had been pretty easy to stay pissed at him.

"He's okay. In rehab. Hopefully, it'll stick." Kevan pasted on her best smile and tried to ignore the look of pity Lynn wore. Thankfully, that was a look Mason never gave her. But it was time to get to work, since the day was about the new homeowners and her band. Not rehashing past tragedies or her fuckwit brother.

All around Kevan, volunteers were getting grouped into specific activities. One for painting walls and trim. Another for landscaping duty. Mason and Jax, along with blondie, appeared to be in charge of digging the hole for the mailbox. And when did those two become so chummy? The one thing missing was the reporters. Strange.

"Why don't we meet the family," Lynn said as she grabbed her and dragged her over to the couple and their three kids.

After speaking with the family for a few minutes, Kevan called the rest of the group over and introduced them. The unbridled appreciation and excitement infected the band and the volunteers. These people deserved this home and were ready to get dirty to make it happen. Kevan checked the time, again. Anxiety chipped away at her cool demeanor. What if no one showed? What if Tina had given them the wrong location? This wasn't just about Manix. The family and Lynn's organization deserved the recognition. The more PR they received, the better the organization did. The better the organization did, the more people they could help.

After checking her voice mail, Kevan called Sindra and left her a message. A dense, uneasy sensation began to settle heavily in her belly. Where the hell were the reporters? The heaviness began to grow as her phone rang. Kevan marched away from the group and answered her cell.

"Hey, it's Sin. Got your messages. I did follow up with the media outlets yesterday. What should I do now?" The usually soft, steady voice of her graphic artist was breathy and panicked.

Kevan let out an aggravated sigh. What the hell was going on? Her pulse raced, and her temple began to throb. *Pull it together. Act like a boss.* "Why don't you call the list of reporters again and find out why none of them are here? It's still early enough in the day that they could run a decent feature."

The long pause on the other end of the phone was not a harbinger of good times. "Yeah. I did call them before I called you back. They all said they'd gotten calls from some guy at Jolt cancelling the coverage for the build."

Some *guy*? Who would do that? Why? "Weird. Did you tell them it wasn't the case and ask to have new reporters sent?" Hope bobbed tentatively to the surface.

"They were all either reassigned or not in. I'm really sorry, Kev."

The dull throb in her temple increased its tempo, and an icy chill of dread began to descend. Shaking off her fear, she took a deep breath. "It's not your fault. Thank you for everything. I really appreciate your hard work."

Frustrated and more than a little dejected, she ended the call. What the hell was going on? And who had pretended to be from Jolt and cancelled her story?

It was hard to hide her emotions; she'd always worn them on her sleeve. Though she avoided Mason, he watched her while she struggled to keep tears from overflowing. It was like he could see through her, right into her heart. Or maybe he knew exactly what was going on and was gauging her reaction. Shaking her head and pushing away suspicion, Kevan tried to swallow her disappointment. She looked around, and everyone seemed busy and happy. Megadeth blared from a sound system the family had set up, and the entire group—family, volunteers, community members, metal band—was hard at work.

The band was there. The house was getting built. The family had become instant fans of Manix and bonded immediately. Unfortunately, somehow the media had been cancelled. And though it looked as if she'd lost this round in the competition for Manix, there was still good work to be done. She looked down at the phone in her hand, and the answer hit her. She'd cover the build herself.

She started taking shots of the family and volunteers and sending them to the band's Instagram and Twitter accounts. Then she added some interview videos and posted them to Vine and Facebook. Because that's how she was. Hit over the head with disappointment after disappointment, Kevan continued to put one foot in front of the other and keep moving forward. Again and again, she adapted and overcame. She'd get the job done and figure out later who had sabotaged her event.

Eventually she tucked her phone away and picked up her hammer. She started pounding nails into her section of the framing, enjoying the freedom of just whacking something. Getting lost in the laborious work, she jumped when Mason's shadow fell across the plywood she was attaching to another board.

"What's up, Bettie?" he asked, the deep timbre of his voice dancing over her skin.

"Nothing for you to worry your pretty little head over." She smirked but checked her phone again by habit, sending another picture, this one of Conner and Marco lifting one of the walls into position.

He drew his knuckles up to her face and dragged them softly down her cheek. "C'mon, darlin', what's going on? Maybe I can help."

A shiver ran down her neck. Oh yeah. He could help all righty. She leaned into his hand before remembering she was in public at a charity event. And not his frigging sex toy. He was on the enemy. Abruptly, she pulled away.

"I doubt it," she said, wondering again if he'd had anything to do with the missing media. He certainly had motive. "And what makes you think anything's wrong?"

"You keep looking around for something. And you've been on and off your phone all morning. What's up?" His sincere smile was not what she needed right now. Or ever. If she didn't grow some courage, she was going to lose this battle.

"I'm fine." She swung her hammer high, struck the nail, and pounded it into the plywood.

"Why won't you let me help you?" He frowned. But he already knew the answer. She could see it in his eyes, reflecting back like a mirror.

She tossed the hammer to the side of a stack of wood and crossed her arms tightly over her chest. "You're the competition. You want what I need. Your success is my downfall. Get it?" Stupid man.

Mason scowled, a tick in his jaw pulsing, and leaned in. He was so close, his warm breath vibrated on her cheek. "Jesus. You think I'm such a heartless dick I'd screw you silly and then throw you under the bus at every opportunity?" When she didn't answer, he said, "I guess you fucking do."

He glared at her for a moment before he shook his head and stomped off. Kevan stared at his retreating back, wondering if he was the culprit or if she was just too jaded to let anyone close.

Mason half listened to the tall, willowy blond giggling about the hammer and nail she was slamming into a wood block. He smiled at her. Why would she volunteer to build a home if she didn't know the difference between a hammer and a saw? So not like Kevan, who was hammering away with a look of raw determination on her beautiful face, completely oblivious to the ogling of every male on the work site, including the group of gym-rat volunteers. Not that he gave a shit. She'd made it clear—he was good enough to screw, but she refused to trust him.

And while Kelli was very attractive and not unlike the women he'd dated in the past, Mason's gaze kept drifting to one curvy brunette with blue streaks and gray eyes, and the most squeezable ass in the history of round, squeezable asses. The sordid things he wanted to do to that perfect ass. *Fuck*. She'd ruined him. No other woman even compared to her sunshine and fucking light. No other woman could spin on a dime so quickly and go from angel to devil either.

Mason decided to pull his head out of his own butt, engage Kelli with an "i," and put on his CEO charm. He was, after all, on this tour for a reason—to save his damn job and get back to normal. Normal. He rolled the word around in his head.

"What's normal?" she asked, and he realized he must have muttered it aloud.

"Exactly," he mumbled. And when she looked up at him with a quizzical expression, he smiled. "Never mind, hon."

Really, though? What is normal anymore? Kevan had fucked up his whole reality as well as his

vocabulary. Normal—nothing was normal post-Kevan
Landry. Nothing. What did he want then, besides her
back in his bed? Nothing. *Yeah, sure, keep telling
yourself that*. Maybe Dan was right. Maybe he did
want more with her.

Looking around, he suddenly realized why Kevan
was so upset and had gone on the attack earlier. The
media hadn't shown up. Why weren't they here, and
why did he have more sympathy for her than he felt
success for himself?

The rest of the afternoon, she did her best to avoid
Mason. She even bolted up the RV's steps and vanished
into the back for her pre-show routine. Like magic, she
transformed into a bizarre, whirling dervish of swirly
skirts, stockings, powders, hair spray, and makeup.

Usually, Mason was fascinated by her dressing-up
ritual. Loved watching the process of her going from
fresh-faced punky girl next door to vampy, vixen queen
of the night. Not tonight. Tonight he needed to know
what had changed that morning. They'd made so much
progress the night before, when she'd opened up to him
about her brother. When she'd let him stroke her cheeks
and kiss her gently. And then later, when she'd let him
make love to her. And then she ran. Now, she couldn't
stand to be near him. Did she blame him for the lack of
media at the build? *Fuck that*.

Mason let her flutter around the RV from bathroom
to bedroom to her curtained bunk and back through
a cloud of cursing and powder, accentuated with
cupboards slamming and frustrated growls. He figured it was best to let her complete her rituals, slam
stuff around, and have her temper tantrum before he

confronted her. When she finally came to rest thirty minutes before they needed to get into the club, she slowed and turned to him.

"I'm gonna go a little bit early and see…"

Patience was overrated. He walked within inches of her and looked down, forcing her to look up and make eye contact with him. Her scent surrounded him, her usual vanilla accompanied with the simple smell of roses.

"What the fuck, Mason," she muttered. He grabbed her chin and rubbed his thumb back and forth over her glossy bottom lip, staring into her eyes.

"Shhhh," he murmured. Her chest heaved up and down rapidly, then slowed as she took a deep breath. They stood there like that for several seconds.

Mason wrapped his arms around her and pulled her pliant body up against his. Her head pressed against his chest. One hand rubbed lengthwise up and down her back, feeling her rigid muscles soften and relax under his fingers. When she sighed, he felt so triumphant he expected doves and butterflies to fill the RV at any moment. He wanted to push her but knew he had to wait. He continued to soothe her with his body and kissed the top of her head.

That woman is under your skin. Dan's words ran through his head. Fucking hell, she was getting to him.

"Tell me," he demanded gently, wanting desperately for her to confide in him. "What's going on in that gorgeous mind of yours? Is it last night?"

She shook her head. "The press didn't show today. I confirmed everything, and nobody showed up. When Sindra called to find out what had happened, the only explanation was a man had called to cancel, and the reporters were reassigned or rescheduled."

A man had called and cancelled. The thin tendrils of suspicion began to unravel and reshape in his mind. Who had called? Kevan's body shook as she took a stilted breath. Still, he waited, sensing she needed to share at her own pace, not be forced by him.

"I was confused. Upset. I couldn't get ahold of her at first. Then I got really pissed," she said. Mason used one hand to unclench a fist from his shirt. He spread her palm flat against his chest and patted it. Her voice was laced with anger and frustration. Wishing he could swallow her pain, at the same time he admired her openness and honesty. She always gave so much more than he ever did. Yet another reason she could never be his permanently.

"I let it eat at me all day until it took on a life of its own." She paused and looked up into his face with sad eyes and lines furrowing her forehead. "I do that, you know." She rolled her eyes and tucked back into his arms, her soft body melting into his. "Give my feelings and thoughts their own lives. Active imagination."

"You think it was me?" Mason squeezed her tighter and couldn't hide the shock in his voice. He hoped he was wrong, but he knew he wasn't. She still didn't trust him. Would she ever?

She sighed again and stared up at his face, worrying her bottom lip, as if evaluating her options for a bigger decision. Like trusting him. If she trusted him a little, maybe they could move forward.

"Yes," she said simply. "I thought it might have been you. And I was pissed. Mostly at myself for trusting someone like you... I mean, trusting a man again." Kevan scowled and pushed both palms on his chest, but he wasn't ever letting her go that easily. *Ever? No. Now. Just for now. That's all I can offer her.*

"I'm not wired like that. I promised a fair fight. Won't go back on my word, Bettie. You're going to have to trust me."

"I realized it couldn't have been you. Tina and Sindra are the only ones with the press list. Someone had to get the list from them, or maybe my email was hacked." She untangled herself from his arms and gently laid a palm to his cheek. "And it's not your style. You'd use the press coverage for your next power play. So, no, I don't think you'd sabotage that kind of opportunity," she said begrudgingly, her eyes watery and distant. "But I can't trust you. I'm sorry. I just can't."

The wistful smile she gave him before pulling away was equal to ripping his heart from his chest and throwing it to the ground. She couldn't trust him, and he couldn't share himself with her. Before giving in to the melancholy threatening to pour down on him, she tugged him toward the door. "Come on, big, bad, handsome man. Let's go have some fun and pretend we're two normal people out for a good time."

Normal. There was that word again. Funny, he didn't think he would ever be normal again.

Chapter 15

MASON WOKE TO AN ANNOYING AND PERSISTENT
vibration. Fuzzy from sleep, he lifted his head and
looked around the cluttered cabin. The RV wasn't
moving, which meant they must be in San Francisco.
The buzzing halted, so he closed his eyes again, needing
a few more minutes of blissful rest. The buzzing started
again. Dammit.

He sat up, rubbed his eyes, and looked down at the
source of his irritation. His phone was lying next to his
pillow. He grabbed it and pushed "answer" before looking at the screen.

"Dillon," he barked into the speaker.

"Mason, it's Simone," a familiar hushed voice said.
"Are you there?" she asked when he didn't answer.

"What do you want?" Although Mason saw no good
reason for pretending she was still his loyal adminis-
trative assistant and he was the powerful boss, regret
immediately clouded his mood. The shift in power
hadn't been her fault or doing. "I'm sorry, but it's early,
and I'm busy. What do you need?"

He heard a long, drawn breath on the other end of the
line. Was she nervous about something? "I only have a
second, but you need to trust me. Do you have something you can write on?" He glanced around and jumped
to grab his notepad and pen from the vanity. Simone
may have been forced to work for Revell, but until then

she had always been a dedicated and loyal assistant.

"Go ahead."

He wrote the name, number, and email she dictated to him.

"Here's the deal. I received a media alert email this morning from a producer at Fuse TV. They're doing a new twist on their popular web show *Metal Heat Meltdown*. They want to feature a rock icon interviewing an up-and-coming band. Manix Curse would be perfect."

"I take it Revell told you about the band?" Of course, the bastard probably went back to the office, complaining about Mason's threats, and then took credit for "discovering" Manix.

"Yes. Well, sort of. I did a little due diligence on my own. Anyway, sir, to get the interview, you'll need to deliver a performance video to them within two days. They'll send a crew out to tape, but they'll require a bigger venue than the clubs you've been playing."

"Like how much bigger?"

"At least twenty-five hundred people," she said, the words floating in the air like smoke before evaporating like his fucking future. "Before you say 'no,' I've already confirmed Manix Curse for tomorrow night at an outdoor theater at one of the community colleges in San Francisco." Oh, great. Not only would he fail, but he'd do so spectacularly.

"Mason. Are you still there?" Her tone was full of concern.

"Yes. There's no way this band can draw that kind of audience outside their local market with so little time." He set the notepad and pen down on the side table and sank back on the bed.

He heard tapping in the background. "I sent you the contact info for the event person at the college. You can do this. You've packed coliseums all over the world with a wave of your magic marketing wand. Twenty-five hundred metal kids is nothing, small potatoes, for you. You *can* do this."

"Simone—"

He could hear low voices on the end of the line. "I have to go. The film crew will be at the venue at six p.m. to set up. You need to make this happen. What do you have to lose?" The line went dead.

Good question. What did he have to lose? At this rate, he wondered if signing the band would even save his job. Jolted by that thought, Mason let it sink in. Would it save his job if he brought the band under the GEM umbrella? And, if it didn't, what would that mean? What did life look like for Mason Dillon without the letters GEM CEO after his name?

Maybe I'll get the girl. Whoa. Two mind-bending concepts in the span of a minute was too much. Probably better to focus on the short-term right now. The very short-term. How to get ten times the number of audience members in to see Manix Curse at a new venue. At the last minute. Sure, no problem.

He certainly couldn't do it alone. Another new thought. *Ask for help.* More specifically, ask the one person who specialized in social media and fan inter-action. Kevan. Between the two of them, maybe they could pull this show together.

When he walked from the bedroom into the living area, she was already making coffee. She leaned against the counter with her back to him, an old-fashioned scarf wrapped in her hair and a cotton, floral shift that reached midthigh, revealing part of the lacy tattoo that wrapped around her leg. Her luscious ass was outlined perfectly through the thin material.

Goddammit. He wanted her. Right now, over the counter, the vision in his head playing clearly. Like an X-rated movie starring Kevan. For a moment, he imagined her wetness shiny on his cock as he pounded into her from behind. He felt his dick stiffen. Shit. Just standing there thinking about fucking her—not even touching her—and his cock was at full mast.

"I heard you on the phone. Made you some coffee. No cream, a little sugar, right?" She glanced over her shoulder. Her gaze blanketed him, and her eyes went from placid to confused to coy. He hadn't seen that look since they'd last been in her bedroom. "Someone's sporting a little morning wood."

Her jibe snapped him out of his trance and into action. He stepped forward, brushing his arm against hers, and heard a quiet intake of air. Good. "Little?" He raised a brow. "We both know that's not true, don't we?"

Her instant blush was perfect. "Oh, good, you put your ass hat on already. Guess I don't have to pretend to be nice."

"Actually, I don't want to bicker with you this morning." He sat at the kitchenette and patted the seat next to him. She deliberately sat across from him. "I have a proposition for you."

She gaped at him. "You've got to be kidding."

He held up his hands in protest. "No, no. A business proposition. I received some information about an opportunity for Manix that could be huge."

Her face dropped. Mason took a bizarre kind of pleasure in watching how different emotions played out on
her expressive face. Would he one day recognize all of
her various feelings?

Ignoring the thought, he said, "But I need your help."

He explained the call he'd received and gave her the
details about the Fuse TV web show. Mason watched as
her wariness faded and her knee began to tap against the
table. Her eyes grew bright, and her fingers twirled an
unrestrained lock of hair, a habit signaling she was deep
in thought or in planning mode.

His eagerness and impatience battled while she sorted
out what he'd told her. Was she interested? Did she trust
him enough to work on a project together? Just as he
was about to interrupt her internal dialogue, she spoke.

"We need to call the Fuse guy and confirm. We
need to create, print, and distribute posters early. Like
this morning. We need to acquire some airtime on the
local college and rock stations. We need to pummel
the Internet with incentives and tidbits about the show.
Really hook the local scene and get people excited."

Holy shit. Not only was she on board, she was already
putting together an action plan. Was it weird that her
über-work-mode persona also made him hot?

When he stared at her, she slapped her hand on the
table and glared at him. "Well? Call Fuse. I'm gonna
call Sindra and get her started on a poster. I need to
take a quick shower." She jumped up and started for the
bathroom, but stopped and turned. She took a step back
toward him. "Thanks."

"For what?" Didn't she realize she was bailing him out?

"For doing this. For the band. For me. Whatever

happens. Thanks for asking for my help. It means a lot."
She cupped his jaw in her soft hand and brushed a kiss
on his bearded cheek.

He was motherfucking speechless. When he thought
he understood her mercurial personality she went and
changed the game on him. Would he ever be able
to predict what she'd do or say next? Probably not.
Probably best to enjoy the Kevan Landry ride for as
long as he could.

Before she pulled away, he clutched her hand and
brought it to his lips. They stayed like that, him sitting,
holding her hand, and her standing next to him until
Ben walked into the cabin for his morning coffee. She
jumped away from Mason, greeted their driver, and ran
off to take a shower.

While she got ready, he confirmed the arrangements
with Fuse as well as the college stadium. Then he went
to the other bus to notify Joe and rally the band. They
would need to get out and spread the word. Once he and
Kevan determined their strategy, they'd assign tasks,
and everyone would hit the pavement.

When she emerged from the back room in jeans and
her hair pulled back, he recognized the odd sensation
that had been building in his chest the last day or so.
There was a certain kind of rightness in all the craziness
around them. The housing build, the shows—everything.
It felt right. Being with her felt right. He actually did
need her help. And it was okay. More than okay.

Empty spaces being filled. By her silly humming, her
constant activity, her color and lust for life.

Kevan said good-bye to whomever she'd been talking to and sat at the table across from him. "Talked

to Sindra." He must've looked confused, because she added, "Jolt's graphic designer. Anyway, she's working on the poster right now. She thinks we're going to run into trouble getting a printer at the last minute. The local big-box printer has some major equipment issue, so she's looking for a small press. But that may be out of the band's budget. So…"

"What? Just ask." He gave her a playful smile. "Since when is coy your MO?"

She laughed, her lip gloss as shiny as her gray eyes. "True. I was wondering if you could pull some big-bossy strings and see about getting someone to print the posters. And then pay for it. We'll send everyone out to plaster the great city of San Francisco."

"Consider it done. We can use a print house here in South Beach. I'll give them a call and let them know to expect the file. I also went over and talked to Joe. Everyone is waiting for us to give them the full scoop and directions." He looked at her pensively, hoping she wouldn't feel like he was trying to take over.

"It's like we were meant to be a team, cowboy," she blurted. Her eyes went as wide as saucers when she realized she'd said the words aloud. "I mean…you know…I meant that…"

Mason reached over and laid his hand over hers. God, every time he touched her it was an education in electricity. Invisible threads of fire sparked from their connection and shot straight to his chest. Though she tried to disguise her reactions to him, he could tell she felt it too. The shift in her expression was obvious as her eyes turned glassy and hooded. Now was the time for work. But later was a whole other animal.

"Told you the other day, we're going to play this out one day at a time. Today, we're a good team. We'll worry about tomorrow when we get there."

She looked up and met his gaze. Taking a deep breath and exhaling slowly, she said, "Okay."

"Kevan," he said, his voice low, "we both know there's something going on between us. Don't know what it is, and I'm not ready to put a name to it. But I'm not going to be able to keep my hands to myself much longer. I suspect you're not either."

"Yeah. That's what I'm afraid of." She stared at where their hands were joined and looked up and smiled at him before she pulled away and opened the laptop in front of her. "I need to start pimping the show online. Give me about thirty minutes to tweet, Facebook, Instagram, reddit, and log on to any local event forums. Then we can go over and talk to the band. Can you email the printer's info to Sindra? I texted you her address." She was in full-blown work mode as she tapped away on her computer, and it was sexy as fuck. How the hell was he ever going to go back to normal? That word—normal—was starting to sound boring and hollow.

Fuck normal.

Hours later, Mason sat outside the radio booth of a local rock station and listened to Marco and Jax talk about their show that night at the Dog Bone Bar and the Fuse TV show while he stared at the high-tech sound board. The lights blinked, providing feedback to the producer. The industry had changed so much in the last ten years. When he'd started out, the boards were still populated with levers and switches. He missed this

interaction, the day-to-day building of a band. He wondered what Kevan was doing, so he pulled out his phone
and shot off a text.

How's it going?

He stared at the screen, waiting for her response like
an eager teenage boy. Fuck it. He didn't care anymore.
He really only wanted to know how she was doing.

Checking up on me, cowboy? ;-)

*Yep. Send me a sext. A pic of your boobs would
be perfect. So I can see what you're doing.*

Ha. Ha. Everyone is out plastering the town
with posters and free passes. Joe hit 2 record
stores (who knew there were still so many).
How're the interviews?

*Great. Jax is really smooth, isn't he? He and
Marco are awesome. Did Tina call back yet?*

Kevan had called Tina earlier to see if she knew anything about the housing build media flop but hadn't been
able to connect with her.

Mason looked up to see Jax and Marco stand and
shake hands with the DJ. His phone beeped, notifying
him of another text.

Yes. No.

He was beginning to suspect that something was very wrong with Kevan's relationship with Tina. She hadn't heard from her former assistant, even though she'd professed her undying loyalty to Kevan despite being let go. That chick was sketchy, but this seemed to be unusual behavior even for her.

1 more interview then back to the RV.

After the show that night, he planned on trying to convince Kevan that they were a good team in bed too.

Chapter 16

Kevan woke wrapped in Mason's well-defined arms, surprisingly comfortable despite their bulk. When was the last time she'd felt so safe and content? She reveled in the solid warmth of him. For about thirty seconds. Then her heart began to beat so loudly she thought it would jump from her chest and run from the room. Her breathing became shallow, and her skin felt cold and clammy. Apparently, she'd fallen asleep sitting on his bed while they debriefed and planned after the show at the Dog Bone. Sleeping with him was far too intimate, especially without sex. The connection between them was becoming too strong. If it had been just sex, then she'd have been able to affect a feline stretch and purr her way back beneath him.

But this, this cuddling, was too much. It had made sense last night when they'd fallen onto his bed in exhaustion. It had felt so perfect when he'd wrapped his arms around her and pulled her tight against his body.

But now the walls of the small room felt even closer, more confining, so she began to crawl off the bed. She spied his neatly folded clothes on the dresser. Neat freak. And another reason of a billion why they didn't belong together.

Yesterday had been a long day, and she decided his morning should start later. She switched off his alarm clock before leaving the room for a shower. Stepping into the small confines of the RV shower stall, she let the warm water cascade over her head and wash away all her confusion. She soaped her body and rinsed her hair, watching the bubbles swirl down the drain. For once, she'd be open-minded and not bait Mason. She would make every effort to act like a grown-up and not a street kid with no manners.

With her new resolve in place, she stepped back into the living area, toweling her wet hair. Mason was already sitting in front of his laptop, talking on his phone, and didn't bother to look up as Kevan entered the room or as she went about her morning routine.

One call led to another and another and then a Skype call with the Hellfire guy. She worked on emails and the band's social media accounts while he talked. Not once did he ask her to join a call or share information. Apparently, the whole Team Landry-Dillon had a one-day expiration date.

Okay, so they weren't working together anymore. It was time for her to get out and promote as much as possible before the show that night. Instead of wallowing in her disappointment and acting like a petulant child, she sent a quick text to the band to meet her and got gussied up. She left the RV quietly, so as not to disturb Mr. CEO as he flexed his marketing muscles all over the place. Since San Francisco was known for its epic music scene, she had no trouble creating a list of appearances for the band before they hit the stage.

Hours later, when the Uber car dropped her off in front of the venue, Kevan was astonished to see a line wrapping around the outside wall of the big, open theater. Luckily, the band members had appealed to several local bands, who were eager to play and showed up with their own loyal fans. The place vibrated with rock-and-roll energy and was nearly packed by the time the show started.

Thankfully, the Fuse TV staff handled all the videography needs. She spent most of the show meeting with fans and local promoters, as well as updating the band's social media accounts. She might have also made an effort to avoid the Suit who seemed to be everywhere she wasn't. This type of bigger show seemed right up his alley, while she was definitely out of her comfort zone and trying not to look like it.

After the show, she stood in the green room, chatting with Jax, while Marco and Conner flirted with some groupies on a couch against the wall, and Mandi sat across from Joe, drinking beer. Members of one of the other metal bands had stuck around and were mingling with the fans and groupies.

"Now, we wait to find out if the show's producers are interested." Kevan twirled a lock of hair, trying not to wonder where Mason had sauntered off to. *Give him his distance*, she kept reminding herself, so they both could do their jobs.

"The way you and Dillon pulled this off. Together," Jax said, shaking his head, a hint of something in his smile.

Before she could respond, Mason stomped into the green room. With his brow furrowed and his lips thinned, he looked kind of pissed. Apparently, he didn't like being ignored any more than she did. She cringed inwardly. No, she'd just been busy doing her job. She turned back to Jax.

It's not like she'd stuck her tongue out at him or

anything, but so much for acting mature and giving him a chance. He'd shot that plan to hell when he'd pulled out his bazooka of indifference and put on his CEO costume this morning.

"Kevan," Mason said with a demanding edge that sent tiny chills racing along her arms.

Looking away from Jax, she turned to see Mason glowering at her. That, in and of itself, wasn't anything new—he'd been glowering at her since they'd met. Well, alternating between charming, glowering, and smirking. Frickin' caveman in fancy clothes is what he was. Although, this time something was different. Something in his eyes screamed "seriously pissed off."

Now we're getting somewhere.

With the tip of her tongue, Kevan moistened her lower lip. Maybe on purpose. Probably. "Hey, cowboy, was that an awesome show or what?" She reached over and patted Jax's heavily inked forearm. "You were amazing."

Jax raised a brow and looked at her with questions dancing in his eyes.

"Go get your stuff, Kevan. I want to talk to Jax."

Her anger spiked, but she laughed. *Is he for real?*

"That's not gonna happen, Mason. I'm busy. And no one tells me what to do." She turned back to Jax and opened her mouth to say something. An arm reached around her waist and pulled her backward into a very big, hard body. Oh God, *his* very big, hard body. The full length of her back made contact with the front of his chest.

Pulling her off to the side, he arched over her and leaned in to whisper in her ear, his breath hot on the back of her neck. "You think I'm angry because you've ignored me all day. I'm not. I get you're trying to pay me back for not being attentive or including you this morning. I won't ignore you again. But it's time to go." She felt her nipples harden and her breath quicken. Surely he could feel her heart pounding against her chest, trying to escape.

"If you're not mad, then what the hell are you freaking out about?" she spit out.

"Gave you the space you needed. Let you take care of business all night. Watched as every man in this stadium undressed you with their eyes. Work is done. My penance has been paid. It's time to go," he growled loud enough for a couple of people to look up from their conversations.

"But—"

He dragged her even farther away from the crowd. "Enough. You're done here, darlin'. Go. Get. Your. Things. I need to talk to Jax. Then I'm going to carry your ass back to our RV, because I can't wait for you to walk there. Then I'm going yank up your dress and rip off your panties."

Kevan's chest heaved, and she involuntarily fanned her face. How had she not realized how hot it was in the room? Had it been so hot in here all night?

"Unless you say no now, I'm going to bend you over the kitchen counter and fuck you until you can't remember your own name. Until all you can think about is me. Do you understand?" All the smart words and clever comebacks she'd formed in her head flew out of her brain. She had nothing.

"Answer me, Kevan. Do you understand?" Almost sweet, even in the midst of his totally unacceptable

caveman behavior—which should really offend her, not
excite her—he was giving her an out.

Butterflies took flight in her belly as she looked up
at Jax, who was watching the scene unfold, the lines on
his face deepening. She nodded. With what felt like a
Herculean effort, she untangled from Mason's grasp and
walked over to Jax.

"It's fine. I just need Mason. I mean, Mason needs to
go over tomorrow's schedule."

With a skeptical look, he nodded and hugged her.
"You know where I am if you need me."

She planted a light kiss on his cheek. Jax was a good
guy and was becoming a great friend.

"I do." She turned and searched the room for her bag
while Mason approached Jax. She hesitated, then realized both men could handle their alpha-selves without
her help. Let them figure it out. She had a bag to find
and a man to bag. In that order.

When Kevan exited the restroom, Mason was already
there waiting. He took two long strides toward her, and in
front of a roomful of people, he lifted and tossed her over
his shoulder like she weighed nothing. She started to protest, to say something about his inappropriate behavior.
But she didn't. Why fight the inevitable? Instead, she laid
her cheek against his firm back when he smacked her
bottom. Hard. Her center flooded with moisture and heat
as the cold sting was replaced with warmth.

Despite her arousal, she yelled, "Ouch, what was that
for? Put me down. Now!" She continued to protest as he
marched back through the room and out the door to the
sounds of catcalls, whistles, and shouts of laughter. She
was so never living this down.

She wriggled and shouted at him the entire two-minute trip of shame to their motor home. His only response was another firm smack on her ass. The spanks infuriated her. How fucking dare he? Unfortunately, her body was rebelling now too. Her core was radioactive—melting.

She'd always enjoyed a little slap and tickle, but had never found a man she could trust enough with her passions and fantasies. Mason didn't require her trust; it was like he instinctively knew what she wanted, what her body craved. Everything he did was designed to drive her crazier and crazier. Even when he got all domineering and bossy. What kind of fucked-up feminist did that make her? She was going to have to turn in her independent woman card when this tour was over. But until then, she was going to enjoy this big, bossy, sexy beast of a man. And his hand on her ass.

When they reached the inside of the bus, the room whirled, and she landed on her feet not seconds before Mason's mouth crashed down on hers. This was not the gentle, considerate lover Mason had been previously. This was all alpha male—hot, strong, and demanding. His mouth pummeled and punished hers in the most erotic and exciting way. He left no corner of her lips, her mouth unexplored. His large hands, wide over her shoulders, ran down the length of her arms until each one circled a wrist. He slowly pulled her wrists together and held them with one big hand while the other sought the bottom of her dress.

"Damn, how many fucking layers does this dress have?"

She smiled against his mouth and gasped when his fingers found her wet panties. He ran his long finger up and down the silky material and slowly pulled it to the side. He moaned when his finger reached into her pussy and felt how ready she was for him.

He pulled his hand free from her panties. Kevan gasped when he unexpectedly and roughly turned her around. Still gripping her wrists in one hand, he leaned down to whisper into her ear. "Do you want me like this, bombshell?" Again, the words weren't there. They stuck in her throat like dry cotton. She nodded, her chest heaving and her legs quivering as he pushed her hips against the kitchen counter with his.

The bus was quiet except for the scrape of metal and then the slither of leather as he pulled his belt from his jeans. Her nipples hardened when she felt the stiff, cold material encircle her wrists. She was pinned. Helpless. But not really. She knew he'd stop the second she asked him, though she had no intention of ever asking him to stop.

"Yes," she hissed as she heard the soft sound of his pants hitting the floor.

"I want you so fucking badly I can't even take the time to get our clothes off." Mason pressed his hardening cock into the soft folds of material covering her ass before he lifted her dress up again and tugged her panties aside. He bit gently into her shoulder as he slid snuggly into her sheath. He was so big, and she felt so full, but needed so much more.

He pulled her dress down over her shoulders. With one hand, he caressed one heavy breast, then the other, alternating between pinching and rolling her hardened buds as he pounded into her body. The pleasure-pain sensation created waves of need she'd never experienced. Kevan wanted to touch him but was awash in sensations.

He'd taken away her choice, and she rejoiced in the comfort of that. Her body bent over the counter, coupled with Mason's firm grip on her hip and the other hand on her breasts, sent her over into a shattering wave. The sounds she couldn't find earlier gathered strength and ripped from her throat as a scream. His name burst from her as her body exploded in pleasure, and stars sparked behind her closed eyelids. But he wasn't done with her and had moved his hand from her chest to her clit and rubbed soft circles until one orgasm collided and grew into another. And still he drove into her, in and out, holding her with one hand wrapped around her hip to keep her from crashing too hard into the counter.

His fingers continued to attack her hard, slippery clit, sliding roughly back and forth. His cock pushed and pulled at a frantic and brutal pace, his hand moving up to her hair, where he wrapped it around his fist. She teetered on the edge, waiting painfully for him to finish her off.

"Come for me again, darlin'," he barely choked out, his voice raw. He tugged her hair as his other hand dug into her hip. "Now."

The tremors in her body built again. He bit down on her shoulder in that one special spot, and she felt her body pulled under and tumbled like the one time she'd been hit by a huge wave in the ocean. She rolled and swirled, her body almost weightless, and heard him growl out her name in a roar.

Kevan collapsed forward, the counter holding her weight. She could feel her hair plastered against her face, her makeup half-rubbed away from their coupling. She didn't care. Not right now. She was fully sated. Exhausted. Fulfilled.

She felt herself turned and lifted. She reached her arms around his neck and pressed her head on his chest. He smelled so good—like Mason. Like a man. When had he removed the belt from her wrists? She wanted to burn this moment into her head, call upon it at a later date, when life was out of control or she needed to be soothed. Kevan felt anchored and grounded. That's what Mason did for her. That's what he made her feel. For once, her hamster-on-the-wheel brain was quiet, settled. Calm.

Such a contradiction this man was. Severe and gentle, brutal and affectionate. She relished the feel of his long fingers that were sure to leave marks on her hip. His marks. Marks signifying his own lust and the desire he felt for her. Right now, only for her. God, she loved how she could make such a controlled man lose all order and melt with passion for her.

Mason moved her to the bedroom, where he gently laid her down on the bed and rolled her to her stomach. He carefully unbuttoned her vintage dress and peeled away the hot-pink crinoline underneath. He tugged off her mangled panties and bra and hung them over the dressing-table chair. The entire time, he brushed back her hair and smoothed his hand gently over her skin, whispering sweet, nonsensical endearments. Her skin so sensitive, each little brush of his fingers sent flickers of sensation down her body.

Mason moved away. The bathroom door squeaked from across the room, and the water in the sink began to run. He returned to the bed, gently cleaned her with a warm cloth, then tossed it in the corner.

He rolled her to her side and looked into her eyes, his angled face shadowed by the darkness.

"Darlin', I'm so sorry."

"For what, Mason? That was incredible. Look at me. I can hardly move." She smiled weakly. Relaxation morphed into exhaustion.

He cleared his throat. If it were any other man, Kevan would swear he was nervous about something. "I forgot the condom. I'm sorry. I have never done that. Ever."

"I haven't either." Her whisper echoed through the quiet room. When he started forward, preparing to say something, she held her fingers to his lips. "I'm on the pill. And I'm clean. I've never been with anyone like that." His eyes widened, and his teeth nipped at her fingertips.

"I haven't either." His three little words filled Kevan's heart with warmth.

"Never?"

"Never."

Pressing her stinging fingertips to her lips, she tried to hide her smile. Well, that was a little surprise. He'd shared himself like that only with her. Only her. Her heart soared, just a little. Maybe more than a little. He didn't need to know though.

"Look, it's okay. It was an accident," she said.

Mason took Kevan's chin in his hand and did what he always did, moved her face to look directly at his.

"Yes. It was, and I am sorry. I never forget protection. I'm apologizing for putting you at risk. Sorry for losing control. But that's what you do to me. And now that I know you're safe, I'm glad I forgot the condom. Fucking incredible to feel you bare around me. You're fucking amazing." Mason slipped his hand around the back of her neck and pulled her toward him as he lay down next to her, covering her body with his much-bigger one. His lips brushed her sensitive mouth, still stinging from his rough kisses earlier. His mouth barely connected with hers.

"Please don't break me," she pleaded against his lips, hating the shake in her voice and the tremble of her lips.

Mason pulled back to peer into her eyes, his expression serious. "Not sure either of us is getting out of this unbroken, darlin'."

Kevan nodded. She sure as hell wasn't. In fact, she was already pretty sure she was in too deep and wasn't getting out without a broken heart.

When Mason moved to take her mouth again, he was all gentle kisses and soft caresses. The result was the same; it always was. He reduced her sassy self to a quivering mass of girl-goo screaming his name in orgasm after orgasm.

Chapter 17

KEVAN WAS GETTING COLD FEET. WITH LAST NIGHT'S concert a major success, she began to doubt the wisdom of accepting Mason's dinner invitation. Was she becoming too comfortable with his companionship? The man was too damn attractive and wickedly smart for her own good. Though she repeatedly tried to convince herself she wasn't looking for anything long-term right now, she still fantasized about a family of her own. Mason definitely wasn't a relationship, happily-ever-after kind of guy. He'd been honest about that from the beginning.

She was tired of pretending Mason was just a boring suit, when he was so much more. Yes, he was working for the same prize she was, but so far he'd played fair. In fact, he'd applauded her efforts and even supported some of her ideas. And yesterday, they had worked side by side, with each of their skills complimenting the other's rather than overshadowing each other's. They'd spent nearly the entire day working at the kitchenette table while the band took the day off to explore and play in San Francisco.

Hints of his kind, yet protective, nature had started to show through his polished veneer. She could take care of herself and had for years. But it was nice to have someone other than Bowen worrying about her. Even if he was the enemy, and his sharp intelligence might be the downfall of her life.

Sure, she'd said "maybe" to his first dinner invitation, not really taking him seriously. When he'd pushed again that morning, she'd figured "Why not?" They were in one of the most beautiful cities in the world, perched on a sparkling bay, filled with colorful music and interesting people.

Any apprehension she'd felt about going to dinner with Mason flew out the window when she stepped into the living area of the RV that evening. He looked up from his laptop, cute black-rimmed glasses perched on his nose, and his mouth dropped open. Apparently he liked her salmon-colored, vintage, sleeveless Dior dress.

"Jesus, woman, thought I had all your personas down, but this one…fuck me," he stuttered, obviously searching for the words as he dragged his tall, broad body to full height.

His enthusiasm emboldened her. "You like?" She spun slowly with her arms spread wide.

Mason shook his head. Her heart dropped. Had she misinterpreted his reaction? "Like? Not even close. You look fucking stunning. Like a modern Veronica Lake."

She felt the warm blush creep up her neck. How did he always know the right words to make her blood boil? He could've named any old starlet. But no, he'd picked the one she loved the most.

"We've been cooped up in this old RV all day. Let's go eat." He grinned, reminding her of a wolf eying his juicy lamb dinner.

Kevan looked around the high-end motor home. The granite countertops, stainless appliances, and plush suede sitting area were far nicer than anything in her little apartment. She rolled her eyes and wrapped her fingers around his thick arm and said, "Yes, let's get out of this dive. It's been horrible being stuck working in this hovel."

Mason grabbed her hand and led her to the car he'd had delivered for their mystery date. They sped off in the opposite direction from the touristy pier area. As they rode along the windy roads, Mason sat next to her, looking delicious as usual in a gray button-down shirt and black slacks.

When they hit a hilly area that was less city and more residential, Kevan turned to him.

"So are you going to tell me where we're going?"

"Yes." And nothing.

"When?" She studied his stern profile, both amused and irritated by his stoicism.

"When what, darlin'?"

"Mason. When are you going to tell me where the heck we're going?" she huffed. The man was exasperating.

He smiled that damn smug smile. "Soon."

"Soon what?"

"I'll tell you soon."

Kevan reached across the console and pinched his nipple through his pressed dress shirt.

"Ouch. Dammit, woman." His face colored red as he batted her hand away.

"Where. Are. We. Going?" She motioned like she was going in for a second pinch. He laughed, the sound wrapping around her like a soft blanket, and he raised his hand to block her fingers.

"The beach. I'm taking you to dinner at this little place right on the beach."

She was so excited, she clapped her hands. "I love the ocean."

The edges of his mouth curled up in that supersexy way of his.

Kevan turned her head toward the window, watching as the buildings grew fewer, the clear, crisp lights of the houses became the backdrop to a pleasant drive. She didn't want him to see how he affected her. How a little play and some simple smiles filled her heart and lightened the burden she constantly carried.

Fuckity, fuck, fuck. He kept doing these thoughtful things for her. Kevan could finally fully acknowledge that she wasn't getting out of this thing unscathed. She wasn't walking away from this man, from the whole Manix Curse deal, with her heart intact. Best to focus on his body, not her heart.

For a moment, she allowed herself to get lost in the fantasy of begging him to stop the car. Then climbing on him in the driver's seat, hiking up her dress. His eyes would widen and fill with lust when he pulled aside her already wet panties and saw her thighs wet with her desire. Maybe he would pull out that big cock of his and drag her down on him. He'd pin her arms behind her and take her hard. As he came in her, he'd nip the spot on her neck—his spot—before she'd careen off the cliff after him.

Kevan shook her head, shivered, and pulled her wrap tighter to hide her hard nipples. Mason stayed silent, but his smile had a sexy tilt. God, she really wanted to have sex with him again. She was trying to remember why screwing Mason was such a horrible idea.

She was beginning to suspect this might be more than

a casual dinner between colleagues. Panic fluttered in her chest when she looked up to find Mason glancing at her. Every time she looked at his face, she was struck by how easy it would be to get lost in those dark hazel eyes and his scruffy, dimpled smile. His reassuring grin shouldn't soothe her worry, but it did. From the beginning, she'd known he was trouble and, yet, here she was again. Fantasizing about rough sex in the car and making a conscious decision to let it all go for another night. She took a deep breath and smiled back.

She plugged her iPhone into the sound system, and the playlist shuffled to Everlast's acoustic "Sad Girl." Whitey Ford's deep voice filled the car with the sorrowful song of an abandoned ex-gang girl. For some reason, she related to the song. The sad, lonely, proud young woman.

She'd allowed herself to be sucked into the vortex of Mason's rugged charm and his seductive magnetism. And when he walked away with her business, and maybe even her heart, she'd be left again, crying her own tattoo tears.

From the corner of her eye, she saw Mason glance at her when the words about the angel, devil, stranger, rebel girl rolled from the speaker. *Yeah, so what.*

"Hey, where'd you go?"

"I don't know what you mean," she said, squaring her shoulders for a fight.

He reached over and smoothed her skirt over her knee gently. "What happened? You were so excited, and suddenly you're all cold."

She didn't say anything. What could she say? He was right.

"No pressure. No work. Remember. Just dinner and enjoying each other's company," he said.

He was right. As usual. Damn man. She nodded, and a reluctant smile threatened to break forward.

"We'll worry about tonight, not the future," she said as her heart sank a notch. She forced a smile, and it must have worked, because he patted her knee and whistled along to the song shuffling on her iPhone through the car's sound system.

Kevan didn't want to think about why he'd chosen to focus on today. She was pretty sure what it meant, but she just couldn't admit it. Because there was no possible future for them. Even if they didn't have the tour and the band hanging over their heads like a guillotine, they still would never fit into each other's worlds. How could they?

He was corporate Ivy League all the way. And she was low-rent street smarts. That would never work in the real world. Kevan could imagine walking into PTA meetings with her hair color of the month and her tattoos next to her big, bad, handsome man in his tailored suit and polished shoes.

Poor little Mason Jr. would be the kid with the weird mom and the perfect dad. Other parents, and probably teachers, would wonder what the hell someone like him saw in someone like her. Maybe they'd assume he'd knocked her up and had to marry her. Whoa. Again, imagination run amok. Cue the witches from *Hocus Pocus* running around in her head. No, that wasn't her future. At least not with Mason Dillon.

She put her hand over his much-larger one and gave a squeeze and a smile she didn't really feel. Tonight would have to be enough. She'd deal with the aftermath of her broken heart later.

Just like always.

Walking into the old Victorian house converted into a restaurant, Kevan marveled at the mix of antiques and modern amenities. Bronze gasoliers in the shape of cherubs dotted the red velvet walls, providing seductive low lighting.

The entryway was narrow and tall, with the walls covered by painted portraits of every size, time period, and style. A gorgeous painted tapestry of a British soldier—circa the American Revolution—hung below a surrealist image of a young woman and a modern piece of a couple entwined. The effect was elegant and relaxed, much like the refined man standing next to her, whose commanding presence was like a supercharged magnet.

The host walked them to a quiet corner of the main dining room, the cozy table draped in burgundy linens and lit by the warm glow of candles. After their orders had been taken and the wine poured, Kevan took a shallow sip from her glass. The cool, tangy liquid slid down her throat, and she hummed in appreciation. "This might be my new favorite wine."

"I thought you'd like it." He took a bite of the warm sourdough bread San Francisco was famous for. "This bread is delicious. You should have some—" Before he could finish, she reached over and gripped his wrist, bringing his hand to her mouth. She never broke eye contact as she took a slow bite of the bread. She let her tongue slide over his thumb before releasing his wrist. The dark look that transformed his face made her feel powerful and reckless. And really horny.

When she shivered, Mason pushed back his chair and moved behind her. He gently dropped her vintage velvet shawl over her shoulders and leaned in to whisper, "I could stare at your hard nipples all night, but I don't want you to be cold."

He kissed the magic spot he'd discovered that first night, and her breath caught as she remembered her fantasy in the car. She trembled again, but this time for another reason altogether.

She smiled at his thoughtfulness. This man was so much more complex than she'd initially given him credit for. She wanted to know more about him, what he liked, where he'd grown up, how he liked to spend Sunday mornings.

After he returned to his seat, she asked, "So tell me about your life. You're kind of an important guy in the business world. This whole touring with a metal band, hands-on marketing thing has to be sort of surreal for you. How does GEM's top gun end up on tour with a secondary-market heavy metal band?"

He sent her a sexy half smile. "When I interned at BEA after I dropped out of Harvard, I spent a couple of years being very hands-on with several of their promising LA-based hard rock and metal acts. Basically, I worked my ass off for very little pay. But the education was priceless and helped me get my first real job in talent development at GEM. And I've been climbing the corporate ladder ever since."

A haunted look flitted across his face but was gone as

soon as the waiter delivered their salads. She wondered at his sad expression. Wasn't GEM his dream? Kevan wanted to wipe the drawn look from his eyes and make him smile again.

"That's it? Pretty short story, cowboy," she said, sipping her wine. "And you really didn't answer my question."

"Which one?"

"The one where Global Entertainment Marketing's top executive suspends time and goes on the road with a talented but second-rate heavy metal band and a quirky, but endearing marketing upstart."

He laughed, a deep, confident rumble that made Kevan feel warm and safe. It made her want to crawl into his lap and snuggle.

"My company has been successful following a narrow business model of pop stars and mid-level R & B acts. Until recently, it worked well, but the industry has changed, and we haven't kept pace. I'm trying something new."

"And that's why you're trying to ruin my life—for something new?" she asked before she could filter her words.

"I'm not trying to ruin your life, Bettie. And we agreed to take it a step at a time. Let's focus on tonight, okay. What else do you want to know?"

"I don't understand why GEM sent their CEO to chase after Manix Curse." She gulped some water. "I mean, you're the top guy at a pretty big company. Why not send someone less senior, less important?"

He finished chewing the food in his mouth. Stalling, probably.

After he took a sip of wine, he said, "Revenues have

been dropping consistently the last four quarters. I've tried to staunch the bleed of money by diversifying our holdings and encouraging reps to seek out new talent. I've worked with marketing to try and change our corporate brand to be more contemporary. But the damage has been done. The ball was already rolling downhill." He took another sip of wine.

She waited for him to continue.

"Despite my best efforts to take the company to another level, the board resisted. But when we recently lost one of our major stars—"

"Bella Cole?"

"Yep. The one and only little diva herself. Anyway, when she bailed to one of the well-funded startup agencies out there—"

"The Argyle douchebags?"

"Yeah." He smiled. "Anyway, the board—or the chairman, really—decided I had to change things or look for another job."

"They're going to fire you?" she whispered.

No. Her breath rattled out of her chest, pinging painfully against the hollowness.

"I came up with a shoot-it-all type of plan to save the company by changing our image and our clientele, and, hopefully, save my job."

Suddenly, winning didn't seem like winning anymore.

She rested her face in her hands. Without looking up, she sighed. "Well, fuck a duck, Mason. We're both screwed if we don't sign Manix."

"Yep."

They sat in silence for several minutes, finishing their salads. Kevan suspected there was more left unsaid than said, but she let it go. She wanted to enjoy the evening despite the dire confession Mason had shared with her. She needed to get him back to his sexy, playful self.

"So tell me how big, bad Mason Dillon was raised."

Relief flooded his face as he rubbed the back of his neck with his hand. "I already told you about my mom. She retired a year ago. My dad was the deputy attorney general for Texas and is now in private practice in Portland. My sister lives in Portland, too, and is a divorce lawyer. She also does pro bono work for the Women's Resource Center in town. That's pretty much it." He swirled his wineglass, the liquid reflecting the restaurant's candlelight and appearing to glow.

"You've got to be kidding me." She looked at him, trying not to let her mouth hang open like a noob. "That's pretty much it," she said in a mocking Texas drawl.

"Okay, fine, what *else* do you want to know?" He scowled, reminding her of a grumpy child.

She shrugged. "Tell me about your childhood."

"Why?" he asked, his face clouding.

She smiled. "Humor me."

The flamboyant arrival of their dinner—three waiters dropping off plates, refilling water and wine—prevented Mason from answering. She let him take one bite of his steak and shrimp before fixing him with a pointed stare.

He sighed. "Born and raised in Texas. Parents are very A-type personalities, very success oriented. They see everything as a negotiation or transaction. They're decent enough people, just not very warm, if you know what I mean."

Kevan nodded. She understood that kind of person completely—driven, emotionally disconnected. Mason didn't seem like that at all. He was stoic most of the time, but when he felt strongly about something, he burned brightly with passion.

Clearing her mind of Mason and passion, she asked, "Is it because of their marriage that you don't do relationships?"

"Let's talk about you. You're much more interesting." He flashed his wicked grin, the one that routinely melted her panties.

Reaching across the table, he offered her a bite of his shrimp; delicious garlic and butter exploded on her tongue. "Mmmmm," she groaned, maybe a little more lustily than she'd intended, but the darkening of his eyes was the reaction she'd been aiming for.

"Your turn, Bettie."

"I used to work tricks out of the Tiki—"

"What the fuck?" His mouth dropped open, transforming his rugged features into a more fishlike gape.

She laughed loudly. "I'm kidding. Making sure you're paying attention. I run the front desk and do the books at Tatuaggio part-time. I earned extra money doing pinup modeling and tattoo magazine shoots. I made enough to get myself through community college and then Portland State with a degree in business marketing, but I still have to work part-time at the shop to make ends meet. Had Tina helping out part-time, but I couldn't keep her on. Sindra is technically an intern, so she works for free." Hopefully, he'd leave it at that instead of digging up all the ugliness of her life. But he calmly cocked an eyebrow and waited. The man was exasperating.

"I told you about my family. Basically it's Bowen and the guys at Tatuaggio." She tried to hide the tears in her eyes by blinking rapidly and turning toward the window a little too late. He saw them.

"I lost my mom to cancer when I was eleven. A little girl still. Bowen is only five years older. He stepped into the roles of Mom and Dad while still a child himself." She paused, letting the past wash over her. "He protected me from my dad's anger and from his creepy friends who noticed when I started filling out and wasn't just a pudgy little girl with fat lips anymore."

Mason's jaw tensed, and she felt the ache of acid in her gut, knowing he felt anger at her past. The shame she usually felt was completely overshadowed by relief. Mason was, at heart, a good man, and sharing her story was the right thing to do.

"Tony has always tried to be there for us. Gave Bowen a job when we needed money. Taught him his trade. Keeps me on when he really doesn't need my help. But really, until now, it's always been Bowen and me as a team. I miss him. He has a gift for creating beauty from nothing—music, painting, mosaics, murals, you name it." Her throat suddenly felt tight, like the present and past had collided and were choking her.

She reached for her wine and took a sip. The sharp but fruity coolness soothed her rising tears. For someone who never cried, she seemed to shed a lot of tears around Mason.

"And now he's fallen into the same pit every other fucked-up man in my family has. Booze and drugs have stolen him from me. Now everything he touches turns to shit." She was about done with the gloom and doom taking over their conversation.

Only after blurting out her entire life, did she worry

she might be sharing too much information. But she wanted him to know. She wanted to tell someone about her life.

"Tell me about your sister," she said.

Mason's smile grew wide. "JamiLynn. Jami. She's a pain in the ass." His words contradicted the warmth cascading over his face. "But I love her."

She imagined briefly a little girl with traces of Mason's strong features, and her heart clenched a little. Just a little. Nothing to worry about.

"Is she like you?" she asked, taking another sip of wine. She rarely drank but was enjoying the warmth and serene cocoon the alcohol created.

His eyes looked directly at her but seemed focused on something far away. After a moment, he answered. "No. She doesn't really look like me. She's short and much prettier. And blond."

Kevan giggled. "I don't know, cowboy, you're one of the prettiest men I've ever met."

His eyes sparkled, reflecting the candles in the dining room, and he laughed. "You have no idea how truly beautiful you are, do you?" Again. This man and his words.

She shrugged. "We're talking about you. Tell me about Jami."

"Jami's younger. As kids we fought. A lot. She was spirited and creative. A little impulsive." His grin widened, barely showing his dimple as he took a bite of his steak. "I think you'd like her. As least how she used to be. In a way you're a lot alike. Anyway, she used to drive me crazy, sneaking out and getting in trouble with her boyfriend, Dallas." He cleared his throat.

"After Dallas, it got really bad for a while, then he bailed. Then she got serious, and school became her priority." He picked up his wineglass and swirled it before bringing it to his lips, lips she wanted to taste again, to feel brushing against her neck.

"I take it you didn't approve?"

"It's not that. I'm glad she stopped partying and was taking her life seriously. But she changed so much. It was like her light just died. My parents didn't approve of Dallas, so they weren't very helpful. They were thrilled when she started acting like them. Jami managed to get through college and then law school." The look of love that shone in his eyes when he spoke of his sister made her heart hurt a little. Oh God, what would it be like to have that intense affection directed solely at her? She mentally shook her head. Now she was jealous of a woman she'd never met?

"What happened?" Kevan asked.

His sigh carried the weight of whatever memories he was holding back. "She got pregnant. He hurt her, and she lost the baby in a bad car accident."

She teared up and reached across to pat his hand. He smiled, a faraway look in his eyes.

"I'm so sorry." They may come from different worlds, but the way he felt about his sister was exactly how she felt about Bowen. This was getting more and more complicated.

Chapter 18

AFTER DINNER, MASON TALKED KEVAN INTO KICKING off her shoes and walking down the dark beach. The moon shone brightly on the water as the waves lapped at their feet. When she pulled away and suddenly twirled around with her arms out, his breath caught in his chest. Her simple joie de vivre made his lungs hurt. *God, can she be more beautiful?*

When was the last time he'd felt such simple joy for anything? Never. She loved life and had no problem sharing her emotions. He believed the world, with him at the top of the list, spent far too much time calculating risk and measuring outcomes. Instead of worrying about odds and repercussions, Kevan Landry lived her life full throttle with no apologies.

Running up, he grabbed her hips from behind and lifted her up before a wave crashed over her legs. Her laugh sent tingles of electricity from his heart to his dick. It seemed that just about everything she did made him as hard as steel.

He set her down, and she turned toward him to wrap her arms around his waist. He dropped a kiss on her pert nose, and she blinked as if considering something. They stood for a moment, the cold water tugging back and forth at their feet, swirling foam and sand in cool circles.

"I'm sorry," she said quietly, barely audible over the crashing waves.

Confused, he asked, "For what, darlin'?"

"For prying. For asking about your job. I know we promised not to talk about the tour or the band tonight, but it's all getting to be a little much. A little confusing."

"Yes, it is." They walked, holding hands, to where they'd dropped their shoes. The cold sand felt good on his feet. Somehow grounding him there in that moment with Kevan.

She dipped down to grab her heels. "It was really sweet of you to bring me here. I promise I won't borrow trouble for the rest of the night."

He stopped and tilted his head. She had the funniest sayings. "What do you mean?"

"It means I won't 'what if' or worry about the competition or next week or whatever."

Mason smiled. He liked the phrase. He liked the way she always had such an interesting take on life and circumstance. Truth be told, he liked her. A lot.

The realization should have stifled him. Stunned him. Choked him with fear. Sent him running.

It didn't. And then he knew. It hit him like the hammer he'd wielded at the housing build. He was falling in love, if not already knee-deep in it.

In fact, he felt almost...relieved. Like he'd been expecting his psyche to hand him that information at any moment.

This just in! Wait a minute, folks, this report can't be true. Yes, it looks like Mason Dillon has fallen in love with the one woman he shouldn't have.

And there it was.

He liked *liked* Kevan Landry. No. He fucking loved her. The warm feeling that ran through his body when she was near, the need to know where she was at all times, the constant craving to feel her skin against his, mark her when they fucked. No. When they made love.

Holy shit.

He really was falling in love with her. How had he not seen this coming? But, really, look at her. Who could spend more than a couple of days with her and not fall horribly, utterly, and hopelessly in love with her? She was brash and funny and beautiful. An angel, a devil, a stranger, a rebel. Like the song.

God, that was her. The sad girl. The strong, soulful rebel. Always there for whatever anyone needed, but then left alone. And a woman like her, so kind and passionate, shouldn't be alone. She needed someone worthy of her strength and her lust for life. Someone who would always be there, make her a priority above all else. He wasn't that guy, though.

Was he?

He was work, work, work—with a little time off to hang with the guys and a little screwing around on the side. Even if they did find a way to be together, he didn't want to end up like his parents, in a cold, planned marriage fraught with terms and good manners, where dinner conversation was centered around work. Wasn't that the way it always turned out?

He wasn't good for her. The sudden realization made his blood turn to ice. He didn't know how to be anyone but Mason Dillon, CEO, and really didn't know how to give love. And there was still this thing hanging over them—the Manix Curse deal.

What was he going to do? It wasn't just his job any longer. No, it was so much more. It was her happiness.

Her business and her brother's wellness. And their
future. He snorted. Like Mason and Kevan could have a
future. Like Kevan Landry could ever fall in love with
the *normal* guy.

"What's wrong, Mason?" she asked, concern marring
her pretty face.

"Huh?"

She squeezed his hand hesitantly and twirled a lock
of blue around her finger. "What's wrong? You look
like your stock portfolio just tanked, cowboy."

"I have a very balanced portfolio." He said it so
matter-of-factly, she laughed. And he shook off the dark
cloud that had descended over his mood. Tonight was
not the night to ponder the big questions.

"Nothing's wrong, darlin'. Let's get you back before
you freeze."

The doubt that had been niggling around the edges of
his brain since he'd been put on notice about his job and
then after meeting Kevan grew stronger, but he shoved
it in with the other "stuff to be dealt with later."

☆ ★ ☆

On the drive back from dinner, a sultry rockabilly beat
playing softly, Mason looked over at Kevan in the passenger seat. She was humming loudly and tapping her
fingers on her knees in rhythm to the strong bass of the
music. She twirled her hair around her index finger as she
often did when she was lost in thought or in her music.

"Kevan?"

"Hmm?" She looked over at him, shadows and light
dancing across her pale skin.

"Who is this?"

"Imelda May. She's an amazing singer from Ireland."

"This song is beautiful."

"Hmm. Yes. It's a little out of character, since most of her music is pretty straight-up rockabilly. It's one of my favorites."

She sang along to the ballad of a struggling couple who made it through some tough times. She had an exceptional singing voice, soft and rich. Add it to the list of features of the most amazing woman he'd ever met.

"*Mo chroí*? It means my love, my darling, right?"

Her cheeks burned pink. "Yes, I think so."

"Can I ask you something?"

"Can I stop you?" She looked sideways at him.

Ignoring her question, he asked, "Did your brother do your artwork?" he asked as he traced the lacy brocade pattern over her knee and on her inner thigh.

"Most of it. Nathan did the lace on my thigh, and Jax did the flowers on my foot. For the big pieces, I wouldn't let anyone else work on me." She smiled at him proudly, almost defiantly.

"No, I wouldn't either. They're really fucking good."

She looked confused. "You like my tattoos?"

"Of course I do. Why wouldn't I?" But he knew the answer before the words were out of his mouth. She was the edgy modern pinup, and he was the boring suit. "I think they're sexy as fuck."

Her smile lit up her face. "You do?"

"You think because I wear a suit to work and went to an Ivy League school I can't appreciate heavy metal, hot women, and tattoos? Really?" That was the real reason they could never be a couple. She'd never see them as compatible.

She shrugged.

"Don't play me," he said. "If I wasn't attracted to you, how do you think I could sleep with you?"

Again, that damn lift of her shoulder.

"Kevan, I meant it that first night when I said you are the sexiest woman I have ever laid eyes on. All of you. Not just that kissable, fuckable mouth, not just your perfectly round ass, or amazing tits. All. Of. You."

She looked down. Apparently fascinated by her hands again.

"I lo…like your wicked sense of humor, your creative business sense, your blue hair, your tattoos, the stud in your nose. I like it all." He'd almost told her what he was starting to feel, that he might be falling in love with her.

Might. Uh, bullshit. Fucking wussy. He was in love with her. And if he told her now, she'd run like a startled deer in the road.

"Remember when you had on your old Social D T-shirt at the housing project?" he asked. She shook her head. "The one that dips down in the back to expose part of the branches wrapping over your shoulder?" She smiled then and knew what he meant. Mason plowed on, riding on the memory. "All I could think about when you were wearing that shirt—and I could see that sexy ink crawling up your back and over your creamy white shoulder—was how badly I wanted to take you from behind. I could see myself bending you over one of the work tables, cupping a breast in one hand, and yanking your pants down with the other."

Kevan gripped the door, and her legs parted slightly. He loved how he affected her with only his words.

Without taking his eyes from the road, he pulled her leg out farther and stroked the inside of her thigh.

"Then what would you do to me?" Her voice was breathy and her eyes glazed.

Still watching the road, he continued dragging his hand up her thigh until he reached the barrier to his true goal. "I was so hard from watching you jiggle and bend in front of me all day, I wouldn't be able to control myself. I would pull your damp little panties to the side or maybe rip them off." She trembled as he lightly caressed the front of her mound through the thin material. Pulling her leg up against the door, she angled her body toward him.

"More, cowboy, I need more," she said, her words released on jagged sighs.

His chest tightened. If only she meant more of him. More than sex. "More what? More of my fantasy? More of my fingers in your wet pussy?"

She moaned and pushed into his fingers. "Both, please."

He should pull the car to the side of the road and bend her over the fucking hood. Do the things he'd told her he wanted to do. He could feel himself lengthening against the zipper of his slacks. Damn woman had had him hard for days now. Like a frickin' teenager.

He pulled her panties to the side and gently stroked between her soaked folds, loving the soft velvet of her smooth skin.

"And I'd shove my cock into you as I held your hips in my hands. I'd fuck you in front of all those workers, the band, and everyone else." She moaned, and he rubbed her hard, swollen nub in short, circular motions as she reached up and pinched her nipples through her dress.

"I'd fuck you so fast and hard that everyone would know you belonged to me." She pulsed against his fingers, her hips undulating on the seat.

"Oh my God, Mason, I'm going to come."

"Come for me, darlin'."

She cried out, and her body went rigid with the powerful orgasm he now recognized as uniquely Kevan. She moaned his name and groaned loudly. He firmly rubbed up and down her soft, wet folds and put his fingers to his mouth and sucked on them, savoring her tangy honey.

"Thank you." God, she said the sweetest things. She was thanking him. Incredible. He smiled around his fingers, relishing the taste of her.

"Thank you, darlin'," he said. Her bow-shaped lips turned up as she grabbed his hand in hers.

"Can I help you out with that rather massive hard-on?" she asked.

He lifted her hand to his lips and brushed his mouth over her knuckles. "Promise me you'll help me out later."

"I promise." And her sweet little smile instantly turned wicked.

Oh, he hoped so. If he couldn't have her heart, he'd take her body. At least for now.

Chapter 19

THE EVENING HAD SPED BY TOO QUICKLY. SHE COULD feel something growing, shifting between them, something alive and organic. She was being drawn into a silky web of trust and affection she found both comforting and oddly unfamiliar, like a cozy but borrowed sweater. It was new, but it was good. His honesty about family and work had Kevan struggling to remember why she disliked Mason so much and why she needed to keep fighting against him. Even the threat of losing Manix was starting to seem less catastrophic than spending less time with Mason.

But then there was Bowen. And she couldn't let her brother down. Better to share a good meal, have some laughs, and get this tour done and over. So when the evening came to an end, Kevan kissed Mason's cheek and said good night.

"Mason, dinner was fantastic. Thank you."

He turned her body toward his and rested his hand heavily on her shoulders. "But?"

She cupped his cheek, and he bent down, his forehead pressed against hers.

"But I'm not getting back into bed with you tonight. It's hard for me to trust. And with the thing with the band, it's too much right now. You're too much."

He drew her body against his, making it even harder to keep her guard intact. She could feel his hard chest heaving against hers as her nipples tightened. Leaning down, he kissed her crown, his lips scalding her, burning his brand into her head.

"I'm not ready to trust you yet," she lied as she pulled away.

He didn't push, and she didn't give.

Yet as she lay in bed, the days unraveled in happy snippets. All with Mason. They'd even worked as a cohesive team, like they'd been partners forever. And dinner *had* been amazing until she'd opened her big mouth and said things she didn't really mean. Perfect. Fantastic.

She rolled onto her stomach, punching her pillow one more time, trying to find a comfy spot.

Oh, fuck it.

"Mason?" she called out into the dark.

"*Kevan.*" He dragged her name out in a singsong voice.

"Are you awake?" *Duh.* "Never mind. Can I come in there? I can't sleep."

"Please."

Decision made, she got up and walked slowly through the open door and stood next to his bed. He pulled the covers down and scooted over to make room for her, patting the empty spot. "Lie down so I can hold you." As her eyes adjusted to the dark, she realized he was shirtless, the shadowy night highlighting the strong contours of his abs and chest. He leaned up on one elbow, curving the muscles on his stomach and his corded arms. The man was delicious.

Without hesitation, she lay on her side, settling her head on his hard arm, and rolled into him. His big, warm body wrapped around her. They were like two perfectly created puzzle pieces. The muscles in her shoulders instantly relaxed, and she sighed as his arm folded heavily across her waist.

"I'm sorry about what I said tonight. Sometimes I'm so afraid someone will hurt me or figure out I don't know what the hell I'm doing, I say things. Strike first and push them away before they can do it to me."

In the inky darkness, she felt him lift his other arm, scrub his face, and put his hand firmly over her hip, his fingers curling around her hip bone. He rested his cheek on top of her head and inhaled softly, but said nothing.

"I do trust you. I mean as much as I can, considering the situation. I don't want to, but I do," she whispered.

Still nothing. Maybe he agreed with her. Maybe he wasn't ready to forgive her lying, impulsive words. "Mason? Did you hear me?"

"Yes, darlin'. I heard you." He slowly inhaled deeply and exhaled again.

"And…"

He was holding her, had invited her into his bed. He had to feel something for her, right?

"And, I wish I could put you in front of a magic mirror and show you how fucking amazing you are. How amazing everyone who meets you thinks you are." The gruffness of his tone didn't match the sweet, complimentary words. "Did I not tell you that the next time we were in bed together and you said derogatory or untrue things about yourself I would punish you?"

She nodded, unable to verbally respond.

"Do you agree that we are in bed right now and you have in fact broken the rule?"

His long fingers gripped her hip and pulled her body

closer to his. Her pendulum of need swung from warm and comfortable to scalding and needy.

When she didn't respond, he asked again. "Kevan, do you agree?"

She finally nodded and felt his smile against her forehead as his exhale rustled her hair. He lifted his hand from her hip and stroked her hair. Softly, at first, then adding more pressure, until his big hand tangled in her hair at the nape of her neck. He moved her face to look at him.

"Open your eyes, darlin'," he said, and she shook her head from side to side.

"I'm afraid." She swallowed the nervousness threatening to take over her brain, expecting him to placate her with words of comfort and soft, gentle caresses like he had before.

Instead, he whispered, "You should be, my beautiful girl. You should be." His chest rose with a long pull of breath before he continued. "I don't know what this is, this thing between us. I know I've never, and I mean *never*, felt this strong a pull to anyone. You confound me. You're beautiful and so insecure. You're creative and intelligent and so inexperienced. You're compassionate, and you're cruel. You're a sex bomb, and you're a compliant, generous lover. You're all these maddening contradictions that don't make any sense, yet make perfect sense." He sighed again. "And I can't get enough of your special fucking brand of beautiful crazy."

He danced his fingers up and down her spine, sending quakes of lust through her torso like jolts of electricity bringing her body to life. "So yeah, you should be afraid. I'm fucking terrified, and I'm never afraid of anything.

The only thing that has ever scared the fuck out of me is the sexy brunette lying in my arms and looking up at me with those stunning gray eyes."

"Mason?" She could hear the quiver in her voice.

"Yeah, darlin'."

She opened her eyes to gaze into his. "I agree."

His gorgeous mouth slowly curled upward, and his eyes took on a predatory gleam. Her rational mind knew she should fear his dangerous evil-sexy smile. But instead, her nipples hardened under her soft nightshirt, and her core tingled, flooding with arousal.

He raised one eyebrow. "To your punishment or to more?"

"Both."

The words were barely out before his mouth slammed down on hers and his hand moved from her back to her bottom. He pulled her body into his as he licked the seam of her lips. She opened for him eagerly as he explored her mouth and held her head angled in his other hand. It seemed as if she'd waited for this kiss for her entire life. He captured her moan with his mouth and tangled his fingers in her hair. Gripping the long strands in his fist, he angled her head into a position that gave him more control over the kiss. As suddenly as it had started, the kiss ended.

When he pulled his mouth away and tucked her into his side, dragging her leg over his thigh, Kevan expected him to grab her and get busy. "I don't think you have any idea the dirty things I want to do to your bombshell body."

His dark promise sent tremors to her clit, making it throb. She squirmed with overwhelming need under his hands, but then his hands stopped moving, and he sighed deeply.

After several minutes, she asked, "Well?"

Mason chuckled but didn't move. "Well what?"

Was he really going to make her say it? "Where's my...my...you know."

"Punishment?"

"Yeah." Was he purposely being coy? *What the hell?* She needed him to take her, brand her as his. And right now.

"Oh, you'll get it. Just not now. Not when you expect it."

"What the—"

He stopped her from finishing by placing his fingers to her mouth. "We're both exhausted. I have your consent. That's enough for now. Fall asleep in my arms."

Kevan wanted to yell and slap at him. If he were any other man, she'd accuse him of being a player. But Mason didn't play games like that. Besides, he was right—damn him. Sleep would be good. And she felt so safe, so comfortable in his bed. She turned her head and placed a kiss on his lightly hair-dusted chest. Her lips tingled from the brief contact, but she tamped down her fierce arousal. They'd said and done enough for one night.

"Good night, cowboy."

"Good night, Bettie."

Tomorrow was another day.

Chapter 20

Bright light seeped in through a crack in the blackout shades, blinding Kevan with a searing laser beam directed into her left eye. They must not have made it from San Francisco to LA yet, because the RV still rocked gently. She stretched and lifted a hand to her face, turning to peer at the sleeping giant with his arms around her. It was a rare moment when she was able to observe Mason without his intense focus on her.

Kevan traced her finger from the crown of his head, across his cheek, and down his long neck, enjoying the contrast of her pale skin against his golden, rougher skin.

Yes, he was pretty, but his body was a man's body, one mapped with the various evidence of an active life. It bore his history as explicitly as any book described a person's story. She traced the tiny visible scars and marks dotting his broad shoulders, arms, and legs. He shifted suddenly and grabbed her fingers as they outlined the thin, jagged scars sprinkled across his forearms and hands. He pulled her in for a sweet kiss, gently caressing her lips with his.

"Where did you get these?" she asked, feathering her index finger along his wrist and arm, enjoying the feel of his coarse hair under her softer skin. He smiled, his eyes filled with sleep and his hair mussed from her fingers. "I was ten. I wanted a new skateboard. You know, a cool one, not a little kid's plastic toy. But my parents didn't think it was practical or educational, so I had to buy it myself."

He pulled her body against his, the smell of his naturally woodsy scent sent signals of lust and contentment to her brain.

"I did everything I could to get that stupid board, including mowing lawns and returning bottles. So one day I was riding my crappy toy skateboard, the one I wanted to replace, to the store with a box full of glass soda bottles on the front. I hit a bump and followed the shattered bottles hands first."

She gasped, cringing at the image of a young kamikaze Mason flying through the air seconds after a dozen glass bottles shattered on the hot summer sidewalk. Choosing to ignore the poor battered and bloody ten-year-old, she focused on the idea of Mason as a child, bringing a smile to her lips. He must have been such an intense, stunning child.

What will his children look like?

Better not go there.

"Did you get the skateboard?"

He shook his head. "Not until high school."

Kevan kissed each little mark on his arms and then continued down his hands.

She pulled the tangled sheet off Mason's waist and pushed it down his legs. Damn, he was fine. *And, looky there, he's happy to see me.* When she looked into his face, the expression in his eyes had turned serious. She smiled and pushed his shoulder back against the bed, eliciting a protesting grunt from him. She caressed the light smattering of hair on his chest and continued her exploration down to his hard abs and hips. Her hand wrapped firmly around his manhood, and his warmth infused her fingers. Slowly, she began to stroke up and down. She scooted down and licked the shaft with the flat of her tongue up to the notched head. Hard, but with a velvety texture.

She circled the head and licked the tip, and the small precum pooled there. Kevan loved the tangy saltiness of Mason. She'd never taken much pleasure in giving a man head. Always felt it was a means to an end, or an exchange for what *she* really wanted. But with him, she thoroughly relished the pleasure she knew she gave him. She craved the power that came with understanding that this successful, gorgeous man was in her mouth, chose to be with her, and she was the one making him growl and cry out her name when he came.

When he moaned again, more loudly, she glanced up to his face before she took him entirely into her mouth and hollowed her cheeks. His eyes were firmly locked on her. He brought his hand to rest on the back of her head as he arched into her and his cock hit the back of her throat. Wanting to please him, she dragged her tongue against his erection.

His hand tangled in her hair as she moved her warm mouth up and down on him. Her nipples tightened with his firm grasp, sending moisture to her pussy. She wanted him to direct her. She wanted him to take his pleasure and show her how to please him.

"Kevan, if you keep going, I don't think I'll be able to stop," he growled, his voice low and dark.

He was close to the edge of losing his tightly held control. She craved that moment. The exact second when they fell perfectly into their roles as if by instinct. She granted him the gift of her power, and he accepted and cherished it. Never had she tasted the perfect balance of sexual submission and control as she did with this man.

She popped the swollen purple head out of her mouth. "Take what you need. I want to feel you unravel."

The words were enough. He wrapped both hands around her head as she pulled him back into her wetness, and he began to fuck her mouth, slow and deep. His hands tensed, and he picked up the pace. Her body felt light, almost meditative as he came in hot spurts into her mouth and down her throat. She swallowed, savoring his salty, all Mason, musky taste.

He pulled her up and stared into her eyes as he held her tightly.

"God, you're fucking incredible." His chest still rose and fell while his legs trembled from the powerful orgasm.

Mason rolled, pushing Kevan onto her back so he could hover above her. He kissed behind her ear and slowly, painfully slow, began kissing and sucking his way down to her breasts, nipping lightly and then sucking harder on each nipple. Nibbling one and kneading the other, over and over, back and forth, until Kevan thought she might explode just from his stimulation of her breasts. He looked up at her with a wolfish grin.

He apparently was aware of the delicious agony he was creating. He bit down on one nipple as he plunged a finger, and then two, into her ridiculously wet slit. She cried out when he began to alternately bite her nipples as he rubbed her hardened clit.

"Come for me, darlin'. Scream my name."

She did. And it was awesome.

★ ★ ★

After Mason's magic fingers gave Kevan an explosive, mind-altering orgasm, they showered and ate, then spent the day working until they arrived in Hollywood. She hurried through her usual routine and was dressed to go in an hour. Mason paced back and forth past the kitchenette table. By now, she was used to his bursts of restless energy. It was similar to the vibe, the surge of energy, she thrived on at live shows. She liked the charge that bounced off him when he was in his hyper state.

She admired him from down the hall. Effortless and handsome with his worn jeans, a pair of black Docs, and a vintage Misfits henley shirt. He looked up and caught her spying on him.

"Okay?" he asked, not really looking for her approval. He knew what she thought of his looks.

Nodding, she tilted her head to the side and pointed to that spot on her neck. "You know you're hot, cowboy. C'mere and tell me if you like this new perfume."

In two long strides, he was holding her by the shoulder and pushing her up against the wall. His tucked his face in behind her ear. "God, you smell so good."

Mason drew in a long breath and rubbed his nose down the side of Kevan's throat to where her neckline turned into her shoulder. That spot he'd discovered and placed his flag in. *Property of Mason. Bite here.*

He pushed the edge of her dress to the side. "I love this place right here." He bit her gently and smiled against her skin when she gasped.

"What the fuck?" He whirled her around quickly. "Holy shit, woman. You can't go out there like that."

She tried to hid her smile. "You can't tell me how to dress, Mason."

"No, I mean, where the fuck is the back of your dress? I can see your whole tattoo and almost your ass crack. No, go change." He pressed his lush mouth in a tight line and pointed to the closet in his bedroom. Their bedroom. She laughed, wondering if he was serious.

"No, Mr. Bossy Pants." Crossing her arms, she stuck her breasts out for effect.

"How the fuck am I supposed to get any business done tonight if I'm distracted by that tattoo and the hot body it's drawn on?" Mason growled. The familiar low vibration instantly made her wet and wanting.

"That's your problem, not mine." She ducked under his arm and grabbed her small clutch off the table. "Let's get this show on the road, cowboy."

Kevan sashayed her hips for his benefit. She couldn't help but laugh at the frustrated groan behind her.

Stepping off the bus, she didn't hide her excitement at being back in Southern California. While San Francisco, with its eclectic music scene, welcomed anyone and everyone with any talent, Hollywood was Mecca to the hard rock, heavy metal world. If you played Hollywood, you'd made it. Hell, bands like Megadeth and Guns N' Roses had started here. She couldn't even list all the groups that had risen to superstardom by playing the rattraps and back-alley dives that lined Hollywood and Vine. Tonight, that group was Manix Curse.

The other three bands playing with Manix Curse were local, bringing their own fans to pack the house. The show had sold out in a day. People lined the sidewalks, and those without a ticket were turned away.

Tonight was all about networking for Kevan. While the opening bands worked the audience into a fever, she had appointments with reps from each band to discuss potential marketing and promotional agreements. All three groups were heavy metal and were perfect for her agency. One was more progressive and built the tension slowly, exploding into layers of music rolling through the room and encompassing everyone there. The second and third bands were more thrash and built on the already enthusiastic crowd.

By the time Manix Curse hit the stage, the crowd was primed for their unique blend of thrash and progressive metal. Watching them play tonight was like watching perfection squared.

The momentum created by the opening bands created a velocity that pushed Manix into the most precise and flawless show they'd ever performed. Basically, they killed it. The crowd loved them. Worshipped them. Add in the easy dynamic between the band members and the intimacy they created with the audience, and the experience was unique and awe inspiring. She loved watching the alchemy—the magic of music. The pulse of the crowd. The sound so loud and all encompassing it obliterated all other thoughts.

Somewhere in the loud and boisterous club, there was a big, bad, handsome man with eyes only for her. All the swaying of scantily clad women, and none of them had the attention of the most gorgeous man in the room. Only she had Mason's full focus. Her nipples hardened and her core dampened as she remembered their morning and afternoon together. The man had supernatural hands. No doubt about it.

Noticing the manager for one of the opening bands, Aortic Pulse, Kevan made her way across the room. He raised his eyebrows in curiosity when she held her hand out.

As he grasped it, he asked, "And who are you, pretty thing?"

She smiled. "Hi, Robert. I'm Kevan Landry with Jolt Marketing. We spoke on the phone."

When recognition flooded his face, he shook her hand vigorously. "Right. Hey, it's really great to meet you. I looked over your brochure, and the band is really interested in talking to you about representation."

Kevan felt the muscles in her shoulders loosen as her chest filled with air, feeling lighter than it had in weeks. "Great. Shall we schedule a meeting or conference call for sometime later this week?"

"I'll call you on Friday, if that works for you. Can I buy you a drink?"

"No, but thank you." Kevan's eyes surveyed the crowd, taking in the clientele, the target market for future clients. But really, she was looking for Mason.

"This your band?" Robert flicked his glance to the stage, where Manix Curse was tearing it up.

"Not yet, but I'm working on it." She winked, shook his hand again, and sauntered to the back of the room, headbanging to the song as it pulsed through the crowd. Narrowly avoiding crashing bodies on the dance floor, she ducked off to the side. Where was he? Usually she could spot him quickly. Or she felt his eyes on her.

Kevan spotted Mason's tall figure in a dark corner, towering over the crowd. He was gesturing toward the shorter man she'd seen him arguing with in Oregon.

Mason's face was flushed, and his mouth moved as if he was yelling. The man seemed to be shouting back, but with a smug smile, almost a sneer, that never left his mouth. Whatever the two were discussing, and *discussing* was putting it lightly, it was not going in the direction Mason wanted. When she got a little closer, she noticed the veins standing out on his neck. He looked angrier than she'd ever seen him.

Who is that man? And why does he have Mason so worked up?

Kevan squeezed through the crowd. Her fast pace was abruptly halted when a strong hand wrapped around her elbow.

"I don't think you want to go there, sweetheart," Joe yelled over the music, close to her ear.

"Why?" she yelled back.

He said something, but it was lost in the wailing guitar riffs. She shrugged her shoulders. Joe pointed to the back hall and led her to the office. Kevan stood with her back to the door, her hands on her hips, eyebrows raised.

"Well?"

"Don't go over there," Joe repeated. "Let Mason work it out."

"Who is Mason yelling at, Joe?"

"Some guy he works with at GEM. Steve something. He's been calling, texting, and emailing the band and me. He even sent Mandi a new Gretsch and promised us an interview with *Metal Maniac* magazine."

The blood in her body froze. Why would some random coworker, whom Mason obviously didn't care for, give Mandi an expensive guitar? Why would he be calling the other band members or promising them anything?

Kevan cleared her throat, trying to dislodge her rising panic. "Wait, what? He works with Mason? Why is he here, Joe?" *And what the fuck does he want?*

He looked up, averting his eyes. What was he hiding?

"Joe?" Kevan asked, her voice low, dark suspicion and fear clouding her thoughts, threatening to choke the air from her lungs and the words from her mouth. "Why is he here?"

"He's been trying to sign the band, Kev. He has been working on them individually, making promises, giving them presents. The whole burrito, kid."

The air left the room. Kevan couldn't breathe. Her head swam with the repercussions of what Joe had told her. *No way, he wouldn't do this to me. Not after today.* She'd been a fool. Thinking he wanted her, that they might find a way to make this whole thing work out. Business was everything to him. It was his life, his identity. He'd told her that just today.

He'd used her and played dirty all along. All he'd wanted was another good screw, and she'd given in every time. Dammit. While he seduced her, his lackey was busy wining and dining the band. All so he could keep his precious CEO job, and now she was left with nothing. The last of her savings gone, spent on Bowen's rehab. Her business sure to fold under the loan she couldn't repay. Her new connections would ditch her the minute they realized Manix was with GEM. Or maybe Mason would steal them too. Worst of all, Bowen shipped out of rehab too soon, and she was left to help him recover.

The cranberry juice in her stomach roiled and threatened to make its way up. Joe was still talking. Saying something about GEM and the rep. The buzzing in her ears prevented her from hearing him. She pushed out of the room, stumbling around a couple in the hall, searching for the bathroom door. Instead, the door opened out into the alley. The smell of refuse everywhere tipped her barf meter over. She lurched forward and threw up against the building.

Once her stomach was completely purged of fluids, she leaned against the brick wall and wiped her mouth with the back of her hand. She looked around at the garbage in the shadows. This was where she always ended up, with the trash. She was either pulling Bowen out of sketchy situations or getting herself into one. On shaky legs, she walked down the alley and into the back lot where the RV was parked.

The utter despair that had taken over her body, her heart, was absolutely the worst she had ever felt. How could he have lied to her? Especially after he knew how much it would hurt her? First Bowen, then the business, now betrayal from the one man she'd let herself trust. Maybe fall in love with. She wanted to rip out the brick sitting in the place of her heart with a feral scream, but she couldn't summon the energy. Nothing.

God, her heart physically ached. And why did it hurt so much? It should be some other part of her body. Her gut should hurt, her head. Just not her damn traitorous heart. Stupid man had gotten under her fucking skin and broken down her walls so he could cut her heart out. Like always.

Well, not really. If she was honest with herself, the

pain she felt from Mason's betrayal, from his lies, was like nothing she'd ever felt before. Ethan had hurt her ego, mostly. She'd wanted to be good enough for someone like him—educated, intelligent, handsome. But really, she'd never loved him. This pain was all new. Searing.

Mason burst from the RV and ran toward her.

"Where have you been? I was worried." She threw her hands up to prevent his arms circling her shoulders. "You look awful, darlin'."

He moved his hand to cradle her face. From somewhere deep, she rallied her strength and held her hands in front of her.

"Don't. Fucking. Touch. Me. Ever. Again," she said, the harsh tone surprising even her.

His face transformed. Wide, open concern turned to shadows in a flash. He understood the razor-sharp sincerity of her words. Understood there was no going back from this new place. Understood he'd lied.

"You aren't even going to let me explain, are you?" His voice was cold. So cold and emotionless. Her chest clenched at the hardness of his tone. She could do this. *Walk away with your pride, Kevan.*

"There's nothing to explain, Mason. You're all about the deal. This business is who you are, right? That's what you said. You, me, that was all novelty…diversion?" Her voice caught in her throat.

She swallowed down the tears threatening to take over again. Rigid. No emotion on his face. Saying nothing.

Please say something. Please tell me I'm wrong. Fight for me, Mason, please fight for me.

"Yeah. Sure, you were a distraction. It was fun, wasn't it, sweetheart?" He shrugged his shoulders.

His distant tone was a knife to her heart, tearing her all the way open. "You threw me under the bus, didn't you? Like I thought you would. Was that always the plan?" She tried to control her voice, but she was yelling. She smacked his chest, but he still just stood there.

"It doesn't matter what I say. You already know the answer, Kevan."

No, tell me you love me. Tell me the band doesn't matter. Tell me something.

"I'm all about the deal. It's who I am. I don't know any better, right?" He scrubbed his hand over his face and hung his head.

The tears were back, rivers of pain and anguish sliding down her face. "I think I could have loved you. But instead, you stomped on my heart with your five-hundred-dollar shoes," she whispered.

"You're so broken, darlin', nothing I do will ever change that." He looked up, his face shadowed and full of sadness. He turned and climbed into the RV.

"Where are you going?" She marched up after him. The dam had broken, and silent tears streamed down her cheeks.

"I'm leaving. They're all yours. I'm done. I don't need them that badly," he said. Kevan watched as the one man she had ever truly loved packed his bags and called a cab. "Keep the bus through the tour. Ben will get you home."

Mason stood close enough for their toes to touch. She hoped he couldn't feel her body shaking. He leaned forward and brushed his lips slowly across her cheek, and she let him.

"Don't ever let anyone tell you you're not good

enough. You're an amazing woman." She felt his breath blowing against her cheek. "Good-bye, beautiful Kevan Landry."

Then she watched him walk away without a glance back. He was gone, but she whispered to the empty RV, "I wasn't truly broken until you broke me."

Chapter 21

MASON STARED AT THE ROAD UNFOLDING BEFORE HIM.
His eyes ached from lack of sleep, and his throat burned
from too much coffee. Thankfully, his heart no longer
hurt. He'd managed to rip it out and toss it along the
highway back to Oregon. Now it was just patched over
with a welcome numbness.

He'd directed the cab driver to drop him off at the
car lot, where he'd rented a sedan for the long drive
back home. After an unforgiving ten-hour drive straight
through the night, Mason pulled over at a rest stop when
his eyes threatened to slam shut. He woke after a few
restless hours of sleep dotted with images of Kevan
screaming, crying, laughing, and pushing him away.
Each scene playing out differently, but always ending
with her whispering the last bullet to his pummeled heart.

I wasn't truly broken until you broke me.

The words were punctured with too much pain to
fix. Too much burn to put out. Her anguish had been so
deep, he couldn't risk one look back at her before he'd
left. There was no way they could have had a rational
discussion about what she thought had happened. Her
past would always be there to overshadow any of his
reassurances and demonstrations of love. She'd never
be able to unpack the emotional baggage she clung to
like armor.

Did you actually tell her you love her, fuckwit?

No, he'd skated right back into the old Mason, the Ice Man, and played it cool. Never said those all-important words, "I love you."

Kevan had had a lifetime of disappointment shoveled on her from everyone, especially men, letting her down over and over again. Mason realized he could add himself to her long list of disappointments.

Kevan's face before he turned away was frozen in his mind. The woman who was always so perfectly put together, from hair to toes, was a hot mess. He'd done that to her. And then he'd run, because he hadn't been able to handle her level of pain. In her mind, they were done before they'd even gotten started. In his mind, he was walking away from love.

Before he realized it, Mason was pulling onto his tree-lined street. He stopped at his gate and punched in the security code. Glancing up at the glass-and-timber remodeled home, once the symbol of his professional pinnacle, now made him shiver with loneliness. What was success and money worth if there was no one to share it with?

Now what was he going to do? Obviously he needed a plan B, since plan A had tanked. Did he hole up in his house and hide from the rest of the world? That wasn't really his style.

How was he going to get out of this shit hole he'd dug? He needed a new path. Once inside, Mason bypassed his extremely comfortable oversized chair and turned down the hall toward his study. He was already calling a number in his favorites before he sat down at his desk and turned on his computer.

"Hey, it's Mason. I need you to draft a new contract."

The next morning, Kevan pulled the glass diner door open, eyes wearily sweeping the crowded room for Dan Carver, the High Energy executive. When the tour had hit Las Vegas, she continued going through the motions—smiling when appropriate, scheduling tweetups, another meet and greet, a promotional stop at a local record store, and arranging the meeting with Dan.

The smell of breakfast—eggs, greasy sausage, and pancakes—assailed her nose. Even the Elvis-themed restaurant, filled with cheery red-vinyl booths set against a glossy black-and-white backdrop couldn't lift her sullen mood. She easily spotted Dan's red hair amongst the vacationing families, hardcore gamblers on benders, and businesspeople. She walked to his booth in the corner of the room, her limbs feeling disjointed and awkward, matching her feelings.

Dan smiled openly as he stood and shook her hand. "Good to see you again. Have to admit I'm curious as to what happened with Mason. His email was pretty cryptic. But I'm more than happy to work with you, Ms. Landry."

At least Mason hadn't advertised their fallout to everyone. But then he wasn't good at explaining anything to anyone.

Kevan smiled stiffly, trying to keep the anguish in her heart from flooding her face and tipping her hand. "You'll have to discuss that with Mr. Dillon."

She slid into the seat and glanced down at the tattered menu, knowing full well she wouldn't be able to stomach any food.

Dan's skeptical expression gave the impression that he knew more than he was saying. He smiled. "My understanding was that another commitment came up."

A young, perky waitress interrupted to take their orders. The distraction bought Kevan a few extra minutes to better formulate her answer. Lying wasn't her thing. And frankly, it was all too much—trying to deal with the heartache, do business, and get through the last couple of tour dates. The lack of sleep and fuzzy haze that seemed to follow her around made it difficult to focus long enough to create a believable lie.

Taking a sip of her coffee, she let the bitter liquid slide down her throat and into the acidic pool of her stomach. "He's a busy man. I'm sure it was something important."

His smile thinned, and his eyes narrowed. "Really? Because I've known Mason a long time, and he's not one to cancel at the last minute. Especially without an explanation."

No shit, buddy. I'd like an explanation, too.

Kevan sighed. Fuck it. "Look, I'm trying to be professional, but I know you're friends. Honestly, Mason and I had a falling out. It wasn't pretty, and it wasn't fun. But he believes in Manix Curse, like I do. So if we could get back to business—"

"Bullshit."

"Excuse me?" she sputtered.

He smiled over his coffee cup, took a sip, and set the cup down, slowly and deliberately. "I said 'bullshit.'"

She stood and reached down for her bag. "I can see this meeting is over—"

Dan reached out and wrapped his hand gently around

her wrist. "No. It's not. Sit down." His smile looked sincere. "Please."

"I don't know what Mason told you, but I'm only here to discuss next fall's Hellfire tour with you. That's it." She sat back down. She needed this for the band. For herself.

The waitress brought her toast and Dan's breakfast, but she couldn't summon the energy to thank the overly peppy woman.

"He told me you're a game changer for him."

What the heck was he talking about? "What?"

That calm, soothing smile again. She didn't know if she wanted to hug him or poke him in the eye with her fork.

"In Medford. At first he acted cool and indifferent, but within a couple of minutes, he pretty much admitted that he cared about you."

Dan's word's banged around her head. *He cared about you.*

"So what?"

"I've known him for a long time, remember? He's never 'cared' about a woman. Never."

He cared about me?

"Well, that's just peachy. He doesn't really care, now." She stopped herself from going further and polluting Manix Curse business with her wrath.

"I thought you should know," he said, looking uncomfortable and grabbing some paper from his briefcase. "Shall we move on to business?"

Instead of acting resentful, he dropped any mention of Mason and got right to the deal. All in all, it was a good package for a new band, that included a percentage of ticket sales, travel, meals, and some co-promotion with several of the sponsors, as well as with other bands on the tour.

Chapter 22

AFTER TAKING A TAXI BACK TO THE CLUB, SHE STOOD in the living area of the tour bus and shared the details of the deal with the band. Her pulse raged, and she tried not to think of Mason and how the credit for the tour was really his marketing connections and genius. The band members reacted enthusiastically, hugging and yelling. Only Jax was a little less excited than the others.

"Dude, aren't you excited? A real tour." She nudged him with her elbow.

Jax smiled. "Yeah, of course. I'm just worried I've been away from work for too long. My client wait list is getting longer. But it's a great opportunity."

Kevan wasn't convinced, but thought he'd be okay once the money started rolling in. But honestly, she could hardly bring herself to care much beyond a superficial interest. "I'm sure it'll be good."

"Okay, Debbie Downer. You seriously need to snap out of it."

She drew back; the effort to hide her misery was getting more and more challenging. "I'm fine. And we were talking about you."

"We were, but now we're done." He motioned for her to follow him outside, where he turned and faced her. "You should call him, you know. We had a couple of interesting conversations, but he genuinely seemed into you. Maybe you mis—"

"What the fuck are you talking about, Jax? You talked to Mason about me? Who do you think you are?" She struggled to keep her voice down, clenching her fists so hard they ached.

Jax grabbed her shoulders and looked down into her eyes. "Calm down. I was making sure he wasn't fucking with you. I told him I'd kick his ass if he did."

"You don't get to do that. My personal life is none of your business. And, for the record, I'm doing just freakin' fine." She turned and stomped back to her RV. Mason's RV.

Kevan hauled her sluggish body up the steps and collapsed at the table. She held her head in her hands. She'd tried to purge everything in the motor home that reminded her of Mason. But since the RV was actually his, the task was impossible. Lifting her head, she glanced around the room. Every corner held a ghost of him or a shadow of a memory with him. Laughing across from her at the table. Pressing up behind her as she made breakfast. Holding her hands against the wall as he ravished her mouth with his talented and punishing tongue.

She stood and reached up over the stove, searching for the bottle of Patrón Mason kept there. Grabbing the bottle and the shot glass he'd bought her in Eugene, she slammed back two quick shots, one after the other. She welcomed the sharp burn down her throat and the warmth that instantly spread through her belly.

Her head swam after the third shot of tequila, her eyes watery and so heavy. Maybe this was the answer to actually getting some sleep. Padding over to the bathroom, she rummaged through her bag and found a couple of over-the-counter sleeping tabs, popped them in her mouth, and swallowed them down with the remaining bit of booze.

Oh God, the ache was still unbearable. Would it ever get easier? Would she ever feel like she wasn't moving under water or breathing steam?

She'd talked to Bowen earlier that morning, and that had helped. Kevan had listened as he'd detailed the goings-on of his rehab stay. He sounded happy. Solemn, but happy. Her brother was starting to come back to life, but he needed more time to get well. He tried to disguise it, but the desperation came through in his calls.

She booted up her laptop and clicked on her email program, thinking about their conversation. She opened on an email from her former assistant, with the subject of Kevan's Itinerary and Promo Details.

Kevan's gaze narrowed as she tried to focus on the words on the screen. Maybe she was already drunk, because the email looked like a copy of the schedule she'd sent Sindra. At the top was a note from Tina to Steve, Mason's coworker at GEM.

Steve,

Attached is the information you requested regarding Kevan's meeting with Hellfire. It appears Mason has left the tour. Kevan still doesn't have any idea we've been working together or that I still have access to her email.

I highly recommend intercepting her meeting with Hellfire. That, coupled with getting

the media off her housing build, might turn the
tide in your favor.

The tour ends tomorrow night in Reno.
Kevan plans to create a bidding war for
the band's recording contract between two
recording labels (maybe more by now) that
specialize in alt and metal genre bands
at the final show. Reps from the labels
MetalEdge and Vallerian have confirmed
they will be in attendance.

I'm hoping you consider this information as
proof of my continued efforts and assets to your
team. I would appreciate if you would return my
calls as soon as possible.

Sincerely,
Tina

Apparently, her former friend and assistant had
stolen her email and conspired behind her back with
the enemy. With the fucking enemy. How could she
do this? Kevan had wondered how her world could
get any more screwed up, and now she had the
answer. Tina.

Numbly, she hit "reply all" and added Sindra and
Mason to the cc.

Tina,

The fact that you accidentally copied me on
your traitorous email only serves to illustrate just
how incompetent an assistant you were. Turn

your keys and laptop in to Sindra immediately.
Don't bother asking for a reference.

Regards,
Kevan Landry

Kevan hit the send button. "And you suck," she said
to the empty room.

Tina's betrayal made her feel worse. While they
hadn't been buddies, she still had considered her a
friend. Her heart had been crushed by Mason's decep-
tion. And she hadn't thought she'd had anything left to
give after that. She was wrong. The knife was stuck in
by him, for sure, but Tina had shoved it in farther. And
then twisted it for good measure. She'd been working
with them the whole time behind her back. And worse—
her heart clutching in her chest—had Mason known?

Was she a fool to have thought she could be more
than a pretty girl with a big personality and bigger
boobs? She had believed she could have more—a business she felt passionate about and a man who loved her
as much as she loved him. Maybe her dad had called it
years ago the first time she'd come home with her heart
in her hands after it had been handed to her by one of the
stars on the high school football team. He'd told her she
needed to accept her lot in life.

But she didn't want to accept that this was all there
was. She hoped the pain would go away some day, and
hopefully, numbness would take over. She'd relearn
how to function in life. Maybe a little colder or a little
harder, but she still needed to work and get by.

She took a deep breath.

Fuck this day. Fuck Mason Dillon. And fuck that heartless shrew, Tina. Kevan Landry didn't need anyone. She'd been going along just fine without any of them, hadn't she?

She made her way to the bed and crawled in, smelling Mason's familiar sent on her pillow. When she closed her eyes, his face was the last thing floating behind her eyelids before she drifted off into a dreamless sleep.

Mason walked into the Global Entertainment Marketing building in the center of Portland's business district with a new sensation gripping his insides. Nervousness. For the first time since his internship interview years ago, he felt unsure and confused about his role in the company. If he was honest with himself, this was the first time in his life where he couldn't foresee the outcome or even what the plan going in should be. He was as close to rudderless as he'd ever been. And a little tired of all these emotions cluttering his usual decisive style.

As he strode through the familiar plush office of GEM, he tried to project a calm exterior. As far as the outside world could tell, Mason Dillon was the fucking Ice Man cometh. He stood tall, wore a tailored suit, flawless shoes, and immaculate, if a little too long, hair. He was the perfect picture of the well-groomed, overeducated CEO, briefcase in hand, greeting his employees and some clients. Other than the tiny skull-and-crossbones pattern on his tie—a gift from Kevan—Mason was all business. On the outside.

The inside was a completely different story. Until he'd met Kevan Landry and went on the wild ride with her and Manix Curse, he had been confident of his next step, always had a plan B, and made sure every path was available to him.

Now, not so much. After a couple of sleepless nights, he'd created two plans he could follow. He could get back on track, starting with firing Steve and forcing the board to expand their clientele. Or he could chuck it all and start over from scratch.

While putting together his strategy, he'd received an email from Kevan. Strange that such a little image in the bottom of his screen could make his heart lurch so strongly. He clicked the icon and was confused by what he saw. The email header indicated it was from Tina, Kevan's flaky ex-assistant, but it was addressed to Steve.

His skin burned with anger as he read through the email. *That fucking worthless bitch and spineless asshole*. Tina had been working behind her boss's back to guarantee Kevan lost the battle for Manix Curse, even after she'd been fired. She'd essentially tried to ensure GEM was guaranteed the contract. Suddenly, he understood it all clearly.

Kevan never had a chance and neither had he. Steve had been there to ensure she was sabotaged at every turn, and Mason—no, GEM—wouldn't lose the contract. Steve had been working against both of them. That's why the little snake had shown up in Medford and then Hollywood. Now Kevan not only believed he'd been working behind her back, but her ex-employee had been doing the same. She must feel utterly and completely alone.

With cracks along the edges of his polished facade, he

walked into the expansive boardroom. The floor-length windows, framed by beige suede-covered walls, looked out over the large pond twinkling in the morning sun. Mason greeted each of the five board members, politely inquiring about their families. He completely ignored the newest addition to their group, the asshole he wanted to slam against the wall. Revell sat there with his normal smarmy sneer, manicured hands folded neatly in front of him on the gleaming conference table.

After they'd all found their seats at the table, the chairman cleared his throat. "We want to congratulate you on your innovative thinking, Mason. You've always been a great leader, but you've demonstrated some ingenious savvy in not only identifying profitable new markets, but also acquiring new talent. Bravo, son." Mason looked at the man he'd considered a mentor, a friend for the last decade. "Steve has assured the board you've secured the heavy metallic band, Maniac's Curse, and a signed agreement is imminent," said the chairman.

Mason laughed. "It's *Manix* Curse, and they play heavy *metal*, Max. And it's hilarious Revell has promised you anything. Because he wouldn't know Axl Rose from an axle rod." Looking around, he saw the confusion on each board member's face. It was almost comical.

John Cleery, the company's other cofounder, took a sip of water and glared at Mason. "What's so amusing? Do we need to remind you that your job is still in jeopardy and Revell has shown competency in your position?"

"You're fucking kidding, right?" The men at the table gasped. Mason had broken a major rule of this little club. No cursing or criticizing board members. "You wouldn't know innovation if it bit you in the ass. I've been campaigning for a diversified talent pool in the company for years. Then you threaten me. So I decided to investigate viable options on my own. Then you send that sneaky little fuckwit to keep tabs on me. This is bullshit, gentlemen." He could feel his face heating up as his anger began to take hold.

"There's no need to be nasty, Mason."

"This isn't me being nasty. Trust me on that, John. I've spent the last ten years earning this company millions in revenue. GEM's success is because of the solid company I've built. So when revenues began to dip, I tried for two years to guide the board into accepting and pursuing a broader, edgier, cross section of clientele. You refused and fought me at every turn."

"Now wait a minute, son—"

"No, Max, I'm done waiting. Let me finish." Mason cleared his throat. "When I took the initiative and made the decision to go after what I thought as the CEO was the best path for GEM, you sent in our most underhanded VP to do your bidding, instead of trusting me to do the job I've done well for a decade."

The coward Steve coughed into his hand, drawing everyone's attention to him. "I was only there to help you get the job done, buddy. Someone needed to stay on task while you were distracted. And it worked, right? All that matters is we got the contract."

Mason clenched his hands around the arms of his chair to keep from springing across the table and pummeling Steve. "No, asswipe. Manix Curse is not ours to sign. They've decided to go with a boutique agency that better understands their market."

Mason watched the smug look fade from Steve's face, replaced with confusion and then rage.

"How the fuck did that happen? I bought them new instruments, promised a media deal. I even fucked Landry's bony-ass assistant, and you still couldn't close the deal?"

Mason pushed up from his seat, knocking back his chair, and stalked to where Revell was seated. At least the little weasel had the decency to appear frightened.

Leaning over so his face was level with his, he grabbed Revell's tie and pulled him forward. Speaking slowly, he said, "Listen to me carefully, motherfucker. If you mess with Kevan's agency again or so much as look her way, I will fucking end you. Are we clear?"

Revell nodded; beads of sweat pebbled his reddening face. Mason released his tie and shoved him back in his chair so forcefully he slammed into the wall with a crash.

Turning to address the room, Mason said, "I quit."

The board members all spoke at once, trying to be heard over the others. Their distress was probably more from not being able to fire him first and less because they genuinely wanted him to stay. He knew Maxfield was proselytizing and grandstanding—his mouth was moving, and his shiny, manicured nails were gesturing—but Mason couldn't hear the words. In his head, all he heard was Kevan's voice playing over and over, like a looping sound bite: "I wasn't broken until you broke me."

He walked out of the room, feeling one hundred pounds lighter. He was done. This part of his life was over. Finished. He felt alone and completely unsure of what to do next, but he knew he'd made the right move.

His life had no structure now, no direction. No fucking plan. No job. No Kevan.

This was probably how Kevan felt. Alone. Shattered. Directionless. He'd walked away from her, thinking he would find a way to fix everything. But he couldn't fix this. He was as broken as she was, maybe even more so.

For once, he didn't have answers and needed to call in reinforcements. Getting into his car, he didn't bother to call, knowing his sister was home. When he pounded on the front door of her quaint bungalow, his sister swung the door open, wiping her hands on a dishtowel. "Hey, what's up?"

Better to get it all out and see what happens. "Jami, I need your help."

After she pulled him into the house and sat across from him on her fancy velvet couch, she narrowed her eyes as if concentrating on a puzzle she could solve. Suddenly, her eyes widened, and a grin blossomed across her stoic face.

"It happened." Her voice wavered. "You're in love."

"Jesus, how can you tell?" Exasperated, but loving how she knew him so well.

"Cut the crap, Mason" He could always count on his sister to cut to the chase. "Spill it. And I mean all of it."

And it poured out. Everything. From the supposed one-night stand to the last fight to the meeting with the GEM board. Jami peppered questions here and there, but she mostly listened to his description of the tour and his relationship with Kevan.

"You really love her, don't you?" she asked quietly.

"I do." He paused. "I love her so much it hurts to breathe, knowing she might not love me back."

"But why wouldn't she love you? I mean, besides all the work stuff, which doesn't even matter."

"We're so different. I mean, she's gorgeous and smart, but we come from very different worlds."

"And that matters how?"

He thought for a second. "It doesn't."

"Then my advice is to go get your girl, asshole." Wow. His little sister almost never swore. When he didn't respond, she yelled, "Now."

"I love you, Jami." He grabbed her and hugged her so hard she smacked his arm.

"Shut up and go fix this, because that's what you do." She shooed him out the door.

He doubted it would be so easy to convince Kevan they belonged together. But he was going to do whatever it took to convince her. He was done pushing all his feelings down and trying to disguise his love as something else. He was going after his girl.

Chapter 23

THE BRIGHT GLARE OF LIGHT BURNED THROUGH Kevan's eyelids, and the noises outside the bus sounded like they were coming through a megaphone, scraping against her skull. Realizing they must be in Reno, the last stop of the tour, she rolled over in the cold bed to glance at the alarm clock glowing 11:23 a.m.

Holy shit. She'd gotten almost ten hours of sleep, the most she'd gotten in months. Kevan cringed at the ache wrapping around the back of her head and burning in her eyes. Perhaps the tequila hangover wasn't worth the oblivion of a few hours of sleep. Already predicting a long day of meetings, sound checks, and what was expected to be an epic, according to Jax, after-party, she sat up and groaned.

Kevan kicked off the blankets and made her way into the restroom to start her last day on tour with Manix Curse. As she stared at her naked, disheveled self before stepping into the warm shower, she realized that the overwhelming sense of doom clinging to her for the last three days had been replaced by numbness. She wasn't afraid, nor was she worried about the outcome or the band's decision? The last thing she really wanted to think about right now was going back to work. And maybe Bowen could come home early and go to meetings, or she could probably get the guys at the shop to run some kind of fundraiser to help with the rest of his rehab. Or she could add some modeling jobs and another part-time job.

Yeah, sure. And I'll get my own personal unicorn, and rainbows will shoot out of its butt.

Nobody really needed her anymore, and she didn't need them. None of it really mattered. She'd follow through on her commitment to the band tonight. Then she'd crawl back to her little apartment and coma sleep for a couple of days before she went to grovel for extra work. Maybe she'd get lucky, and Tony would give her more hours or need some more pinup tattoo shots for the shop or their signage. Everything would go back to the way it was—the same. It would be fine.

She tried to pull a deep breath into her lungs, but the air caught in her throat. She choked down the inevitable sobs threatening to bubble up. Again. The Chevelle's line "send the pain down below" ran through her head. *Yep, shove that shit right on down.* But it was so hard. So hard to forget his hands in her hair, his mouth on her neck, his arms around her body. Damn. Maybe her heart did still twinge a little. Would she ever get the smell of him off her?

The band was still at their sound check, so Kevan took her time getting ready. Their first appointment was an interview at a local Reno radio station. After a short acoustic set at the local college, they'd do their show and top it off with the huge end-of-the-tour party. She'd been working all the social media angles for the past week, building up to tonight's show at the Knitting Factory. Old and new fans were pumped about the band's appearance, and the venue manager expected tickets to sell out.

Any other day, she'd be proud of the schedule, proud

of what she'd accomplished. Today, she couldn't bring herself to care. She faced the harsh truth of betrayal by her friend—and Mason, probably the one true love of her life. There, at least she'd admitted it. She had fallen in love with the straitlaced suit. It was humiliating enough that he didn't love her back. Hell, she was used to that, but she had actually trusted him to "fight fair." Kevan now had confirmation she was a complete failure in love and in business.

She turned off the water and pulled herself out of the shower. She leaned her forehead against the wall and stopped fighting. One more time she let the relief of the tears come. Just this once and then she'd let go and move on. She let the salty tears streak down her face. Yep. One more good cry and she was sure she'd be better.

While running the towel over her wet skin, a thought flitted through her sluggish and tear-drowned brain. What if Mason *hadn't* screwed her over? What if he'd actually had an explanation for the mess the other night? She never had given him a chance to explain. For a moment, she didn't feel so heavy, so numb. For a moment, she clung to the idea that there was a possible future for her and Mason.

But no. He would have said something then, when she had accused him. It was too late now anyway. The bridge had been burned. She laughed to herself, the sound echoing off the small stall. That bridge had been exploded in a scene from a blockbuster action film. But maybe she could still salvage the contract and get her family back together. Be there for her brother like he'd always been there for her.

She finished toweling off and wrapped her hair up in a big, wet bun before throwing on some jeans and a T-shirt. After making some coffee, she plopped down in front of her computer to work. She went through the motions—emailing, calling, and working on a tour announcement press release—until the afternoon rolled around and it was time for the band's promo appearances.

Manix was in rare form during the radio show and the short acoustic set at the college. The band's enthusiasm actually lifted Kevan's spirits. She even threw Jax her best sassy smile when he constantly shot her concerned glances and told her twice that they needed to talk. Then she'd done everything possible to stay out of his path.

With two record-label executives in the audience, she'd made every effort to dress in her regular attire and affect a professional appearance. She wanted the band to be successful, even if they were ambivalent about her part in their future. She owed the guys the best representation possible. When Kevan made a promise, she always did her best to follow through. So many people broke their promises to her, and she did the opposite. It was part of her moral code. If she didn't, then what did she have left? Not a fucking thing.

While the opening band played, Kevan introduced Joe to each of the record-label reps. The three men chatted, and a pitching war started between the two execs, reminding Kevan of a not-so-long-ago campaign in Joe's office. The memory twisted in her, sharp and fresh.

Excusing herself, she headed for the bathroom but found her path blocked by a very good-looking, very tall, tattooed drummer. If the look on his face was any indication of his mood, she was in for a lecture, or inquiry, or something. He regarded her with narrowed eyes and a pretty damn serious set to his jaw when he wrapped his fingers around her arm and pulled her into the back office.

"It's time for our talk, Kevan," he said as she tried to pull her arm free from his grasp. "Now."

Jax pushed her toward the worn love seat and turned to lock the door. He leaned his long, muscled body against it.

"What the fuck, Jax?"

"What the hell is going on with you?" The muscles in his jaw tightened, and his eyes went sharp.

"I told you I'm fine. All right?"

"You're a terrible liar, Kevan Landry. In case you've forgotten, I was there during the Professor Fuckhead shit. I was there when Bowen was beat to hell by that asshole. And you were upset." He crossed his inked arms. "But I've never seen you like this. What's going on?"

Kevan sighed, vowing she wasn't going to cry. Not again. "We had an agreement, Jax. And he lied—about everything. I thought I was falling in love with him. And I thought he was starting to love me too. But it was all a lie."

He shook his head, disbelief clouding his features. "No, he told me early on he was serious about you. He got very possessive. Kind of pissed me off at first. But he asked me to give him a chance. With you."

"When? What are you talking about?"

"Mason told me he really cares about you and he wouldn't hurt you. That's what I was trying to tell you when you got pissed."

He cares about you.

She shrugged. "He lied."

"Are you so sure?"

"He made me fall in love with him and then went behind my back to steal Manix away from me. We had this stupid agreement." Kevan stood and paced in front of the couch. "We were going to compete for you fair and square. Just him and me, no company resources, no outside help." She stopped and looked up at him, blowing a loose blue curl out of her eyes with a burst of air. "I believed him. Like the fucking idiot I am."

Jax shoved his body off the door and reached her in two long steps. He grabbed her shoulders. "Look at me, Kev."

Slowly, she looked up, trying to force her face into a mask of defiance, until she saw the compassion washing from his.

"His asshole board of directors sent that guy behind Mason's back to make sure he closed the deal. When Revell reported back about your arrangement, they decided to take it into their own hands." Jax tilted his chin, daring her to call him a liar. Realization slid from her scalp down her back like an ice cube.

"He didn't know," she whispered. Not a question. A statement of understanding. "But what about Tina?"

Jax frowned. "What about her?"

"She was working with the GEM guy. Before and after I let her go. She acted like it was no big deal. She understood. Blah, blah, blah. Did Mason know she was stabbing me in the back?"

He laughed. She scowled back. "I'm pretty sure Mason would have shut that shit down if he'd found out. He made his feelings about you pretty clear. After

LA, he sent an email to Joe, saying he was withdrawing GEM's proposal, and you were a far better choice for the band. Sounds like he withdrew because someone from his company interfered and broke your agreement. Seems fair to me."

The acid in Kevan's belly threatened to crawl back up. "Then why did he leave me and the tour? Why didn't he stay and explain?"

Had she even given him the chance to explain?

"Don't you think you owe it to him to find out? Do you love him?"

She nodded. She had assumed Mason was betraying her, and he'd let her think it. She had proved she didn't trust him, and that's all he'd ever asked of her.

"Then you need to go after him, make this right."

"Even if I do love him, Jax, we're so different. Each time I put myself out there, I get screwed. Every time. What if it's me?"

"Stop with the pity party, Kevan. It's not your style. Sometimes you have to take the big risk. Did you really ever put yourself out there for fucking what's-his-professor-jackass-name? You're better off without him, but did you?"

"No, I didn't. But this right here is the exact reason I don't get my hopes up."

"If it wasn't meant to be, it wasn't meant to be. And honestly, Mason would have to be a fucking dolt not to want you. You're the full package—sweet, sexy as hell, smart, the real deal." Jax leaned over and kissed her cheek. "I'm not even sure he deserves you. But someday I hope someone looks at me the way you looked at him."

"I really screwed it up, didn't I?"

"Hey, I don't know. But I gotta get onstage. Think about what I said." Jax turned to walk out the door before she grabbed his hand and tugged him back. She wrapped her arms around his neck and pulled him in tight for a hug.

"Thank you. For everything."

Two hours later, Kevan was in the middle of the end-of-tour party in a casino hotel restaurant. Still nursing a hangover, she sipped her standard cranberry juice, trying to hold a conversation with the record exec from the hardcore label. His name was Benji or Banjo or something. He was clearly interested in the band and had even been talking to Joe about a full album and supporting tour after Hellfire.

Everything she and Mason had worked so hard to accomplish for the band had happened. They'd increased their fan base, they'd engaged fans in the different communities they played, and she'd managed to ramp-up both their traditional and social media engagement. They'd even exposed Manix to new markets by visiting college campuses and playing free, impromptu acoustic sets.

Yep, they'd been so successful. But at what cost? Was a broken heart worth their success?

Unfortunately for Kevan, she was no closer to coming to a conclusion about what to do about Mason and the whole damn kerfuffle than she had been after the conversation with Jax. She looked up from Brody? Benson? Bailey? Yes, Bailey. He slurred his words as his glassy eyes appraised her and he raised a beer to his lips. He liked her. He'd told her so with both his words and his grabby hands. Thought she was a "pretty little thing." Said they should celebrate Manix Curse in style back in his suite at the Circus Circus. Yeah. Like that was gonna happen.

He wasn't bad looking. Actually, he was kind of cute, and she wanted nothing but to forget all about the big bear of a man that haunted her every thought. Maybe she could lose herself in some random affection. Bailey looked at her expectantly. He must've said something and was looking for a response. Should she give her demure, coy smile? Or the more overtly sexual one? Or, how about the polite one that said she was flattered but not interested?

No matter how she tried to focus on what was happening around her, in that very moment, she couldn't stop thinking of Mason. Mason hadn't lied to her. Mason hadn't thrown her under the bus. Mason hadn't tried to ruin her. In fact, he'd walked away from the whole arrangement and basically handed her the band. Why hadn't he tried to explain? Why just leave without a fight?

Maybe she was the one at fault. She'd expected his betrayal from the beginning. And he'd known that. Her sadness and anger had created a toxic cocktail she'd swallowed down and spit back at him. Her pain had clouded everything. And she'd chased him away with cruel words and a total lack of faith in him. In them.

Damn. She jumped up, catching her tottering glass before spilling juice all over. Understanding seeped into her bones in the midst of giggling fangirls, beer pong, and loud metal music. What had she done? Mason hadn't run out on her because he was a liar and a cheater. The one man she'd ever truly loved hadn't left her. She'd left him before he could do it to her.

Across the room, Jax must have caught the perplexed look on her face, because he gently patted the girl on his lap, and she stood, pouting. He smiled and kissed her cheek, then walked toward Kevan with a smug look on his handsome face.

"Well, gorgeous, are we done here or what?"

"I think so."

"Took you long enough. Let's get the fuck out of here and get your ass home."

Chapter 24

MASON'S PLAN WAS NOW CLEAR, HIS PATH DEFINED. Using his hands-free phone system, he called Joe.

"I was two seconds from calling you," Joe said, followed by a good-natured chuckle.

"Yeah? What about?"

"A meeting. Want to talk to you about the tour and look at our options."

They spent a few minutes catching up on the end of the tour and discussed the possible recording contract. Joe was a good guy. He really seemed to have the band's best interests at heart.

"You know, I'm wondering when you're going to ask about Kevan." Joe's usual cheerful tone turned serious.

"How is she?" Mason asked, surprised.

"Your girl is walking around like a zombie. She thinks she has everyone fooled, but she's just putting the time in, smiling when appropriate and playing the good marketing and PR rep that she is. Last night, your record guy was pawing and panting all over her. She was polite but then suddenly hopped up and left. Practically ran from the room with Jax."

A branch of cold dread wound up his spine and squeezed. Mason knew she was home, since an email had popped up on his phone, alerting him of the RV's return. But he hadn't known she'd left with Jax.

"She hasn't called me." He paused. Perplexed and

unsure what move to make next. "For once in my life, I don't know what to do."

Mason understood her misery. He lived his own version. He hoped she could hold it together until he could fix all this. If she would let him.

"My suggestion is to grovel, beg, bribe her. Whatever it takes. That girl is special. You know it. I know it."

Mason laughed. "Oh, I'm fully aware of Kevan Landry's special something. But I don't know how to fix this."

"Come to the meeting. Bring your A game."

Afterward, Mason made a lengthy call to his attorney with some specific instructions regarding his employment termination, as well as some issues about his future plans.

He hung up as he pulled into the parking lot behind Tatuaggio. He reached over to the passenger seat for the printout he needed and a CD fell out of his bag as he grabbed the beaten leather briefcase—a gift from Jami when he'd received his business degree. He picked up the disc and started to throw it on the seat, when he recognized the pretty rockabilly woman on the cover. Imelda May's *Mayhem*. Kevan loved Imelda May and had everything she'd ever recorded. He'd admired her lovely voice and the upbeat tempo of the music. Kevan loved her voice but also her style.

He turned the disc over in his hand and recognized Kevan's impatient scrawl on the note taped to the back.

To my own Big, Bad, Handsome Man. This copy is all for you (just like the song). —K

Kevan must have bought the CD and slipped it into his briefcase for him to discover at a later date. A surprise. Cunning, sweet girl. She was so...so what? Giving? Considerate? Impulsive? Sexy? Beautiful? Yes, yes, yes, and yes. Check all of the above. Even then she'd been thinking about him and his offhanded comment that he liked the music. Had anyone ever paid that much attention to his wants or his interests? No, never. Just her.

A knot formed in his chest. Mason chided himself for letting her go, for walking out without fighting back. In all his life, he'd never given up so easily. He'd been so angry that she hadn't trusted him enough to listen to him. The hurt in her eyes and the quiver in her voice had nearly brought him to his knees. He didn't want to be the cause of any more anguish for her. So he'd walked away, his anger and hurt dictating words he'd never meant. Not giving up, just to regroup and figure out how to win her back. He gripped the steering wheel tighter. Except, dummy, Kevan would look at it as desertion. Another user and abuser leaving her alone.

Time to fix this shit.

After hours of lying on his stomach, the buzz of the tattoo machine, combined with classic rock playing over the speakers, had dulled the constant ache in his chest. The sharp piercings of the tiny needles had permanently etched away the past and drawn, literally, a new future on his back.

"Endorphins are something else, aren't they?" Tony asked, breaking Mason's almost meditative state. "Numbs all kinds of pain."

Mason grunted.

The older man chuckled and wiped something across Mason's back. "But some aches can't be fixed with ink, my friend."

"I know where you're going with this," Mason said. "And I'm not trying to fix anything with a tattoo, Tony. I just want her to see how serious I am."

"How serious are you?"

"Have you ever been in love?" The buzzing stopped as he heard Tony clean the needles and switch colors.

"Yep." The machine started humming again, and he felt the needles stab into his skin. "Callie. The orneri-est, bossiest ballbuster you ever met. Loved her from the day I met her, when I was a twenty-three-year-old hell-raiser, until the day she died of breast cancer three years ago."

"So you know, then," Mason said quietly.

"Yeah. I know. I know Kevan is pretty fucking spe-cial, and she deserves to be treated like it. Life's not easy for women like her. Women like Callie. They've had to work hard to stay ahead, and they don't like to ask for help. Ever."

Mason grunted. No shit.

"But you'll thank the universe every day you have her in your life. Every damn day." Mason could tell Tony was thinking about his deceased wife, the love of his life, as he lathered on the ointment and taped plastic wrap over his shoulder. "You're all done, big guy."

His muscles tight from lying on the massage table for so long, Mason got up and stretched his arms and rolled his head from side to side. "Thanks, Tony," he said, catching the artist's gaze. "For everything."

Tony's laugh rang out in the empty shop. "What's your plan?"

Mason paid him and smiled. "Gonna go get my girl."

Less than an hour later, Mason stood and watched Kevan come through the door to Joe's office. He could see her through the glass wall of Joe's conference room. She put her back to him as she stopped to hug and then chat with the receptionist. It gave him the opportunity to admire what a truly magnificent backside the woman had. When she glanced over her shoulder, their eyes connected, hers narrowed in question, then sadness. Today, she was even more stunning than when she'd almost landed in his lap two weeks ago. Mason was sure his fantasies of her glorious curvy body and full mouth had grown to imaginary proportions. Nope. Not even close. She was so fucking beautiful, striding into the room with her head held high, he could feel his cock harden just looking at her. Suddenly, he wasn't the fierce businessman, he was a crushing boy again.

And she was falling, again. This was starting to become a trend. Kevan falling. Mason catching. His hands grabbed her small waist and steadied her until she laid her hands flat against his chest and pushed back. Mason couldn't help smiling at her bravado. His girl, so fucking proud.

"You need to stop wearing those heels, darlin'. You're gonna hurt yourself."

"I don't need you to keep catching me." So defensive. Definitely not a good sign.

"But I will. Keep catching you, I mean."

She tilted her head to look into his eyes, then swiftly

turned to shake Joe's outstretched hand and exchange greetings before sitting at the table next to Mason and across from Joe.

"The band's not here, because they're still catching up on their sleep. The tour took it out of them." He winked. Both Kevan and Mason nodded. Yep. Took it out of all of them.

"I'm gonna get to the point here. We, Manix Curse and their management"—he paused and smiled— "would like to thank both of you for being good sports and coming on the road with us with no notice. Your enthusiasm and professionalism is both noted and appreciated." His tongue drew across his lower lip, and his hand fiddled with the pen on the table.

"First, it's important you know we have no intention of employing the services of Global Entertainment Marketing. They are too big for our band and don't have the right experience, or culture, to support and promote a heavy metal band."

Kevan exhaled, and Mason tried to hold the smile threatening to transform his mouth. She should be feeling relief and hope right about now. Maybe waiting for the "but…" And here it came.

"But—" Joe looked from Mason to Kevan. Mason could see her shoulders slump slightly. Poor Kevan, there was always a *but* for her. He looked directly at Mason. "But, we were extremely impressed with your connections; the tour and sponsorship opportunities you presented were phenomenal." He paused. Mason heard Kevan swallow but didn't dare turn toward her or pat her like he wanted to. No, he had to allow her to maintain her shield. For now.

"And Kevan"—Joe turned toward her and glanced at a sheet of paper in front of him on the table—"your skills with social media, public relations, and building the band's fan base far exceeded any expectation we ever had. You are truly amazing. I mean, look at these numbers." He pushed the sheet of data across the table between Mason and Kevan.

Mason knew Kevan's nature was biting at the bit to ask questions, push Joe to reveal his decision. *Just wait, gorgeous. Patience.* But she held her tongue and made the effort to peruse the sheet of numbers she was already very familiar with. Her face was a mask of interest, but her long neck was rigid, and her knee bounced under the table.

When she looked up, Joe continued, "And now that Mason has left GEM"—Kevan's head whipped around to look at Mason, her eyes saucers and her full, pouty mouth open in an *O*—"we'd like you to consider joining forces, together, as our marketing and public relations team." And there it was. The zinger.

Her head snapped back to Joe so quickly that Mason mused she might get whiplash.

"I don't understand. You want both of us to work for you?" She turned to Mason and whispered, "And you left GEM?"

He blinked slowly but said nothing.

"What? Why?" she stuttered. God, she was so beautiful. "Because of Steve?" He nodded. Still waiting. "And Tina?"

He smiled.

"But you loved your job, Mason. It was everything."

"No, Bettie, not anymore."

Joe stood. "I'm sure you have a lot to discuss. I'd like a call by tomorrow morning to let me know whether you're interested in my proposition. And we can get together later this week to discuss the details."

Joe made excuses—something about needing to catch up on legal work—and ushered them from his office. Without saying a word, they walked to the parking lot.

Ah, I love walking behind this woman. Because right there was the coup de grace, the woman's ass. She looked over her shoulder and caught him staring at her butt, definitely not for the first time. She gave him no indication of her feelings. Her walls were up nice and tight.

As she stomped to her beat-up Volvo, Mason caught her arm and handed her the small stack of stapled papers he'd been holding.

"You have exactly one hour, Kevan, and then I'm coming for you."

"We should talk first. I just…I mean…I'm…" she stuttered.

"We will. In one hour, I'll meet you at your apartment."

"What does that mean, Mason?"

"It means you have one hour to read this and then we're going to talk." And God willing, *fuck like rabbits until the end of time.*

She took a long, deep breath and sighed. "But I need to tell you how I feel. About you."

Was that bad or good? How did she feel?

"You have an hour, beautiful, and then your time is up. I'm not waiting any longer." He turned and walked to his car. Only this time, he glanced back at her over his shoulder, held up his index finger, and gave her his best, most reassuring smile.

Then he got into his car and drove around for a while before pulling into a guest spot in Kevan's apartment building parking lot.

Mason glanced at his watch. Only thirty-seven more minutes to go. Tick. Tock.

Chapter 25

KEVAN STARED AT THE SILENT TELEVISION ACROSS the small room. She should probably read the papers before Mason showed up. And she knew he would show up. What was it in his eyes? A new challenge? A certain way to tell her he was finished with her and cut her loose for good? She deserved that after assuming he'd broken their deal.

She should be prepared for whatever he wanted to discuss. But she couldn't bring herself to read the stack of neatly printed pages sitting on her lap. So afraid of what they might contain, she laid them facedown.

Just in case.

When she'd marched out of the conference room, she'd been ready to have it out in that parking lot again. Only this time, she was going to be brutally honest—tell him the real and the ugly. Mason needed to know that he owned her heart and that she was dumb drunk crazy in love with him. No more holding back. But she hadn't gotten the chance.

When he'd handed her the stack of papers and left, she'd worried she'd read him all wrong. He could be looking for closure and, being the kind of man he was, he wanted to face her when he told her.

Damn. Damn. Damn.

What if it wasn't love she'd seen in his eyes at the meeting?

Fuck. Fuck. Fuck.

She was sure she couldn't live the rest of her life with this horrific, gaping, heart-shaped hole in her chest. Nope, that would suck. If he didn't want to work together, if he couldn't love her like she loved him, what was she going to do? The thought of continuing on like she had the last few days made her groan aloud. That wasn't living. When had she turned into such a friggin' pansy?

She took a deep breath. No, she'd be fine. Sad, but fine. She'd figure out how to work with him on the Manix account, and she'd get her brother back.

Kevan jumped when her phone buzzed on the table. Thinking it might be Mason. Or Joe. Or Bowen. She picked it up to read the text. Mason. Eight simple words that could mean so much.

Time's up. I'm coming for you, mo chroí.

Well, there it was. Time to face the music. She was going to lay it all out for him. Tell him she loved him too much to accept anything less than the same from him. Or, maybe she wasn't. Maybe she was too afraid of the pain.

Two minutes later, Kevan stood staring at the gorgeous man in front of her, shoulders slumped forward, eyes red, lips thinned and grim. Even miserable, he was the most handsome and masculine man she'd ever seen. Everything her body and heart had ever desired.

She was done pretending she didn't want him, that she didn't need him. She was done pretending to be someone else to protect her tender heart. She was hopelessly, madly, insanely in love with this bossy, maddening, brilliant, kind man.

And she was going to tell him. She just hoped it wasn't too late. How could she ever have thought she could live without him? Without his fancy suits and manly man smell of woodsy goodness and fresh soap? Without his wolfish smile and the predatory way he looked her up and down before devouring her? This man had gotten into her blood from his first overwhelming kiss. No, before then. If she was honest with herself, she had belonged to Mason Dillon as soon as he'd brushed his beautiful mouth across her knuckles and said, "I've got you. Don't worry. I won't let you fall."

Because she fell and he caught her. That's what he did. Every. Single. Time. She'd pushed him away, chased him off, as often and aggressively as she could, and he'd still come back every time.

He stood there, expectantly. Waiting for her to say something. Or to invite him in. She wanted to throw herself into his arms and live the rest of her life there, but she knew he wasn't ready for it. She wouldn't be able to hide her true feelings for him for long, but she loved him enough to know she couldn't keep him. She loved him enough to take the ride with him and then let him go.

They needed to talk about the papers he'd shoved into her hands. He'd looked as if he needed a response to them. But she'd been too afraid to look at them.

He scrubbed his hand down his weary face, and the side of his perfect mouth curled up slightly. "You didn't read the contract, did you?"

Shaking her head, she stepped back to let him in before she humiliated herself by groveling at his feet. She motioned to the vintage lilac-colored couch she'd picked up at an estate sale two years before.

"Why, Kevan? Why didn't you read it?"

She swallowed down her fear and cleared her tear-clogged throat. "I was afraid."

"Of what, darlin'?"

He looked almost sad as he moved to sit on the farthest end of the couch. Was he trying to get as far away from her as possible? Maybe she should have read the papers, prepared herself a little more.

"Of you, Mason. Of my feelings for you." He moved to say something, but she held up her hand to stop him.

"I think you like me. And I think you might even want us to work together."

The smile spreading across his face made her heart sink.

This was it. Regardless of what was printed on the small stack of papers, she needed to tell him how she really felt. "I'm so sorry. I know I have no claim on you, but you have one on me. On my heart." She looked down at her hands, afraid of the truth in his eyes and what it would do to her. "I'm crazy stupid in love with you, Mason. I have been since that first night at the club when I practically fell into your lap. I'm so in love with you my heart hurts when you're not near, and I can't stand one more moment without telling you the truth."

The tears were coming now. Great, she was telling him how madly in love with him she was while her face was beginning the contortions of the most epic ugly cry ever.

When he didn't say anything, she sighed heavily. What did a woman like her—chaotic, messy, loud, impulsive—have to offer a solid, professional man like Mason Dillon? Diddly squat. That's what.

She looked at the papers scrunched in her hands and then risked a glance at him. He sat there staring at her, his expression unreadable. He nodded at the papers.

"Read the contract, Kevan," he said simply.

She nodded. *I can do this*. She laid the paper-clipped stack on her lap and tried half-heartedly to smooth the wrinkles out. His long hand touched hers gently, stopping her movements. "Read it. Please."

She did. She read every single word through the blur of her tears. She sloppily wiped her nose on the sleeve of her silk blouse, ignoring the deep chuckle from the elegant man sitting by her side.

When she reached the end of the document, she took a deep, shuddering breath. And reread it from the beginning.

★ ★ ★

Mason sat as quietly and patiently as possible, hoping the legalese of the contract would sufficiently explain how he felt about Kevan. His pounding heart threatened to jump from his chest, and his lungs refused to breathe evenly. He needed her to know that regardless of how she felt about a long term-relationship, he was ready for one. In more ways than one.

Would she want the same thing? She'd said over and over she couldn't trust a man like him—someone not from her inner circle, someone from the more traditional business world she liked to keep herself separate from. What if it wasn't a cover to protect her battered and lonely heart? What if she really wasn't interested in something more? He couldn't even imagine a world without Kevan Landry in it.

The damned insufferable woman slowly read over each page as if savoring every word. And when she reached the end of the document, she flipped it back over and started reading it again. On the third time through, he grabbed the document off her lap.

"Woman," he snapped in exasperation.

She jumped. Looking up, she grinned through her ruined makeup and runny nose. And she was breathtakingly beautiful. How on earth had he ever thought a few times with her, a few weeks, would ever be enough? It would take him years to explore every facet that was the perfect diamond of Kevan Landry. It would take forever to get below the top layer of her complexity and beauty.

"What does this mean, Mason?" Her voice so low, he had to bend forward to hear her. "What does this mean?"

"What do you think it means?" He held his breath, waiting for her answer. *Please let her understand*.

She looked away, like she was peering into the future and not at her colorful wall. "I think you're asking me to be your partner," she started slowly. "I think you want us to work together."

When she glanced back at him for confirmation, he nodded encouragingly. He could feel his grin stretch across his face, but it quickly dropped when he recognized the shadows of sadness still hiding in her eyes.

"Isn't that what you want—for us to be partners? You're amazing. So creative and innovative. We'd make a great team," he said.

She nodded and moved to stand up. He pulled her closer to him. Why was she acting this way? "I don't understand. You said you loved me. Don't you want this, Kevan?"

She smiled wanly. "I do. I really do. It's just..."

"What? What more can I offer? I'll give you anything, darlin'."

"Your heart, Mason. I wish I could take anything and everything you're willing to offer, but what I really want is everything. And I don't think anything less will be enough."

Oh God, he was such a fool. He'd tried to approach this spirited woman with a business deal. Like his parents would. She didn't want a cold, emotionless contract. *Moron*. She was all hearts and rainbows and color and unicorns. She needed declarations of love, the grand gesture.

"Look, I'm new at this. Let me try again." He pushed off the couch and bent his knees so he could look up into her eyes. Taking her hand in his, he brought it to his lips and gently brushed his mouth over her knuckles.

"Since the very first time you fell into my arms, my body and my heart have belonged to you. I can't explain it, but it's almost like my soul knew it was missing something and that you would make me complete. I had all these empty spaces in me that you filled up. Do you understand what I'm saying?"

"I think so, but I think you need to *fucking* say it... you know, so I'm sure." She smiled her kittenish smile. *My girl is back*.

He ran his hand up her back and tangled his fingers in her hair. "I love you, Kevan Landry. I want to be your partner—in business and in life. I can't imagine living another day without you in it. I want to share everything with you." He angled her head to the side, exposing her neck. "I want you to have my babies. I want to tattoo your name across my heart. I want everything you can give me. And more." Each word he accentuated with a brush of his lips against her jawline, down her neck, and across her shoulder.

He'd laid it all out for her. It was up to her to have the courage to pick it up and make it her own.

Kevan's skin pebbled, and he felt her shiver. "Oh God, Mason, we're so different. You're so professional and normal, and I'm, I'm…"

He continued his slow kisses until he reached her lips. "I'm not here to fix you, Kevan. I love you just the way you are." He felt her grin grow under his mouth. "The most perfect crazy, beautiful, creative woman for me."

Her soft hands tugged at his shirt and made their way up his chest, sending chills down his spine. "But I'm always cold, and you're always warm."

He rolled his eyes. How could he not at his silly woman? He sat back down on the couch and pulled her closer, yanking her blouse over her head and tossing it behind him.

"You can warm your cold hands on the warmth of my heart, darlin'," he said, his accent thick and his voice deep.

When she threw her head back and laughed from her belly, he unbuttoned his dress shirt and set it on the arm of the couch.

She stood and turned, revealing her luscious ass to him. Coyly, she looked over her shoulder and pulled the zipper down on her skirt. "And I'm all cool and awe-some, and you're all boring suits and meetings." She let her skirt fall and stood there in her lacy bra and panties. He stood and ran his palms down her body, outlining her curves with his fingers.

Turning her, he smiled before slowly grasping the back of her neck to guide her soft lips up to his. He didn't devour her this time. Instead, he savored the feeling of their barely touching lips. He kicked off his shoes, and with his free hand, he rid himself of his pants and boxers.

Her hands stroked his arms. "And you're all classy and athletic, and I'm all tottering heels and klutzy."

Her hands stopped abruptly when it reached the large bandage taped over his back. Kevan gasped and covered her mouth with her hand. "Mason, what did you do?"

He turned and reached over his shoulder to pull off the bandage, revealing a stunning and colorful modern pinup tattoo across his shoulder blade and down his back.

"It's beautiful." She looked up into his expectant face and smiled.

"It's you, Bettie. It's all for you. Forever. Because, honestly, I can't remember a time when I haven't loved you."

He deftly unsnapped her bra and dropped it on the floor. He wrapped his hand on either side of her rib cage and leaned forward to take a round rosy aureole into his mouth, loving the way her body instinctively arched into his. Without warning, he turned and sat on the couch, the soft chenille caressing his fevered skin. Mason trailed two fingers slowly around one breast, then the other, and then down to her core. He slid her panties aside and plunged his fingers in, rubbing his palm against her slippery nub. Her body bowed and fell forward, onto his lap, where his hand steadied her so he could lean forward to kiss her.

She smiled against his mouth, and he whispered, "I will catch you every time you stumble and fall, darlin'. Every fucking time."

He yanked her thong down, positioned her over his lap with her legs straddling his hips, and arranged her body, her swollen cleft aligned directly over his hard cock.

"I know. And that's why I love you." She lowered herself slowly—painfully and exquisitely slow—impaling herself and surrounding him in her warmth.

Her eyes found his, and she seemed to stare directly into his soul. She saw him, the real him, and he saw her. Holding tightly on to Kevan's hips, Mason lifted her up and pulled her back down, driving in over and over, murmuring his love for her on every thrust.

Reaching up, he found her breasts, cupping one in each hand as she continued to control the building storm around them. He leaned forward and pinched one nipple and bit the other. Her body arched, and she began to move with an almost frantic pace, stretching for the finish line. Feeling the tingle too quickly in the base of his spine, he reached down between their slick bodies and rubbed her clit with his thumb and index finger. Her cry of pleasure and the sharp bite of her teeth on his shoulder became his undoing as he threw his head back and growled out his orgasm.

Panting, he cupped her face in his hands and said, "I was so lonely and didn't even know it before you found me. But it was you who made me realize how empty my life was. It was you who was strong enough to show me the man I'm supposed to be."

Tears streamed silently down Kevan's face. He leaned forward to kiss one away.

"Marry me, Kevan. I can't live another day without waking up next to you."

She smiled and leaned into his hand. "But, Mason, I don't even know where you live."

"Doesn't matter. We'll live wherever you want."

She giggled, then her smile dimmed. "You didn't really break me, Mason. I was so broken before you, so unhappy and alone. I knew I could trust you, and yet I refused to. I won't ever doubt you again. I love you."

She laid her head on his shoulder and wrapped her arms around his neck. Her smooth skin, still damp from their lovemaking, was a balm to his once-cold heart. Marriage to this woman would never be easy; she would always keep him on his toes, but he couldn't think of a more exciting adventure than a lifetime with Kevan Landry.

Epilogue

KEVAN STARED AT HER REFLECTION IN THE GLASS
door before Mason swung it open and ushered her into
New Beginnings. He grabbed her hand and tugged
her toward the reception desk as she scanned the open
room for any sign of her brother. Not being able to visit
Bowen the last two and a half months had been difficult. Their phone conversations had gotten lengthier
and more regular the longer he stayed in rehab, but the
center had prohibited more visits until he'd been there a
full month. And now, three months later, it was time to
bring him home.

She practically vibrated with excitement. And just a
little anxiety. How many times had Bowen looked her
right in the eye and given her that charming grin while
lying through his teeth? Hell, near the end, most the time
he hadn't even needed a reason. He'd lie just to lie. For
the heck of it.

Mason kissed her forehead. "It's going to be fine,
darlin'. You'll see."

He squeezed her hand and stepped forward to ask the
receptionist to check them in and call Bowen. As she
scanned the room again, a tall man stood in the meeting
area and shoved his hands in his pockets. He peeked up
through long black hair and she locked her gaze with
eyes like hers. But instead of seeing the hollow husk of
Bowen she'd visited several weeks ago, there stood her

tall, strong brother. His hair was a little shaggy, and his head was tipped down, almost shy, but it was Bowen.

A squeal tumbled from her lips, and her feet were racing across the room before she could stop herself from jumping into his arms. Someone was crying. Deep sobs sounded around her.

When she heard her brother whisper, "Don't cry, Kev. I'm okay. Shhhhh," she realized the cries were coming from her. She wanted to wipe her tears away, but she couldn't imagine letting him go. Ever. She pulled her arms tighter around his neck and breathed deeply, dragging in a stilted breath. Gone was the stale acidic smell of booze and general unwellness that had followed him like a fog for so long. Bowen smelled like Bowen again: an earthy smell with hints of orange or lime or something citrusy.

"Bo, Bo, Bo," she chanted while he stroked her hair until he set her gently on a couch against the wall and turned toward Mason.

Her brother jabbed his hand forward. "Bowen." She looked back and forth between the two men who owned her heart, both standing with feet wide and tight smiles, wariness clouding their eyes as they shook hands.

"So you're Dillon. The guy who broke my sister's heart, then glued it back together again." Bowen crossed his arms, sleeves of colorful ink flashing from under the cuffs of his shirt.

"I love your sister. Did from the beginning. And I'm not going anywhere."

She reached across to grab Mason's hand. Bowen intercepted her hand first, turning it back and forth so the pink diamond sparkled under the harsh florescent lighting. A smile lifted the corner of her mouth. Mason had had it specially designed. A reworking of an antique setting with modern stones. A declaration of his love and an artistic version of them—contemporary and vintage, sassy and bossy, forever set in a circle on her finger. And it was so sparkly that Mason had insisted she turn the ring in toward her palm when she drove so she wouldn't be distracted by the shine. It's not like she actually hit that woman on the sidewalk. Sheesh, one near miss and everyone starts getting all paranoid.

"This makes you happy?" Bowen asked, looking up from her hand and pinning his laser eyes on her. "He makes you happy?"

Kevan could feel the skin on her face stretch as that damn smile took over. Again. "So freaking happy."

Bowen brushed his hands on the front of his pants. "What can I say? I guess it's cool with me." He shifted to catch Mason's eye, and Kevan felt her pulse race. Now what? "But I'm back in the game, my friend. You don't get to hurt her again."

Mason stepped forward and smacked Bowen on the back. "No worries there. I'll kick my own ass if I so much as muss one of her lovely blue hairs." He laughed. "Truth is, Kevan can take care of herself. You raised her right."

She rolled her eyes. "Oh, for fuck's sake, you guys, let's get out of here."

Bowen leaned down and picked up his duffel bag, then threw his arm around her shoulders. His strength was back. He must've been using the exercise room there. Something close to hope tingled in her fingertips and toes.

"Where we going?" he asked as they walked toward the exit.

"Home," both Mason and Kevan said at the same time.

Bowen nodded but didn't ask for details. Good. He'd figure out soon enough that they had a new home. A new life. One that had started the day Mason had joined Jolt Marketing and they'd signed Manix Curse as their first major client.

They were no longer alone, individuals forced to navigate the treacherous real world on their own. They were a family. And family was everything.

*Here's a sneak peek at book two in
Kasey Lane's sizzling Rock 'n' Ink series*

BEAUTIFUL MESS

JAX LOOKED AROUND AT THE ASSEMBLAGE OF PEOPLE sitting around the conference table. At the head sat his band's manager, Joe McKellan, marketing reps Kevan and Mason, and his band, Manix Curse, which included their singer Marco, bass player Conner, and his little sister, guitar wunderkind Mandi. This was everything he'd worked toward for the past several years: success as an artist, sitting on the tip of a rocket about to launch them into the rock and roll heavens where he'd be a heavy metal god.

He glanced at his phone. In about two minutes the one chick he'd never really gotten out of his system was going to walk into the conference room, contractually obligated to share breathing space with him. Boo-fucking-ya. Maybe he'd get the chance to mess up her perfectly coiffed lady bun. Maybe he'd turn on the charm and get her to go out again. One more night together. For old times' sake. Because one more night was all he'd ever get once she unburied the truth about their breakup.

Right on cue, Joe's new receptionist led Jami toward the conference room where they all waited for her. What would she say when she realized he was in the band?

Did she already know? Tingles of anticipation sparked up his spine, not unlike the spikes of adrenaline he felt zipping through his body before a show.

Had Kevan and Mason told her he'd be there? Probably.

They all stood as she walked through the open door wearing a pristine pantsuit and matching heels. She was giving off that school principal vibe in waves, but he knew what hid beneath her overly practical clothes. White-hot fire burned under all that navy-blue ice.

She smiled, the type of smile most would accept at face value as genuine. But he could tell the smile didn't quite make it to those cerulean-blue eyes; it was a practiced, lawyerly smile. And as she began to shake hands with everyone and make her way around the table, Jax knew without a doubt this was the all-business Jami, the one she showed the rest of the world. He wondered again if the hair in her tight bun at the base of her neck still felt soft and satiny like silk. Would it snag on his calloused fingers when he ran it through his hands? And, more important, was it still long enough to wrap around his fist as he took her from behind?

Whoa. Time to cool your jets. Business first. Fun later. If he was lucky.

He cleared his throat, trying to shake the image of her heart-shaped ass under his palm as she searched for her brother and then Kevan. Then…wait for it. *Bam!* Her gaze fell on him like a fucking hammer and she nearly dropped her briefcase.

So that would be a no. They hadn't told her. Interesting.

Jax couldn't hide the knowing smirk that spread

across his face. He'd bet dollars to doughnuts the three of them were the only ones in the room to see her smile falter and the lines momentarily mar her otherwise smooth forehead. Oh yeah. He liked ruffling her feathers. He liked it a lot.

Regaining her composure, she held out her slim hand, her nails short, shiny with clear polish. A funny thing for him to notice because he was a guy and all, but she'd always done that to him, made him notice the little things.

"Jackson Paige, a.k.a. Jax Pain." Her lip curved up and the dimple in her cheek popped. The gleam in her eye said so much more than her words. "Mason and Kevan neglected to mention you're in the band."

His much larger hand swallowed hers and he tugged her arm. Just a little. Not enough to physically throw her off balance. "JamiLynn Dillon, esquire." And then without thinking about it—because if he'd thought about it he wouldn't have done it—he pulled her all the way in for what looked like a chaste hug between old friends. But he could feel her slight tremble and hear the catch in her breath. God, he'd forgotten how tiny she was. How voluptuous and small and how the curve of her body fit perfectly with his taller, leaner one. And her smell. Flowers. Sweet, simple flowers. A soft edge to the sharpness she tried to portray to the world.

"Hello, sunshine. Miss me?" he whispered in her ear, brushing his mouth against her soft lobe. The sharp intake of breath and the way she melted into him before she pulled away meant he could still affect her. Good.

She laughed with a confident twist to her sultry mouth. He bet only he could hear the slight tremor in her voice or see her throat move like she was swallowing dirt. "Well, I see Jackson hasn't changed. Much."

As everyone chuckled and shuffled back into their seats around the table, she sat between Mason and Joe. Jax sank in the seat directly next to his sister and across from Jami while actively avoiding eye contact with Mandi.

Mandi's glance flicked back and forth between Jax and Jami. Jax narrowed his eyes and shook his head, a warning to his pixie-sized sibling with the big mouth. But she smirked and her eyes shone with glee. Dammit. Surprisingly, she didn't cackle evilly or rub her hands together in excitement.

"So, Jami…may I call you Jami?" Mandi asked as Jami's smile stayed pasted to her face like an emoji sticker. "I know you're Mason's sister, but how exactly do you know my brother?"

"We met in law school."

"Ohhhhh, you're that—" Jax grabbed Mandi's knee under the table and squeezed hard, but not before Jami's blond and perfectly arched brows furrowed, creating a single line, like a question mark, between her eyes. Although he hadn't told Mandi about Jami, per se, he had told her about "some chick" he'd been with in law school. That it hadn't ended well. Mandi probably assumed the mystery college girlfriend was the reason he was a serial dater. She'd be correct in that assumption, of course.

"Yes. I suppose I am." Jami's lips went firm as she pulled the band's contracts out of her bag and turned to Joe, the decision maker and official suit of Manix Curse. "I've gone over the contracts Joe had delivered earlier this week. While there is some predatory language and terms we'll definitely want to negotiate, the three offers are fairly solid and have the potential to be quite lucrative. Of course, we're still waiting for the formal offer and contract from the record label. I don't expect those until next week. At that time we'll counter, if necessary."

Jax sat silently while she talked, but stretched his legs under the table, bumping her foot with his and making her fumble her words briefly. She never glanced at him, but he could tell his presence was getting to her.

He should quit messing with her. Let her go and do her job without interfering, But fuck, she was hot when she put on her bossy lawyer pants and took control of the meeting.

Joe smiled, but then again he was always smiling, so it was kind of hard to differentiate his moods. "Excellent. Then you're interested in joining the Manix team as counsel?" When she agreed, he slid a stapled stack of papers her way. "This is the signed contract of our agreement, along with the retainer we promised. But, as specified in the contract, you get paid when we get paid."

"Great. Shall we go over some of these points while the entire band is here?" she asked.

☆ ☆ ☆

Hell's bells.

Jackson Paige was, in fact, Jax Pain, the drummer of Manix Curse.

That thing in her chest tightened around her ribs, making it hard to breathe.

This new little development was further complicated

by the fact she'd been hired by the band to negotiate their tours, sponsorship, and recording contracts.

As she slowly rinsed her hands in the sink and checked her updo for any out of place strands, she pretended it didn't make a difference. She had a way of doing things—rules, structure, plans—that worked for her now. A life that made sense. And Jackson had no place in the calm order of her life. None. He was a blustering tornado that would rip apart anything good and calm she had, leaving behind only a mess. And his effect on her panties had nothing to do with real life. It was something she needed to note and then forget. She took a deep breath, allowing the oxygen to fill her lungs and relax that pinch in her chest.

By the time she found herself striding back down the hall to grab her briefcase from the empty conference room, she'd quelled the pounding of her heart to a slow tempo. She could do this. The soup of emotions boiling up from seeing him at the tattoo shop and again today would go away. It would. She would be okay. She was not a frivolous, impulsive girl easily swayed by tall, muscly tattoo artists, let alone superhot musicians. She was a damn lawyer. A respected member of the judicial system, a sworn officer of the freaking court.

Jami didn't like all these messy feelings. She'd gotten used to being in control. She looked down at the front of her suit as she smoothed her jacket. Her outfit screamed conservative attorney. Or it asserted it politely, but resolutely.

Stepping into the conference room, she looked around for her bag. Not on the table. Not on the chairs. Dammit, she was usually more together than this. She was turning around to go back through the door and see if someone had left it in the reception area when she heard the *snick* of the door closing. She snapped her head in the sound's direction and a very tall, very sexy Jackson stood there, swinging her bag from his hand.

"Looking for this, sunshine?" His smile was wide, but slightly predatory, and his eyes narrowed in challenge. He needed a shave. Well, another man with that amount of scruff would need a shave. Jackson, on the other hand, looked knavish and naughty as heck with his shadowy stubble and messy hair. Hair that was longer than it had been in school and shorter on the sides, brushing the collar of his gray-striped button-down shirt. The edges of what looked like swirls of blue water peeked up over shoulder and across his collarbone, tickling his neck. He had his long sleeves rolled to mid-arm. Color filled his forearms to his wrists, with the tongue of what appeared to be a dragon licking over the top of one hand. The muscles in his corded arms tensed and danced when he shifted her bag.

Why did she find him so damn hot, burning all rational thought from her head with just a glance, just a touch? Why him? She saw guys every day with his same look and never gave them space in her head. There was something in the relaxed but coiled way Jackson held himself that exuded pure sexual charisma. All rock-star charisma.

A rock star that had left her. Without explanation. Without a reason.

"Yes, thank you," she said tightly, reaching for her bag. He swung it out of her reach, pulling it to his chest.

Without warning, the room whirled as he grabbed her

shoulders and spun her. Her back hit the door with a soft *thunk* and she heard, rather than saw, her bag fall to the floor. She couldn't move, couldn't look away from his piercing gaze, which might as well have been a knife the way it cut her open, exposing her. Heat from his body washed over her, blanketing her skin, overwhelming her. He didn't touch her anywhere but her shoulders, where his long fingers dug into her flesh, branding her through her jacket and blouse. They stood there staring at each other, her hands at her sides. Then he reached up and drew his index finger from her ear down along her jaw, sending sparks flinting off her body. Her nipples pulled into hard buds, almost painful as they ached for his touch. If she wasn't careful, those sparks were going to start a fire she wouldn't be able to put out. She couldn't afford to lose control. Not now, and not ever again.

Breathe. Breathe. Breathe.

She wanted to close her eyes. Wanted to lean into his touch and let him take her over, like he always had when they were together. But she couldn't give in.

Not anymore. Not again.

When she moved to speak, to stop him maybe, he drew his finger over her lips, causing her to gasp. She sucked air into her lungs…air she so badly needed but couldn't quite get enough of. Big mistake since his smell—that clean, salty scent he always had, like minutes earlier he'd jumped off a surfboard after riding waves—kicked her sense memory in the gonads. And everything she'd been trying to forget about him came flooding back, making it hard to ignore the flutter in her belly.

Jackson shook his head and an unruly lock of hair fell forward over his eye, lending him a sinister and mischievous look, like the forbidden devil he was. The air between them grew thicker, weighed down by ghosts of the past and a lust that had never gone away.

He leaned down, touching his forehead to hers. "I can't ignore the thing between us, Jami. Can you?"

Yes. She certainly could and would. But then she did something completely unexpected. Something she hadn't planned or even considered. Because if she'd thought about it for even one second, it would never have happened.

She wrapped her hands around the back of his neck and tugged his mouth down to hers. It was a light, sensual brush of her lips against his, but the little flutter she'd felt earlier that had been barely a blip on the Richter scale became a full-scale earthquake, threatening to destroy everything. And yet she didn't care. It wasn't enough.

Though she continued to tease his lips with her own, Jami needed more. All rational thought, all control, all her rules flew out the window and were replaced with a dark need she recognized on a visceral level and thought she'd obliterated a very long time ago. The mask she affixed firmly every day to keep order in her life fell off the second his mouth met hers. It completely disintegrated as soon as her tongue decided to lick the crease of his lips and turn a seductive taste into a feast of mouth fucking. Instantly he took over and his fire consumed her. Like it always had. It would consume and then leave her like so much dusty ash on the floor.

A groan, a deep, low moan, sounded in the room and Jami's eyes snapped open. The groan came from her. No. Not again. This was not how this thing was going down. She was years over Jackson Paige. Years. Over. And now his band was her client, which definitely meant no kissing. Sweet or sexy didn't matter.

What the hell was she doing kissing Jackson? A cold, sharp clarity wrapped itself around her. She pulled away and ducked under his arm, and the separation felt more like a slap than it should have. A look of confusion marred his handsome face for a moment before it was replaced quickly by his don't-give-a-shit-take-it-or-leave-it grin. Of all the looks he gave, she hated that one the most. Though, at that moment, she was grateful for his cocky response since it was a reminder of exactly why she shouldn't be kissing him.

Her hands fisted against her hips. "I'm sorry. I was clearly out of line. We shouldn't be doing this, Jackson. We shouldn't be doing any of this."

"I disagree. I think we should do it some more," he said as he stepped forward. She held up her hand, stopping him.

"You gave up that right when you left me without an explanation or even a good-bye. Not even a 'screw you' so I knew where I stood. Nothing." She cocked her eyebrows, waiting for something. A response. Some shame. Anything.

But his expression never changed when he swept his hand through his hair. "Fair enough, but let's not forget you basically just fucked me with your mouth, sunshine. This isn't over."

Guilt and desire and anger mingled hot in her throat. "Oh, yes it—" She stopped abruptly when he stalked toward her and leaned down, sending shivers up and down her arms.

Jesus, what was wrong with her?

"No," he said, close enough she could feel his breath feathered against her cheek. "You're right about one thing. We do have some unfinished business."

"Jackson." His name was an exasperated sigh on her lips. "You're a client now. So even if I did want to know why you ran off, and even if I did want to take it further, I can't. We can't."

The half-lie half-truth rolled off her tongue easier than she'd thought it would. The truth was that he was a client, and they really shouldn't mess around. But the other side of that coin was that she really just wanted him to pick her up, hike up her skirt, and pull aside her soaked panties before he plunged his big dick into her over and over again until he gave her what she knew would be the best orgasm she'd had in a very long time.

But that wasn't going to happen, because no matter how badly she wanted him in her bed again, he was no good for her. It had taken her far too long to get over him, and the recovery had almost been as bad as when she'd been a screwed-up teen. In a way, maybe it had been worse.

"That's where you're wrong. We aren't done." He pressed his face to her throat. Her breath hitched as he ran the bridge of his nose up her neck and then bit her earlobe. The surprising nip sent sharp pricks of desire straight to her already aching nipples. He pulled back and chuckled before turning around and glancing over his shoulder.

"That's where *you're* wrong," she said. "We were done a long time ago. That was your good-bye kiss."

Something dark flashed in his eyes before he pasted that damn smirk back on his face. "See ya soon, counselor."

He strode casually out the door and into the empty reception area, leaving her raw and exposed, nerves sparking and jumping like live wires.

Like he always did.

☆ ☆ ☆

Word must have gotten out that Manix Curse was playing the Tiki again because the club was nearly at capacity, wall-to-wall flannel and denim as far as the eye could see. Everyone from his middle school girlfriend to his high school art teacher had come up to congratulate him on the band's success.

It was cool. But frankly, it was fucking exhausting always being on. Always smiling and acting the good ol' rock star. It was bullshit. Half the time he felt like a poser and the other half he just felt tired. Until he got up onstage behind his drum kit. Then everything else faded away—the crowd, the lights, the women. All the chaos narrowed into a fine laser point where the only thing that mattered was the music, his band. They became a fluid, unified entity.

Jax rolled his drumsticks in his hand and playfully tapped out a beat on his much shorter sister's pink head. Mandi, apparently, didn't appreciate his brotherly affection and attempted to punch him in the stomach, despite the fact that she was a dinky little squirt with fists the size of his big toes.

"What is it about you guys and punching each other?" A familiar, husky voice broke through Zakk Wylde's remake of "Ain't No Sunshine" booming through the club.

Jami. She'd actually come.

His head snapped up and his blood felt like lava, burning him from the inside out as it flowed faster through his veins. Unfortunately, his shock gave the dinky devil next to him an opening to punch him hard in the gut, doubling him over with a cough.

"What the hell, Mand?" He choked, trying to stand up straight and hold his belly. But his sister waved at Jami, smirked at him, and ran off toward the greenroom.

He turned back to Jami and realized she was wearing a short jean skirt—short enough he could see her creamy thighs—and a sleeveless plaid cotton shirt. And even more surprising, if that was possible, she had it unbuttoned far enough that he could see the top curve of her full breasts, held tightly in a lacy tank top. She was hotter than any woman he'd ever laid eyes on.

She threw up her hands. "Well?" She huffed, blowing out a breath that lifted her loose, long blond hair. Long, gorgeous hair that he hadn't seen down in five years. He smiled, trying really hard not to look predatory. He couldn't help it. Despite her douchebag parents and her odd attachment to everything boring and beige, his body instantly reacted to hers. She looked awesome. But instead of telling her so, he motioned with his finger for her to spin. He had to know how long her hair fell down her back and what those black heels she was wearing did to her pert round little ass.

She tried to hide her blush, which he always found so cute, but slowly turned, her arms still spread wide. How she could be such a wild vixen in bed and still get embarrassed at a little lascivious attention was pretty damn funny. When she started turning, he realized he wasn't the only one watching her swivel her hips as she circled. He turned his glare at the table of assholes eyeballing Jami and the two standing against the bar. The blond goddess in front of him remained completely clueless to her audience.

It was only a moment before her back came into view. Her hair wasn't as long as it was back in school. Oh no, it was longer, curling over the round lift of her ass. Enough hair to grab and wrap around both fists as he imagined bending her over and driving into her. His chest tightened and he took a step forward. Placing his hands on her shoulders, he felt her tremble under his touch. He loved that feeling. The way he affected her. No matter how much she fought their connection and their past with her words, her body betrayed her lust. Every. Damn. Time.

Jax bent over her, letting his hand trace her shoulder, down her collarbone, and brush the side of her breast before spreading across her soft belly. He loved Jami's body. Always had. Her insane hourglass figure made him drool. Even when she hid it in boxy suits and wore her no-nonsense bun and lawyerly demeanor. She oozed sex innately. She knew it. Fought it. But not tonight. Tonight she wore it on her sleeve. Owned it.

And Jax was just arrogant enough to believe it was all for him. "Did you wear this for me, sunshine?" he whispered into her ear and ran his tongue over the soft curve of her lobe.

She stiffened for a fraction of a second before melting back into him and shaking her head. Such a little liar. He smiled against her neck, her soft, flowery scent filling his lungs like it was oxygen itself. "Did you come to get your panties or did you come to see me play?"

"Both." Her words were low, a smoky whisper. "I thought it would be a good idea to hear my client's music. And you do have something that belongs to me."

"You'll have to stay for one to get the other." He ran his nose along her neck and bit her softly. He didn't need to feel her up in the middle of the dingy club to know her nipples would be hard as two little bullets. Experience and her sharp intake of breath told him that.

"Please stop."

He turned her in his arms and looked down into her blue eyes. "I will if that's what you really want. Or we can pretend the past doesn't exist. For one night." Wrapping her long hair around his fist, he angled her head where he wanted it. Where he needed it.

"I'm going to kiss you now."

"In the middle of all these people?"

"Yeah."

Her eyes widened and while she seemed to consider it, he ran his hand along her neck and cupped her face. She nodded, hissing slightly when he gave a sharp pull on her hair. He heard the band announced as Conner ran past him and bumped him with his shoulder. "Time to rock and roll, playboy!"

Jax took Jami's mouth. There was no other way to describe it. He took her full, bow-shaped lips under his and tried to convince her with his tongue to stop screwing around. There was no subtle build up, no gentle touch of lips brushing together. He needed to fucking kiss her again. And hard. So he did, leaving no question as to what he wanted from her, fucking her with his tongue and rubbing his hard cock against the soft give of her body. He was going to combust into flames if he didn't get back inside her sweet curves soon. He moaned into her mouth and held her tighter when she mirrored his desire with a low groan of her own.

The lights flashed and dimmed as he contemplated how quickly he could get her into Shelby's office without breaking the connection. Reluctantly, he pulled back, noting the dazed, glassy look in her eyes and how hard she pulled her hands around his neck. *Good*. He slowly tugged her panties from his pocket and tied them around his wrist. Before she realized what he'd done, he pulled his drumsticks from his back pocket, twirled them in the air, and winked.

Then he turned and ran up toward the steps of the stage, wondering why he was always running away from her and not toward her.

✳ ✳ ✳

"Did he just wrap a pair of women's underwear around his wrist before going up on stage?"

Jami turned slowly, still in a Jax-induced haze. Her friends Ella and Gabby stood behind her. Oh shit, had they witnessed the whole scene play out between her and Jackson? That was exactly why she shouldn't be here. Why she had to stay away from him. He was dangerous. He made her think wearing a short denim skirt, heels, and a tiny top were good ideas. That coming to a heavy metal show in downtown Portland was a good idea. Or that letting a tattooed, pierced six-foot-four wall of narrow, twisting muscle wrap her hair around his fist in a packed bar and kiss her breathless was a good idea.

It wasn't. Not a good idea. Definitely a very bad idea.

She stared at her friends. What had Ella asked her?

Behind her, a guitar began to play a slow, pulsing melody. Soft, sweet, building to something bigger. More solid.

The steady beat of a bass drum. Then more drums.

Ella and Gabby pointed to something on the low stage behind Jami. The band. Of course, the band was starting. More specifically, Jackson's band, her client, Manix Curse, was beginning their set. Her heart dropped into her belly. She swiveled around, her eyes tracking the hundreds of hands with their fingers held up in heavy metal salute.

The lone spotlight shone down on the tall and shirtless Marco Dane as he tossed back his mane and bellowed to the sky about the cruelty of love. His perfect torso was already glossy with the sheen of sweat. But it was the tall, rangy man beating the drums with feral efficiency that made her blood boil with prurient lust. His head hung low, but his short, messy hair was already dark with sweat despite the fans circulating air around the stage. Conner leaned into a mic in front of Mandi and they joined the chorus.

Jami watched in awe, mesmerized by the pure, raw power of the four band members and how seamlessly, yet viciously, they tore apart and reconstructed the song. She'd never seen anything like it. Never heard any band with such vitality and brutality and, yet, a dash of melody. Even in her wilder youth, when she'd snuck into every concert and club possible, she'd never seen anything quite like Manix Curse.

Not one for crowds or other people actually touching her, Jami barely registered the audience members pushing into her, clamoring for a closer look at Manix Curse. Or even the couple of losers that attempted gropes before Ella—or she assumed it was Ella—slapped away a restless, errant hand.

The band abruptly ended their song and the crowd went wild, screaming their names and favorite songs into the chaos.

Marco laughed—or growled, more accurately—into the mic and the women in the crowed squealed. "You guys here to see Manix Curse?"

The crowd screamed louder.

"You here to rock the fuck out?"

They yelled louder still.

Then Jackson raised his head and searched the crowd. The smirk that transformed his face when his eyes locked on Jami's could only be described as wolfish. The voice in her head began to whisper again, filling her with all kinds of dark and dirty thoughts. Because gone was the laid back, easy going Jackson everyone knew. In his place was the man she'd met years before.

Sexy.

Dangerous.

Pure sin.

And her blood turned from liquid into steam and evaporated from her body, leaving her a hollow shell of need.

He flipped his sticks around his fingers in a manner that, for some unexplained reason, made her panties wet. Then he pointed one stick at her, and sure enough, her freaking panties were wrapped around his wrist like some ridiculous rock-and-roll talisman. People turned to stare at her, obviously wondering what, or who, had caught the playboy drummer's eye, but she just stared at him.

He yelled into his mic, "One, two, and three, and four!" before breaking into a fast-paced beat. His long arms moved so quickly she could barely keep up with his movements, except for the flexing and undulating of the well-defined muscles in his shoulders.

Lord above, the man was sheer muscle and raw sex.

When an elbow flew past her head and nearly hit her temple, she realized her friends were trying to drag her out of the way of the mosh pit that had opened up like a tempestuous storm in the middle of the club. She let them lead her to the edge of the crowd.

Gabby turned to her, her cheeks pink and her green eyes wide. "Dude, what the fuck was that?"

"That, my dear friends, was Jax Pain. Drummer extraordinaire and bad boy tattoo artist. He's the whole thing," she said as Jackson flipped his head back, his hair wet with sweat, but still so hot. So freaking hot.

When Jackson's eyes connected with hers, everything in that room just disappeared. Like in a damn movie. Only this movie's soundtrack was set to a heavy metal grind and not some Top 40 ballad or hokey country song.

"I will find your darkness," Marco growled into the mic. "And add my own."

Mandi's fingers slowed and her guitar cried, drawing out the melody.

"I will drag you into the light."

Jackson's arms moved at a more languid pace, his muscles flexing and twitching, the movement nearly hypnotizing.

"Because now I know for sure."

Conner's bass line pummeled the audience—building, digging deeper, climbing higher.

Marco looked up through his mane, a huge lion of a man, and screamed, "You were meant to be my home!" at the same moment Jackson jumped up, kicked his stool back, and pounded his drums in a blurred fury.

The air in Jami's lungs left with a whoosh. She couldn't breathe. And despite the loud wall of sound circling her like a hurricane, she could hear the swooshing sound of the blood pulsing through her ears.

Jackson was glorious. A magnificent metal god.

As the song ended and he ran up with his band mates to take a bow, he brought his wrist—his panty-covered wrist—to his nose and smiled that untamed one-sided grin again, before running off stage.

By the time the band wrapped up their three encores and the bright overhead lights illuminated the club again, Jami was making her way toward the door with Ella and Gabby. Suddenly a damp, tattooed arm wrapped around her waist and she felt herself pulled into a solid, slick body.

Before she could yank herself free and reprimand the ass messing with her, Jackson's dark voice whispered into her ear. "Say good night to your friends."

Her nipples hardened as if on command and the heat she'd been feeling all night in her chest dropped down between her legs. He pulled her tighter, snug against the hard cock pressed against her back.

She didn't even consider the remote possibility of saying no. Maybe tonight she'd give into her lust for him. A shiver crawled up her neck and her heart raced. Maybe one night was what she needed for closure.

Jax was on a performance high and wanted nothing more than to pounce on Jami. They were stopped by three different women before he finally pulled her into the owner's office and kicked out a couple making out on the couch. He'd barely slammed the door behind them before he twirled her and pinned her up against the door, his hand on the fleshy globes of her sweet ass. He growled when she wrapped her hands over his shoulders and pulled herself up his body, her legs winding naturally around his waist.

She'd once told him his sheer strength and size had always made her feel safe, protected. That she always found it erotic as hell. He felt just the opposite right then, like he might be too close to losing control. Like he might be the farthest thing from safe.

His rock-hard cock throbbed against the zipper of his ridiculously tight jeans. Somewhere in the back of his adrenaline-infused brain, he knew it was wrong to rub his show-sweaty body all over her sexy but tidy outfit. All he cared about was touching her, feeling her, feeling the hot glove of her pussy around him again. He was tired of waiting, of playing games.

"You were taunting me from the stage weren't you, sunshine?" He rubbed his scratchy beard along the edge of her jaw. The sharp intake of her breath followed by the increased pulse in her neck told him two things. One, she was as turned on as he was. And two, he could have her right then and there if he wanted. A part of him wanted that very much. "Eye-fucking me the whole time."

She didn't answer for a moment. Their panting crowded the air between them.

"I was in awe," she said finally, her voice sounding low and hoarse, like velvet wrapped around his cock. He pulled back to look into her eyes. "I didn't expect... I didn't know... I..." She stared up at him, the blue of her eyes so vibrant it looked almost lavender, but she looked so confused and lost.

"You were so beautiful, Jackson. So powerful. I had no idea that your music—that you—were like that. I mean... I don't know. I just didn't know."

He smiled and licked her neck, stopping to nibble her ear. His normally articulate lawyer seemed flummoxed, at a loss for words. "Men aren't beautiful."

"You are. And, oh my God, so freaking sexy."

He chuckled. "I love how ready to be fucked you are right now, and you still can't swear properly."

She pinched his shoulder. He squeezed her ass with his hands. Hard. She gasped and leaned forward, pressing her mouth to his. "Then stop talking and fuck me, bad boy."

He sucked her full bottom lip into his mouth and bit. "So now who's getting bossy?"

"Jackson!" she pleaded. And he liked the edge in her voice—jagged with lust and need. "I want you."

I want you.

There it was again.

"Want you too, babe, but not here."

And then Jami did something that blew him away for the second time. She pouted, sticking out her luscious bottom lip again. "Why not?"

He yanked her hips toward his body and leaned down,

whispering against her lips, "I'm going to take you home and rip your clothes off. Then I'm going to take my time relearning every curve, every sweet crevice. Slow. So fucking slow. Then I'm going to devour you."

"Yeah?" she asked, her voice breathy and nearly a croak.

"Yeah."

"We need to get the hell out of here."

Jax watched as Jami practically ran from the room, her perfect ass swishing back and forth as she tugged him through the loitering crowd and nearly ripped his arm out of the socket when he was stopped and congratulated for the fifth time. Who knew such a tiny woman could be so strong?

He loved her impatience. It was hot as hell. He'd let her drag him around the club for now, but as soon as they were through the door she would be all his.

And he wasn't walking away this time. Not for anything.

COMING MARCH 2017

★ ★ ★

BEAUTIFUL CRAZY PLAYLIST

In order to find my quiet place, I often have to don headphones and drown out the world around me. Sadly, classical music isn't my jam (gives me a headache), so I try to play music that inspires me and fills me with the emotion required for a specific scene. Below is a partial playlist of the music I listened to while writing *Beautiful Crazy*. For a complete playlist, please see my website (www.kaseylane.com).

"Light a Way" by Volbeat
"Big Bad Handsome Man" by Imelda May
"World in Flames" by In this Moment
"Alias" by In Flames
"Collapse" by Zeds Dead (featuring Memorecks)
"What's Mine Is Yours" by Sleater-Kinney
"Sound of a Revolution" by Sonic Boom Six
"Can't Help Falling in Love" by Elvis Presley
"11:11" by Rodrigo y Gabriela
"The Bleeding" by Five Finger Death Punch
"Dear God" by Avenged Sevenfold
"Into the Ocean" by Blue October
"Lullaby for a Sadist" by Korn
"The Outlaw Torn" by Metallica
"Top Yourself" by The Raconteurs
"Grow Old with You" by Matthew Mayfield

—Kasey

★ ★ ★

ACKNOWLEDGMENTS

It's been my private dream to be a published author for a long time. It wasn't until my husband, Jeff, finally told me to stop talking about it and go do it that I signed up for a SavvyAuthors NaNoWriMo event. It turns out I had some stories to tell.

This book would still be growing old on my laptop without the help of so many people. It really does take a village. It started with my husband, the hero of my very own happily ever after, and ends with my incredibly patient and awesome editor, Cat Clyne, and all the talented people at Sourcebooks. From my first editor and friend, Blake Leyers, to my first beta reader and the sister of my heart, Melody, to my oldest friend and favorite tattoo artist, Nikki. My agent, Cate Hart (who has the uncanny ability to communicate anything in Dave Grohl gifs), was the first person to see past the stilted early draft and see my potential. She pulled my voice from my head and helped make Kevan and Mason real. My original critique partners, RJ Garside (my first writer friend and biggest supporter) and Jade Chandler (we learned together along the way), helped turn me into a real writer and told me the hard truths about what needed to change and what didn't. My newest CP, Kaylie Newell, is my literary BFF, twinsie, and PIC. I adore you and am thankful every day for your friendship. I will always be grateful to my SISters and their support, especially my conference wife, Sarah Vance-Tompkins. Without my weekly coffee shop meetings of the Hope Junkies, I would still be creating in a vacuum. Thank you for your friendship and counsel Kaylie, Maisey, Gwen, Megan, Lisa, Holly, and Vella. And lastly, the never ending love of my entire wonderful, crazy family, especially my parents, Robin and Walt, and my amazing kids, Abigail and Max. Without my family's support, I wouldn't have been able to steal enough time to write, rewrite, revise, rinse, and repeat.

This book is for all the misfits, the survivors, the music lovers, the believers, the freaks, and the geeks. You are my people. ♥♥♥

ABOUT THE AUTHOR

Award-winning author Kasey Lane writes sexy romances featuring music, hot guys with ink, kick-ass women, and always a happily ever after. A California transplant, she lives with her high school crush turned husband, two smart, but devilish kids, two dumb-as-rocks papillons, and a bunch of bossy chickens in the lush Oregon forest. Visit her at www.kaseylane.com, where you'll find her swearing too much and talking about the San Jose Sharks, tattoos, and Jack White.